THE COMPLETE CASES OF VAL EASTON

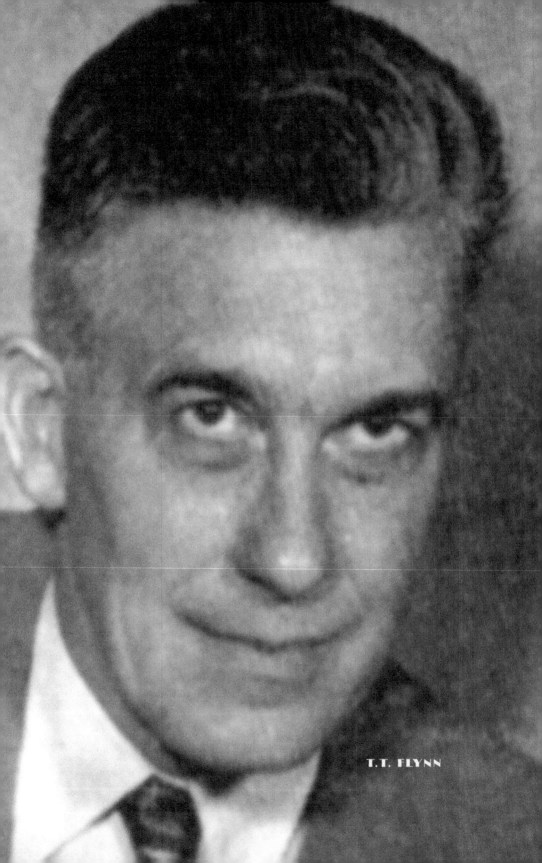

T.T. FLYNN

THE COMPLETE CASES OF

VAL EASTON ™

T. T. FLYNN

ILLUSTRATIONS BY
JOHN FLEMING GOULD

STEEGER BOOKS • 2020

TABLE OF CONTENTS

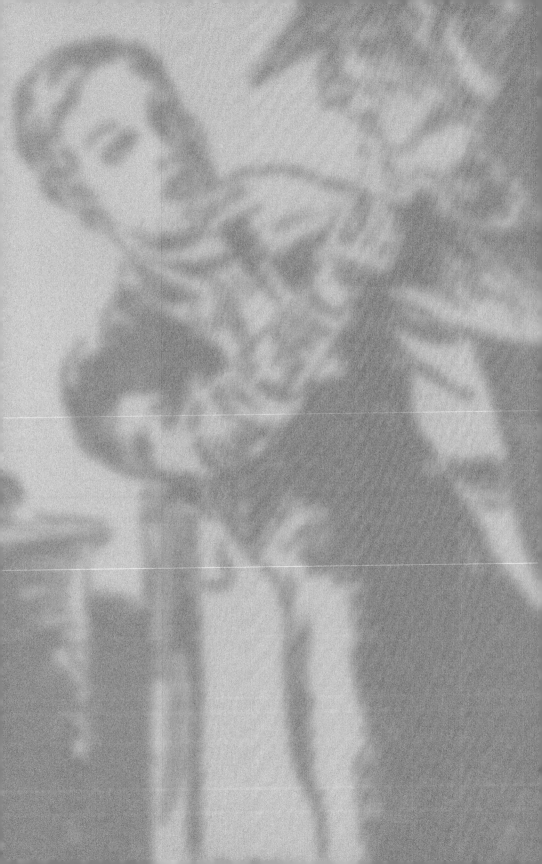

THE BLACK DOCTOR

ACROSS A WORLD-WIDE
CHESSBOARD OF MYSTERY AND
DANGER HE MOVES HIS HUMAN
PAWNS—THIS GHASTLY MAN-
MONSTER WITH THE GREEN-
FLECKED EYES. AND ONLY VAL
EASTON, CRACK SECRET SERVICE
OPERATIVE, KNEW THE DEFENSE
TO CHECK HIS GHOULISH
GAMBIT—CORNER THE BLACK
DOCTOR IN A MURDER MATE.

CHAPTER ONE

S13

IT **WAS** the last evening on the *Laurentic*, the last dinner before quarantine, and the slow progress up the bay past the Statue of Liberty and into the river where snorting tugs would skilfully guide the big liner into her berth. Six days out from Southampton, the *Laurentic* had found five days of bad weather, of plunging seas and gale-swept decks. Four days in which fully half the passengers had remained below, shunning decks, games, amusements—and food.

But all that had passed magically. The skies had cleared. The sweeping seas had smoothed in the sunny calm that followed. And now the big dining saloon was crowded. Val Easton ate with only half an ear on the table conversation.

His mind was on other things. The mission that had taken him to London and Rome, by way of Paris, and then back to London again. The weeks of piecing together tiny bits of information to make the pattern which took shape in his final report. It had been good work too. The cable from his chief, calling him back to Washington, had said so.

A fragment of the conversation jerked his attention back to the table, without sign of it showing on his lean features.

The full-bosomed woman at the head of the table—a Mrs. Beamish—had said aggressively: "The whole thing was bosh! In wartime, perhaps. But not now. Spies are as old-fashioned as the dodo bird." And Mrs. Beamish glared around the table as if daring anyone to take issue with her over the matter.

They were, Val realized, talking about the picture that had been shown the evening before. One of the latest thrillers built around the adventures of a famous woman spy during the War.

The needle was bending toward her wrist.

Most of them had seen it. The discussion at once became heated. The most outspoken was the blond young Mr. Miller at Mrs. Beamish's left, who looked like a poet just out of college, and who stood by his convictions heatedly.

"Of course there are spies," he protested. "They're always working. You read about them all the time."

"And see silly pictures about them," Mrs. Beamish declared sarcastically.

"That picture was based on historical facts," he said with the positive assurance of youth. "Whether you liked it or not, it happened. Why—why, any of us here at the table might be a spy! I might be one, working for a foreign government." And visibly set up by the thought, he looked gallantly across the table at the pretty girl on Val's right.

VAL SMILED inwardly. It seemed funny, this talk about spies. Almost like a fiction story. Something sinister and diabolical about it. He wondered if he looked the part. Wondered too, what would happen if this tableful of peaceful travelers were apprized of his identity, and could look for a moment into the roiling currents of international intrigue.

But Mrs. Beamish leaned forward with a glitter in her eye. "Young man," she asked sharply, "did you ever see a spy?"

"Er—well, no."

"Ahhh!" said Mrs. Beamish with a cutting smile, and leaned back in her chair as if that settled everything. And young Miller's weak retort of "How would I know one if I saw him? They don't go labeled," made no impression in her self-satisfied armor.

There was a chuckle from the slender, middle-aged Englishman who had sat at the end of the table every meal, beaming through rimless eyeglasses and talking books and authors to whomsoever would listen. Carmody was his name, a book salesman on a business trip to the States.

Now he smiled and bobbed his head as he leaned forward and spoke.

"I fancy Mrs. Beamish is more than a little bit right. This is not wartime, nor is there the wide interest in such things that we had in the days of the old worldwide Imperial German spy service. My firm, by the way, has published two books on such things and I can—er—modestly claim to know something about it. Spies are practically as dead as the dodo. We have about as much chance of finding one here at the table as we have of missing our dinner in New York tomorrow evening." And Carmody beamed at them all.

The young man retorted sulkily: "Just the same, I'm still betting on spies. You might be one yourself."

"Ha ha, so I might," Carmody chortled. "And if you'll drop around to the nearest bookstore as soon as you land, at least I'll guarantee you a corking good book on the subject. Make your hair stand up no end if you believe everything that's in it."

"I don't have to read a book to have my mind made up," young Miller said darkly, and applied himself to his dessert with irritated jabs of his spoon.

Val said to Carmody good naturedly as he left the table: "I may get that book myself. I've always been curious about such things."

"Do," Carmody beamed. "At least it's jolly good reading. Almost made me wish I had been one myself back in the days when they were taken seriously."

A trim, blue-uniformed young man from the Marconi room came in, paging, "Mr. Easton. Mr. Easton."

Val lifted a finger; the blue uniform met him and an envelope was placed in his hands. "Radiogram, sir."

Val tore it open and deciphered the coded message with the ease of long practice.

V EASTON
ON BOARD SS LAURENTIC
CONTACT S13 BEAMISH ASSIST IF NEEDED
SIGNED GREGG

Sheer amazement almost made Val wheel around and glance back at the table. The signature "Gregg" was the code word for the chief, housed at the right elbow of the State Department in Washington. Its sense was plain. Its information stunning. And for the thousandth time Val was swept with admiration for the perfection of the intricate and far-flung web of which he was only one strand.

S13—Beamish.

Only one meaning to that. That full-bosomed, majestic woman, who had sat at the head of the table day after day on this crossing, was a part of the same web. That woman who looked like the stodgy, opinionated wife of some equally stodgy business man; that severe matron whose tall, slender daughter had appeared once briefly on deck with her, was—*must* be—a clever Intelligence operative.

Val smiled wryly at the thought of how he himself had swallowed her aggressive declaration that no longer did such people exist.

Why had she done it?

And Val paid her the compliment of believing that there had been a purpose behind it. He tucked the radiogram in his inside coat pocket and strolled out on deck.

HALF AN hour later Val found Mrs. Beamish standing by the rail, peering pensively down at the endless ribbon of foam-flecked water that rushed astern. A blue coat was wrapped around her ample figure, a chiffon veil held her hair in place against the rush of the night breeze. Even now his critical scrutiny found it hard to believe she was the one Gregg referred to. He leaned against the rail beside her, said casually: "S13."

"What?" Mrs. Beamish demanded in a startled voice.

Val repeated it. She frowned at him. "Young man," she asked tartly, "is this a new way of flirting with an old woman like me?"

"Gregg suggested it," Val said idly.

"Hmmmmp!" said Mrs. Beamish shortly. She drew her coat closely around her shoulders, adjusted her veil slowly, turned and eyed him deliberately. A smile slowly broke over her angular face.

"So you're the one?" she said. "My, my—and to think we've been eating at the same table. Gregg radioed that one of his men would see us this evening. Come down and meet Nancy. She's been feeling bad the whole trip."

"Your daughter?"

Mrs. Beamish sniffed. "Bosh! It makes good atmosphere. Whoever would suspect an old fogy like me? I wish Nancy Fraser was my daughter. She's a girl in a million."

"Nancy Fraser? I've heard of her."

Val had indeed. Nancy Fraser, tales of whose daring ingenuity were already becoming classics of the Intelligence Service. An adept at disguise, a quick thinker, a beautiful girl, fearless, resourceful and blessed with uncanny luck was this Nancy Fraser.

MRS. BEAMISH, preceding him into the cabin on B Deck, said: "This is our man, Nance. Mr. Easton, Miss Fraser."

The girl who slid effortlessly to her feet from the bed almost took Val's breath away. She was softly feminine at first glance, a beauty with fine cleancut features, slightly sun-tanned. Her chin was firm and her mouth fairly wide, with a humorous quirk at the corners. She was a platinum blonde, and her silky hair, cut short, was waved close to her head in a style almost mannish.

He was to learn later that there was a reason for that. But at the moment he was conscious only of the calm, boring gaze of a pair of the bluest and deepest eyes he had ever seen. They took him apart in one swift look, examined the pieces—and approved. For she smiled and gave him a firm hand.

"I'm glad to see you, Mr. Easton. Sit down. This has been a rocky passage for me. I'm still a little wobbly."

"I was surprised to get Gregg's radiogram," Val told her as he seated himself. "I suppose something is up?" Nancy Fraser's smile faded as she sank on the edge of the bed. She nodded. "Something is up. I coded Gregg a resume of it, and he radioed back that he would have one of his men who was on the ship get in touch with me. I've been waiting for you."

"I would have guessed every other man on the ship," said Mrs. Beamish with a critical look at Val. "You're such a nice, harmless-looking young man. I thought you might be a college professor or a bond salesman."

The front of Nancy Fraser's silk negligee trembled as she laughed softly at Val's wry smile. "Don't mind Norah, Mr. Easton. She's apt to break out with some startling remarks."

"Hmmmp!" said Mrs. Beamish. "I say what I think, when it suits me."

Nancy Fraser became serious once more.

"Here's what we're up against, Mr. Easton. I'm working on a delicate matter. As near as I understand it, the stage is all set for some world-shaking moves that haven't even been hinted at in the newspapers. Anything may come out of it. The Shanghai business was only a move in a bigger game. Japan, Russia, England, France and Italy are all holding different hands in the Far East. Our government is vitally concerned. Treaties, agreements, protestations by statesmen are all for public consumption. Behind that the real moves are being made. The different foreign offices are the only ones who really know."

"And some of them don't know as much as they'd like to," Val commented.

"Exactly. None of them do. Each one is afraid of what the others may be doing. I doubt if the Intelligence Services have been half as busy since the War as they are now. Wires, cables and radio services are being tapped. Confidential codes being broken down and deciphered. Mails are being watched. Intelligence operators planted where they can get at the contents of diplomatic pouches, and scores of men in high position are being watched day and night for some clue as to what their governments are driving at. It's a mess. World peace, or another war that will make the last look like a kindergarten exercise, are in the balance."

Val knew all that. But he liked the crisp way this Nancy Fraser went to the heart of the matter. He was seeing another side of the beautiful girl who had cordially greeted him. A woman, this, who was steely hard beneath her femininity; who thought straight and to the point.

"Where do you come in?" he questioned bluntly.

"At the moment I'm following a man who stands high in the British diplomatic service. A man who is coming to the States on a secret mission. He is traveling incognito as a Mr. Galbraith. I am confident he is carrying secret papers or instructions that can't be entrusted to the mails or cables."

"Who is he?"

"Sir Edward Lyne. A tall, thin man with a close-clipped black mustache."

"Haven't noticed him."

"Probably not. He has kept to his cabin most of the trip."

"That seems simple enough," Val said, offering his cigarettes to the two women, and holding a light for them.

Nancy Fraser leaned back on one arm and nodded. "It is simple enough. Only—we're being followed too."

Those last sharp, vibrant words brought a sudden tang of danger into the atmosphere of the cabin. Val snapped alert, eyed her keenly.

"Who is following you?"

Nancy Fraser shook her head. "That's the trouble," she confessed. "Neither Norah nor I have been able to find out. But someone knows who we are, or suspects us. Our cabin was entered one of the few times we both were out of it. Entered, searched cleverly and left exactly as it had been."

"How did you discover it?"

Norah Beamish smiled proudly. "That girl is a wonder, Mr. Easton. She never leaves her room without fixing it so she knows at once whether it has been disturbed."

"A few little ends of silk thread that are never noticed when they are displaced," Nancy Fraser explained. "To make certain this time, I questioned the stewardess closely. She had not been in here."

She didn't have to say anything more. Too well Val understood why she was disturbed. It was bad enough to match wits with dangers one was aware of. But there was nothing more unnerving than to find that one's disguise had been penetrated, that unknown danger lurked close, and to be unable to discover it and take precautions. Until Nancy Fraser found out who had searched her cabin, she must suspect every one on the boat, must look for anything to happen at any hour of the day or night.

"Suspect anyone?" he prompted.

"No. We're up in the air."

The room had a narrow window opening on the promenade deck. A window halfway up, with the drawn curtains inside swaying slightly in the wind. And just as Nancy Fraser answered him, a harder gust than usual blew the right curtain aside, Val's eye caught a fleeting glimpse of a shoulder shifting hastily back to one side.

Someone was out there listening!

CHAPTER TWO
DEATH ON B DECK

VAL MADE a catlike lunge to his feet, reached the window in a silent stride, and grabbed through it. As he expected, the shoulder was just outside. His fingers dug hard into the rough woolen doth, and he jerked hard to bring the lurking figure over where he could see the face.

The other made no sound. But the hard edge of a taut palm struck the bone just above his wrist a terrific blow. It was *jiu-jitsu*, skilfully, savagely and instantly applied. His hand went numb and useless, and the blinding pain shot above his elbow.

With a twist the shoulder tore away and was gone.

Val jerked his arm in, biting his lower lip against the gasp of agony that rushed to his teeth. Nancy Fraser had come to her feet alertly and was staring wide-eyed as Val whirled toward the door.

"Someone listening out there!" he threw at her, and jerked the door open with his good hand and rushed out on deck.

The promenade was brightly lighted. At least a score of people were visible from the back of the long sweep of deck. But most of them were leaning over the rail; the others were strolling astern. No one at the moment had his eyes fixed on the spot. And the deck was empty!

A deck bay was a few yards away. His man must have gone there. But when Val reached it he found the bay empty and none of the chairs occupied. The companion door at the back was closed. He opened it, looked into the passage beyond, and swore under his breath. His man had moved fast and surely. Had gotten away. Val was forced to admit that fact after a few moments' search.

He met a steward in the passage, asked the man sharply: "Did you see a man come through here a few moments ago?"

His tense manner drew a curious look from the white-jacketed little Cockney.

"Ayn't seen a soul, sir."

"Sure?"

"H'I don't myke mistakes, sir. A man cam't afford to w'en 'e's holdin' down a nick on a top'oler like the *Laurentic*, sir. Is there something wrong?"

"Nothing," said Val, turning back. "Thank you."

NANCY FRASER had put on pumps and a coat that covered her negligee. She was standing near her door when Val returned. She met him with a questioning look.

"He got away," Val admitted unwillingly. "I was a fool to grab at him through the window like that. But I wanted a quick look at his face. He gave my wrist a crack that paralyzed it, and was gone."

"You didn't see him at all?"

"No."

"Let's take a turn around the deck," she said abruptly. "We've made a mess of things. Whoever it is knows you're with us now. I wish we had thought of that."

"I shouldn't have gone to your cabin," Val admitted. "Wouldn't have if I'd known what was up. But I didn't suspect it was this bad."

"Norah knew. She should have stopped you. And I should have closed that window. But we all make mistakes. I wonder how much he overheard."

"We weren't talking loud."

"Loud enough. I'm afraid," she said gloomily. "Darn it, the cat's out of the bag now. I'm much worse off than I was when I radioed Gregg. It's terrible! We've got to find out who it was."

"Line up a few hundred first-class passengers and look them in the eye, I suppose?" Val suggested.

"Your ideas are about as good as mine."

"This is the last night. On shore we may be able to do something about it."

"And maybe not. Don't you see we're both practically useless now until we get at the truth of this?"

They made the circuit of the deck twice, and finally Val suggested: "You might as well turn in. I'll stay up later and keep my eyes open. I'll let you know if I see anything."

Her handclasp was cool and firm, her "good night" brief, but her smile warm. Val walked away thinking about her.

AT MIDNIGHT the deck lights were dimmed. The strollers began to thin out. Val stayed out, for he was not sleepy. For hours he had been thinking about Nancy Fraser and this new bit of business. Who was so interested in her? What did it mean?

In other professions one might have shrugged the whole matter aside until something else happened. But not in his and Nancy Fraser's. If they didn't think at least two jumps ahead of the other party the results might be disastrous.

A steward passed with a tray holding a pot of coffee.

"Bring me a pot of coffee," Val told him.

And the steward touched his cap. "Yes, sir. Soon as I get back, sir."

Val leaned on the rail and stared out at the vast expanse of sea heaving slowly under the moonlight. Light steps came to his side. It was Nancy Fraser.

"I couldn't sleep," she said under her breath. "I wondered if I would find you out here."

"I'm having coffee in a few minutes. Care for some?"

"Sounds good. It might help my memory. I've been lying in bed trying to think of any suspicious move I've seen since I came aboard. I'm stymied."

"Ditto," Val admitted.

They waited there at the rail, talking low. Nancy said finally: "I thought you had ordered coffee."

Val looked at his wrist watch and saw that twenty-five minutes had passed as they lingered at the rail. "That steward must have forgotten it," he said irritably. "Let's look him up."

They walked slowly back along the deck. And suddenly, without warning, a woman screamed with shrill hysterical fear!

Nancy Fraser stopped short, her hand gripping Val's arm convulsively. "What's wrong?" she gasped.

The scream had come from ahead of them. Near the rear of the dimly lighted promenade Val saw two feminine figures backing toward the rail.

"I'll see," he jerked out under his breath, and leaving Nancy Fraser to follow, he ran toward the spot. He met the two women hurrying toward him. Two middle-aged spinsters. He had noticed them before during the trip. And now they were badly frightened. One was near hysteria as she turned and pointed back to the spot where Val had first seen them.

"There's something wrong there!" she cried shrilly. "I s-stumbled over an arm sticking out of the doorway! I—I think someone is d-dead!"

"Wait here!" Val ordered sharply. "If anyone's dead you can't be hurt!"

He found the door a moment later, and as he came up to it saw an arm thrust out at the bottom. A white-clad arm, sticking straight and motionless into the dim light of the deck. An arm that lay on the floor, its rigid fingers grasping talonlike at the empty air.

Val swore softly under his breath. It was a ghastly sight. For that arm seemed to be reaching, groping with desperate futility for something that had withdrawn beyond reach.

He stooped and lifted the hand. The flesh was clammy and cooling already. It was flaccid, limp, with that slackness which comes only from one thing. Whatever the arm had been reaching for, it had found only—death.

The door was ajar. The cabin inside was dark, silent.

Doors were opening along the deck; passengers were looking out. Nancy Fraser joined him.

"What is it?" she asked breathlessly.

Val reached inside for the light switch. "You'd better not look," he advised. "This won't be nice."

"I've probably seen worse sights," she retorted coolly, and looked in past his shoulder as the light flashed on inside.

WHATEVER SIGHTS Nancy had witnessed before, they had not hardened her enough to stop the gasp of horror which burst from her. Even Val himself could not take it coolly. The steward whom he had accosted half an hour before was lying there on the floor before them. Lying, twisted on his side, knees pulled half up, one hand clutching the front of his white jacket and the other reaching out through the door in that frantic, gruesome gesture. And on the doorsill his face was turned up to them drawn and crimsoned with congested blood, mouth open, tongue protruding, and bulging eyes set in a horrible sightless stare.

"He's dead!" Nancy said huskily.

Val nodded. "Yes. Dead all right. This is the man I ordered coffee from. No wonder he didn't bring it!"

Looking beyond the body, he saw on the floor the tray the steward had been carrying. It had been dropped. Cup and saucer were shattered into bits. The pot lay on its side, the dark brown contents making a long stain on the rug, surrounded by a snowy sprinkling of sugar.

"He died almost, as soon as he entered," Val muttered. "Didn't even have a chance to put his tray down. Dropped it cold."

His eyes ran over the body as he said that. There was no sign of blood. And no marks of a struggle either. Except for the spot in front where the starched white cloth was caught in convulsive fingers, the coat was neat and trim. Even the man's carefully combed black hair was in place.

It had been smoothed down with hair dressing, and was as sleek as it had been when he had walked along the deck.

Nancy noticed all that too, for she said: "It must have been heart failure."

"Looks that way," Val agreed.

A deck officer came running up in the van of half a dozen passengers closing in on the spot. "What is it?" he panted.

"One of your stewards must have had a heart attack," Val said, standing aside so that the officer could get a good look.

The bronze-cheeked, broad-shouldered young man pushed the door open all the way and stepped inside.

"Here's what's this?" he uttered in a startled voice. "Wake up, sir!" And over his shoulder: "The man must be a sound sleeper!"

Stepping in too, Val saw what he had missed with the door partly closed and his attention centered around the doorway. The bed was occupied by a man clad in blue silk pajamas.

"That man's not sleeping!" Val said sharply.

The young deck officer swore softly. "He—he's dead too!" he said shakily.

In fact, it was hard to see how the officer had been mistaken in the first place. No man would be sleeping that way. For the occupant of the bed lay in a twisted, contorted position also. One hand clutched his throat. The other had hooked around a pillow drawing it tightly against his side as if he had grabbed wildly at the nearest thing. The covers had been kicked down. One more roll would have taken the body off on the floor. And the mouth was open, the tongue protruding, the features congested with blood exactly as the steward's were.

Both men had died the same way.

All that Val got in a glance. And in the same moment he recognized the man on the bed with dumbfounded surprise. It was Carmody, the cheerful British book salesman!

CARMODY'S BODY bore no marks of violence either. No wounds. No blood. The death that had come to him as he lay in bed was the more ghastly and mysterious because of it.

"I'll get the captain and the ship's doctor here!" said the deck officer hoarsely. "Watch the cabin will you, please? Keep these people out." And as he stepped out, the young man closed the door as far as he could and said appealingly to the passengers gathering outside: "Please return to your cabins."

But by the excited remarks that drifted in, none of them paid any attention to the request. Val bent over the bed and touched the arm clutching the pillow. It was rigid. Frowning, he tested one of the legs. *Rigor mortis* had already set in. The flesh was cold.

It was not logical. He turned to the steward. That body was still flaccid, and the flesh was warm in comparison with the body on the bed.

Val fumbled for a cigarette, and then thought better of it and stood staring from one to the other. Both men had died in the same manner. One body was cold and set with *rigor mortis* and the other was warm and limp. It did not make sense.

There were cases, Val knew, where *rigor mortis* set in quickly. But this death that had come in the same manner to both men would not react so differently. There was only one conclusion to draw. The steward had been dead for half an hour—Carmody had been dead for hours.

And yet both had died in the same manner! Both had died horribly, yet without marks of violence! The door opened and Nancy slipped in and closed it behind her. "They're gabbling out there like a flock of excited chickens and roosters," she whispered. "What's the explanation of all this?"

Val shrugged helplessly. "I'm wondering." He told her what he had discovered. "D'you know this man?" he asked, jerking a thumb toward Carmody.

"No."

Carmody's coat and trousers were neatly hung up; his shoes were together on the floor, his shirt and tie and underwear on a chair as he had taken them off and arranged them. Under the bed was a gladstone bag, apparently undisturbed. Everything else in the cabin was in order.

The window was closed. A fragment of memory sent Val to the door. In the outside of the lock was a key with a small wooden handle to it—the steward's master key which he had apparently used to open the locked door.

Val shook his head in answer to the questions that were thrown at him by the people outside, and closed the door again.

"It's got me stumped," he confessed to Nancy. "There's a gruesome mystery here."

And when, a few moments later, the captain and the ship's surgeon entered, Val explained how he and Nancy happened to be in there, and pointed out what he had found.

Captain MacCreagh was a burly, weather-beaten man who still carried the dogged gruff manner of old sailing days. Doctor Simms, the ship's doctor, was short and slender, with a neat Vandyke and shell-rimmed glasses. He made a swift examination of the bodies, and then pulled the steward's outstretched arm in enough to let the door close tightly.

Captain MacCreagh had been watching impatiently. Now he demanded: "What do you think of it, doctor?"

The doctor polished his glasses with the middle of a handkerchief. "Mr. Easton is right," he said slowly. "These men did not die at the same time. That one on the bed has been dead for hours. And this steward died very recently."

"What killed them?"

THE DOCTOR fitted his glasses precisely on his nose, glanced at the bodies, and then at the captain. "I would suggest an autopsy, captain. Neither of them has been wounded in any manner, as far as I can see. They have all the appearance of dying from suffocation, yet there are no marks about their throats to indicate any violence which would cause that."

"In other words," the captain snorted, "you don't know anything about it."

The doctor was unruffled. "Precisely," he answered calmly. "I have never seen anything quite like it. The window is closed. The door was apparently locked, or the steward would not have used his key from the outside."

"That means," Val pointed out quickly, "that the steward was delivering an order to a man who had been dead in his locked cabin for hours."

The captain glared at him. "Then who ordered it?" he snapped.

"Perhaps the autopsy will show that," Val smiled.

"*Hmmmmph!*"

The captain stepped to the door, opened it, beckoned the deck officer, and growled: "Check up on the order that was brought here by this steward. Find what time it was given and who ordered it." And when he closed the door again, the captain said: "I wonder who this chap is."

Val mentioned what he knew of Carmody which was little enough.

"We'll search his effects and see if there's anything more," the captain decided. "He ought to have his passport and some papers. His people will have to be notified by radio, and asked what to do with the body. Blast it, I hate a business like this! It's bad for a ship's reputation."

Val suggested: "Right now it's more to the point to find out what killed them."

"You talk like a detective."

"I'm not," said Val calmly, and let the matter rest there. But he and Nancy Fraser stayed as the captain and the doctor hurriedly searched the cabin.

They found a billfold and some small change, a pocketknife, a fountain-pen flashlight clipped inside the coat, passport book and several letters, a key that opened the locked gladstone.

The captain's thick fingers fumbled through the clothes inside. With a grunt he drew out an English army-model automatic pistol and two extra clips filled with cartridges.

"*Hmmmph,*" he said, tossing them on the bed. "What does he want to carry these for? Army model too. I guess that's all. No—what's this?"

The captain drew out a small thin black leather wallet. As he opened it a little silver badge dropped to the floor. He let it lie as he looked inside. The wallet was empty and he tossed it and the silver badge on the bed also.

"That's all," he said. "And not much. His address is on the passport. That will be enough for my purpose, I guess."

Val hardly heard him. His glance had riveted in startled surprise on the badge the captain had picked up. And Nancy Fraser's had done the same thing. Their eyes met for a moment and it would have taken many words to interpret the meaning that flashed between them.

For Carmody, the smiling book salesman, had been proved by that badge to be a Secret Service agent of the British government!

CHAPTER THREE

COLD STEEL—WELL DONE

THERE ARE times when terror can be quiet, insidious, hidden. So it was now. Murder had been done. Coldblooded murder, unbelievably clever in its execution. How it had been done Val Easton did not pretend to know at the moment. Why, he might never know. But from the instant he was aware of Carmody's real mission, he knew it hooked up with Nancy Fraser. The man who had been lurking outside her cabin window was the one to explain this.

And if Carmody had been removed so skilfully and ruthlessly, why not Nancy Fraser and her companion? Why not himself, now that he was identified with them?

The deck officer returned.

"The coffee's easy to explain, sir," he told Captain MacCreagh. "This chap Carmody left an order with the steward to bring him coffee around midnight every night. Seems he was troubled with insomnia, or something like that. Couldn't sleep if he didn't have his coffee in the middle of the night."

"He'll have no trouble sleeping now," the captain remarked grimly. Doctor Simms fingered his Vandyke thoughtfully. "Queer. Mighty queer," he murmured, glancing at the bodies.

"What?" the captain rasped.

"This steward's death. Carmody had been dead for hours when the man arrived with the tray. The cabin was dark and the door was locked. It isn't reasonable to suppose that the killer remained in here all that time."

"No," admitted the captain testily. "He'd be a fool to do it."

"Exactly. The steward arrived, unlocked the door, stepped in—and died almost instantly. There was no struggle. There could not have been any noise, or someone out on the deck would have heard it. He simply died on the spot as Carmody had done. From the position of the body I would say he died as he was trying to back out the door."

"Dammit, man, something happened to him!" the captain snorted impatiently.

"I can't suggest what it was," Doctor Simms remarked coolly.

And there the matter rested.

While preparations were being made to put the bodies in the morgue, Val casually glanced at the papers which had been taken from Carmody's coat. He found nothing that might help him, and left the cabin a few moments later with Nancy Fraser.

They walked half the length of the deck before either spoke. Then Val said soberly: "It looks pretty bad."

"I think I'll stay up tonight," Nancy said calmly. "I don't want to be found that way in the morning."

Val shot her a quick look. "You think it touches you?"

"Don't you?" she countered.

"Perhaps...."

Nancy said with conviction: "I'm not timid, but I have a hunch this is far worse than anything I've been up against before. This isn't wartime. Murder isn't on the cards now. An ordinary espionage agent wouldn't try a thing like that. It's creepy, ghastly."

"American and British agents are out," Val said soberly. "Carmody didn't seem especially dangerous to me. I think you're right. You've walked into something bigger than you think."

"Big enough for—murder," said Nancy slowly. She chuckled softly in a way that showed her nerve was unshaken, and laid a steady hand on Val's arm. "At least, my friend, we should be thankful we know as much as we do. We might have gone ahead blindly—and drawn the same thing. Tomorrow is another day. We'll see...."

TOMORROW WAS another day, of bright sunshine over the fantastic, serrated skyline of New York, as the big liner plowed slowly up the bay.

During the night the ship had been in the grip of suppressed excitement. The bodies had been removed to the ship's morgue. The room had been locked and sealed. Wireless messages had crackled forth to shore. Passengers had been questioned, scrutinized. And at quarantine detectives hastily summoned from shore had come over the side with the ship reporters. Flashlight pictures of the cabin were taken; thumbprints were photographed. Passengers were diplomatically interrupted at their packing and last-minute preparations for going ashore, and questioned suavely. The newspapermen probed like hawks.

Val and Nancy were questioned by newspapermen and detectives. Their stories were brief and of little help. Of their business, or the man who had been lurking outside Nancy Fraser's cabin window nothing was said.

Carmody, it appeared, was a man who had little to do with anyone, outside of those he met at his meals. He had had no trouble with anyone, had no intimates.

Val himself had radioed Washington in code before daylight, giving such details as he knew. And Washington had replied in code. Val took the message to Nancy Fraser.

V EASTON

ON BOARD SS LAURENTIC LONDON DISCLAIMS KNOWLEDGE OF CARMODY OR INTEREST IN HIM SAVE AS BRITISH SUBJECT YOUR IDENTIFICATION AS INTELLIGENCE AGENT ERRONEOUS ON NO ACCOUNT LET IT INTERFERE WITH MATTER IN HAND WORK TOGETHER UNTIL FURTHER INSTRUCTIONS

SIGNED GREGG

When Nancy had read the decoded words, Val tore the message into bits and dribbled them over the rail.

"Chalk up another puzzle on your list," he said drily. "If Carmody isn't a British agent, what is he? What was he doing with that badge? And why was he killed? It's more tangled than ever if we take that honor away from him."

"Could it be possible," Nancy suggested "that London is pulling Gregg's leg? Won't admit Carmody's their man, for fear it might tip their hand on something they're anxious to keep hidden?"

"Quite possible. It's been done plenty of times before. Carmody's dead. They can't help him now. And again, they may have told the truth."

"The badge?"

"He might have found it."

Nancy tossed her head. "Badges like that aren't left lying around for people to find. What about his gun?"

"People carry guns."

"It's an official issue."

"Might have found it too," Val grinned.

"Your suggestions grow worse," Nancy told him.

Val lit a cigarette. "We're cleared on it, anyhow. Gregg seems a trifle annoyed. Suppose I pick your man up when he leaves the Customs and get in touch with you at your hotel? Give you a little leisure that way. I don't think we'll be held on board. They won't detain a shipload of people without evidence."

"That would be nice," Nancy nodded. "We'll go to the Blockman."

No one had shown any interest in them that morning. And yet Val could not shake off the feeling that he was being watched. He tried every trick he knew to prove it, and got nowhere. The feeling persisted, irritating him finally. Nerves, he told himself. And yet he knew it wasn't. They were both under silent, insidious scrutiny, and there was nothing worse.

And the thought of Carmody horribly dead behind a locked door made things no better.

VAL HAD been right about the ship's passengers. Among them were many influential people who could not even be considered as suspects. The men from shore were as baffled as the ship's company had been. They had no clues, no concrete suspicions. Names and addresses were taken, and other data, but nothing else was done. The debarkation was under way in full force shortly after the ship was moored in her berth.

Val had looked up Galbraith, studied the man from a distance. He was typically British in a quiet, unassuming way. A sparse, medium-built man in tweeds, with a long, pale, unsmiling face, a neatly trimmed mustache, an indifference to his surroundings that bespoke much travel. He conversed with no one, kept to himself. Carmody's death, of which Galbraith evidently knew, aroused no visible interest in the man. Val, following him that morning on a stroll around the deck, noticed that Galbraith did not even glance at the door of Carmody's cabin.

And Galbraith's manner when he left the ship was leisurely and indifferent. He went to the "G" section in the Customs line-up, stood by indifferently while his kit bags were examined, and then followed a porter and the bags to a taxi.

Val had managed to have a few words with the man in charge of his own luggage. His bags were mysteriously passed and whisked out of line. Val caught a taxi ahead of Galbraith. Outside the pier shed he ordered the driver to wait. A few moments later they were following Galbraith's cab.

Galbraith did not look back, seemed not to suspect he might be followed.

Val kept watch behind to see if any cab was noticeably following him. But in the crowded traffic it was almost a hopeless gesture.

Galbraith went directly to the Rosecrans, one of the big hotels overlooking Central Park from Fifty-ninth Street.

He entered the lobby behind his luggage in time to see Galbraith step into an elevator. The card registration system was in use at this hotel. There was no way of telling what room Galbraith had been given. Val smiled disarmingly at the clerk, and tried a random shot.

"My friend, Mr. Galbraith from London, told me on the boat he was going to register here. I'd like a room near him, if possible."

"Mr. Galbraith has just registered," the clerk replied. "Let's see—I can give you Room 717. That's just across the corridor from him. Mr. Galbraith is in 716."

"Excellent," Val nodded.

As soon as he was settled in his room he telephoned Nancy.

"Norah and I will come over there and register," Nancy said. "If he goes out, follow him. We must know whom he sees."

But Galbraith did not go out at first. He had a caller. Through his door, which had been left ajar an inch or so, Val saw a gray-clad back as the visitor was admitted to Galbraith's room. Just a glimpse, and then the door closed on them as Galbraith said formally: "How do you do, Mr. Ramey?"

The two were closeted in Galbraith's room for half an hour. In that time Nancy Fraser and her companion registered and Nancy telephoned from their room on the third floor. Val told her of Galbraith's visitor, suggested she be ready to tail him when he left.

Val was sitting inside his door when Galbraith's visitor stepped out into the hall once more. He heard the man say unctuously: "Tomorrow night at Oakridge then. Follow those directions after you reach Washington and you can't miss it."

And the fleeting glimpse through the cracked door showed a stocky, pasty-faced fellow, whose downsnapped hat brim shaded features that were as unctuous and oily as his voice had sounded. Before he was a dozen paces down the hall Val had closed the door and was at the telephone, calling Nancy's room. "All right—catch the next elevator," he rapped to her. "Blue suit, pudgy, pasty face, brim of gray hat snapped down."

"Right," said Nancy briefly and her receiver clicked.

Val was smiling thinly with satisfaction as he lighted a cigarette and resumed his watch at the door again. Galbraith's visitor would have a hard time shaking her. But as he conned over his one hasty glimpse of the fellow his smile faded to a thoughtful scowl. Ramey was a queer person to be calling on Sir Edward Lyne, to give Galbraith his right name. If long experience in judging people at a glance held good, Ramey was a shyster, tricky, smooth, untrustworthy.

Tomorrow night at Oakridge—near Washington.

What was behind that rendezvous which had been arranged?

GALBRAITH LEFT his room shortly. He walked down Fifth Avenue and over to Times Square, slowly window shopping. He went to two of the Times Square newsreel theaters, window-shopped some more, dined leisurely and walked back to the hotel, with a leg-weary Val Easton still within sight of him.

Val called Nancy Fraser's room when he got in. Norah Beamish answered instantly, and her voice was sharp with worry.

"You haven't seen Nancy?" she queried anxiously.

"No. Isn't she in?"

"I haven't heard from her since she went out this afternoon," Norah informed him. "Do you think something could have happened?"

"I doubt it," Val reassured her. "She'll show up in a little while. Have you eaten?"

"I had some food sent up," Norah told him. "I won't leave the room until I hear from her. She may telephone."

"If she does, let me know. And if she comes back, have her telephone my room at once. I'll leave word at the desk if I go out."

Galbraith seemed set for the time being. Val hastily stripped, took a hot shower and dressed again. He found himself wondering about Nancy Fraser. Had something happened to her? She was the kind of girl who would take chances. Val found it impossible to forget those two still forms on the *Laurentic*, grim warning of the price of carelessness.

He had barely finished dressing when knuckles rapped sharply on the door. Val answered it with a feeling of relief. It must be Nancy, returned finally and came up for a word with him. He opened the door with a grin on his face.

And....

The grin faded to astonishment. A black-coated waiter confronted him, bearing a cloth-covered tray.

"You've made a mistake," Val told him. "I didn't order anything."

The waiter looked doubtful. "Mr. Easton, isn't it?"

"Yes."

"This is right then. A young lady telephoned down and said to bring this order to your room. It's for two. I believe she is supposed to share it also."

"Oh," said Val blankly. "All right, bring it in."

His reaction was pleasure. This was such a thing as Nancy Fraser would do. Thoughtful of her. Eat while they talked. She was back then, and everything was all right. And he wondered what news she was bringing.

The waiter had a small folding rack under his arm. Opening it, he set the tray carefully down. He was a swarthy, poker-faced man with powerful shoulders bulging inside his black jacket and wrists which protruded out of sleeves that were too short.

"The young lady said to cook the steak well done," he declared. "Will you see it now, sir?"

From the moment the fellow had entered the room, closing the door behind him, Val had been struggling with a feeling of bafflement. Something was out of place in this picture. Wouldn't Nancy have telephoned him, after all, as soon as she got in? And he hadn't been under the shower more than a few minutes. Hardly long enough to have a steak well cooked and a full meal sent up to the room after she returned.

And there was something else....

Suddenly he got it. How the devil did the waiter know that the woman who ordered the dinner over the telephone was a young woman? He couldn't know.

And the man's coat was too small, his face was tanned where a man used to working indoors would be pale. And a degree of insolence had come into his manner. He leered at Val across the tray as he whisked the cloth away.

One look was enough to tell Val that his suspicions had been right. For the dishes that had obviously contained food a short while before were empty now, and in the midst of them lay a large flat automatic.

Val jumped for that gun instantly.

It was a long chance—and it failed. A muscular hand closed over the gun and its muzzle jerked up and met him.

Val stopped short, arms tensed at his sides. For a moment silence held the room, while Val's eyes locked with a pair of dead slate eyes which stared at him with a cold unwinking gaze. Politeness, mockery, pretense were gone now.

"Lift your hands!" the other ordered across the littered tray.

"What's the idea?" Val countered.

"Shut up! Don't argue! Put your hands up!" As he spoke the other stepped around to Val's side. The gun was steady in his hand and his manner was venomous. A slight foreign accent tinged his words.

Slowly Val raised his arms.

"Turn around!"

Val did that too. And a second later steel crashed against the side of his head brutally. Everything went blank, black. He pitched forward to the floor.

CHAPTER FOUR
THE HOLLOW NEEDLE

THE LIGHT overhead was still burning brightly when Val's eyes opened again. He was stupid for a moment, senses whirling, pain roiling in his head. He couldn't think what it was all about.

And then he remembered. The waiter—the cloth-covered tray—the gun—the stunning blow against his head....

The tray was still sitting on the rack in the center of the floor before him, the white cloth tossed on the floor and the soiled dishes mocking him.

The waiter and his gun were gone. The room was silent, deserted.

And there by the side of the bed Val sat in the straight-backed chair, tied hand and foot with lengths of fine silk cord.

His ankles were fastened to the legs of the chair and his arms were tied behind it. Silk cord was lashed about his wrists so tightly the circulation had been cut off. His hands were numb. Cloth had been stuffed into his mouth and tied in place by a towel, making an extremely uncomfortable but highly efficient gag.

He was helpless, miserable and impotent.

As his predicament burst over him, Val's first reaction was a struggle to free himself. He quickly saw it was impossible. He couldn't rub the gag out of his mouth and call for help. Over his shoulder he saw that the window had been closed and the shade pulled down.

THE PHONE was on the other side of the bed. By the side of the door was the bell button that would quickly bring help. Only a few feet away—and yet it might have been as many miles.

Val raged at himself for a moment. He had been a fool to be caught off guard that way. And yet it had been smooth work, well planned and executed. Whoever had done it had known about his connection with Nancy Fraser; had known that Nancy was out and might be back any time.

Only one man could have known that—the one who had been watching them on the *Laurentic*.

What was the reason for it? Not Nancy. She was out of the hotel. Hardly Norah Beamish, on a lower floor. Galbraith then! Galbraith across the hall, where Val's door commanded his, where no move could have been made without danger of interruption.

He didn't know how long he had been tied here in the chair before regaining consciousness. It might have been minutes, or an hour or more.

In that time what had happened to Galbraith?

Val eyed the telephone narrowly. If he could inch the chair around to it he might tip the phone over. Using his toes and throwing the weight of his body at the same time he managed to shift the chair inch by inch, But it was slow, hard work. Perspiration broke out on his forehead.

And in the midst of that the telephone suddenly buzzed.

Val cursed behind his gag. That was Nancy or Norah. And he couldn't answer. It was maddening to know help was so near and be unable to summon it.

The telephone buzzed again and again and then stopped. He hadn't covered a quarter of the distance to the instrument. Stubbornly Val kept on.

And then a few minutes later a key grated suddenly in the door. A bareheaded, broad-shouldered stranger stepped into the room, took one look and uttered in a startled voice: "Hey—what's this?"

From behind his back Nancy Fraser darted into the room. Relief broke over her face as she saw Val staring mutely at her. With a swift little rush she reached his side, snatched the towel down and pulled the wadded cloth out of his mouth.

"Thanks," Val mumbled through cramped lips.

"Who did this?" Nancy asked tensely.

"Fellow disguised as a waiter. Get across the hall and see if Galbraith's all right. I think they got me out of the way because of him."

"This looks mighty funny to me," the broad-shouldered stranger said ponderously. "You hurt, buddy?"

Val had him placed by now. A hotel detective, already muddled, and uncertain about everything.

"I telephoned as soon as I got in," Nancy said swiftly. "When you didn't answer I queried the desk and they said you hadn't left any word there. I suspected something was wrong, so I got the hotel detective to come up here with me and unlock your door."

Nancy whirled around on the detective. "Cut him loose from there!" she snapped. "Where's your master key?"

THE MASTER key was produced with a puzzled frown. Nancy snatched it and made for the door. "Hey, where you going with that?" the detective protested.

But Nancy whirled out of the room without answering either of them. The detective turned after her in indecision. "Is that dame gone nutty?" he uttered plaintively.

"Cut these damn ropes!" Val snarled. "Don't stand there like a lunkhead! Get me out of this chair!"

The fierce command in his voice brought the desired result. The detective's thick fingers fumbled open a small pocketknife, and he hacked at the cords. Val was chafing his wrists and wringing circulation back in them as the detective stooped over and slashed at the cords around his ankles.

Val staggered to his feet.

From across the hall keened a cry of distress that broke off sharply in a choked gasp. Nancy's voice!

Val plunged for the doorway without stopping for the gun in his bag. Galbraith's door was standing ajar. He crashed it open with his shoulder and plunged into the room—into a scene of confusion and violence.

The place had been looted hurriedly. Bureau drawers were out and their contents tossed heedlessly on the floor.

Bags had been slit open with a sharp knife and searched hastily. The closet door was open, the bed turned down. And Galbraith's body lay huddled in the center of the floor.

All that went unheeded. For before him Nancy was fighting off a tall, stooped, black-caped figure which clutched her throat with one long talonlike hand as it tried to wrench its other hand from Nancy's desperate grip.

They staggered around as Val entered the room.

A pale, ghastly, cadaverous face turned toward Val. He was aware of a parted, writhing mouth, of blazing, green-flecked eyes, of teeth that showed momentarily like fangs.

It was the face of a monster, a fiend, lashed by murderous fury, indescribably venomous, vicious, dangerous. Some horrible fate had been in store for Nancy. The hand she clutched so desperately held no gun, no knife, no club. Its talonlike fingers were tensed about the small, gleaming barrel of a doctor's hypodermic. And the long sharp needle was bending in toward her wrist with all the shuddery menace of a deadly serpent's fang.

As the door slammed shut behind Val he threw himself at that sinister black-caped figure. A swift turn brought Nancy between them. She was hurled violently back, her grip tearing away.

Val's arm saved her from a bad fall.

Behind him the house detective hammered violently on the door, bawling: "Open up, inside there!"

"Look out!" Nancy gasped warningly. "He'll kill you!"

Her words were too late. A hand plunged under the black cape as its wearer backed toward the open window. It came out with something that looked like a small, shiny metal fountain pen. But the instant he saw it leveling at them Val knew better.

He tried to shove Nancy behind him, and was too late. There was a dull *pop.* A whitish ball of vapor leaped at them, expanded rapidly, enveloped them....

And suddenly they were blinded with tears, coughing, choking, sneezing and fighting for breath. Helpless, Val backed toward the door, sweeping Nancy with him when his arm touched hers. He was thinking of that vicious hypodermic needle and the man who wielded it. They were at his mercy now.

It had been long since Val Easton had known such fear. And it was for Nancy Fraser, not himself. When the tear gas cleared out of the room, would she be stretched out there on the floor also?

The door was shaking before the assault of the house detective. The commands to open up were growing loud and furious. The tumult guided Val to the door. That dick had a gun. His hand found the knob. And still nothing had happened to him as he turned that knob. For some reason the black-caped attacker was holding back.

The door was shoved in violently against him, knocking him off balance.

"By God, what's the idea of all—" the house man bawled as he charged in, breaking off into a fit of sneezing and choking before he could finish the question.

VAL WAS mopping at his streaming eyes with his handkerchief, trying to see. The dick blundered into him. The hard muzzle of a gun poked roughly into his ribs.

"Watch that gun, you big ox!" Val yelled. "You'll shoot the wrong person!" The gun was pulled away. "Come out in the hall!" Nancy choked. Val stumbled out after her. And there, away from the insidious gas, they gained a measure of control and sight.

The house dick was standing in the doorway, mopping at his eyes and swearing under his breath. Peering blearily at Val, he raved: "Did you shoot that stuff off?"

"Do I look like it?" Val retorted. "Is that fellow in the room yet?"

"What fellow?"

"Tall chap with a black cape."

Peering through the doorway, the dick said angrily: "There ain't no one in there! Hell—is that him on the floor?"

But it was Galbraith's body he spoke of. It had not moved since Val first saw it. Air was pouring through the doorway, driving the last of the gas out the window. Wiping his eyes and peering as b st he could, Val edged into the room. The tall, black-caped figure had vanished!

From nearby rooms other guests had poured out into the corridor, gathering around the door now. A woman caught sight of Galbraith's body on the floor and gave a stifled cry.

"Get back, you folks!" the house man ordered through his teeth.

Val looked out at them. "Did anyone escape from this room?" he demanded.

One of the men said flatly: "I was looking when the door was opened. You two men and the young lady were the only ones who came out. What happened?"

Val hurried over to the window without answering. It was open, and when he looked out he saw four stories below the dark roof of an adjoining building.

It was to this window that Nancy Fraser's assailant had been backing when Val last saw him. He hadn't gone out into the hall. He wasn't here in the room. He must have gone out of the window.

But the sheer side of the tall building offered no refuge. There was no ledge by which he could have gained an adjoining window. No fire escape near. No ladder of any kind, up or down. And yet it was the only way he could have left the room. Val whirled on the house man, jerking a thumb at Galbraith's body as he did so.

"The man who did that went out the window!" he rapped out. "He may have fallen. I can't see the roof down there very well. Better search it and the building underneath. And the hotel here. He was tall, thin, wore a black cape and dark suit."

So fast and furious had everything happened that this was the first chance for more than a fleeting look at Galbraith. Val dropped to his knees beside the motionless body as he spoke.

Galbraith lay on his face, one arm under his head, the other thrown out awkwardly. He was dreadfully still and limp. Had no pulse in neck or wrist. And as Val lowered the lifeless wrist, his gaze was caught by a tiny smear of blood just below the coat sleeve.

Taking care not to disarrange the body before the medical examiner viewed it, he bent over and scrutinized the spot closely. Skin and flesh had been punctured by a needlelike instrument. A drop or two of blood had welled out before the wound closed. An area of flesh around the spot, no larger than a dime, was discolored slightly. That was all. And yet Val shivered as he rose to his feet, rubbing his hands slowly together. He was thinking of that glistening hypodermic needle in those talonlike hands....

The hotel dick was staring at him with wide eyes. "Is he dead?" he queried, nodding at the body.

"Very," Val answered drily. "Better call the police. And then get down after that man!"

The detective had closed the door against the curious in the hall. He stepped to the telephone, called headquarters and reported the matter. And then swung around and glowered at Val and Nancy.

"I didn't see anyone else in here," he said deliberately. "I'll just wait here with you two until the coppers come."

CHAPTER FIVE

THE BLACK DOCTOR

IT TOOK Val a moment to realize that he and Nancy Fraser were under suspicion. And when he did a wave of anger rushed through him.

"You fool!" he said crisply. "Can't you see we didn't have anything to do with this? I was tied up in the other room, and Miss Fraser was only in here a few seconds. You heard her cry out, didn't you? And you got a dose of the gas that chap left!"

"No one could have got out of here," was the stubborn answer. "If there was a guy, he jumped, and he's down there on the roof dead. And if there wasn't, you two can explain it to the cops. Better sit down there on the bed an' make yourselves comfortable."

Nancy Fraser met Val's angry glance with a philosophical shrug. "He's gone by now, anyway," she said. "We might as well make the best of it. I've got something to tell you."

While talking with the detective, Val had been conning over something else in the back of his mind. That pale, furious face with the blazing, green-flecked eyes had been strangely familiar. He was certain he had not seen the man before, and equally certain he knew something about him.

Nancy's face was pale from the shock she had just experienced, but her voice was steady. "That man," she said under her breath. "Did you ever see him before?"

"No. But I've a feeling that I should have," Val confessed.

"I saw him once in Switzerland," Nancy declared. "He was pointed out to me in Geneva. That was Carl Zaken, better known as the Black Doctor."

"Good God—the Black Doctor?"

"Yes!"

And neither of them needed to say any more.

Through the shady, secret channels of international espionage, tales of Carl Zaken, the Black Doctor, seeped like fantastic nightmares. He was in the way of becoming a legend to those who dealt in such matters. There were men willing to swear that no such person existed, but they did not know the facts.

No country claimed the Black Doctor, and he served none more than momentarily. Master spy, incredibly clever, cold-blooded, ruthless, a wizard in disguise, the Black Doctor gave orders to a wide-flung web of desperate characters. That much was definitely known. How many people received those sinister orders, only the Black Doctor himself knew.

At times he worked alone, and at others as many as a score had helped him. His influence was like an evil miasma. When murder suited his ends, he killed with technical skill. If torture would help, he used torture with all the fiendishness of expert medical training. He was an adept at languages and disguise. And his favorite role was that of a doctor, friend of man and trusted by everyone. For, so rumor had it, Carl Zaken had once been a doctor.

He dealt in information for the most part, stopping at nothing to get what he wanted, and selling the results to the highest bidder if he could not use them better himself.

"Are you certain he was the Black Doctor?" Val urged in amazement.

"The man who pointed him out had been caught by the Black Doctor once. He'd never forget him, and warned me never to. We only caught a glimpse of him, but I marked that face for good. This was the man." Nancy smiled wryly. "And I had to meet him without a gun."

"What happened?"

NANCY GAVE a little shudder. "He jumped at me just as soon as I slipped through the door. I caught one glimpse of his face and that hypodermic in his hand, and knew what I was up against. I tried to scream for you, and he caught me by the throat. All I could do was try and keep that needle away. There was murder in his face. It—it was ghastly."

"And a good thing you dodged it," Val said soberly. "Galbraith evidently didn't."

"Was that what killed him?"

"Needle puncture in the wrist. If he'd had time, he'd probably have cleaned the smear of blood away, and there would have been another mystery for the police to solve."

"You think he was on the ship?"

"Who else?"

"But why kill that poor devil, Carmody?" Nancy asked.

"Ask the Black Doctor. He must have a good reason. He's after something."

"What?"

"God knows. Galbraith here knew—and he's dead."

"Do you think he got it?"

"He tried hard enough," Val said, looking around the looted room. "I don't know. Evidently he was still busy when you walked in on him." Val's jaw set. "He killed that chap on the boat and Galbraith here in cold blood. It wasn't a question of putting him out of the way while he searched the room. He simply slaughtered him and then went about his business. Evidently came all ready to kill."

"Was he the man who tied you up?"

"No. Must have been one of his men. And clever work it was. The fellow came to the door disguised as a waiter, saying he had brought a meal you had ordered for us. I let him in without thinking, and when I did tumble that something was wrong it was too late. He had a gun on me then. Knocked me out and trussed me up."

"I can't understand why they didn't kill you," Nancy said. "It would have been easy enough."

Val rubbed his forehead and shook his head. "Lord knows," he admitted. "It would have been easy enough all right."

They were silent for a moment.

"That pseudo waiter must have left a trail around the hotel here some place," Nancy muttered.

"I'm not worrying about him," Val shrugged. "I'm wondering what this is all about. Why kill Galbraith and search his room here? He could have done it just as easily on the boat. Even the Black Doctor doesn't go around killing people for the fun of it. He could have left Galbraith alive just as well as he did me, if he had only wanted to look through his things. What about that chap you followed? He had evidently made a date to see Galbraith somewhere near Washington tomorrow. He was an oily-looking bird."

"Wasn't he?" Nancy agreed. "And a suspicious one, too. I think he was afraid someone might be following him. He tried all the tricks to shake anyone off."

"D'you think he saw you?"

Nancy rubbed the side of her nose carelessly and shrugged. "I've cut my teeth at that sort of thing. I'm pretty sure he didn't see me. After riding around town, taking the subway, ducking into a movie and out a side exit right away, he finally went into a telegraph office and sent a wire."

"Who to?"

"I didn't have a chance to find out. I wanted to see what else he did."

"The little bloodhound," Val grinned. "Did you?"

"I did. He popped into a telephone booth in a cigar store, and then took the elevated to Battery Park and went through the Aquarium."

"What?"

" 'Pon honor. He looked at all the little fishes like he was going into his second childhood. And then met a man and woman back in one of the dark corners and talked at least fifteen minutes with them."

"What did they look like?"

"It was shadowy where they were standing," Nancy said. "I couldn't see them well. And my man left first. I had to tag him, He chivvied back uptown on the 'El' again, got off at Forty-second Street, hailed a taxi—and I lost him there. I couldn't get another cab quick enough. Any other time there would have been a dozen on hand."

"It doesn't matter. He's going to Washington."

Nancy arched a delicate eyebrow. "How do you know?"

BEFORE VAL could reply the door burst open and admitted the hotel manager, patrolmen and detectives. The law took charge of the situation; and the ponderous house detective stated his case flatly.

"That lady there," waving his hand at Nancy, "comes down and says will I come up and open a door for her. She thinks maybe there's trouble. And when I do that gentleman is tied up in a chair. While I'm cuttin' him loose she takes my key an' runs into this room. He follows her an' they slam the door in my face. I don't know what happened in here, but when they opened the door the room was full of tear gas an' that body was on the floor. They tried to tell me there was another guy in here who knocked him off, but I didn't see no one. There wasn't no way he could have gotten out. So when they tried to run me off the scene after this guy they claim was in here, I call headquarters an' sit on the lid."

Though no direct charge was made, the house detective's story was damning as he told it.

A brusk, lantern-jawed detective seemed to be in charge of things. He had examined the body and made a quick survey of the room while the house man talked. Now he stepped to the window, looked out, and turned on Val and Nancy.

"No one could have gotten out that window!" he rasped at them. "What's the straight of this?"

"What's your name?" Val asked coolly.

"I'm Lieutenant Ives of the homicide squad. And since this is murder I warn you to make your statements correct."

"Step into the bathroom with me, Lieutenant Ives," Val requested curtly.

Ives hesitated, fingered his lantern jaw, and then said gruffly: "All right, if it'll make you feel any better."

Val closed the door behind them and met Ives' scowl with an icy stare.

"I didn't bother to reason with that addle-pated fool who suspected us," he said icily. "I'm going to tell you what happened; and then I want to get away as quickly as possible. You can check us at Washington, of course."

Val palmed a small badge for Ives to see. The detective took one look at it and whistled softly. His manner changed abruptly to fraternal courtesy.

"I couldn't know," he apologized. "What's the lowdown on all this?"

Val told him what had happened.

"What's your interest in this fellow who got bumped off?" Ives asked when he finished.

"That doesn't matter," Val refused him. "A lot of things don't matter right now. The man who killed him went out the window. May have gone up a rope ladder to a window above, or slid down a rope to that roof below."

"Where's the rope then?" Ives demanded skeptically.

"A hard flip from below on the rope would have loosened the hook over the window. You may find marks on the sill made by a hook. I'd suggest you try and trace him, and look over this hotel for a check on the pseudo waiter who took me in."

"I don't need to," Ives commented. "Coming up in the elevator the manager told me they had just found a waiter who had taken a meal up to Room 701 and hadn't returned. They found him tied up and minus his coat. The tray and dishes he had brought up were gone also. The fellow who had occupied the room had checked out ten minutes before. All the waiter could say was that as soon as he brought the tray into the room he was knocked out, and when he came to, stuffed under the bed, two men were eating the meal as if he wasn't there. He didn't get a look at them."

Val thought with unwilling admiration that the Black Doctor would have the nerve to stop and eat part of the meal, which had evidently been ordered to get the waiter and tray where they could be used. But he said nothing of that. Too much information might throw obstructions in their way. For there was small doubt in Val's mind now that this murder of Galbraith was only a move in another, bigger game that the Black Doctor was playing. And it was that game in which he was most concerned. Time enough when it was uncovered to think about bringing the Black Doctor to book for murder.

Ives took out a little black book and wrote down the description of the Black Doctor and the man who had impersonated the waiter. He asked for more information. Val referred him to Washington. Ives gave up with a shrug.

"I don't know what it's all about," he confessed. "You evidently know what you're doing. I'll call headquarters and they can let the commissioner decide what to do."

"Tell him to get in touch with Washington at once," Val ordered. "We've got work to do. Later on we can return for testimony."

"It's unusual," Ives warned.

"Washington will settle it."

AND WASHINGTON did settle it in a bit less than an hour, such was the power of that secret arm of the government which Nancy Fraser and Val Easton represented.

Neither of them knew exactly what had flashed back and forth over the wires; but Ives himself, still at the hotel, answered a telephone call, and told Val with a wry grin: "I guess you two have got something on the ball all right. Orders from the commissioner himself are to let you go and forget about you for the time being. So long—and luck to you."

"We'll probably need it," Val said.

VAL REGARDED the penciled message which he had obtained from the manager of the telegraph office. It had taken pressure to get a look at it against all rules of the company. But it told him what he wanted to know.

> J.B. Tillson,
> Oakridge Manor,
> Hartsville, Virginia.
> Party arriving tomorrow.
>
>   Signed, Ramey.

So Galbraith had intended to meet Ramey at Oakridge. Hartsville, Virginia, was close to Washington. The answer to everything must center there.

He returned to the hotel and looked in at Nancy Fraser's room on the way to his own.

"Pack up," he said with a grin. "There's just time to catch the next plane to Washington."

Norah Beamish shifted her ample form on the edge of the bed and said tartly: "Nancy needs a good night's rest. She's been through an ordeal, young man."

"That's right," Val said contritely. "Get your rest then and I'll run along."

Nancy had just been powdering her nose when Val stepped in, and a nice nose it was too, he noted. She tossed the powder puff on the dresser and stretched slender arms over her head, yawning luxuriously like a lazy cat.

"Nonsense," she said cheerfully. "I'm just getting warmed up. You must stay here and get the rest and we'll run on."

Norah Beamish charged to her feet like a formidable battle cruiser getting under way.

"Leave me here?" she snorted. "My great aunt's transformation you will! Do I look like an old grandma who needs to be parked in the corner? The idea! I won't have it! Where're those bags, Nancy? Get packed, young man! We'll be ready!"

Though Nancy had disavowed fatigue, when the wide-winged monoplane swept off the lighted landing field with a roaring rush, climbed high, and swiftly dropped the blazing panorama of lights that were New York back over the horizon, she promptly closed her eyes.

Norah Beamish sat behind her with a defiant tilt to her chin. When Val looked at her he received a visible sniff. Plainly Norah held him responsible for the suggestion that she be left behind to take her ease.

Val grinned, and then glanced across the aisle at the smooth curve of Nancy's throat. Her eyelids lifted and she smiled lazily at him, and then they closed and she seemed to doze.

What a girl, Val thought. Nerves like steel, inexhaustible energy, ready to tackle anything. She had come through an ordeal that would have reduced most women to nervous hysteria. And now, knowing that they were pitting their wits against Carl Zaken, the dreaded Black Doctor, she was dozing as peacefully as an untroubled child.

He felt a slight tightening of his throat as he remembered again that heart-stopping moment when death had grazed her wrist. And hard on the heels of that Val felt a cold chill as he wondered what lay ahead for her before this business was done.

The Black Doctor had not earned his reputation without cause; and somewhere at this very moment he was moving craftily through the mystifying web he was spinning about them.

CHAPTER SIX
MYSTERY AT
OAKRIDGE MANOR

BY FAST passenger plane the service from New York to Washington is a matter of less than two hours air time. Considerably less. And if a long-distance telephone call has been made from the New York airport, resulting in a speedy automobile waiting at the Washington airport, the time elapsed from Central Park to upper Pennsylvania Avenue is phenomenally low.

It lacked five minutes to midnight when Val, Nancy Fraser and Nora Beamish stepped into that sedan and were gruffly greeted by the heavy-set, saturine man behind the wheel. It was Gregg himself, as unknown and overlooked by the world as were the actions of that subtle force which he controlled.

"You people are playing hob with my sleep!" Gregg snarled as he sent the car through the gears with a rush and they whirled off the air field. "One would think I had nothing to do but stay up nights and nurse a lot of agents joyriding around the world. Let's have the straight of all this. I couldn't make heads or tails of your gabble over long distance a while ago, Easton."

That was Gregg's way, and no one who took his orders paid any attention to it for very long. Behind it Gregg was fanatically on the job, as witness his presence here tonight, when he could have remained in bed and sent any of a score of men in his place. His presence too, was testimony of the importance he placed on the curt reference to the Black Doctor that Val had made over long distance.

Val sketched what had happened as they rolled swiftly toward the heart of the city, with the slim white-lighted shaft of the Washington Monument spearing the heavens to their left, and the floodlighted dome of the capitol ballooning toward the sky off to their right.

Gregg sucked a cigar and listened closely, grunting to himself now and then. At the end he blew his horn viciously at another car that seemed about to pass in front of them, flicked cigar ash out the car window, and spoke.

"Carl Zaken, eh? I'd give my liver to get him. He's caused me trouble before. Get this—there'll be hell and furies over this business. Two English citizens murdered, one on a ship flying the United States flag, and the other in New York. We can't pretend to know much about it, or the fact that we've been watching one of their men will be known. Can't have that. If they catch on we're suspicious of this chap who called himself Galbraith, they'll start hunting for the source of our information. It'll be embarrassing. Blast it!"

"What was Galbraith after?" Val asked bluntly.

"Don't know," Gregg said equally bluntly. "We got a tip that something unusual was in the air, and a man was being sent over here *sub rosa* empowered to spend as high as a million pounds for something. That's a hell of a lot of money, if you'll excuse my English, ladies."

"Hmmmph!" Norah snapped from the back seat beside Nancy. "I can do better than that, Jim Gregg, as you well know. Go right ahead."

Val grinned in the darkness, remembering that Nancy had said Norah Beamish had once been Gregg's private secretary.

"Huh? Er—all right," said Gregg, thrown off his stride for a moment. "As I was saying, I cabled Miss Fraser to pick this man up and see what he did. And all this other has broken out of a clear sky. It's hard to tell what to make of it."

"I'd do a lot for a million pounds," Norah observed acidly. "Doubtless this Zaken would do the same. Has that occurred to you?"

"Galbraith didn't have a million pounds on him!" Gregg snapped. "He was only empowered to offer it."

"If you were to offer me a million pounds—" Norah said, undaunted.

"I wouldn't," Gregg growled. "But I'll offer you a suggestion. Let Easton give me his views on the matter."

"Well, I like that!" Norah commented indignantly. "Ouch, Nancy, stop poking me with your elbow."

The silence was thick for a moment as Gregg restrained himself with an effort. "Norah Beamish," he said ominously, "pipe down."

"Oh, all, right," Norah said sulkily.

A MATCH flare lighted Val's red face as he held the flame to a cigarette. "Zaken is after that money," he stated, tossing the match out the window. "If it's worth that to someone else, it's worth it to him. He can cash in on it."

"If he gets it you're all fired," Gregg said calmly. "This thing is getting out of hand. I want Zaken in custody before he gets a chance to do any more harm, and I want to know what Galbraith was after over here. Those two murders will go unsolved until we have all that. There'll be complications. You say you haven't the slightest idea what happened to Zaken?"

"He vanished out of the room," Val said slowly. "His man had the room directly above that. By the time I could do anything it was too late. Both were gone."

Val paused and looked out of the window.

"Yes?" Gregg urged.

"I don't know what Zaken was after in Galbraith's room," Val admitted, looking at him. "Or why he killed Galbraith. But I've got a good hunch that wherever Galbraith was heading for, we can expect Zaken to appear, sooner or later. He gained no money immediately by killing Galbraith. And, from everything I've ever heard about the fellow, he never kills unless there's a good reason for it."

"Where does that get you?" Gregg countered impatiently.

"I know where Galbraith was going."

"Ahhhh—you do?" Gregg suddenly chuckled and laid an approving hand on Val's arm. "I knew you wouldn't let them run you out on the end of a limb and saw it off. Now, let's have the rest of it."

Val remembered Norah Beamish sitting quietly in the back seat and letting him talk. "This isn't really my case," he reminded. "Miss Fraser may like to handle it her own way."

"Ridiculous!" Nancy jeered. "The thing had gotten out of my hands. Where would I be if you hadn't barged into Galbraith's room just in time? I'm helping you now, and bother all the modesty."

"She's right. Let's have it," Gregg agreed.

"I don't know where this Ramey comes in, with his dodging around New York, or what to think of the couple he talked to," Val admitted. "But the next move seems to be at Oakridge Manor. I came down here tonight as quick as possible to do that. If Zaken shows up there we'll collar him and get the truth."

"Why all the rush, if you're going out there tomorrow?" Gregg queried irritably. "You could have let me sleep."

"Going out tonight," Val told him. "It's only about an hour's drive. We'll stage an auto breakdown and go up to the house in search of a telephone. Or I'll say that Galbraith was found dead in New York with that address in his pocket, and pass as a newspaperman asking for information. And in the morning you can post men around the place, working with the information I get tonight."

Gregg considered. "Good enough," he decided. "But don't mention Galbraith. Let them expect him. Just look around the place and play dumb. It ought to work. They'll know nothing about what happened in New York tonight, of course."

They had traversed the long length of Pennsylvania Avenue as they talked. Gregg turned in to the curb at Fourteenth and the Avenue, opened the door and stepped out.

"You might as well take this car," he said. "I'll taxi home and get some sleep. I'll take you with me, Norah. You're probably tired out."

"You will not, Jim Gregg," Norah said defiantly. "Don't think because you O.K. my pay check you can order me around all the time. I'm going out there with Nancy. If there're any car breakdowns and shenanigans I'll fit right into the picture as the helpless mother—what are you laughing at?"

"At the idea of anyone thinking of you as helpless!" Gregg choked. "God help the people at the Manor! They don't know what's landing on their doorstep. And I warn you, Norah, if you bungle anything you'll come back in the office and take dictation. Good night." And Gregg departed hastily, still shaking with laughter.

"The old hyena!" Norah said heatedly, glaring out the window. "I'll make him sweat for that."

HARTSVILLE WAS a small suburban town south of Washington, some thirty minutes of fast driving. Houses were dark and wanly lighted streets deserted. But a gas station and a drugstore were still open for business. In the drugstore Val asked casually as he bought a package of cigarettes: "Know of a place around here called Oakridge Manor?"

"Sure," was the prompt reply. "That's the old Mason place out on the river road. Fellow by the name of Long bought it a few years back and tacked that name on it."

"What's he like?"

"Don't see much of him," said the druggist as he rang up the sale. "Queer sort of man, I hear. Don't welcome visitors. And when people want to be let alone around here, folks most generally let 'em alone."

"How do you get there?"

"Six miles out on the highway, and you turn to the left. It's about three miles down the river road, I reckon. Kind of lonesome country back in there, although the road is used a heap. Long's land backs up clear to the Potomac. You'll see a sign over his gate."

Val thanked the man and went back to the car. As soon as they got away from the little village it became apparent that the druggist had not been wrong when he had described the country as lonesome.

Mist was rising off the river, swirling across the stabbing headlight beams in ghostly streamers. The damp smell of the river bottoms off to the left of the road poured in through the car windows. Great oaks and poplars grew alongside the road, and they passed many stretches of scrub-pine woodland. Now and then a small house was visible behind a whitewashed picket fence, but for the most part the country seemed deserted.

Norah Beamish said flatly: "I don't like this country. It gives me the creeps. I didn't know you could get this wild so close to Washington."

"You should have stayed in the city and gone to sleep," said Val.

It was the wrong thing to say. "Young man, I know my business!" Norah crushed him. "I may have the creeps, but I'm as good as any man we'll find in this section. Nancy, give me a cigarette."

A match flared; and Norah Beamish had taken perhaps half a dozen puffs from her cigarette when a stout wire fence on the left of the road suddenly gave way to massive stone gate posts with a wooden arch between them. A lettered sign hanging from the arch said: OAKRIDGE MANOR.

Val cut the ignition and brought the car to a stop at the side of the road.

"Here we are," he said. In the sudden silence which wrapped them his voice sounded with startling clarity.

Nancy chuckled softly. "Broken down and everything. And where is the house?"

The fog was thicker, if anything, rolling its damp breath through the open car window at Val's side, swirling through the yellow glare of the headlights like endless tenuous tentacles. The distant boom of frogs pulsed dismally on the night. It was a lonely, deserted spot.

Norah Beamish said with conviction: "Anyone who would park himself out in a place like this for very long must be a trifle addled. If anybody had told me this morning on the ship that I'd be here tonight, I'd have hooted them down."

Nevertheless she followed Nancy with alacrity when Val stepped out and opened the rear door.

"You can wait in the car," Val told her.

"Young man," Norah answered majestically, "if Jim Gregg can't tell me what to do, it's useless for you to try. I came here to play a helpless old mother and I'm going to hobble up to that house and play her. Save your breath."

"Hobble on," Val surrendered. "Let's go. I can't see the house, but it must be back there somewhere."

"Are you taking a gun?" Nancy questioned.

"Hardly need one," Val assured her. "After all, we can't possibly be suspected. And with—er—a helpless mother along, we'll fit the part perfectly."

"Nancy shan't stir one step from this car without a gun in the party," Norah said firmly. "She's a helpless girl—and I don't like the looks of this place. It gives me the creeps."

"A gun it'll be then," Val agreed cheerfully. He leaned in the car, pulled his bag out from their luggage, and slipped his automatic in his pocket. On second thought he added the flashlight he always carried somewhere in his effects.

THEY WALKED back to the gate and headed along the driveway into the fog. The hoarse booming of the frogs gradually grew louder, and by that Val knew they were approaching the river. Huge old trees lined the driveway, stretching heavy branches out over their heads. Once the fog parted briefly and he caught sight of a gibbous moon hanging high in the sky. But for the most part they walked blindly in the mist, which blotted and enfeebled the beam of his flashlight.

And the walk seemed endless.

"I don't believe there's a house around here," Norah panted finally. And then said something not entirely lady-like as her heel turned on a stone and she lurched against Val. "Drat it!" she grumbled. "I should have put on hunting boots!"

Val himself was beginning to wonder how much farther they would have to walk. This estate of Oakridge Manor seemed to be endless. The drive made several turns, seeming to run almost in the shape of a sprawling "S." He judged the house was invisible from the road. And then without warning a dark automobile appeared before them; and beyond it the lighted windows of a large house emitted a sickly glow through the mist.

"Thank heavens we won't have to wake them up," Norah remarked with relief.

Val turned the flash into the machine. It was empty; and bore D.C. license plates. Oakridge Manor, he judged, was having visitors this night. All the better.

The drive widened into a big circle in front of the house, with a flower bed in the center, and they could make out dimly the looming bulk of a large Colonial mansion, with a wing at each end. They started around the flower bed; and suddenly Norah stumbled again, and gasped sharply as she jumped quickly aside.

"What is this?"

Val's light was on it a moment later—a huge Great Dane dog lying dead on the driveway with a trickle of blood staining the ground in front of its chest. It had been shot, and had not been dead long as Val discovered when he touched it with his foot.

The sight shocked them out of their calm. "I don't like this!" Nancy whispered sharply.

"I'd like to get my hands on the man who killed that beautiful animal!" Norah exclaimed indignantly under her breath. "Look at him—poor thing!"

Val looked at the house instead. Looked warily. Of a sudden the drear silence had taken on an ominous quality. He couldn't say why. After all, there were a score of reasons why the dog might have been killed. It might have been a strange dog, for instance, trespassing in some way. But nevertheless the feeling persisted.

"Perhaps you two had better go back to the car," he suggested under his breath.

"We'll stick together," Nancy told him quietly.

"I'm not afraid!" Norah Beamish insisted defiantly. "It takes more than a dead dog to upset me. Go on."

Val hesitated, and then against his better judgment led the way to the front door. It was made of heavy planks, with small diamond-shaped panes of leaded glass at the top. Curtains inside cut off the view beyond. He found a big wrought-iron knocker breast high, and used it. The clanging sounds seemed to echo back through the house, which despite the lights was strangely silent.

The knocking was not answered. He repeated it. And while he waited, he roved the beam of the flash around the big dark front porch. Not ten feet away the bottoms of a pair of shoes caught his eye.

It was a man, lying there on his face, with the bone handle of a knife sticking up grotesquely from under one shoulder blade!

CHAPTER SEVEN
THE WOMAN UPSTAIRS

NANCY FRASER saw that sight past Val's shoulder an instant later. Her fingers bit into his arm as she pressed close to him. "Is—is he dead?" she asked unsteadily.

"Looks that way," Val muttered, stepping forward to the side of the motionless body.

He stooped, caught a shoulder and turned the face up. The flashlight showed a dapper, well-dressed young man with a sharp face, prominent nose and tousled black hair. It was no one he had ever seen before.

Norah had moved to the spot also. She did not cry out. She was calm as usual. "Nancy—I think we had better go back to the machine."

"What do you think is happening here?" Nancy asked Val swiftly.

"Haven't the slightest idea," he confessed. "But it looks bad."

Just then the front door opened, letting a bright swath of light out across the front porch.

Val whirled around, sliding his hand into his pocket.

A broad-shouldered, heavy-set man stepped out into the light and peered at them. He had a gun in his hand, and as he stared at them the weapon slowly lowered to his side and he asked gruffly: "What's this?"

"I think you're the one to do the explaining," Val countered, walking toward him. "Who killed that man?"

"You aren't the sheriff?" the stranger mumbled, looking at the two women.

"No. I'm not the sheriff."

"Then who the devil are you?"

Norah Beamish ranged alongside Val, and there was not the slightest trace of a quaver in her voice as she said firmly: "Our car ran out of gasoline down there on the road, and we came in here looking for a telephone or enough gasoline to take us on."

The man who stood there in the light had a wide flat face, with lumpy, muscular jowls, blue-black with a close-shaven beard. His eyes were narrowed, his mouth was a tight line and his manner suspicious as Norah Beamish spoke to him. But the suspicion gradually left.

"Out of gasoline, eh?" he said.

"Yes," Norah answered calmly. "Have you any to spare? And while we're asking questions, what is that dead man doing there? It's—it's horrible."

VAL KEPT his hand on the automatic in his pocket. He was aware of the narrowed eyes resting on the pocket for a moment, and suspected that the fellow knew what was in it. But the fact seemed to make no difference. They couldn't look very suspicious with Norah Beamish standing there very much the *grande dame,* asking imperious questions.

"I guess it does look pretty funny to find a thing like that on a front porch, doesn't it, madam?" the man chuckled. "The fact is, I'm waiting for the sheriff now. I thought when you knocked it was he. You see, this fellow, whoever he is," with a jerk of his head at the body, "was prowling around here tonight with at least one other man. The dog ran out barking at them, and they shot him."

"They should have been shot themselves for that!" Norah sniffed.

"My sentiments exactly, madam," she was assured. "I heard the disturbance and ran out to see what was the matter. One of them took a shot at me in the dark. I made a good target against the light, I imagine. The bullet just missed me. See where it hit the side of the door?"

He turned and pointed to a small round hole in the wood at the side of the door which Val had not noticed when he knocked.

"And so you stabbed him?" Norah queried, wide-eyed.

That drew another chuckle. "No, madam, I did not stab him. I had stepped out without my gun, and I ran back inside and slammed the door. It was 'Big Buck,' the nigger yard man, who threw that knife. He's quite handy with one, and he had dodged out at the side of the house when he heard the noise. Standing there, he saw one of the men run up on the porch and take a stand at the side of the door with a gun in his hand. Evidently waiting for me to show myself again, madam. Buck didn't know what it was all about. But he knew I was in danger, and when I started to open the door again, having gotten my gun, Buck threw his knife. Unfortunately with fatal effect. The man fell. And his companions must have gone one way while Buck went the other. When I stepped out on the porch with this revolver, I found the fellow breathing his last, and it took me ten minutes or so to get the straight of the matter. I've telephoned the sheriff, and he said he would get out here as soon as he could.

"And that," said the man drily, "explains the gory scene, madam. If you people will step inside you may use the telephone, and save yourselves the unpleasantness of being out here with him."

With a polite inclination of his head he indicated the doorway hospitably.

"Thank you. We will do that," said Norah firmly, and she sailed inside before Val could say anything to her. Nancy looked at him inquiringly.

Val swiftly conned the facts. "You say there were two of them?" he asked.

"At least that many."

"And the others ran?"

"I haven't seen anything more of them. I guess they didn't know how many men were out there in the darkness throwing knives, so they left while the leaving was good," the man chuckled again.

GALBRAITH HAD been intending to come here. He had been killed. Now violence had appeared at this house a few hours later. Was it the work of the Black Doctor, Val wondered. Was this house unaware of the danger threatening it? Had the Black Doctor, or some of his men, been closing in on it and been checked by an unexpected knife thrown put of the darkness?

It looked that way.

The mystery was growing thicker at every move, but this was the chance he had wanted to get inside the house. Val nodded slightly at Nancy and followed her into a wide, spacious hall.

"My name is Easton," he said calmly as their host joined them, closing the door behind him.

"Tillson is my name, sir," the other answered promptly.

This was the man, then, to whom Ramey's wire had been sent. But what about Long, the city man who had bought the place several years before, according to the owner of the drugstore back in Hartsville? Val had been wondering about that all the way out. Long owned Oakridge Manor, yet Ramey had wired a J.B. Tillson. Did they live here together? Were they partners, friends? Those were questions he wanted to ask, but didn't dare to, under the circumstances.

"You are the owner, I presume?" he suggested.

And received a negative shake of the head.

"No. Mr. Long is the owner here. He's upstairs in bed with a broken leg."

Norah Beamish had been looking around as they talked. "You have a nice place here," she complimented.

"Thank you, madam," Tillson bowed. "I think it is myself."

He was a curious combination of hard-boiled sophistication and ultra-polite civility. The fact that a man lay dead on the front porch did not seem to disturb him in the slightest. In fact he seemed amused, if anything. Val surprised a quirk at the corner of his mouth that was suppressed almost instantly. And since the telephone was not pressed on them at once, he talked casually.

"Do you have a farm here?"

Tillson shook his head. "Only a vegetable garden. I guess there isn't enough money in farming these days to tempt John. And since he has enough money to live on he lets the place lie as it is."

"I imagine the women folks are upset by this business tonight," Norah Beamish observed shrewdly.

"There are no women in the house," Tillson told her. "John is a bachelor, and my wife is in California."

"Where all wives should be," said Norah.

Tillson was the perfect host as he smiled at her sadly. "There are different opinions about that, of course, madam. I miss Mrs. Tillson a great deal. Won't you ladies sit down? Mr. Easton, the telephone is in the back of the house. I'll take you there. Better get the call in before the sheriff gets here."

Talking to this man, looking about the spacious hall, listening to the peaceful quiet of the old house, Val had felt increasingly that something was wrong.

All this did not hook up with Galbraith's errand to this country; with Gregg's declaration that the man had been empowered to spend a million pounds; with the British agent that had evidently been tagging Galbraith; and the cold-blooded way both men had died. What could one of the great powers find interesting in this spot? In this man Tillson or his friend who lay upstairs with a broken leg? What did New York have to do with this peaceful lonely spot on the banks of the Potomac?

And while those thoughts had flashed through Val's mind, he was wondering about Tillson also. For despite the ultra politeness, the soft, almost genial manner of the man, the effect fell flat. He didn't look like a country gentleman, or a man who would be satisfied to hibernate in a quiet spot like this. He looked hard, cold, clever. And every once in a while there was a glint in his eyes, a catlike scrutiny of his surroundings, a cold, quickly caught inflection of his voice, that bore out that impression.

NO, THE man didn't ring true. The situation didn't ring true. There was peace in the air. But it was a taut, quivering peace, a quiet that seemed charged with electric tension.

Instead of quieting the nerves it put them on edge. Val had a very definite feeling that all this pleasantry might change instantly to tragedy.

And against all the facts he had marshaled there was the evidence of the dead dog and the lifeless corpse out there on the front porch. That dead man belonged to the cities.

He wasn't a casual country prowler. He didn't belong out here in the mist-filled night, far from houses or people—unless the facts were right. Unless there were more to all this than appeared on the surface. Unless Galbraith had been intending to come here, and the Black Doctor was also interested in the place.

That was evidence that could not be disputed. Val wished the women were back in the machine, heading toward Washington. He was, he told himself, a fool for bringing them out there. He could have done the job just as well himself.

"I'll use your telephone," he agreed briskly. "And then we'll go out to our car and cause you no further trouble."

"It is a pleasure," Tillson assured him. "It does this house good to have women in it once in a while."

And the words were barely out of the man's mouth as he turned to the door on his right when the quiet of the house was rudely shattered by a rush of feet upstairs. And following that came the high, shrill, terror-stricken cry of a woman....

They all froze in their tracks, staring toward the top of the wide sweeping stairs that led up to the second floor, whence that scream had come.

Val's eyes dropped to Tillson, whose head had hunched forward and whose face had darkened with an ugly scowl.

That was all the proof Val needed of his suspicions. Tillson had lied flatly when he said there were no women in the house. And that woman who had screamed was in mortal terror or great pain. It drove a shiver down his back.

"What's wrong up there?" Norah Beamish uttered explosively, swinging around on Tillson.

It all happened in seconds. Later on Val was to wonder why he hadn't moved fast enough. But he didn't have a chance, couldn't guess what was going to happen.

After the scream cut off sharp, the running feet still pounded upstairs. They reached the head of the stairs and started down.

The four of them standing below in the hall saw the feet, the legs, the whole figure of a man dashing down the stairs. He was hatless, coatless, shirtless—a sleek, pudgy form half running, half falling down the stairs in his mad haste.

His hair was rumpled wildly; blood was streaming from the corner of his mouth, spattering the white front of his under shirt and his arms. And one hand brandished a gleaming revolver.

With a shock Val recognized Galbraith's New York visitor—Ramey!

Only now the sleek unctuousness of the man had given away to wild, uncontrollable fright and desperation. His face was twisted in a mask of terror as he catapulted to the turn of the stairs.

"Get back!" Val cried at Nancy Fraser. His arm swept her roughly back against the wall.

And an instant later, as Ramey reached the turn in the stairs, their ears were deafened by the report of a gun. It was Tillson shooting. Standing there calmly, jaws clenched until the bunching muscles ridged out. His gun spat once—twice—three times....

Ramey's legs gave way under him. The terror-stricken mask of his face suddenly looked horrible as it was struck by a bullet. His body raced forward, the gun flying from his fingers.

And as Norah Beamish lost her poise and screamed aloud, Ramey's limp body tumbled and bounced and slid to the floor of the hall at their feet.

CHAPTER EIGHT
THE £1,000,000 SECRET

THE ODOR of burnt powder was strong on the air. Their ears were ringing from the shattering explosions in the confined space of the hall. And ghastly death there before them was stark evidence that they were not dreaming.

Val turned on Tillson, tugging at the automatic in his pocket—and met the steady muzzle of Tillson's revolver. Behind it he saw a new Tillson. A man no longer smiling, polite. The narrowed eyes were cold and hard. The flat face was a mask that was not good to see.

"Put your arms up!" Tillson ordered through his teeth.

Val hesitated only a fraction of a second. Proof of what might happen if he did not was too close at hand. He jerked his hands from his coat pocket and lifted his arms in the air.

"You—you cold-blooded killer!" Norah Beamish gasped.

"Shut up!" Tillson ordered her roughly. "You talk too much, old lady!"

"Old?" Norah choked. "Why—why—"

"Do I have to shut your mouth for you?" Tillson asked coldly.

"Norah, be quiet," Nancy ordered clearly. She stepped to Norah's side and laid slender fingers on Norah's arm.

Tillson gave her a cold grin. "You have, some sense, young lady," he remarked.

"You haven't acted as if you had," Nancy told him in the same cool voice. Her deep blue eyes were boring at the man as if she were trying to look behind his face and see things that had not become visible heretofore.

Tillson sneered at them. "Gas!" he said. "Ran out of it right by the front gate. It was convenient, wasn't it? And too bad."

"Your name isn't Tillson," Nancy said coolly.

"No? What is it?"

That was what Val was wondering. The whole picture had changed. He was trying to get his bearings again, linking up the facts to make a new picture. And while he was doing that someone else came to the top of the stairs and descended leisurely.

Val saw black-clad legs, a white shirt, with sleeves rolled up—and a tall, stooped figure descended into view. A pale, cadaverous face looked down at them as the newcomer halted at the turn of the stairs and surveyed the scene for a moment with an inscrutable smile on his lips. The bony arms below the rolled-up sleeves were covered thickly with dark matted hair. And the long talonlike fingers of the right hand held a keen, gleaming surgeon's scalpel.

Nancy uttered a choked cry. Val swore under his breath, and a chill crawled down his back. For that stooped figure holding the little gleaming knife was Carl Zaken, the Black Doctor.

"So?" said Zaken mildly, gesturing with the scalpel. "These are our visitors. This is a surprise."

And the very mildness of his voice made the words sound worse. For Val and Nancy had seen what the man could do, and had heard tales of what he was capable of.

Standing there holding the surgeon's scalpel he looked like a smiling fiend.

Norah Beamish's harsh whisper to Nancy was audible to all of them. "Who—who is that man?"

Nancy's face was pale. Val saw the fingers of her free hand curling tightly into her pink palm, and guessed the terrific effort she was making to keep a grip on herself. But her voice was steady as she spoke.

"That is the man who attacked me in the hotel this evening. His name is Carl Zaken."

"Oh!" said Norah weakly, and for once she seemed at a loss for words as she stared up at Zaken.

Zaken leaned against the railing, toying with the scalpel. He betrayed no surprise at Nancy's knowledge of his identity. His greenish eyes seemed to blaze and glow as the light from the hall fixture struck into them.

"What were you doing to that fellow?" Val asked harshly, nodding at Ramey.

"We were having a little confidential talk," the Black Doctor said smoothly, and his lips parted in a ghastly grimace and he slowly tapped the back of the scalpel against a thumb.

"You mean," asked Val thickly, "you were torturing him?"

"Persuading," Zaken corrected. "Unfortunately he knocked my man down, seized his gun and tried to leave us, forgetting entirely his woman friend. But then, cheap criminals of his type think only of their own skins."

ALL THE tales Val had ever heard about the Black Doctor flashed before him now. He understood the terrible fright and agony on Ramey's face as he had plunged down the stairs. This lonely house was being given over to things too horrible to contemplate. And Nancy was thinking the same, for he saw her smooth white throat flutter as she swallowed convulsively.

"He was in New York this afternoon," Val said mechanically.

"Yes. He and his friends should have stayed there instead of hurrying here as soon as he was through with Sir Edward Lyne," Zaken said contemptuously.

"You came quick enough. How did you get out of that room and down here in Virginia so fast?"

Zaken grimaced again with amusement. "I have found that he who moves fastest moves safest, Mr. Easton. Leaving the room was a small matter. My man, who had tied you up so I would not be interrupted, had lowered a thin silk rope from his room just over Sir Edward's, to call our late friend by his right name. I left you via the rope, the fire escape from the roof below, and a taxicab that I hailed at the mouth of the alley. I picked my man up at the hotel entrance a few minutes later. We passed the police car as we turned into Fifth Avenue. A fast ride out to a chartered plane. A faster trip to Washington and out here. Voila— and the thing was done. I presume you came by plane also?"

Val nodded. "I didn't expect to find you here," he confessed bluntly.

"*Touché*—the surprise is mutual. I did not believe you had been able to find out where Galbraith was going. I killed him for that reason—so the matter would end there for you—and him. Had I suspected otherwise I would have used lethal gas."

"Like you used on those poor devils aboard ship," Val charged swiftly.

Zaken gestured delicately with the scalpel. "The steward was an accident. The gas lingered in that closed room longer than I thought it would. He walked into it. The wind must have blown in through the door he left open and aired the cabin thoroughly before he was discovered. You found no trace of it?"

"No," said Val shortly.

"Just as well," Zaken murmured. "It is very deadly. It had to be because of the small amount I was able to inject through the keyhole."

"Why do it?"

"He was a member of the British Secret Service, dispatched as an unofficial guard over Sir Edward Lyne. We bumped into each other on deck that evening, and I think he recognized me. I couldn't take chances. You understand how it is in delicate matters like this, Mr. Easton?"

"In a small way," Val agreed sarcastically. "I suppose you found out what Lyne was after when you searched his hotel room. And then put him out of the way because you needed him no longer."

"But I knew what he was after," Zaken declared humorously, showing his fanglike incisor teeth as he smiled. "But I did not know where it was. You are quite right about the rest. I simply—ah—eliminated competition which might have proved embarrassing. He would have come here at once, of course. You would have followed—and my plans might have been upset. I have only three men with me. The whole matter broke so suddenly I barely had time to get passage on the same boat with Lyne. No matter what I pay for information, my sources are not always infallible." Zaken's casual manner changed abruptly. "Bring them upstairs," he commanded. "Shoot the first one who makes a wrong move. Are you sure they're alone?"

"Yes. I was waiting near the gate when they stopped their car."

Zaken nodded, waited until they were almost up to him and then preceded them. He turned to the left at the top of the stairs and led the way to the back of the house, to a long, high-ceilinged room with a great bay window, curtained now, opening out into the night.

Standing beside the door and furtively fingering a swelling eye was the man who had posed as a waiter only a few hours earlier. "Did you get him?" he asked Zaken uncertainly.

"Yes," returned Zaken coldly. "And the next time you grow careless, Stubbs, it will be the end. I stand for blundering no more than once."

"Yes, sir," Stubbs replied uneasily, his eyes dropping before the greenish glare that transfixed him. And pallor swept over his face as Zaken led the way into the room.

IT WAS an upstairs library, with book-cases along the walls, comfortable chairs, and a large brick fireplace against the end wall. Over the fireplace hung a large copy of the Stuart painting of George Washington, and the inscrutable eyes of the stately figure seemed to look down and ponder this strange scene that was taking place.

Six people were seated in that room, as strange and heterogeneous a collection as Val had ever seen. Every one of them was marked with the sickly brand of fright and terror.

Sitting in the bay window were two; a pretty, slinky, tawdry young woman dressed in flashy clothes, who was slowly rubbing an angry red wrist; and a hard, sophisticated man of about thirty, wise, worldly, and at this moment pale and haggard as he wet his lips and stared at them.

On a bench beside the fireplace were a lanky negro in overalls and a fat negress, the whites of their eyes rolling.

Two chairs near the end of the library table held a stiff, severe, waspish woman of about forty-five, and a small, slight man with a bulging forehead and shrewd eyes, a strange mixture of intelligence and pomposity. He was haggard also, with sunken, feverish eyes and a limp appearance, as if worry and fear had crushed him.

STANDING NEAR the doorway, a gun in his hand, was a cool, self-possessed man in his early thirties, his face cast in a shrewd cold mold, with a cruel mouth under a small black mustache. He looked foreign—was foreign Val found out a moment later.

For Carl Zaken, continuing with the same mocking politeness, gestured at them with a scalpel. "The people you came to see, Mr. Easton. Study them at your leisure. In the window there we have Miss Dolly Mae Hall, as perfect a sample of your shopworn New York night-club siren as one could wish to find. Her specialty is understanding love, and she seems to be good at it."

Val saw the pompous little man with the bulging forehead wriggle uneasily in his chair, and glance fearfully at the severe woman at his side, who pursed her mouth and glared at him.

Zaken flashed them a humorous glance and went on.

"With her is 'Badger Bill' Marcus, a sterling partner, I understand. Those two negroes work about the place. And in these chairs by the table we have Professor Henry Long and his gentle wife. This man guarding them is Vollonoff, who has been with me for some years, under one name and another. You recognize these three, Vollonoff? Easton, Miss Fraser, and a Mrs. Beamish, of the American Secret Service. They worked faster than we thought possible. Don't underestimate Easton and the girl, Fyodor. They are dangerous."

Vollonoff flashed a cold smile under his black mustache. Val judged him to be almost as dangerous as Carl Zaken himself.

"The man you saw on the front porch," continued Zaken, "is Sammy McGee, alias Tillson, a partner of Ramey and Marcus. The story, as I gather it to date, is that Professor Long, to celebrate the successful culmination of several years' work, and the undoubtedly trying company of his wife in this isolated spot, went to New York to taste the bright lights. Or, as I have heard your countrymen say, 'to throw a bust.' He drank not wisely but too well, talked indiscreetly about what he had been working on and had accomplished, and in that alcoholic daze found himself in the grip of an undying passion for Dolly Mae. They progressed to her apartment—control yourself, Mrs. Long—the flesh is weak at times.

"The play that was staged must have been masterly, Easton. When it was over Professor Long found himself apparently laboring under the onus of having shot his new love's husband, with Ramey, one of her men friends in the role of rescuer, who hustled him away from the police net to safety. It developed that the price of continued safety and silence was a share in the fortune that Professor Long stood to gain from his invention.

"Under duress Professor Long was constrained to turn the marketing of his invention over to the gang controlled by Ramey, which had him in its grip. They sent Sammy McGee down here under the name of Tillson to keep an eye on the professor and make certain he did not forget that at any moment he might be hauled back to New York for murder. And Ramey took up the marketing of the invention, not with his own country as any patriotic citizen would do, but with the British government, who could be counted on to pay almost any price for it. The upshot of the negotiations was the hurried dispatch of Sir Edward Lyne, with instructions to look into the matter and offer anything up to a million pounds on the spot if he considered the claims correct."

Carl Zaken shrugged.

"And that's where we came in, Easton. Ramey had evidently stipulated a secret rendezvous in New York with the man sent over, with more directions there. His intention was to bring Lyne down here, convince him, wait until the money was paid over, and probably decamp with all of it. After giving Lyne directions, he and his confederates hurried down here instantly. We found them here when we arrived. The dog barked as we came up and had to be put out of the way. McGee rushed out, and Vollonoff dispatched him with his usual skill. And so we came in and went to work. I had just finished a little session with Ramey in the other room, finding out that Professor Long has been canny enough to keep the final drawings of his invention hidden. And now I am ready to take that little matter up with him."

ZAKEN SMILED without mirth as he stood there in his shirt sleeves, drawing the gleaming little knife through his fingers. Professor Long's face went grayish as he met the grimacing smile the Black Doctor gave him.

Mrs. Long sprang to her feet and cried shrilly: "You'd better leave Henry alone! You—you'll suffer for this outrage, whoever you are!"

Vollonoff stepped forward and shoved her roughly back in her chair.

Val hardly saw the play. His mind was on the astounding revelations Zaken had made apparently under the impression that he knew almost as much about it. What could that shrinking, pompous little man with the bulging forehead control that would be worth almost any price to a foreign government?

He said casually: "I doubt if Lyne would have offered much for it. And you probably won't get anything for your trouble, either."

"No?" Zaken mocked. "Not for the answer to the problem that every general staff in the world has been seeking for fifteen years? An infallible range finder that will locate and bring correctly to bear anti-aircraft guns by day or night, or in fog? Your own army engineers have been working on it for years. And according to Ramey, the professor here has solved the problem with a sensitive finder that picks up the spark emanations from the motor timer, calibrates their distance and height and speed by instant triangulation, and brings the guns hooked up to the system to bear instantly. With it a fleet of bombing planes can be located whether seen or not, and shot down at once. It will make the country that controls it safe from aerial invasion. Think what that will mean to England—to know that she is safe from attack by air! Millions saved in defensive air fleets, and probably the winning or losing of the next war.

Japan, with her great cities near her island coasts, will pay any price for it. The general staffs of every great power will be bidding wildly for it, once the information gets out that Carl Zaken can turn that invention over to them."

And Val knew with a sickening feeling, that the man was right. If this Professor Long had perfected an invention like that and it looked as if he had—no price was too much to pay for it. And Carl Zaken, master spy would offer it to the highest bidder. The chances were that some other country would get it, possibly a future enemy of the United! States. In this lonely house tonight a world issue was being decided. And in the balance were only himself, Nancy Fraser and Norah Beamish.

Zaken's mocking glance was on him. "You don't agree?" Zaken questioned.

Val shrugged. "Perhaps. D'you think Long will tell you? He doesn't look like the type of man who would give as important a secret as that into the wrong hands."

Professor Henry Long sat up and spoke for the first time. "I'm not!" he burst out passionately. "I didn't know what Ramey was going to do! He said he was dealing with our government! I won't turn it over to another country! I won't...."

Zaken showed his fanglike incisors in another grimace. "Your sentiments do you credit, professor. We will see what a short consultation will do. I have been very successful in the past as a persuader. Kroner, bring him in. We won't embarrass the ladies by doing it in here."

The powerful fellow who had posed as Tillson pushed to the professor's chair without a word, seized his arm and hauled him up. When the little man tried to struggle, he received a blow in the face that knocked him limp and mumbling. And in that state, while his wife wailed shrilly and the others looked on with horrified helplessness, the professor was half dragged, half carried out of the room.

The Black Doctor slowly scraped the edge of his scalpel across the matted hairs of his left arm. The gesture was casual, but the effect was ghastly as he grimaced and turned to follow.

"I shall write Gregg tomorrow and compliment him on his agents," he said to Val and Nancy. "A pity I can't let you live to tell him about this. But a million pounds is too much to risk...."

CHAPTER NINE

GAS TRAP

NORAH BEAMISH cast a venomous glance at Vollonoff and went over and tried to comfort the nearly hysterical Mrs. Long. Twin spots of color were vivid on Nancy's face as she looked at Val silently. Stubbs stood outside the door, fingering his gun. Vollonoff lounged inside, his eyes watching every move they made. The couple in the window seat huddled together miserably. And the fat negress began to mumble, "Oh, Lawd—Oh, Lawd— Oh, Lawd...."

A piercing shriek suddenly rang through the house, the cry of a man in torment and agony.

Professor Long's wife gasped and fainted, which was perhaps best, for more shrieks followed.

Norah Beamish whirled on Val, her eyes blazing. "Can't you do something about it?" she cried.

Vollonoff smirked expectantly.

And Val stood there with his shoulders slumped, the picture of dejection. "And get shot for trying?" he answered Norah helplessly. "You saw what happened to that chap downstairs."

Norah glared at him. "I thought you were a man!"

"Val—" said Nancy helplessly.

"It's no use," Val said wretchedly.

"We're going to die anyway," she reminded through stiff lips.

"Perhaps they'll let us go if we promise to let them get away. They could tie us up—"

"Oh!" Norah blazed contemptuously.

Even Vollonoff was affected by this show of helplessness. "Sit down," he advised, with a curl of contempt on his lips. "Not so dangerous, after all."

Val shrugged helplessly and turned toward the nearest chair. And as he passed slowly in front of Nancy, with his back to Vollonoff, words slid almost inaudibly from the corner of his mouth. He didn't even look at her to see what their effect was.

Nancy's face suddenly twisted in helpless grief. She fished for a handkerchief and dabbed at her eyes as she turned toward the other end of the room.

"He c-can't help us," she wept. "Come over here with me, Norah."

Norah stared at her in amazement and then swiftly followed her. "Don't you cry, honey," she begged bruskly. "There's a way out of this."

"No, there's not!" Nancy wailed.

Val could see them as he pulled the chair around to sit down. But an instant later he heard Nancy gasp: "Catch me! I'm—I'm…."

And Val snapped the chair off the floor, whirled around and hurled it with every ounce of strength in his body. As he had planned, Nancy's gasp had drawn Vollonoff's attention for a second. Vollonoff sensed what was happening—too late. As he jerked his head back the edge of the chair seat caught him squarely in the face. The gun in his hand roared deafeningly, missing. And an instant later Val was on him, smashing his fist over the top of the falling chair.

The jar of the blow rocked Val's arm clear to the shoulder. And it drove Vollonoff reeling backward, knocked out cold, the gun falling from his hand.

Val ducked into the protection of his body, caught Vollonoff under the arms and heaved him at the doorway. Stubbs, leaping into the room in confused surprise, caught the full impact of Vollonoff's weight, and for an instant was tied up in confusion there in the doorway.

"Here!" Nancy cried at Val's side. She thrust Vollonoff's gun into his hand. She had seized it off the floor. Her eyes were shining, her voice thrilling in its disregard for danger.

"Get down on the floor!" Val rapped at her as his fingers closed over the revolver. A wave of confidence swept through him. No longer were his hands tied by futile helplessness. The very thought of the odds against them, and the consequences if he failed, brought strength.

The revolver leveled just as Stubbs hurled Vollonoff's falling body back into the room and raised the automatic in his hand. Both guns spat at once. A cold, searing sensation raked Val's side. He knew he had been shot there. But Stubbs reeled around, clasping a shattered elbow. And then dodged out of sight beside the door before Val could fire again.

A LEAP, a kick, and the door crashed shut. An instant later Stubbs poured a fusillade of shots through the door. But they all went wide, hitting no one.

Everyone had come to their feet. The negress began to shriek in terror.

"Shut up!" Val yelled at her, and when that had no effect he ignored her.

He heard Carl Zaken's voice shout in the hallway. "What happened in there?"

And Stubbs replying shakily: "He knocked Vollonoff out with a chair, got his gun, and shot me in the elbow! I'll bleed to death!"

"And good enough for you!" Zaken snarled. He broke off into French, cursing Vollonoff and Stubbs for ignorant fools. "Clumsy pig! Son of a goat!" Zaken shouted. "Watch that door! Don't let them get out! They can't get away! I'll fix them! With gas!"

Nancy and Val both understood the words. The rest did not. Marcus asked uncertainly: "What'll we do?"

"Gas!" Nancy whispered to Val. "It won't be tear gas this time!"

"No," Val agreed bruskly. "He's gambling high tonight. He'll slaughter the lot of us as quick as he can now."

Nancy looked at him desperately. "What will we do? We can't get out that door."

"Here! Watch the door! Don't waste the bullets! We'll need them!"

Val grabbed up a chair, stepped to the great bay window and began to swing the chair vigorously. Glass crashed and fell away before it. A few seconds of that and the windows were cleared away.

WRAITHS OF fog swirled in. The croaking of the riverside frogs sounded very close. He judged the house sat almost on the river bank. He turned around and snapped at the others:

"Get out on that roof! Quick! Your lives may depend on it!"

Professor Long's wife was still unconscious in her chair. Val picked her up and strode to the window. He had to wait a moment as Marcus and his girl friend and the two negroes scrambled through, ignoring the jagged edges of glass. None of them waited to help him. Val hadn't expected it. Their nerves were too shattered by terror. He heaved his burden through and lowered her roughly to the roof below. She would have a measure of safety out there.

Norah Beamish and Nancy were at his side, waiting for orders. Norah's eyes were shining too. "Young man," she cried, "I apologize!"

Outside the door Carl Zaken's voice snapped in French: "One side, pig!"

"Give me that gun!" Val husked to Nancy. He fired two shots at the door. Couldn't see whether he had hit anything or not.

Vollonoff stirred on the floor just before he fired. The sound of the shots seemed to bring him out of his daze. He sat up groggily. And an instant later Nancy caught Val's arm and pointed to the doorway.

"Look!"

Through one of the bullet holes in the door thrust the glistening point of a sharp needle. From its end a tiny spray of liquid spurted into the room. And that spray dissolved into a bluish vapor as they stared at it.

"Out that window quick!" Val urged. He whirled Nancy around himself, and started her with a shove.

And as he waited for them to get through to safety, Val saw a sight he never forgot. Vollonoff was staggering to his feet just in front of the door, his eyes on them with dazed surprise.

"Look out!" Val shouted at him. "Come over here, quick!"

Instead Vollonoff turned around to the door, obviously intending to escape. And the first dissolving wave of gas closed about him. Vollonoff's hand shot to his throat. He strangled. Too late he realized what was happening and turned toward the window.

The gas cloaked him like an evil halo now. He staggered, his face turning purple and his eyes starting from their sockets. His mouth opened to cry out—and only a horrible strangling issued from it. Vollonoff took one lurching step toward the window, and then tumbled forward on his face, kicked and lay still.

Val ducked out the window, white-faced and shaken.

"God!" he husked to Nancy. "No wonder that steward couldn't get out the door! Get down off this roof before it starts to drift out the window. One good whiff of it seems to be all that's needed."

HE DRAGGED Long's wife to the end of the roof. She recovered consciousness as he did that. The negro was down on the ground. The negress slid off, hung by her hands a moment, blubbering, and then dropped the short distance to the ground and was caught by her companion.

"Pass her down to me," Val ordered Nancy.

He dropped the same way. Nancy and Norah Beamish lowered the protesting woman and he caught her. Nancy and Norah followed. And while they did that Marcus and his girl companion made the drop successfully. They were all safe.

"Get back out of sight and stay there!" Val said to Nancy and Norah. "No more foolishness! I'll see what I can do."

He raced through the damp mist to the front of the house, gun in one hand and his flash in the other. The front porch was still and quiet. A wink of the flash showed the dead body lying where he had left it. The front door was closed.

But as he looked, it was jerked open from inside and the man who had opened it once before stepped out. Val shot at him and missed. The man jumped back inside, slamming the door.

Val waited tensely, wondering what would happen next.

It came from behind; running feet poked out of the fog and closed in on him. Val faced them crouching, wondering with a sick feeling if Carl Zaken had lied, and had more men out here in the night.

But a voice shouted: "That you Easton?"

It was Gregg. And as Val relaxed and lowered the gun, Gregg came running up with half a dozen men. "We heard the shouts," he panted. "Having trouble?"

And all Val could think of at that instant was to say foolishly: "I thought you were going home to sleep."

"Got to thinking that this was too important to leave up in the air till morning," Gregg told him. "I called some of the men and started out here to get the lay of the land myself, and station them. We saw your car back there by the gate and had started to look the ground over when we heard something that sounded like shots. And then we heard you shoot here again. What happened?"

"Two of you go around and watch there!" Val ordered before he replied. "Shoot anyone you see trying to leave. Anyone outside is all right."

"Do that!" Gregg ordered hastily.

And as two of the men ran, Val hurriedly gave Gregg the highlights.

"Surround this house!" Gregg snapped to the rest of his men. "And shoot to kill. We've got one of the most dangerous men in the world cornered."

The words were hardly out of his mouth when three quick shots barked at the back of the house.

Val sprinted for the front door, and Gregg pounded after him, gun in hand also. Val opened the front door and peered in cautiously. The hall was empty. Ramey's body sprawled at the foot of the stairs. The interior of the house was still. Ominously still. Deathly still. But as he and Gregg stared in, the door at the back swung silently open. Carl Zaken leaped into the hall with a catlike movement, holding a gun in each hand.

He saw them at the same instant and jerked the two weapons up.

Val shot him first. Emptied the revolver in a tearing burst as fast as he could pull the trigger. Zaken went down, shooting wildly and futilely. He tried to rise on his two hands, dragging his guns with him. And slumped forward again. And then with a sudden movement he threw them weakly from him.

"*Touché,* Easton," he called weakly, turning a ghastly, pain-racked face toward the doorway. "I told Vollonoff you were a dangerous man."

And so it ended. Zaken's other two men had been trapped at the rear of the house, where they thought no one was watching, shot seriously and captured. They found Professor Long upstairs in one of the bedrooms, half dead from fear rather than pain. A few moments later, downstairs, he thrust a roll of drawings in Val's hand.

"Here," he said weakly. "Keep these. I—I never want to see them again. I'll take whatever the government offers for them."

Gregg's men, after performing hurried first aid, were already loading the wounded into their car, which they had brought up to the house and the body of Carl Zaken went with them.

Gregg was saying to Norah Beamish: "Want to ride back with us?"

"Nonsense!" Norah snapped. "I'll go with Nancy and Mr. Easton. Nancy needs me."

There was a slight inscrutable smile on Nancy's face as she said: "I think I'll be taken care of all right, if you want to go, Norah."

For a moment the older woman looked at Nancy shrewdly. And then she, too, smiled, and sighed. "I'll go with you, Jim Gregg," she said. "I think I'm getting old after all. Nancy doesn't need a mother tonight. Do you, Nancy?"

But Nancy was smiling at Val and didn't hear her.

TORTURE TAVERN

LIKE A GHASTLY YELLOW
SPIDER CHANG CH'IEN HAD SPUN
HIS MURDER WEB, AND ONLY
VAL EASTON, SECRET SERVICE
OPERATIVE, KNEW WHERE
EACH STRAND LED. KNEW THAT
GOLDEN-SKINNED HALF-CASTE
PEND HAD JOINED FORCES WITH
THE DREAD BLACK DOCTOR AND
TURNED AN ANCIENT INN INTO A
TORTURE TAVERN, A HOSTELRY OF
HORROR AND DEATH.

CHAPTER ONE

S 47 TALKS

THE NEW YORK LIMITED paused briefly at Manhattan Transfer while an electric locomotive replaced the steam engine which had brought it from Washington. Smoothly it moved off toward New York. The scant baker's dozen of passengers in the Pullman where Val Easton sat began preparations for departure. The porter scurried up and down the aisle with whisk broom and shoe rag, and luggage he was stacking in the vestibule.

Val Easton remained quiet. Station arrivals were an old story. Most of his time was spent on trains, steamships and occasionally passenger planes, quartering the globe on those vague nonpublic bits of business which were of interest to the Secret Service.

As Manhattan Transfer yards dropped behind, the train secretary entered the Pullman, paging quietly: "Mr. Easton, Mr. Easton.

Val held up a finger.

"Telegram, Mr. Easton," the secretary said, handing him a yellow envelope.

Val ran his finger under the flap and glanced at the contents. "No reply," he said. And when the secretary had moved off Val considered the message again with frowning concentration.

—and something circled Val's neck from behind.

IT WAS in code, from Washington. Long practice in decoding such missives gave him the contents almost at a glance.

VAL EASTON
EN ROUTE NEW YORK LIMITED

S 47 ERICKSON NEEDS HELP STOP CONTACT
IMMEDIATELY CARE NARCOTIC HEADQUARTERS
GREGG

Gregg was the code word for the chief in Washington. It was known that he had another name, but those who called him chief, and all whom he contacted in the course of business, knew him only as Gregg.

Val drew a small notebook from his inside coat pocket, flipped to a middle page and scanned a notation.

The nice old lady with the paper-wrapped packages across the aisle would have been horrified had she known the history of that penciled scrawl, the events to which it was the key. Intrigue, violence and murder were centered on that innocent page.

It was an address copied from a slip of paper found on the body of a murdered man—Vollonoff, the right-hand man of Carl Zaken, the dread Black Doctor of international espionage. Vollonoff—who had met death intended for Val Easton and Nancy Fraser in lonely tidewater Virginia a few short nights before.

Carl Zaken was in a Washington hospital. Vollonoff was dead. But the Black Doctor had not worked alone. There were others.

That penciled notation was the only clue.

Val pocketed the notebook, and walked into the front vestibule, tearing the telegram into bits as he went. Opening the vestibule door slightly, he scattered them to oblivion.

For some five minutes he stood smoking a cigarette and eyeing the flat desolate Jersey meadows, across which the train was plunging in the late afternoon sunlight. Now and then the porter stacked luggage behind him, and passengers hurried through. Val ignored them. His mind was on the job ahead, on all that had happened since he had crossed the trail of the Black Doctor that last night on the *Laurentic* before docking in New York.

Few people realized that the art of espionage and counter-espionage had not ended with the cessation of war. Rather it had increased as turmoil and distrust flourished among the nations of the world.

It was at a time like this that the cleverness of men like the Black Doctor brought highest returns. Master freelance spy, cold-blooded and ruthless, giving orders to a wide-flung web of similar characters, he had more value than an army corps to the country who purchased his services.

But Val Easton himself had brought down the Black Doctor.

Many types were included among the passengers on that train—and of them all Val was probably the least assuming. He might have been a lean young college instructor, a brisk bond salesman. There was about him no suggestion that he was one of the most valued units in the American Secret Service. That was part of his stock in trade.

The lights came on as the train plunged into the Hudson Tubes. Val returned to his seat, sat quietly as they emerged from the tubes with slackening speed to stop finally beside the long platform in the Pennsylvania Station.

In the great main waiting room above, Val ordered his redcap to wait while he looked up a telephone number, entered a booth and dialed it.

"Erickson there?" he asked… "Put him on."

"Erickson speaking," a voice said a moment later.

"Easton talking. Gregg wired me on the train to get in touch with you." Erickson was a stranger. His voice had a short, brusk tempo. "I was expecting you," he said. "I talked to Washington on long distance an hour or so ago. They said you were on the train."

"I'm going to the Severin Hotel. Better meet me there," Val decided. "Ask for Henry Jones of Baltimore."

"Right," Erickson agreed.

A TAXI rolled Val to the Hotel Severin, on Forty-third Street, half a block off Times Square. He registered as Henry Jones, of Baltimore, was assigned a room on the eleventh floor. He hardly had his bag open when the telephone rang. The desk said: "Mr. Erickson is in the lobby."

"Send him up," Val requested.

Erickson was a short, stocky man with a square jaw and heavy straw-colored eyebrows. His manner was brisk, his handclasp strong, his glance frankly appraising. "I've heard of you," he said. "Er— I expected to see an older man."

"Sorry. That will come later," Val smiled. "Have a seat… Cigarette? No? What's the picture?"

Erickson sat down. "I've been watching the Elite Hotel over in Brooklyn," he explained.

"Yes—Gregg told me it was being done," Val nodded. "But I'm a little puzzled as to what the narcotic people have to do with it. I didn't know they had been brought into this."

"They haven't been, exactly," Erickson explained. "I was on the local narcotic detail for a time and I know the federal men. It seems they're interested in this Elite Hotel too. It's ever near the Brooklyn docks, run by a naturalized Pole named Weitzkorn."

"I read the first report," Val nodded. "Caters to men off the ships, dock and harbor workers and transients, doesn't it?"

"That's right. There's a speakeasy next door, too. This Weitzkorn is under suspicion of working with a drug ring. Harbor right at his elbow and men coming off the ships all the time, makes it a natural station. That's where the narcotic men come in. They've had a man planted in the hotel for two months now. He's supposed to be a mate looking for a ship, which are scarce these days. They've got the finger on a couple of punks—but they're after the big shots."

"Interesting—but what is the connection? We're not interested in a drug ring."

Erickson shoved his hat toward the back of his head, placed hands on his knees and leaned forward earnestly.

"When I found the narcotic boys were snooping I buzzed them. Their inside man has been keeping an eye peeled for me. Day before yesterday he tipped me off to a bird who'd been there three days and smelled phony. Quietly dressed, seems to have plenty of money. Keeps to his room most of the time, and he's had several visitors. None of the regulars around the place seem to know him—but Weitzkorn, the owner, licks his boots."

"What name is he registered under?"

"Jacques Prideau, from San Francisco."

"Probably assumed," Val suggested. "His description?"

"Slender, rather dark. Looks like a Spaniard to me."

"Know anything else about him?"

"I tailed him last night," Erickson said.

"Good. And then—"

"He took a surface car to the subway, and shuttled at Grand Central to Times Square. Acted jumpy, like he was afraid someone might be tailing him."

"Spot you?"

Erickson smiled scornfully. "I cut my eyeteeth at that fifteen years ago. If he spotted me I'll start peddling papers on Forty-second Street."

"All right—and at Times Square—"

ERICKSON'S SMILE turned rueful. "He ducked into one of those three-floor chop-suey palaces on Times Square. Went clear up to the top floor—I know that." Erickson snorted. "But when I got up there he had faded. Not a sign of him! I didn't ask questions, for I figured if he had the drag to duck like that the Chink waiters would spot anyone interested in him. I tucked away a bowl of suey—and then laid close outside until after the joint closed. He never did come out." Erickson shrugged. "And this morning, early, the plant in the hotel wised me that this Prideau blew in about eleven last night. He left that suey joint by another entrance while I was watching the front."

"Chinese restaurants don't suggest this business we're interested in," Val frowned.

"Maybe not," Erickson admitted. "But that ain't all. Get a load of this. I laid for him again this morning. He went out about nine—and made straight for that Chink layout again. I didn't go in this time—but I'm willing to swear he didn't leave by the front. At twelve-thirty I called the narcotic office from the cigar store on the corner—and their man at the hotel had sent in word for me that Prideau had returned about eleven. Can you tie it? He's got a regular beat to that suey hashery—and he vanishes as soon as he gets inside."

"Interesting," Val agreed. "But it sounds more like dope, which is no concern of ours. In case everything has not been made clear to you, we are trying to round up the remnants of a dangerous group of secret agents who were working with a Carl Zaken, sometimes known as the Black Doctor. We found a blank slip of paper on the dead body of one of Zaken's men. G-2 Laboratory applied reagents and brought out the name and address of the Elite Hotel. The invisible writing indicates that Zaken or his men used that hotel in some manner. Zaken was not a drug dealer. He is a spy, a procurer of secrets for the country that will pay highest for them. We are not interested in drug activities."

Erickson said doggedly: "This Prideau is the only one so far, we can suspect. He's unknown to the narcotic men, and he's a pretty stylish bird to be staying at the Elite without a reason. Besides, I haven't told you all."

"I've been wondering why you needed help."

"I lammed back to the Elite," Erickson continued. "Prideau usually stays in all afternoon. Today he went out about one-thirty. Walked down the docks about a mile. There's a small boat pier there, run by an old fellow who rents rowboats. He owns an old launch, fast by its looks. Prideau talked to him about ten minutes and then turned back to the hotel. I let him go, and dropped in and buzzed the old man. Pretended I wanted to rent a boat. He had rowboats, but said the motorboat had just been rented for a couple of nights, paid in advance."

"Drugs," Val guessed.

"No," Erickson denied. "I thought of that. If it was drugs for the ring—they'd have their own motorboat. A dozen if they wanted them. Weitzkorn could have produced one. But he didn't. I asked myself why," Erickson said earnestly, "and I think I got the right answer. Snow boats might be known to the police, liable to suspicion in the harbor. Suppose somebody didn't want to be noticed? They'd hire a strange boat—like Prideau did."

Val considered a moment, and nodded. "Something in that. If Prideau is one of Carl Zaken's men," he said, "I can't see his interest in a launch—unless he intends to slip aboard some ship and quit the country."

"That's why I telephoned Washington," Erickson confessed. "Prideau can't be very afraid of detection or he wouldn't wander around in public. I thought I'd better get further instructions. The chief told me you would take charge."

"Yes. We'll see what this Prideau is up to this evening," Val decided. "If he is Zaken's man, we want to know; and if not the sooner we find out the better. We'll want a fast motorboat."

"I can have one assigned from the harbor patrol," Erickson offered quickly.

"No—better not. No publicity if we can help it. Can't tell what will happen and who will talk. I'm more interested in what this fellow does than taking him into custody. If he is one of the Black Doctor's men I want to use him as bait to get any others. You know the water front—try to get a boat with plenty of speed as quick as you can. Tie it up near this wharf and we'll tag along tonight."

Erickson got to his feet. "I think I can get one quick," he promised. "I'll call you back." He moved toward the door.

"One other thing," Val reminded, following him. "Any man of Carl Zaken's is dangerous. Bring a gun."

Erickson set his blunt jaw. "I'll handle him if there's trouble," he grunted.

CHAPTER TWO

THE DEATH FOG

THE COOL evening brought fog rolling up the bay on a gentle inshore breeze. Val Easton sat in the thwarts of the motorboat and swore under his breath as the minutes slowly passed. He hadn't counted on this. It was black, still, where the motorboat rocked slowly to the bay swell. The gaunt creosoted piles of the small wharf loomed up at his right. Little wavelets *slap-slapped* against the hull underfoot. The smell of salt and fish and creosote hung low and heavy above the water. The fog swirled damply past his face. Looking up he could see writhing, dirty yellow streamers moving against the shore reflections. Out in the harbor the ghostly, intermittent bellows of fog whistles marked groping water traffic.

The rickety pier was dark, deserted, lonely. A single small light bulb before a shanty office at the shore end, shed feeble illumination.

The old man who owned the little flock of boats rubbing together on the opposite side of the pier was gone for the evening.

Erickson was standing inside the high board fence which shut the water front off from the street at this point—standing to see if Prideau came through the gate this evening.

It was nine P.M. already.

Val began to wonder if they were not wasting the evening. They had no certain assurance their man would appear. It was a bad night to be out on the bay. Small boats were easily run down in this kind of weather.

And yet, for surreptitious business, it was perfect.

The boat was tied by a small ladder near the end of the pier—almost impossible to sight unless one walked directly over it and looked down—and yet not too far from shore to miss the rusty creak of gate hinges opening.

Val heard the hinges, muffled through the fog and lapping water, and tensed. The murmur of a voice reached him through the fog. And then, unexpectedly, startling, a stifled, choked scream rang out! It carried a ghostly timbre.

Val leaped to his feet.

Just that one cry—then silence, deep, eery, ominous. Worse than an outburst of noise, that silence. Erickson would have called out had he been all right.

Val swarmed up the short wooden ladder, dragging an automatic from his coat pocket as he went.

"Erickson!" Val called. "Where are you?"

Erickson did not answer—and, as he started for the gate, Val froze in his tracks, staring in unbelief. An uncanny chill pricked the short hairs at the back of his neck.

In the wavering shadows at the shore end of the wharf a woman was standing, regarding him intently. Her figure was barely visible—but her face, pale, soft, beautiful, like a cameo framed in jet-black hair, swam through the writhing fog wreaths.

Her cheek bones were high, her mouth red, vivid as the color of an East Indian flame tree—and her features as expressionless as those of a musing Buddha.

She was an Oriental. The high cheek bones, the strange beauty as striking as that of a lotus flower in full bloom, left no doubt. Through the slow drifting fog her face seemed magnetic, incredibly lovely, mysterious, hypnotic.

And something encircled Val's neck from behind—thin, strong as a tenuous band of steel, biting deep, cutting off wind and speech as he was jerked back.

A hand caught his right arm as he tried to shoot. The automatic roared—and missed.

And in the red, hazy curtain dropping over Val's senses the pale, beautiful, exotic face swam—vanished.

THAT WAS the last thing Val saw, the last coherent thing he knew. His neck seemed severed by the cord garrotting him. He was falling into the whirling crimson haze.

Far away a woman's clear, musical voice remonstrated. "No! Not this one too!"

But he might have imagined it.

Long time later he heard the throb of an engine—and then the shrill blasts of a police whistle—close....

Reality came with a hand roughly shaking his shoulder, a blinding glare when he opened his eyes. He was on his back, an electric torch shining down in his face. A voice rasped: "This one's coming around all right!"

Hands jerked him up. The torch beam, the light before the shanty, showed two bluecoated patrolmen. The scene still seemed unreal. The light was there—and the shanty was there—but that lovely mysterious face was gone.

Had he dreamed it, Val wondered? Dreamed too the clear musical voice interceding for him?

Strong fingers dug painfully into his arm. A brusk voice demanded: "What happened here? Who got that guy outside the gate?"

"What is it?" Val muttered—and abruptly his mind fastened to that question and clarified to cold reality. "Take me to him," he demanded.

They led him through the gate. The torch swept the ground. Erickson lay there in a grotesque huddle, his pallid face staring up horribly into the gray clammy fog.

A slender, bone-handled dagger protruded from Erickson's throat.

Val knew then he had not dreamed it.

The patrolmen were truculent, suspicious, accusing. "Who is he?" they demanded.

"Who stuck that knife in him?"

"How many of you were here?"

"Who lammed off in that boat?"

Val hardly heard them. Less than half a minute had passed since he had been jerked to his feet. The drone of a speeding boat engine had sounded close then. It was still out there in the fog, drawing away.

"How long ago did you hear that shot?" he snapped.

"Three or four minutes," the man on his right growled. "You came around as soon as we shook you. An auto drove off just before we got here. Whose was it?"

Speaking fast and distinctly, so there would be no argument, Val said: "Can't tell you. Didn't know a car was there. I'm working out of Washington—Secret Service. The men who did this just left in a motorboat. You can hear it out there. We had a boat ready to follow them. It's out at the end of the wharf. There's a chance to get them yet! Come along!"

To the credit of the two bluecoats, they wasted no time in argument.

"He may be phony—but I'll give him a whirl," the last speaker decided instantly. "Notify the harbor squad, an' keep an eye on the body, Tom. Come on, mister. My name's Hannigan. Where's this boat?"

Val dropped into the launch and listened for the receding engine out there in the fog. It was quartering down the bay. He started the motor as Hannigan cast off. Water roiled, frothed at the stern. The hull quivered as they swung out of the slip and gained speed. The bow began to lift and smash through the harbor swells, sheeting spray to right and left.

A small searchlight was mounted on the bow decking. Val found the switch and the silver shaft bored into the swirling fog. Hannigan rocked to his side and shouted in his ear: "Who're we going after? Who knocked off your sidekick?"

"Don't know. How long will it take the harbor patrol to get out here?"

"Can't tell how far away they are."

THE BOOMING blast of a whistle broke forth just ahead. Low-placed deck lights winked out. Their searchlight pushed through the gray damp veils to the squat hull of a harbor tug plowing sturdily into the river. Val twisted the wheel—they burst through the tug's swell in a plunging spray-drenched rush and swept under the stern.

"Watch it!" Hannigan yelled. "A dinky boat don't stand much chance in the bay a night like this."

"A good swim would top the evening off."

"Hell—I can't swim!" Hannigan yelled ruefully.

Val cut the motor and comparative silence fell. The myriad lights on shore were invisible. The ghostly searchlight beam gleaming on restless black swells only emphasized their isolation. The boom and shrill of warning whistles drifted from many points in intermittent bursts.

Hannigan touched Val's arm. "What's that?" he asked.

Bearing off more to the right, less faint than it had been, was the distant muted snore of a motor.

"We're pulling up on them," Val said, and started the engine again.

Gone now was any thought of stalking the craft ahead. One thing only Val wanted—to get the man who had driven that bone-handled dagger into Erickson's throat.

And yet he was puzzled. Who was that strange exotic creature who had stood there in the fog? What was she doing there? And what was she?

Chinese? Val had to admit that he couldn't be sure. Strange, aloof, mysterious, she was not of the West, he was certain. Beyond that he couldn't guess. One of the Black Doctor's followers? Erickson had turned up the mystery of Prideau and the Chinese restaurant. She tied in with that; but he had never heard of one like her connected with the Black Doctor.

Was it Prideau who had knifed Erickson and used that garotte? A livid welt and painful neck were still mementoes. Yet it was the girl who had interceded for him.

Half a dozen times Val cut the engine for short seconds while they picked up the beat of the motor ahead, a little closer each time.

And then, with startling abruptness, the gray steel wall of a ship's side loomed up before them. Val snapped off the ignition, spun the wheel. They swept around parallel to the ship's side, bumped hard against a lowered companionway.

Hannigan grabbed it and burst out: "Hell—this ship's anchored! We're down by quarantine! Where's that boat we've been following?"

They both listened, heard nothing.

"It stopped around here," Val said under his breath. "I'm going aboard. Something funny here."

No watchman was on deck by the companionway. The fog crept damply through the dim glow of an occasional deck light. The ship seemed silent, deserted, sleeping.

Val moved forward, where lights were visible on the forward well deck. So many lights seemed queer. He was wondering about them when a catlike figure suddenly rounded the corner under the bridge superstructure and confronted him.

The surprise was stunning, the quick glimpse unnerving. Val saw a tall, powerful, half-naked figure with dark muscles bulging sleekly. The man overtopped him by inches. He glimpsed a full-lipped mouth, glaring slant eyes, smooth black hair. A yellow god—a yellow demon that recoiled an instant at sight of him—and instantly flowed into a noiseless crouch. A hand gripping a long knife flashed up with all the menace of a flickering snake's tongue.

The stripped body launched at him.

There was no time to plan. No time to dodge. Death had suddenly exploded out of the night.

Val dropped instinctively, almost flat to the deck. The knife slashed viciously over him. A plunging leg struck hard against his shoulder. The savage rush catapulted the other in a staggering plunge against the rail.

VAL SURGED to his feet again as the saffron-skinned figure whirled back at him. A desperate lunge—and his hands caught the knife wrist as it started to lash out once more. His shoulder drove the other back against the rail again.

For a moment they struggled fiercely, breath exploding through their lips in short gasps. And then to Val's horror the wrist he gripped began to slide through his hands. It was coated heavily with grease.

The other was heavier, more powerful also. His forearm struck Val's face, snapping his head back. A brace, a lunge, and they both reeled away from the rail. The slippery wrist moved inexorably through his double grip—and in the fog-filled half light the keen knife blade moved with grisly certainty toward his throat.

Inches away the slant eyes glared into his face. The full lips curled away from sharp teeth in a primitive snarl. No mercy in that face.

It all happened in seconds—yet bewilderment flashed through Val's mind in that time. Who was this grease-coated giant? What was he doing on deck this way? Why didn't he call out for help?

No time to get Hannigan now. He couldn't even try for the gun in his pocket. Val did the only thing possible. He suddenly threw himself back, dragging the other after him.

It was an old *jiu-jitsu* trick. He struck the deck hard, and the other crashed down on top of him.

Val struck rolling, his right knee coming up, and the force of the fall hurled the other clear on over him. Dimly, as that happened, Val heard two sharp, shrill whistles ringing through the night.

He rolled over, bounced to his feet, snatching for the automatic in his coat pocket as he came up.

Even quicker than himself was the feline recovery of the glistening giant. And then a strange thing happened. The two shrill whistles rang through the night again, on the other side of the ship.

A bawled warning suddenly sounded further back on that side. "Ahoy there! Keep off! What d'you want?"

The hand that held the knife snapped back, flickered forward—and so fast did the knife come that Val hardly saw it. His dodge was instinctive as he raised the automatic. An instant before it roared in his hand a sharp blow against his shoulder swung him off balance. The shot went wild, and the knife clattered down on the steel deck plates at his feet.

He had missed—and like a saffron ghost the other was running toward the opposite rail. Val stopped his second shot as he saw the dim figure plunge over the rail without stopping. And as he went a short harsh cry came from him in some strange tongue.

Faintly Val heard him strike the water.

And then pandemonium broke out.

A gun barked sharply. A burst of two shots answered. The voice that had spoken before bawled lustily: "Man leaving! Stop that boat!"

The spinning roar of a gas motor drummed against the night.

Looking down into the forward well deck Val saw men erupting from the fo'castle head—men in all stages of dress—yellow-skinned men with slant eyes, jabbering, gesticulating as they ran to the rail to watch.

Val turned, ran back toward the companion, tumbled down to the boat.

"What happened up there?" Hannigan yelled.

"Shove off! That boat we want is leaving!"

Hannigan asked no more questions. Their own engine spun alive a second later. They gained headway, raced past the blunt bow, where a great rusty anchor chain stretched taut into the water. Val tipped the searchlight up and glimpsed the bow lettering.

Nartega, it said.

Then they were past to open water. A second searchlight beam split the fog off to the left and enveloped them in dazzling brilliance. His own light picked out the other craft, sheering off with a white curl of water at its bow.

The sharp concussion of revolver shots drummed beside him as Hannigan crowded close and fired at the fleeing craft. They fell in behind it, passing out of range of its searchlight, which blacked out.

Hannigan thumbed fresh cartridges in the cylinder of his gun.

"Keep close!" he yelled. "I'll stop 'em!"

Their own searchlight still held the other craft. In its radiance Val saw a dark figure rise at the stern and lift a long-barreled weapon. He thought it a rifle at first—but Hannigan saw it too, caught his arm and bellowed: "Get down! Turn that light off! It's a Tommy gun!"

A LIVID pulsating tongue of flame leaped from the muzzle of that weapon ahead. The air was suddenly filled with whining death.

Their searchlight went out with a crash. Wood split, splintered off the forward coaming. Something clipped the edge of Val's ear, a bullet ripped through the cloth of his coat sleeve as he dropped flat beside Hannigan. And over them the leaden hail of death still whined, still smashed into the hull, puncturing the planking in a dozen places.

Val reached up to twirl the wheel. It spun uselessly. He flipped the ignition off and the engine stopped.

The gunfire ceased a moment later. They lost headway quickly. The racing craft ahead drew off to the port side as their own boat swayed off her course.

Hannigan was swearing luridly.

"Got me through the shoulder!" he raged. "Flesh wound, I think, but it's beginning to hurt like the devil!"

"They're gone for tonight," Val admitted regretfully. "And we're perforated like a sieve. Let's see that shoulder. Here—I always carry a fountain-pen flash at night."

A bullet had cut through the upper muscles of Hannigan's shoulder, missing the bone fortunately. The wound was bleeding freely. Using their handkerchiefs for bandages, Val did what he could to stop it. His own shoulder had been grazed by the keen knife which had slashed through his coat. It was not bleeding much. He turned his attention to the boat.

A bullet had cut the rudder rope. The swells were slopping through several bullet holes. Below the waterline the hull was still sound. He found line in a locker and patched the rudder rope crudely.

The other craft was long out of hearing when he finished. Their searchlight glass and bulb were shattered.

Running slow they made their way back to the anchorage and managed to pick up the *Nartega* again. Her deck was lighted now, men were at the rails. They made the launch fast to the companion and in a few minutes gave explanations and got the story.

The *Nartega,* from Bordeau to Shanghai, by way of New York and the Canal, had developed engine trouble off quarantine and anchored for the night. The small boat Val and Hannigan had been following had stopped offside. The watchman had challenged it.

Val had clashed with the lascar fire-room crew. A hasty check-up showed one of the lascars was missing. That half-naked, grease-coated form had been ready for a plunge in the cold waters of the bay.

"Chink-running!" Hannigan said disgustedly.

Val said nothing—but he wondered. The lascars clustered below on the well deck had all professed ignorance of everything. But the memory of the girl he had glimpsed briefly on the dock, and that half-naked giant who had savagely attacked him had nothing in common with these ignorant jabbering coolies on the deck below.

The lanky chief mate, in charge, due to the captain's absence ashore, willingly complied with his request and had the wireless man flash a message ashore asking the harbor police to intercept the launch dashing up the bay and watch the Elite Hotel.

That was about all that could be done. Hannigan's shoulder was bandaged out of the *Nartega's* first-aid chest. He could do well enough with that until he got to a doctor. Val's ear was only scratched, his bandaged shoulder not stiffening much. Since the launch had to go back up the bay anyway and the fog was thinning out, they took their bearings and started back.

THE NIGHT'S work was not yet ended. Prideau was not the type of man to trouble himself about getting one miserable lascar fireman into the country. This night's ruthless doings did not explain Prideau's trips to Times Square, his residence at the Elite Hotel, the cold-blooded disregard of murder that had been shown. And it did not explain that striking, mysterious girl.

They went to the Elite Hotel first. Val and two city detectives with a search warrant.

The Elite Hotel was a squalid, five-story brick building with a dim, linoleum-floored lobby. A yawning clerk grew sullen at sight of the detectives, took them up to the room unwillingly when shown the warrant.

Prideau's room held only a pigskin gladstone bag of excellent quality. Half a dozen steamship and hotel labels had been scraped off. But the evidence remained that Prideau was a man of the world, given to extensive traveling.

The bag yielded clothes and a leather-cased toilet kit of ebony, chased with silver. The room contained no clues. Careful examination disclosed no false bottom or compartment in the bag.

"Looks like we're stuck," one of the detectives commented. "This guy was smart enough not to carry any evidence."

Wiser in the ways of espionage, Val concentrated on the leather-cased toilet set. The ebony backs of two military brushes seemed a trifle thicker than necessary. Holding one close to the light he discovered a thin line between the bristle back and the ebony case into which it fitted.

Borrowing a pen knife, it was the work of a moment to pry out the bristles and a thin slab of hard rubber into which they were set. An eighth of an inch space lay behind it, backed with sheet lead to equalize lost weight.

"For the love of Mike!" the other detective exclaimed, as Val lifted out several fine sheets of tissue paper. "Wasn't he the tricky one?"

Val spread the sheets out on the bureau top. Three—each one covered by a tracery of fine lines with scattered words written in.

The detectives stared over his shoulder. "Looks like someone went screwy and tried to draw a jigsaw puzzle," one declared.

"Maps," Val said, "sketched hastily from memory, I'd say. The words are French. Here—this is a building—chemical, it says. Here's another labeled chemical. This line around everything looks like a fence. This is a gate. Here's a powerhouse.… A railroad spur. This building by the gate is labeled offices. And here—this area outside the gate is marked Commercial Street."

"Philadelphia!" the detective at his right shoulder exclaimed. "I used to live there. Commercial Street's down in the south part of town, near the river. Lots of factories along there."

"So," Val said thoughtfully. "Prideau was interested in a chemical plant in Philadelphia, eh? It shouldn't be hard to locate."

"What good's a chemical plant in Philly goin' to do us? You won't find the bird who knocked off your sidekick hiding out there."

"Hard to tell what's there," Val mused. "It may be interesting. I'll keep these sheets for the Secret Service. If they're needed for evidence they'll be available. I suggest you have this place watched in case our man returns. And I'll leave you now. I have other things to do yet tonight."

CHAPTER THREE
SUEY-HOUSE SET-UP

A **TAXI** dropped Val in Times Square. He had said
nothing about this place to the police for obvious
reasons. Erickson's murder was local business. This chop-
suey place tied in with matters that might be far more
complicated, need the utmost secrecy. Times Square at this
hour of the night had lost some of its light, its seething life
and gaiety. Theater fronts were darkened, shop windows
dim, the restless sidewalk crowds and massed lines of traffic
had thinned out. Newsboys were hoarsely shouting early
morning editions. The occasional nighthawk cab rolled
swiftly on its way. Pedestrians walked briskly. The lighted
windows of an all-night restaurant beckoned wanly.

Val found the Shanghai Low restaurant without any
trouble. It occupied the second and third floors, was
reached by a flight of brass-bound stair treads in a dimly
lighted entranceway. The second floor was dark. One
lighted window was visible on the third floor where the
window shade was up a few inches. He crossed the street
and strolled to the entrance.

A short furtive Oriental was standing inside the swinging halves of the entrance door. On sudden impulse Val
stepped inside. The Oriental quickly took a cigarette from
his lips and peered from under the brim of a limp cap.
He was middle-aged, Cantonese by his slight stature and
features.

"Are they open upstairs?" Val asked casually.

The other shook his head. "Eight o'clock tomollah."

The beady black eyes surveying him seemed to grow more intent. "Close up till tomollah," the other grunted. "Whaffor you want know?"

"I'm curious that way," Val said. "Let's go up and see—" And in the same breath his sharply outflung arm knocked the little man away from the wall—knocking him sprawling against the brass-bound stair treads. "I was looking for that," said Val. "Called for a warning, didn't it? About to push this loose nail head in the molding, weren't you? We won't touch it. Let's go upstairs."

The saffron-skinned guard got to his feet silently, staring at the gun which had appeared in Val's hand. The little byplay in the entrance had not been noticed by anyone outside. Quiet reigned at the top of the steep flight of stairs.

"Whaffor you come like this?"

"You'd be surprised. No tricks now."

And to make certain of that Val took a handful of the other's coat collar and stayed behind him as they slowly climbed the stairs. A door opened from the small, carpeted landing at the top. It was closed, locked.

"Open it," Val ordered.

"No can do."

Val shook him. "Don't make me go through your pockets for the key."

His manner must have carried conviction. A key was produced, slipped in the lock, turned. Val pushed his prisoner warily through the doorway.

VAL HAD been in many Chinese restaurants like this. A small glass counter and cash register by the door, rows of tables occupying two rooms, several potted plants and some cheap Oriental decorations furnishing atmosphere. A single dim bulb over the cash register furnished the light.

No one appeared. Directly ahead of them a flight of stairs went up to the third floor. Val took his prisoner up them.

A partition had been taken out and one large room formed this upper floor of the establishment. A stronger bulb shed brighter light through the big room. No one was visible up here either. Val looked around curiously. This was the place where Prideau had been followed—the place he had vanished abruptly.

There were no more stairs by which he could have ascended any higher. No visible doors gave exit from the room. A heavy smell of food and incense pressed close about them. A large fly buzzed loudly against the ceiling. The silence was profound.

His unresisting prisoner stood sullenly. No help there. Keeping the other's coat collar in his fist, Val began a tour of the walls. Cold logic was behind the move. Prideau had vanished in this room. With other diners present he would hardly have risked a secret panel.

THERE WAS an old fashioned fireplace in the back wall, relic of some far-off day when this building had been used for other purposes. Not that.

Behind the stairs was an open alcove, curtains bunched on each side. At a glance one could see it was used for hanging coats and hats. "What's in there?" Val asked.

"No savvy." But the prisoner's beady black eyes flashed queerly. He made a move to go on past the alcove.

"Not so fast." Val took him in.

Wooden paneling formed the back of the alcove. One look and Val knew he was on the right track. Paneling was an open invitation to search for a secret door. He put his palm against it and pushed. The paneling gave slightly at the side.

"I thought so," Val muttered—and stopped. Through the paneling had come the murmur of a voice.

The panel would not give or slide. It might take an hour or more to find the control. Smashing it was out of the question.

"Open it!" Val ordered.

"No savvy."

Val shifted his grip to the back of his prisoner's shirt collar—and twisted. "Open it!" he said through his teeth.

Thirty seconds of that was enough. Muted, strangling, gasping, the other lifted a hand to the last clothes hook on the right side and twisted it. The panel swung in of its own accord.

Pitch blackness confronted them.

Enough light seeped through the alcove to show a rug and a chair beyond. Val dragged his man through, and then stopped short. This room was even warmer than the one they had left. The air was heavy with the fresh fumes of tobacco smoke. Not a sound came from the blackness which surrounded them. But the air had the electric feel of human presence.

He hadn't counted on this. His prisoner was taut, straining in his grasp. Realizing they were silhouetted against the glow in the alcove, Val moved aside. His leg struck another chair. Something moved furtively across the room.

Val couldn't see what it was, and yet he suddenly knew beyond doubt that they were not alone in the room. The silence was creepy, ominous.

And then it happened.

To his left there was a swift stir of movement. As he whirled to face it something smashed hard against him—

his face, shoulders, chest, driving him back off balance, knocking him dizzy.

He was dimly conscious of his prisoner tearing free, shouting angrily. Weaving drunkenly, Val was suddenly enveloped in thick folds of cloth. Short, crisp orders snapped out. He was conscious of light glaring on the other side of the cloth. Hands grabbed him from behind. The automatic was torn from his fingers. He was tripped, slammed down to the floor.

A woman's voice, calm, clear, spoke sharply in Chinese. At the sound of it Val's dazed thoughts swept back to that fog-bound Brooklyn wharf. It was the same girl.

"Get her out of here!" a man panted above Val. "Someone may be following him, Chang."

"You fool!" the clear voice snapped angrily. "Don't speak my name! This man who was guarding the door says he came alone."

"Can't help what he says," the voice above Val grumbled. "He wouldn't be coming alone."

"Let me see who he is."

Val was jerked to his feet, the cloth whisked of his head. Blinking, he found his arms held by two short, stocky Cantonese in black silk coats. Beside him, holding his automatic, frowning, stood a slender, thin-faced man with sensuous lips and a small black mustache. Val's automatic was in his hand. His face was cold, cruel.

His jaw dropped as he saw Val's face. "*Sacré!*" he swore in French. "This is the man we left on the wharf!"

AND VAL recognized him by Erickson's description— Prideau, of the Elite Hotel. But it was to the man beyond Prideau that his eyes went and clung. Despite the well-tailored blue suit, the impeccable shirt and tie, the carefully combed black hair and cork-tipped cigarette held carelessly between long golden fingers, Val recognized with a shock, the half-naked, grease-coated coolie who had leaped at him on the deck of the *Nartega*. The giant catlike build was there, the same sickle-shaped scar in the corner of one eye, which he had fleetingly noticed in those desperate seconds, and forgotten. The same man—and yet a different one. It was hard to believe this well-groomed man he faced could be that filthy lascar.

The cork-tipped cigarette lifted, and the other inhaled leisurely while his eyes ran over Val.

"It was this young man, Prideau, who almost stopped me leaving the *Nartega*." There was an uncanny, rhythmic, purring quality about the voice, a sense of latent force and power. The English was flawless, the manner mild—and yet behind it all was iron force and ruthlessness.

All that Val got through senses still partly dazed. Something warm trickled down his face. He saw red blood on the front of his coat. On the floor where it had fallen after crashing against him lay a heavy teak chair inlaid with mother-of-pearl. More blood trickled into an eye, half blinding him. That chair had almost brained him.

Prideau, recognizable by Erickson's description, said irritably: "He's Secret Service."

"Search him," said the man called Chang.

Prideau did that swiftly, skilfully. In Val's inside pocket he found the three sheets of flimsy. An angry oath burst from him. "I knew it! They've been through my things!"

A round teak table, its edge inlaid with mother-of-pearl, stood in the center of the room. Chairs ranged around it; ash trays holding cigarette ends showed where the group had been sitting when Val entered. The girl had left the room before his eyes were uncovered. Chang, Prideau, the guard who had been down at the street—no longer furtive—and the two black-coated Chinese were the only occupants of the room beside Val.

Chang's expression did not change at sight of the tissue sheets. He lifted the cork-tipped cigarette to his full lips, inhaled deliberately and trickled smoke slowly from his mouth. "Your name?" he said suddenly to Val.

Val shrugged. "Jones."

"A lie," Chang said matter of factly.

Val shrugged again.

"You belong to the American Secret Service, Mr.—ah—Jones?"

"You flatter me," Val said drily. "Is there such a thing?"

"What were you doing at that dock?" Prideau snapped.

"Looking for drug smugglers," said Val blandly. "We're breaking up your little drug ring at the Elite Hotel, gentlemen." He wondered if they would believe it. He forced a thin, triumphant smile to his lips.

Chang inhaled again. His face was a yellow mask. "Drugs," he murmured softly. His glance slid to Prideau. An unspoken message passed between them. Prideau visibly relaxed.

Chang smiled. "You are a very clever man, Mr.—ah—Jones. I believe now your narcotic service is as efficient as rumored. We shall have to change our plans quickly. A risky business, this drug-running. No?"

"You'll find it so before you're through."

So, smiling, each bluffed the other. Chang was covering something up. Drug-running and a chemical factory did not fit together.

Chang glanced at a thin wrist watch.

"We waste time. You are dangerous. It desolates me that you must be held incommunicado."

Prideau exclaimed harshly: "Put him out of the way! I don't trust him. Murder has been done tonight."

"I am not a fool," said Chang. Then he spoke in Chinese, rapidly, musically.

The man who held Val's arm answered, nodding agreement. The two of them forced Val toward a door across the room.

Chang said with a faint sardonic smile: "Some men are too clever for their own safety. Good-by, Mr. Jones."

THEY TOOK him down steep, dark steps unfamiliar to his stumbling feet, flight after flight of them. The lifeless air was heavy with the odor of incense and the Orient. Val thought of the garotte that had been slipped about his neck once tonight. So easy to do it again in the thick blackness cloaking these warrenlike passages. A sharp turn—a strangling moment of horror—and the end....

He thought of the devious twisted threads which so far had been unraveled, and wondered to what grim end they led. He thought of that lovely exotic girl, indifferent to murder. He thought of Prideau, dangerous as a snake in his coldblooded sophistication, and of that catlike, golden-skinned man called Chang, who had appeared so amazingly out of the grimy stokehold of an incoming ship.

And lastly Val thought of Carl Zaken, the Black Doctor, the master spy, guarded in his hospital room in Washington. Did the girl, Prideau and Chang have anything to do with Carl Zaken and his always sinister plans?

They stopped. A key grated in a lock. A door swung open before them. Val was shoved into damp, musty blackness.

His arms were still pinioned firmly, but one hand lifted from his right arm for a second as the man on that side closed the door and groped for a light switch.

Val dealt all his cards in one explosive moment. Lashing back with his right arm, his clenched fist smashed into a face.

The man squealed loudly. His grip slackened.

Val shook it off. Pivoting like an exploding steel spring, he hooked the same fist to the other side. The dull smack of that terrific blow was loud in the darkness. The shock of it numbed his hand, traveled clear to his shoulder. But that surprised Cantonese, clinging so tightly to his left arm, vanished with only a strangled gasp.

The dull impact of his body against the wall was followed by his sprawling collapse on the floor.

The second man was shouting in shrill alarm.

Val felt a silken cord flick against the side of his head. He had been right. They had intended to garotte him silently and callously.

Val hurled himself forward in a flying tackle that drove the fellow to the floor.

The wiry Cantonese fought like an eel, writhing, clawing, struggling to wiggle free. Val swarmed on top, located his head and struck with both fists again—again—again....

The struggles suddenly weakened, slowed....

Val found the throat, jerked up the head, and drove it against the floor. The body under him went limp.

Panting, he sprang to a crouch, listening. His own strident breathing was the only sound he heard.

Matches were still in his pocket. He struck one. The flaring yellow glow outlined a dusty concrete floor, the brick walls of an underground cellar. The two black-coated

Cantonese who had led him down here for murder were lying limp and motionless before the doorway.

Val caught a leg and hauled the second one away from the door. He wondered if they were armed—found they were. Short, ugly, snub-nosed automatics. He struck another match, found the light switch and snapped it on. He was in a store room filled with boxes, old furniture. A few feet away a second door was set in the brick wall. Val ignored it, opened the door they had entered, went back the way he had been brought. Up the steep flights of stairs through the pitch blackness, an automatic in each hand this time, poised to shoot if necessary.

He met no one on the stairs, and came once more into the room from which he had been taken—and found it deserted. Prideau. Chang and the furtive little Cantonese guard had vanished.

The paneled door was still ajar. He walked through into the third-floor dining room, quiet and still as he had found it. The same fly still buzzed loudly against the ceiling.

Val ran lightly down to the second floor, and found no one there either. Not until he reached the curb did he glance at the two automatics, and stop to draw a deep breath. As he looked back at the dim-lit doorway from which he had emerged, it was hard to believe all that had happened in this most public spot of New York. Hard to believe he had been so near death with the law almost within shouting distance.

Val walked swiftly toward Forty-second Street in search of a policeman. There might yet be time to round up that small group he had last seen three floors above. But even as he went he remembered Erickson's story of those who had gone in the front entrance and failed to come out that way.

And before another thirty minutes had passed, Erickson's story was substantiated. Not one of the men he had met in that building was discovered by the police. Even the two men he had left sprawled in the basement were gone. In a nest of rooms and passages behind the third floor of the building they finally located another flight of stairs, another passage leading out at the back into a narrow courtyard and through another door onto the side street. Their quarry had vanished and there was no way of knowing where they had gone.

CHAPTER FOUR

HARMITE

NOON NEXT day found Val in Philadelphia. Telephoning the Chamber of Commerce, he quickly had the information he desired. Only one chemical plant answered his description—Harmsworth Chemical Products, Inc., far down in the south part of the city near the docks.

A taxicab took him there. And as the cab rolled up to the place Val saw that he was right. There was a high wire fence, the two-story office building inside the gate, the powerhouse smokestack beyond a maze of other buildings which hummed with activity.

The office of Nathaniel Harmsworth, president of the company, was located at the plant. Val sent in his card, waited briefly, was ushered in to that gentleman.

Harmsworth was a solid, gray-haired man on the late side of fifty. He wore rimless noseglasses, looked exactly what he was—a substantial, prosperous manufacturer. It was hard to believe he could be connected with the events of the preceding night. Harmsworth's first words supported the idea.

"Your card says Secret Service, Mr. Easton," he remarked. "I am puzzled as to what you can want with me."

"Can you give me a reason," Val asked, "why a sketch of your plant should be in the possession of a man suspected of espionage?"

"The devil! Espionage?"

"Yes."

Harmsworth leaned back in his desk chair, removed his glasses. His face was suddenly grim. "Our research department, Mr. Easton, perfected last winter a perilous gas so deadly that it frightens us to think about it."

Val leaned forward, searching Harmsworth's face. "Do you mean," he questioned carefully, "a new poison gas has been discovered?"

Harmsworth nodded. "Yes. Accidentally. We manufacture, among other products, ethyl iodoacetate, a so-called tear gas, and during the war turned out dichlorethyl sulphide, the familiar mustard gas, for the army. But the lethal qualities of this accidental find are so terrible in infinitesimal concentrations that we have no hesitation in declaring it one of the most ghastly weapons ever thrust into the hands of mankind. Two of our chemists have already died from contact with minute quantities which would have been negligible in any other known gas."

"A terrifying picture, Mr. Harmsworth."

Harmsworth's square face was solemn. "I can't talk about it and not be terrifying. I have been a practical chemist all my business life. We have heard much of lethal gases since Nineteen Eighteen, gases that would wipe out whole populations. All bosh! Mustard gas in a ratio of one to one hundred thousand parts of air requires an exposure of almost an hour to do damage to the lungs, and that not necessarily fatal. Hydrocyanic acid, used by the British and the French, caused immediate death in concentrations of one to two thousand parts of air. But this new discovery is lethal in the ratio of one to thirteen million. Apparently there is no protection against this gas, which for laboratory purposes we have called Harmite."

Val did not bother to mask his incredulity. "No protection, Mr. Harmsworth?"

"None!" stated Harmsworth harshly. Discussing it seemed to stir in him a mixture of pride and repugnance. "Harmite is colorless and odorless, and possesses to an astounding degree the ability to penetrate clothing and be absorbed through the skin. The victim is dead before he even suspects the air is tainted. Before he even breathes it, in fact. And the infinitely small concentrations required make it a simple matter to drench large areas. We have tested it out on farm areas and controlled groups of sheep."

"Who knows about this?" Val asked quickly.

"We tried to keep it a secret," Harmsworth told him regretfully. "But such things have a way of getting out and spreading to interested quarters. Already we have had offers from three sources, of sums ranging into the millions for the formula, if it measures up to rumor."

"Who made them?"

"I can't say," Harmsworth smiled thinly. "Anonymous in each case. But I can guess foreign governments were behind them. No one else could be interested."

"What did you do?"

"Refused, naturally," Harmsworth said bluntly. "For a variety of reasons—not the least of which is lack of desire to see myself and family exposed to an attack by Harmite in case of war. If it ever becomes necessary to use Harmite in war, I want my own country to have the benefit."

"Does Washington know about it?"

HARMSWORTH SMILED ruefully. "I took the matter up with the army. A great deal of red tape was involved. Not the least factor is an overwhelming sentiment in this country against the use of gas in warfare. Our negotiations have only progressed to the point where they have detailed an army chemist to work with our research department in refining the phases of manufacture. At present it is a rather involved and complicated matter to turn out large quantities. We are trying to simplify that."

"It would seem to me, Mr. Harmsworth, that feeling the way you do about it, you would have destroyed the formula."

Harmsworth admitted candidly: "It occurred to me. But what one man can discover, another can. How do we know that some foreign laboratory will not stumble on the same thing? The harm it would do us in the long run would be vastly greater."

"Probably so," Val admitted. "I suppose you have the formula written out?"

Harmsworth nodded. "Yes, we keep a master formula in code locked in the treasurer's safe across the hall."

"Where anyone can steal it."

"The safe is substantial and little exposed to theft, since we keep no great sums of money there. A watchman is on duty all night. People are in the building. We are working three shifts right now. It is no secret."

"I'll make arrangements to have two men watching your safe tonight," Val promised. "If anyone tries to get that formula we want them."

"I'll feel easier," Harmsworth confessed. He got to his feet abruptly, his face lighting with pleasure. "Hello, Trudie," he greeted. "All ready?"

"I didn't know you were busy, Dad." The girl who had entered the office smiled apologetically as Val rose and turned toward her.

"My daughter, Mr. Easton," Mr. Harmsworth said.

Trudie Harmsworth was pretty, gay, slender and vigorous. "Sorry to bring filial duties into a busy office," she smiled at her father. "But I'm shoving off to Washington with Sis, and couldn't leave without saying good-bye."

Harmsworth stood smiling for a moment after his daughter left.

"Great kid," he confided. "Mother's dead and she's about everything to me." He caught himself, looked sheepish. "About this other matter, if there is any trickery in connection with the Harmite formula I want it cleared up."

"We're working on it now," Val assured him. He put through a long-distance call to Washington, got two men detailed to watch the Harmsworth plant.

Skinner, Gregg's confidential secretary, had other news. "We've been trying to locate you. The chief wants you here this evening. Better take the next train."

"It seems I'm slated to follow your daughter, Mr. Harmsworth," Val said as he hung up. "My chief wants me in Washington." He shook hands with the chemical magnate and caught a cab for the railway station.

"VAL! QUICK—HERE!" That sharp, urgent call reached Val as he was passing the White House. He was near the curb where glowing lamps dispelled the new darkness. The taxi which had swung in to the curb stopped as he stopped and he saw who had hailed him.

It was Nancy Fraser—Nancy of the platinum hair and deep-blue eyes, whose daring and ingenuity were already becoming classics of the Secret Service. Nancy, who only ten days ago had faced death at his side. He could see her in the dim interior of the cab, one slim white hand on the door as she leaned toward him.

"The nicest thing that's happened to me today," Val said to her.

No answering smile curved Nancy's red lips. "Get in," she urged sharply.

As Val sank on the seat beside her and closed the door, Nancy leaned forward and said to the driver: "Take us down Fourteenth Street and around the ellipse slowly. And close that window back of you."

Not until the sliding glass panel had been moved over so they could talk with privacy did Nancy speak. In those seconds Val studied her and thought her more lovely each time he saw her.

Her fine, clean-cut features, her firm little chin, her stunning mop of platinum hair waved close to her head, made Nancy unique among women. It was hard to link this small, slender bit of femininity with the amazing Nancy Fraser of international espionage.

Nancy leaned back in her corner with a sigh of relief. "What luck, finding you there on the sidewalk! It was like wishing for the moon and suddenly having it dropped in your lap—green cheese and all."

"Kind of you to class me with the cheese," Val bantered. "Why all the excitement?"

They were passing the squat gray pile of the United States Treasury now, and the cab turned into Fourteenth Street and rolled with traffic streaming past the long-columned side of the Treasury. Nancy leaned toward him and said earnestly: "Someone is following me."

"Who?"

Nancy shrugged. She was wearing a light evening wrap and no hat, and her shrug was as graceful as all her other movements.

"I haven't the slightest idea," Nancy confessed. "It is a big limousine—I saw it under a street light—and it has been behind me ever since I left my apartment. One headlight is brighter than the other. I don't like it, Val. I've changed my destination, and was just wondering what to do when I saw you."

"No one would be following you unless they knew who you are," Val decided.

"Hardly," Nancy agreed. "And very few people have any idea who I am. Do you suppose it has anything to do with—the Black Doctor?"

Startled, Val said: "The Black Doctor?" His mind flashed back to Erickson, lying in the fog with a knife in his throat. Was this more of it? "Zaken is safe enough," he said with a strange lack of conviction.

"He didn't work alone," Nancy reminded. "And he promised more. You broke his pride, Val, when you shot him down. As long as he has life he will be trying to even the score—with both of us."

"No one is allowed to see him. He hasn't a chance to do any plotting," Val pointed out. He thought a moment. "I'm in a hurry. Got an appointment with the chief. Let me out at Thirteenth and the Avenue, just around the corner. I'll get the number of the car that's following you and look into it."

Five minutes later the cab rolled up Fifteenth Street, swung into Pennsylvania Avenue, let Val out, and went on. Val was idling by a lamp post at the curb when a car with one bright headlight and one dim one turned out of Fifteenth Street and purred past him.

It was a limousine, large, sleek, expensive, with a hunched Oriental at the wheel. There was light here on Pennsylvania Avenue, enough to strike into the interior and show the face leaning close to the glass, staring out at him.

And Val Easton caught his breath at the sight. It was a woman, pale, soft, beautiful. Her face like a cameo framed in jet-black hair on which an ornament of brilliants gleamed like cold, fiery diamonds. Her cheeks were high, her mouth vivid, her incredibly lovely face expressionless.

He would have known her anywhere—standing in the foggy shadows on the rickety wharf—or seated in that expensive car.

Their eyes met for a moment. Her head turned slightly to watch him as the limousine rolled past. The same magnetic, hypnotic look.

She sank back out of sight as Val ran after the car. It accelerated sharply. The tail-light blinked out. And there ensued the strange sight of a well-dressed young man dashing down the middle of Pennsylvania Avenue in hopeless pursuit of a speeding machine.

There was no traffic policeman on duty at Fourteenth Street at the moment, no cars in sight. By the time Val got a taxi beside the Willard Hotel and followed the trail of the limousine to F Street it was out of sight. He had the driver go down F several blocks; and then, seeing that the search was hopeless, told the driver to turn back.

His pulse was still pounding with the shock of it. That vivid, exotic face was the last thing he had expected to see here in Washington, and the fact that she was following Nancy Fraser made this thing even more mysterious.

The quickly veiled tail-light had blotted the license number. Val hurried into the nearest drugstore, called detective headquarters and asked that the limousine be picked up on sight.

It was a tense and greatly disturbed young man who walked the short distance to his appointment with the chief.

CHAPTER FIVE
MONSIEUR GARRE
OF THE SÛRETÉ

IT WAS a bare room, as austere and noncommittal as the seated visitor in the desk chair. A slight, intent man in his forties, he gestured as he spoke rapidly, and now and then touched the waxed ends of his small black mustache.

Gregg—for so the world knew the master of this austere room—was gruff, heavy-set, saturnine. He sat listening in silence.

Val Easton opened the door on that silence. "Sorry I'm late," he said to the chief.

Gregg said: "This is Monsieur Hilaire Garre of the French Sûreté, and, shall we not say, the French Secret Service? Mr. Valentine Easton, Monsieur Garre."

White teeth flashed under Monsieur Garre's black mustache as he stood and bowed slightly, half-consumed cigarette between his fingers.

Gregg motioned Val to a chair, said when he was seated: "Monsieur Garre is looking for a man called Chang Ch'ien, part Chinese, part Burmese, with a dash of English. We seem to have no knowledge of him. Has he ever come to your attention?"

Val stiffened, thinking back to the events of the past forty-eight hours. He said cautiously: "Perhaps you'll give me an idea?"

Hilaire Garre leaned forward and rested a clenched fist on the edge of the desk. "We consider Chang Ch'ien one of the most dangerous men who ever entered French territory," he said earnestly.

Garre's eyes half closed; for a moment he seemed to be looking far beyond the room.

"Chang Ch'ien," he repeated softly. "His early history is a mystery. It is rumored he is the son of a beautiful half-caste Anglo-Burmese woman who was taken under the protection of a powerful Manchu mandarin in the state of Szechuan, far up beyond the Yangtse gorges. Chang Ch'ien was a young man when the Dowager Empress died and the Manchu dynasty collapsed. The story says that he and five Manchu retainers left Szechuan in one of his foster father's junks crammed with family treasure—and from that day he dropped out of sight." Hilaire Garre spread his hands apologetically. "But that is only rumor."

"Fairly complete background for a rumor," Val suggested.

"A missionary who knew the family in Szechuan at the time saw Chang Ch'ien in Paris not long ago, and claimed to recognize him by a peculiar scar at the corner of his eye. The story finally found its way into Chang Ch'ien's dossier. It does not matter. Chang Ch'ien, the man, exists."

Val asked carefully: "Why do you want this Chang Ch'ien, Monsieur Garre?"

"For murder. Monsieur Easton; and for crimes worse than murder. Our underworlds of Paris and Marseilles and Bordeaux have been called depths of iniquity—yet there are men and women in those dregs who grow pale at the name of Chang Ch'ien. He is a myth, a legend, a terror few have seen and many felt to their sorrow. It is known his wealth is great, his influence far reaching. It is of record that at various times his infamy has touched depths we know nothing about. The Sûreté is seeking Chang Ch'ien for the murder of a Frenchman."

"I see," said Val, as more parts of the puzzle slipped into place. "What makes you think your man may be in this country?"

"Two reasons, Monsieur Easton. By brilliant detective work he was traced to Bordeaux the day following. There a famous *cocotte* was found murdered in her sumptuous apartment, which was alleged to have been supported by the wealth of Chang Ch'ien. In her fireplace we found scraps of burnt paper which had not been reduced to fine ashes. It was a blunder, messieurs. Analysis found one written word that had clear meaning for us."

Gregg cleared his throat. "Monsieur Garre was on the phone from New York today, Easton. This is why I called you back."

"The word," said Hilaire Garre slowly, "was Zaken."

"Carl Zaken?" Val snapped.

Garre nodded. "Exactly. Carl Zaken—the Black Doctor. That day in Bordeaux, two ships cleared for the United States; one for New Orleans in ballast, and one with general cargo for New York and Shanghai, with a lascar crew. She docked this morning in New York. I arrived the day before on the *Ile de France* from Cherbourg."

"And did you get your man?" Val asked, knowing the answer already.

Hilaire Garre's shrug was eloquent. "I was on the dock when she made fast. *Alors*, messieurs—no man was aboard who might have been Chang Ch'ien. The ship had anchored in the lower bay for six hours because of engine trouble. Sabotage by some member of the crew, it was decided. There was a heavy fog during the evening. A small boat came alongside and signaled and a member of the fireroom crew leaped overboard and was taken away. It was undoubtedly Chang Ch'ien."

"Have you heard of a Chinese woman being connected with him?" Val questioned.

HILAIRE GARRE spread his hand expressively. "Who knows what women have been linked with Chang Ch'ien? There was the *cocotte* at Bordeaux, although we do not know what their relations were. Business, perhaps. In Paris it is known that Zaken was finally brought to earth by your most capable Secret Service, messieurs. We have linked Chang Ch'ien with Zaken. It is our belief he has come to join Zaken."

"Zaken," said Val, "is a guarded prisoner in one of our Washington hospitals. It was thought for a time he would die. The courts are waiting for the doctors to certify his fitness for trial. He will draw a death sentence—or be in a prison cell before long."

Gregg broke his silence gruffly. "Easton is the man who shot Zaken down."

The dapper little Frenchman caressed his chin for a moment. "We too in France know Zaken, perhaps even better than you in this country, my dear Monsieur Gregg. You have accomplished a brilliant coup, but I assure you most emphatically that Zaken has no intention of dying or occupying one of your most excellent prison cells."

"He'll take his medicine," Gregg promised gruffly. "I would suggest your Chang Ch'ien made a trip for nothing, if he planned to join Zaken."

"Perhaps," said Hilaire Garre politely, "but both men are not without resources. I cannot even assure you Chang Ch'ien came alone. France has other seaports, other ships have left her shores. Chang Ch'ien commanded money and men in France and other countries. Would it not be strange if he chose to leave all that behind, and enter a new country, penniless and alone? I suggest his move was planned."

"It would seem strange to some," said Gregg pointedly, "if he chose to leave all he has built up within the borders of France."

"No," denied Garre emphatically as he jumped to his feet. "What more natural, messieurs? In France his game has become too—what is it you say in your colorful American slang?—hot for him! It was but a question of time."

Garre took a nervous step away from the desk, and wheeled back, slapping a fist into an open palm.

"We of the Sûreté have been criticized for our methods, messieurs, but it is our way. Call it Gallic temperament, if you will. *Voila*—we have the facts, we think like the criminal, we strike through the mystery for the truth. And, messieurs, I am convinced that Chang Ch'ien has moved to more sinister deeds. Where is the wealth and power of the world concentrated? In your country, my friends. And you will pardon me for being frank? America sleeps while dangerous men enter and vanish among her millions with freedom to plot and act such as no other country allows."

Garre leaned forward and tapped the desk emphatically.

"Chang Ch'ien, my friends, has come to reap the harvest of your carelessness. His plans are the plans of Carl Zaken. It will be a sad day for America if they are not stopped. Justice in France is swift, merciless. Give me Chang Ch'ien and I will take him back to the guillotine."

The fiery outburst of the dapper little Frenchman was impressive. Gregg lifted his telephone and spoke briefly into it. "Connect me with the Sheldon Hospital." And when the call was put through, he said: "Is Mr. Zaken still in his room?... Thank you." He hung up. "Zaken is in bed under guard. Any attempt at communication with him will be instantly reported."

"Good!" Garre agreed. "There will be an attempt. It is an imposition, messieurs, but this evening might I have the pleasure of seeing Zaken?"

"Easton will take you now," Gregg agreed. "We are at your disposal in this matter."

Hilaire Garre's acknowledgment was graceful, urbane. "Anything done in the name of France is appreciated by the humblest citizen of France, messieurs."

SHELDON HOSPITAL, in the southeast sector of the city, was surrounded by blocks of old red brick houses. Huge shade trees towered from the curbs, their arching branches interlacing over the streets. As the taxicab sped over the smooth asphalt, Val's thoughts went to the hospital ahead, to the man, Carl Zaken, bedded in a private room, guarded by a plainclothesman.

Death would have been small payment for that pale, cadaverous creature with the green-flecked eyes, whom the world of espionage knew as the Black Doctor. But the death so often dealt to those who had stood in the Black Doctor's way had ironically passed him by. Now, held for murder, guarded night and day, bedridden, helpless, he still had become dangerous, menacing, in the threat of reunion with the sinister Chang Ch'ien.

Val had not made his report to Gregg, had not intimated to Hilaire Garre his contact with Chang Ch'ien. This was a matter of utmost secrecy.

Val asked, without much hope of a truthful reply: "What information did Chang Ch'ien get away with?"

Hilaire Garre replied with more frankness than he had thus far shown.

"I myself do not know; but we have a common profession, *n'est-ce-pas?* Yes, there were papers missing from the body of a clerk of our naval ministry. Memoranda of vital importance to France in these disturbed times."

"Have you considered the United States might be interested in Chang Ch'ien and his information?" Val suggested, while his mind went to Nancy Fraser, to those things he had not divulged to his companion.

"We're not innocent," Garre chuckled. "War is not threatened between our countries. In the setting sun lies danger. The spy who offers his services for money would be a fool to traffic with the West when double, triple the price awaits him in the East. Name of a name! Am I not right?"

"Afraid so," Val admitted, "Here's the hospital, and your friend, the Black Doctor."

The cluster of brick buildings before which they stopped occupied half a city block. Dimly lighted windows stretched to right and left, four stories high. An entrance hall gave into a softly lighted reception lobby where a stiffly starched nurse behind a flat-topped desk smiled as she recognized Val Easton.

"Good evening, Miss Hanson," Val greeted, for he had come to have some slight acquaintance with her in former visits. "Everything all right in Zaken's room?"

"I believe so," Miss Hanson nodded brightly. "We will be discharging him in a few days. He has a visitor."

Val stopped short.

"Orders were no one without proper authority was to see him. Who is it?"

"It's quite all right," Miss Hanson assured him. "It was—" she consulted a pad before her—"Detective Kimberley from police headquarters."

"No one from police headquarters has any business seeing him, Miss Hanson."

"He showed his badge, Mr. Easton, and said he had come for a statement from the—the prisoner. He carried a briefcase."

"Ring police headquarters and ask for the detective bureau," Val snapped at the flustered nurse. And as she lifted the telephone and obeyed quickly, he questioned: "How long ago did this man go up?"

"About twenty minutes." Miss Hanson surrendered the receiver.

"Sheldon Hospital speaking," Val said curtly. "Have you sent anyone to get a statement from Carl Zaken who is being held here?... Thanks."

Val's face was grim as he handed back the instrument. "They know nothing about it," he said to Garre.

"Name of a thousand devils! I suspected it! Mademoiselle, will you have the goodness to describe this man to me?"

Miss Hanson's eyes were wide with astonishment, her face alarmed. "Why—why, he was a rather tall man," she faltered. "I didn't notice him particularly. Other visitors were here at the desk, and he wore a hat pulled low over his eyes. He asked which room Mr. Zaken occupied, and smiled as he identified himself. I thought everything was all right. There—there is a detective in the room, you know."

"Yes, I know. Queer about this, Garre. You haven't heard anything from the room, Miss Hanson?"

"No," said Miss Hanson, visibly upset.

"Come along," said Val to his companion. And as they strode into a rubber-matted corridor, Val said: "You don't think—"

"Chang Ch'ien," Garre replied grimly.

"The detective in the room will be suspicious. His orders are strict."

"Child's play to Chang Ch'ien," said Garre, snapping his fingers.

"Think they are planning an escape?"

"I do not think. I wait to see. You are armed, my friend?"

"No," Val admitted. "I didn't look for anything like this. The detective on guard has a gun." Val turned up wide stairs beside an elevator shaft. "Quicker time this way. It's on the second floor."

Hilaire Garre's eyes were glistening, his small black mustache seemed fairly to bristle as he patted his coat under his left arm. "I have a gun, monsieur. Perhaps I was foolish—but now, no! Have I your permission to shoot if it is Chang Ch'ien?"

"If he resists arrest and you're sure it's your man, don't let him get away."

They came out into a second rubber-floored corridor, quiet, dim. A white-enameled metal table and chair stood at a turn in the corridor; fever charts, thermometers and the various incidentals of the night nurse were there. But the nurse herself was not.

"Everything seems to be all right," Val judged. "It's the end room on the right. Here, better give me that gun. I'll go in first."

As Val finished speaking the end door on the left of the hall opened and a white-clad nurse stepped over and entered the door opposite.

"She's in Zaken's room now," Val said as he slipped in his coat pocket the small automatic Hilaire Garre handed him. "Wait until she comes out and we'll see how it is in there."

"Mais, oui," Garre agreed. "Excellent."

The door of Carl Zaken's private room abruptly opened. The white-clad nurse fled into the hall, darted toward them. She bore every indication of panic. Recognizing Val, she gasped: "In there! Something terrible has happened!"

CHAPTER SIX

THE BLACK DOCTOR STRIKES

BLOOD HAD drained from the nurse's cheeks. Her glance held horror. Hysteria was near the surface. Any woman less rigidly trained would probably have succumbed to the obvious shock and fainted. Val caught her elbow, steadying her as she swayed.

"What is it?" he queried calmly.

The little nurse passed the back of her hand over her eyes and visibly shuddered. "A dead man!" she whispered. "I lifted the covers—and there he was!"

Her story was not exactly clear. Val wasted no time in questioning her. "Wait here!" he commanded.

A moment later he was in the room where he had last seen Carl Zaken helpless in bed, with a watchful detective seated near the door. White, sterile, scantily furnished, this room, and the detective who should have been on duty was gone.

A sheeted, blanketed form lay on the white iron bed, the covers drawn up over the head.

At first glance it might have been Zaken. Val turned down the covers. Despite the warning, breath sucked sharply through his teeth. The fully clad headquarters man lay huddled there on the bed, his face congested, his eyes bulging grotesquely.

A glance was enough. The man was dead.

Hilaire Garre muttered an expletive in French. "Chang Ch'ien's hand has been here!" He pointed. "Look!"

The detective's hands were at his throat, taut as they had been in the last instant of life. The fingertips were hooked under a braided silk cord sunk deep into the neck muscles.

The mute story was plain to read. One could visualize the affable visitor, the ready story, the lulled suspicions—and the sudden drop of the cord around the victim's neck, the savage twist from behind stopping speech and bringing death despite frantic struggles.

Hilaire Garre said in a low voice: "Strangulation from behind. If the cord is twisted right, the neck is broken. In any event death is quick. An Asiatic did that. It is the way of thuggee—the robber caste of India. For centuries they have killed this way. Chang Ch'ien killed so in France—silently, bloodlessly, with all the cunning of an Oriental."

No longer was it possible to doubt that Hilaire Garre's quest was not founded in fact. Chang Ch'ien had come to America—to Carl Zaken, the Black Doctor.

And their infamous alliance had been sealed with murder!

Strangely, at that moment, Val's thought flashed to the pale, beautiful, expressionless face framed in jet-black hair, which for a moment on prosaic Pennsylvania Avenue had drawn his mind out of itself, sent his imagination whirling off into the dread unknown. This, then, was the unknown evil—threatening, stained with the red thread of death as vividly as her lips had been with carmine.

The clash with the Black Doctor in the night mists of tidewater Virginia had been the beginning, not the end. Now, linked with the cold menace of the legendary—but all too real—Chang Ch'ien, the threat of Carl Zaken had leaped to monstrous proportions.

Val stepped to the open window and looked out.

THE HOSPITAL buildings formed a rough U, with a boiler house in the top of the U and a driveway leading out past it. A small, shaded light shed a dim glow on the irregular cement court in the center of the U. A truck was parked down there, ashcans lined up before the boiler house; but the court itself was empty of life.

No ladder leaned against the window. The jump was too far for anyone to make, with hard cement below.

Val said to his companion: "Will you go down in the court and look around? Question anyone you see?"

"Mais, oui," Hilaire Garre assented swiftly, and hurried out.

The little nurse was more composed when Val rejoined her in the corridor. "He is dead?" she questioned.

"Quite dead. Did you see the man who went in there?" Val asked her.

"Why, yes," she assented nervously. "I was sitting at my table, and he asked which room Mr. Zaken was in, and said he was from the police. He—he looked like a foreigner."

"An Oriental?"

"He could have been, but his English was good."

"Did he knock before he entered the room?"

Again the little nurse shook her head. "Everything was quiet. Two of the rooms rang for me, and I was busy from then on. I usually look into that room every hour. This time when I entered, the detective was not there. I thought perhaps something was wrong with the patient and the guard was looking for me. But when I turned the covers down I found him there in the bed—" The little nurse shivered again at the memory.

"Was Zaken able to walk?"

"A little."

"Could the two men have come out this way while you were in one of the other rooms?"

"I don't think so," the little nurse denied promptly. "I always leave the door ajar while I am in a room, so I can see anyone passing in the corridor. We like to know who is moving about. No—I am certain no one went out this way."

"Get a doctor up here and report the matter to police headquarters," Val said. "I am going out in the court."

He found Hilaire Garre at the corner of the power house talking to a man in dirty overalls. Garre reported briskly: "This man was inside at his duties. The engine in there makes a noise so that one hears nothing. My friend," said Garre to the overalled one, "this opening past your building is the only way out of here?"

" 'Less'n you go through the buildings," said the engineer without much interest.

"No chance of them having left by the upper corridor without being seen," said Val. "They wouldn't risk hiding inside until they got a chance to slip out. Come with me."

The street behind the power house was dim, quiet. The familiar red brick houses stretched along the opposite side, many with lighted windows. A laugh broke the quiet of a porch over there.

Val crossed and found a young couple seated in a swing. They answered his questions readily.

Yes, an automobile had been parked across the street by the hospital driveway. They had noticed two people come out of the driveway and enter the car some ten minutes ago. One seemed to be assisting the other. The automobile had driven off and they had forgotten about it. The street was dim; they had not noticed the make or color of the sedan. Black, perhaps....

Rejoining Garre, Val said: "They drove away from here ten minutes ago."

"We will not find them this night," Garre said gloomily. *"Nom de Dieu*—it is a catastrophe; the Black Doctor and Chang Ch'ien are together! It was all planned. *Sacré*—what a witches' brew they will concoct! They must be stopped at any cost!"

"They will be," Val promised harshly.

THE POLICE appeared at the hospital immediately, and made little headway. It was established that the man had been large, speaking with a curiously clear, musical voice. Gloves of some dark material had covered the hand which gripped the leather briefcase he had carried, and which had vanished with him.

The investigation was headed by a lieutenant of detectives, Sullivan, a lank, experienced man, who frowned continually between gray, bushy eyebrows. Sullivan said bluntly to Val: "The Secret Service knows more about this than we do. I understand the full story of this Zaken has never been given us, and we were keeping watch on him merely as a matter of form and jurisdiction. But this—"

here Sullivan's square jaw set hard—"is our business. Our man has been murdered; and by heavens we want all the dope we can get!"

"There isn't much to give," Val told him. "Zaken was an alien, caught holding up one of our citizens who had certain papers that were valuable. He killed one of his own men in the scrimmage, and was being held for murder."

Neither Val nor Hilaire Garre mentioned Chang Ch'ien for obvious reasons.

Lieutenant Sullivan was dissatisfied, but baffled. It was possible, the interne on duty admitted, for Zaken to get about to a limited degree. His condition had been improving rapidly; he might have been better than a cursory examination disclosed, reserving strength for just this occasion. He would have been a well man in a few days.

"A well man," Val repeated bitterly to Hilaire Garre. "And I counted him out of the way for good."

"*Hélas*—so it goes," Garre shrugged.

A white-capped nurse glided up to Val at that moment. "Mr. Easton?" she queried.

"Yes."

"A Mr. Gregg has just called and wishes you to go to the detective bureau at police headquarters as quickly as you can."

"Did he say what he wanted?"

"No, but he sounded urgent, Mr. Easton."

They left the hospital together, Val and the dapper little French Secret Service man.

Garre mused aloud: "The Black Doctor will not be caught again so easily, my friend."

"No," Val agreed curtly.

Garre mused on. "He and Chang Ch'ien... name of a name! I try to see why it is they form the liaison—and I am stupefied. Something big, vast, I sense it, yet I cannot put the fingernail on it."

"Come with me, and we'll talk this thing over later," Val suggested. "An extra head will help, since you know them both."

"But surely," Garre agreed quickly. "I was hoping you would consider my interest."

Gregg was on his feet in the office of Daly, the night captain of detectives. Gregg's face was set. He showed more than his usual feeling. "Hell's popping tonight!" he snapped at Val. "Nancy Fraser and a woman companion have been abducted!"

Val swore with the shock of it—for a moment silence fell as he stared at Gregg.

"What happened?" he asked. "Who was with Nancy Fraser?"

Gregg looked queer. "A Miss Harmsworth."

"Good Lord! Not Trudie Harmsworth from Philadelphia?"

Gregg nodded. "Her father telephoned this afternoon. I had a long talk with him. He was disturbed, apprehensive. He informed me his daughter was in town, and asked me to keep an eye on her. I had Nancy Fraser go out with her tonight."

"Good Heavens, sir, I wish you'd told me about this before. I—might have been of some assistance."

TWO WILD-EYED young men burst into the office as he finished speaking. Both were in their middle twenties, wearing dinner clothes. They were pale, haggard. Their eyes were bloodshot and watery. Coats and trousers were wrinkled, stained, covered with dirt.

The first one, a tall, handsome chap with clean-cut features, burst out wildly: "Have you discovered anything yet? Good God—this is ghastly!"

"Take it easy," Daly counseled calmly. "We're doing all we can. I sent out a general alarm over the city, and reported the matter to the Maryland and Virginia State Police. Tell me exactly what happened. Your telephone call from Tacoma Park was a trifle incoherent."

The young man gulped, drew a deep breath. "I'm Walter Mitchell," he said rapidly, harshly. "This is my friend, Mr. Kinnard. Miss Harmsworth and myself are—er—halfway engaged. She arrived from Philadelphia this afternoon and agreed to go out with me tonight—and later called and said she would have a companion, and did I know anyone to escort the other young lady. Charley here filled in. We were going to the Mayflower, but at the last minute decided to go out to the Blue Cock roadhouse in Maryland."

Val interrupted: "Did anyone else know your change in plans?"

"No," Mitchell denied. "They were made at the last moment. We went out to the roadhouse, dined, danced a little; and then started back. The carburetor went bad after several miles, and we stopped. Charley and I got out to see what we could do—and while we were looking at the motor an automobile stopped behind us. A man walked up and asked if he could help. And then, without warning, he exploded tear gas in our faces." Young Mitchell clenched a fist and swore. "God—if I could get my hands on him!"

"We'll do that," Daly reminded coolly. "Go on."

"While we were staggering around half insensible with the pain in our eyes and blind as bats, they tied and gagged us!" Mitchell said hoarsely.

Gregg put in: "They?"

"Yes. There was more than one. When we could see again we were lying in the woods beside the road. We rolled out on the road, into the light before our car. A passing machine stopped and freed us. The girls were gone. I heard the other machine drive off toward Washington while I was blind from the gas."

"Would you recognize the car or the man who spoke to you?" Val asked.

"No. All I saw was its headlights," Mitchell confessed hopelessly. "It was too dark to see much of the fellow who came up to us. I remember one thing. He dropped his 'r's' when he spoke, and had a curious inflection to his voice."

"Chinese?" Hilaire Garre asked softly.

"Why—yes. I believe you've hit it!" Mitchell cried.

Kinnard, who had not spoken; until now, said savagely: "I got a good look at the headlights of that car. One of them was a lot dimmer than the other."

"I knew it!" Val exploded to Gregg. "Chang Ch'ien!"

Of the six in that room, only three understood the exclamation. Hilaire Garre nodded. Gregg had regained his impassivity. Daly shot him a sharp look.

"Chang Ch'ien?" Daly echoed. "What's that?"

"Doesn't matter now," Val remarked. "I know that car. It's a black limousine. Get it and you'll have this cleared up. I asked earlier in the evening to have it picked up."

Young Mitchell cried hoarsely: "We've got to find them! Good God—I—there's no telling what may be happening to them!"

Gregg laid a hand on the young man's shoulder. "It probably isn't as bad as you think," he said kindly. "If Easton knows that car he has a pretty good idea of what's behind this."

Mitchell snatched at the thread of hope. "D'you think so?" he begged.

"Yes. After Captain Daly is through with you, notify Miss Harmsworth's sister, and all of you keep calm."

"I'd like to believe you," Mitchell gulped.

"He's right," said Daly. "And there's nothing more you two can do just now. Stop in the next office and leave a telephone number."

Daly went out after them.

HILAIRE GARRE looked bewildered. "I do not understand," he confessed. "Is it that Carl Zaken and Chang Ch'ien have struck so soon?"

"Evidently," Gregg assented. He ran fingers through his gray-streaked hair, gnawed at his under lip. "Looks plain enough," he growled. "Zaken wanted Nancy Fraser—and they took both girls." Val slapped a fist into his palm. "Those plans of the Harmsworth factory—and then Harmsworth's daughter. Tonight—it can't be coincidence."

Gregg's eyes narrowed. "Notify Harmsworth," he ordered abruptly. "Use Daly's telephone. I want to talk to Daly."

Val put the call through to Philadelphia, and when Harmsworth was on the line, broke the news.

Nathaniel Harmsworth's voice roared over the wire from Philadelphia. "Abducted? Good God! Who got them? What are you people doing about it?"

"Everything we can," Val assured him. "Try to keep cool. We're certain nothing has happened to them yet."

"Keep cool!" Harmsworth shouted. "How the devil can I when my daughter has been kidnaped! She may be dead now! They may be ill-treating her!"

"Not a chance of it," Val said with more assurance than he felt.

There was a moment's silence at the other end of the wire. When Harmsworth spoke his voice was more controlled. "What are you people doing?"

"I'm at police headquarters," Val told him. "A general alarm has been sent out over the city and Maryland and Virginia. We have a clue to the car which carried them off. If there are any developments I'll notify you immediately."

"Do that," Harmsworth pleaded. "I'll stay near the telephone."

Gregg and Daly returned as Val hung up. Daly was saying: "They had at least three quarters of an hour start. Frankly, I doubt if that machine is on the streets or roads now. It will be picked up if it is. Every car with a dim headlight is being stopped and checked."

"It's important that this be kept out of the newspapers," Gregg said.

Daly shrugged. "It might be done. We've only asked that the car be picked up and brought in."

"Do it," Gregg requested. "This isn't public business."

Daly grunted, reached for a pipe on his desk. "You chaps are always hush-hushing. I don't suppose you want to tell me?"

Gregg smiled thinly. "Rather not. It's a little too complicated to go into, and too damned important to spread around. I'm going over to my office. I'll have a man there all night. If you get anything let me know at once."

Daly agreed to do that. Val and Hilaire Garre went out with Gregg.

Gregg sighed as he strode off along the sidewalk. "This is a hell of a mess, gentlemen. Just when you think everything is quiet and well in hand, it breaks out in half a dozen places. We're dealing with an organized group. They've struck all along the coast here so accurately that it must have been all planned to the last detail."

Garre murmured: "Chang Ch'ien and the Black Doctor could operate all over the country—and in Europe at the same time, messieurs. They have secured something valuable, beside the persons of the two young ladies, *n'est-ce-pas?*"

"Not yet," Gregg denied hastily.

"*Oui,*" Garre said discreetly, and thereafter remained away from that subject. A gentleman, Val decided. Zeal for his own country did not move him to impose on the confidence which was being vouchsafed him.

CHAPTER SEVEN
CHANG CH'IEN

THOUGH OUT of Washington most of the time, Val kept a small apartment as a headquarters and a home to return to. It was just off Connecticut Avenue, not far from the British Embassy. The elevator was not working after midnight. He walked the three flights to his door, heavy-hearted, baffled.

Despite all the confident things he had said to Nathaniel Harmsworth he knew Nancy Fraser and Trudie Harmsworth were in real danger. This was no ordinary kidnaping. The thing had been executed like clockwork.

And the threat of the Black Doctor and the mysterious, sinister Chang Ch'ien was growing hourly.

So thinking, Val let himself into his apartment, and stepped into the living room, reaching for the light switch. Suddenly he froze, sniffing the air.

The usual faint aroma of tobacco had been replaced by the sweet, heady odor of incense. His finger found the light switch, snapped it on. His wary glance found the room empty.

There was no mistake about the incense. A hammered-brass ash tray had been in the middle of the small refectory table against the wall. It was resting on the edge now—and in it a small round piece of black incense was emitting a wavering spiral of blue smoke.

The light overhead gleamed through layers of slowly rising vapor drifting about the room. It had a thick, cloying, laguorous odor, heady, almost smothering. The room felt stuffy; yet at the same time there was no temptation to open the window. It was strangely pleasant just to stand and inhale....

With an effort, Val shook off the feeling and stared about. Who had been in here and lighted that incense?

A vague sense of danger crept over him, and then slowly died away as he filled his lungs again and again. The sensation of pleasant well being crept over him. The couch and pillows against the wall invited. He had been up a long time. It would be perfect to relax here and think everything out.

Some hidden sense of warning flashed cold reality through Val's mind at that point. He wasn't reacting normally. Someone had entered his apartment—yet he only wanted to sit down and think it over. It must be the incense—drugging him....

Yet it took a distinct effort to force himself to the window. His hand was on the long drapes—when they opened before him, and a slender figure stepped out.

Long later the picture was still in Val's mind. Pale, soft, beautiful—the girl he had seen twice before stood there. Only tonight, close up, through the confusion gripping his senses, her strange exotic beauty seemed like a flame, dwarfing every other woman he had ever known. The sparkling ornament of brilliants was still in her black hair. Her high cheek bones, her mouth vivid as a flame tree, her delicately formed features and her creamy skin against the drapes made her like some lovely lady out of an old Chinese print.

A hush fell between them as, perfectly composed, she looked at him, smiling faintly.

VAL BROKE it, with an effort. "What do you want here?" he asked.

Her faint smile lingered. Val's mind leaped back to the night before as the same clear musical voice said: "I let myself in your door with a skeleton key, Mr. Easton. I hope you do not mind?"

And Val didn't, although one part of his mind—a very small part—knew that behind her loveliness there must be evil.

"Who are you?" he heard himself asking.

She replied, with the faintest shade of mockery: "Won't you make me welcome? I am Tai Shan. I have come to help you."

Later Val could appreciate the exquisite irony of that. Even now he got a flash of it. For his hand went to her arm, and he forced himself to say grimly: "I've been looking for you. Where are those two girls?"

She was not disturbed by his grip. Indeed, the faint smile deepened on her vivid lips. She spoke three words in a strange language. Later he was to know it as Mandarin.

Two mighty hands fell on Val's elbows from behind, snatching him back a step—two steps....

He was like a child in that grip. Turning, he saw, towering behind, the pale, almost blond features of a giant Chinese. Surpassingly ugly, one side of his face drawn into a set leer by a great vivid scar, the man stared past him at Tai Shan.

And Tai Shan gestured ever so slightly. Val was pulled back step by step until he stood beside the refectory table, and the swaying column of blue incense.

Tai Shan followed slowly. "You see, I mean you no harm. I saved your life once, Valentine Easton. I am your friend."

Through the drifting veils of incense her beauty blurred—as it had through the fog wraiths on that lonely wharf. The cloying perfume, stronger than ever, brought an overpowering sensation of peace. Tai Shan must be all right. Her visit here seemed perfectly in order. She was a friend, come to help....

Another slight gesture of her hand freed the grip on his elbows.

"I have waited two hours for you," Tai Shan complained.

And through Val's swimming thoughts came keen regret that he had kept this woman waiting. "How did you know where I lived?" he muttered.

"I know many things," Tai Shan assured him. Her voice was like a musical soporific. "I know that you have been looking for two young ladies. I have come to take you to them. You will go with me, won't you?"

Back, far back, the sense of hidden danger stirred feebly again, and then vanished. This lovely Tai Shan could only have come to help, as she said. All the rest was a mistake.

As from a great distance Val heard himself saying slowly: "Let's go."

Tai Shan addressed the giant Chinese. She took Val's arm. They left the apartment. A big sedan was standing at the curb before the building. The giant Chinese padded silently up behind them, slipped into the seat beside Val and closed the door. They rolled away instantly.

A soft bandage was slipped over Val's eyes. From that moment he had no idea where he was going. It was enough that he was riding beside Tai Shan, his arm inside the curve of her arm, his shoulder against her soft shoulder. She brought peace and the mystery of the East—she inspired confidence....

"You have wondered why I saved your life?" Tai Shan inquired.

"Yes."

"I have heard about you," said Tan Shan. "And I have watched you when you were not aware of it. Death is not for you, Val Easton. You are young, life is before you, great things to be done if you will bend yourself to them."

At the moment it seemed she was right. A sense of latent power rose strong in him. "What shall I do?" Val asked.

Tai Shan sighed. "You will see," she said.

THEY DROVE one mile—or twenty miles, turning frequently. Blindfolded, drifting into a languorous daze. Val neither knew nor cared. But gradually a change was taking place. The fresh cool air of early morning was diminishing his agreeable lassitude. A growing distrust of this Tai Shan at his side crept over him. The feeling that all was not right became stronger with each passing moment. Behind the eye bandage Val's forehead wrinkled with effort to comprehend what it was all about.

In the midst of that the car stopped. The giant on his right opened the door, stepped out. Tai Shan said: "We have arrived."

Tai Shan followed him from the car, took his arm, guided him forward, cautioning him to lift his feet for steps. A door opened before them, and as they passed through the dull, booming note of a gong sounded in some distant place.

"A warning," Tai Shan said in his ear, "that a stranger has entered the house of Chang Ch'ien."

A strange odor of the East met them as they walked forward, the aroma of incense and sandalwood, of heavy perfumes, mixed with the sweet, biting fumes of opium smoke. Behind them padded the giant Chinese guard.

They brushed through draperies that rustled stiffly to their touch. A bright light struck through the bandage. Tai Shan's hand stopped him.

A calm, clear voice said in flawless English: "You have done well, Tai Shan. Uncover his eyes."

Blinking, Val found himself standing in a circle of light pouring down from a point directly over his head. The ceiling was high, the floor was of highly polished wood, the light gleamed back in a thousand yellow lancets from heavy cloth-of-gold tapestry covering the walls.

Val looked for Tai Shan. She had disappeared. The giant, scar-featured guard who had come with them was gone. He was alone in that silver circle of light.

In the darker shadows beyond, a tall figure slowly moved forward, speaking in the same calm, clear voice, a familiar voice. "Welcome to the humble house of Chang Ch'ien, Mr. Easton."

There was an uncanny, rhythmic, purring quality about the voice, an overwhelming sense of latent force and power, a feeling that the mind behind was projecting out, enfolding the will to which it was addressed.

Perhaps the night air had sobered Val sooner than intended. He was even able to catch a faint touch of mockery, as if Chang Ch'ien were talking down once more to one who was helpless, pliable.

And with the last word Chang Ch'ien stepped into the outer rays of light, moving with the effortless ease of a great cat.

It was the same man—the lascar whose knife had barely missed his throat, the man who had passed sentence of death on him in that shabby Chinese place of business on Times Square.

Once more the silken robes and fictionized trappings of a wealthy Chinese were not there. Chang Ch'ien was dressed in the somber black of correct dinner clothes. A long, intricately carved ivory cigarette holder lifted in sinewy, supple fingers, Chang Ch'ien inhaled lazily, smiling as he looked through the smoke which drifted up past his face.

Each feature was as fine and clear-cut as though from tinted marble. The mouth was wide, full-lipped, the cheek bones high, wide, the eyes only slightly slanted, and the smooth black hair sweeping back from the forehead was black and shining. The curious scar which Val had noticed twice before, of which Hilaire had spoken, was there at the corner of the right eye, small, sickle-shaped. It drew the corner of the eye up still further into the slightest sardonic cast. Light in contrast with the somber black coat, Chang Ch'ien's skin on closer scrutiny had a faint golden tinge.

It was easy to understand now why Chang Ch'ien was the myth, the legend, the terror. Cunning lurked behind that lazy smile; ruthlessness and cruelty lay dormant like velvet-sheathed claws. Men of many types had passed before Val Easton's eyes, yet never had one who so personified sheer satanic power as did this Chang Ch'ien.

It shocked his mind to wakefulness; like a dash of cold water.

Chang Ch'ien spoke again in his clear, purring voice. "You do not answer me, Mr. Easton. Is it possible your mind is drugged into vacancy?"

"So I was drugged?" Val asked. And found that it still took an effort to speak. He could think of the present, but the past and the future were still blurred.

CHANG CH'IEN gestured easily with his long ivory holder. "I see I was mistaken. You will forgive the drug, I know—even though I am trifle proud of it. My own discovery, Mr. Easton—a very unusual blending of the widely used hashish and the little known Arabic khat, the Flower of Paradise, as its devotees term it. In the form of incense it brings paradise and forgetfulness for a short time."

"I see," Val muttered.

"No," Chang Ch'ien purred amiably. "I doubt if you see clearly. I underestimated you before. I did not know you were the Valentine Easton of whom my friend Carl Zaken speaks with the utmost venom. One who can outwit and earn the hate of so brilliant a man interests me. And the member of any nation's Secret Service who can captivate the fancy of so wise a woman as my sister, Tai Shan, intrigues me. You are honored in your hates and fortunate in your loves, Mr. Easton."

Startled, Val said: "Love?"

"In the poetic sense," Chang Ch'ien agreed with a faint amusement. "At first sight, if I am to believe all I hear. A remarkable girl, Tai Shan. At times I do not understand her. Woman, the eternal riddle, *n'est-ce-pas?*"

"I don't know your sister," Val parried.

"You shall," Chang Ch'ien promised. "Fate casts the dice, and men dance to the numbers. I am a great believer in destiny, Mr. Easton. You are a chivalrous man. What would you do to save a woman's life—and possibly your own?" Chang Ch'ien waited with a mocking smile.

"What woman?"

"Not so chivalrous," Chang Ch'ien sighed. He stepped back silently—and a moment later the metallic note of the gong vibrated through the room.

"Look," Chang Ch'ien directed from the shadows. The golden curtains at one side of the room parted. Nancy Fraser and Trudie Harmsworth moved slowly into the silver circle of light.

"Val!" Nancy cried—and with a swift step reached his side and caught his hand, as if the touch brought her hope and strength.

Both the young women were pale and shaken. And it seemed to Val that Nancy's fresh beauty brought a note of vibrant cheerfulness into the cloying fog of evil.

"Are you both all right?" he demanded.

Trudie laughed with relief. "Miss Fraser said you would find us right away."

Still clinging to Val's hand, Nancy laughed shakily. "Perhaps I was a little more confident than I felt. How did you do it so soon, Val? Who is with you?"

Unnoticed until now, Chang Ch'ien moved noiselessly out of the shadows, smiling thinly. "Since trust can only be born of great affection," he said smoothly, "it desolates me to dash your hopes, but Mr. Easton is here at my request."

Nancy's glance sought Val's questioningly. "Is he—right?"

"Yes," Val confessed.

Trudie Harmsworth faced Chang Ch'ien defiantly. "My father will make trouble about this!" she blazed with the reckless confidence of youth. "He'll spend every dollar he has to hunt you down like animals, you—you contemptible, yellow-skinned cad!"

Chang Ch'ien stood like some smiling, black-garbed, golden-skinned incarnation of evil. "I see you have the typical aversion to people of my race," he purred. "Let us trust you will change your mind. You both will return to the room where you were. I merely wanted Mr. Easton to satisfy himself that there was yet time to save your lives."

Chang Ch'ien stepped back into the shadows. The gong rang once more, metallically. The golden tapestry parted. Two slender, impassive Chinese, wearing neat blue business suits, moved into the room. One laid a hand on Trudie's arm. She threw it off, crying: "Don't touch me!"

"You are safe until tomorrow," Chang Ch'ien said smoothly. "Go peacefully, young women. And in case Mr. Easton contemplates violence, he is covered by a gun."

Nancy looked at Val questioningly.

Val nodded heavily. Nothing else to do.

The golden drapes closed behind them.

CHAPTER EIGHT
TORTURE TAVERN

CHANG CH'IEN drew a thin cigarette case from the pocket of his dinner coat, and turned it in the sinewy golden fingers of one hand. "Let us hope your chivalry is stimulated," he smiled. "I offer you their lives—two pale lilies of priceless worth," and here the mockery in Chang Ch'ien's voice was plain.

"And in return?" Val asked.

"Only the Harmsworth formula," Chang Ch'ien said blandly. "You will write and assure a distracted father what a small price will bring his daughter's return."

Chang Ch'ien opened the thin cigarette case, extended it. "Will you indulge?"

Val took one of the cork-tipped cigarettes, accepted the light Chang Ch'ien proffered.

"And if Harmsworth is unwilling to do that?" Val questioned.

"He will, with your insistence," Chang Ch'ien smiled. "Had it not been for you we might have tried to get it another way. But when you appeared at the Harmsworth plant we knew you had cleverly checkmated us there. Surprised, Mr. Easton? I assure you our sources of information are complete and flawless."

"I doubt," Val said flatly, "that Harmsworth would ever surrender that formula, even if threatened through his daughter." A slight haze seemed to drift before his eyes, causing Chang Ch'ien to grow taller, his voice to recede.

Val suddenly realized that his mind was beginning to fumble again, as if fogged by alcohol, or drugs. Drugs! The cigarette he had been smoking must be guilty. Val took it hastily from his lips, with a mighty effort steadied his thoughts.

The monstrous, wavering figure before him shrank to normal size. He heard clearly when Chang Ch'ien smiled once more and said softly: "But if the formula for Harmsworth's new gas is not surrendered he will be a man without a daughter. And you will be a man without the woman you care for. Later we will have the plans some other way. We must have them. Do you understand? Carl Zaken and I have planned a new world—a world where the yellow man will be—"

A harsh voice broke through the room. "Are you insane?"

Chang Ch'ien started, wheeled to face the tall stooped figure that shuffled painfully into the glare of the light, on the arm of the giant scar-cheeked Chinaman. And even Val felt his pulse skip a beat as he looked into the pale, ghastly, cadaverous face whose green-flecked eyes surveyed them both malevolently.

Carl Zaken, the Black Doctor, stood before them.

And if Chang Ch'ien was a golden-skinned terror, the Black Doctor was a monster, a fiend, indescribably vicious, venomous, dangerous. Here stood the man whose name had for years seeped through the shady secret channels of espionage like a miasma.

NOW, RESTING one hairy-backed hand on the supporting arm beside him, and obviously in pain, the Black Doctor showed teeth like fangs as he snarled again at Chang Ch'ien in a rasping voice. "You fool! What do you mean by confiding in this man?"

And Chang Ch'ien visibly shrank before the malevolence directed at him. One had only to look to know who was master.

"He is drugged," said Chang Ch'ien quickly. "The cigarette…. I only impressed upon his mind the futility of resistance."

"He is not a coolie to be threatened. Drugged or not, he's dangerous. And beside, he is mine. I have a little account to settle…."

The green-flecked eyes flamed as they ran over Val. Death seemed to creep low and close in that golden-tapestried room.

Chang Ch'ien stirred restlessly. "The account can wait. This man came under the protection of Tai Shan."

Carl Zaken bared his teeth. "Protection—for him?"

Chang Ch'ien spread his hands.

"I promised Tai Shan—if he will throw his lot in with us, he will be spared."

Carl Zaken raised talonlike fingers to his forehead, beaded with sweat. His smile was ghastly. "I am still a sick man," he said with an effort. "But I see I am needed. I heard you speak of a letter. I will see that he writes it. Take him downstairs."

For a moment they stood, the pale cadaverous Black Doctor and the golden-skinned giant with the sickle scar at the corner of his slant eye. A silent struggle flashed between them, dramatic in its very quiet.

Chang Ch'ien yielded. His hands spread out, he bowed slightly. "I trust your wisdom, my friend."

Carl Zaken laughed, a derisive grimace, unpleasant to see. "You'd better," he said cryptically. "Call your men."

Chang Ch'ien stepped into the shadows without answering. The awesome note of the gong rang once more. And in quick answer to it the two men who had removed the young women from the room appeared once more.

Chang Ch'ien spoke to them in Chinese. They closed in on Val, dragged him to the spot where Nancy Fraser and Trudie Harmsworth had disappeared, into a dim-lit corridor beyond. Carl Zaken followed on the arm of the scar-cheeked giant.

They went along that hall, past a flight of stairs leading up, turned to the right beside the stairs and descended other steps, down....

It was a grisly repetition of that similar descent in the heart of New York. Only this time the presence of the Black Doctor blotted out what hope might have been present. Carl Zaken was not the man to forget those moments in tidewater Virginia, when guns had crashed and his well-laid plans had smashed before his eyes. The lead slugs healing in that pain-racked body would not soon be forgotten. There would be no second escape.

They came into a cellar, dank, musty, cold. A cellar hoary with years, where spider webs hung thick, and the gloom of past generations lay thick as the dust on the old brick walls.

The padding feet of the men who led him, the shuffling tread of the Black Doctor sounded loud in the dismal quiet. Great flagstones underneath looked cold, bleak, in the lifeless rays of two dim bulbs overhead.

Near the end of the passage they stopped. The scar-cheeked giant stooped and lifted an iron ring embedded in one of the flagstones. He twisted it twice, and then heaved. The great flagstone pivoted on its center with a dull scraping sound, revealing a black pit and a flight of brick steps leading down.

The Black Doctor's laugh echoed eerily in the stillness. "We tried for three hours before we solved the secret of that iron ring, Easton. Clever to have to twist it before the flag unlocks, eh?"

"Very," Val agreed drily. "What is this place anyway?"

"It was an inn, I believe, some years before your Civil War. And later was used as a prison—or so I have heard." Zaken chuckled. "The old hostelry must feel honored to have guests once more. Though I fear its hospitality must take a slightly different form from what it did in the past. Torture Tavern might be an apt name for the new management to put on its signboard."

Val shivered at the implication behind Zaken's words, but descended the brick steps without remonstrance. When he was at the bottom, a switch clicked somewhere behind him and a light went on overhead. A long, narrow corridor stretched before them. This sub-cellar was even danker, gloomier than the passage overhead they had left. The bricks underfoot were dark with subterranean seepage. The ghastly form of a big gray rat scurried across the shadowy passage and vanished.

Carl Zaken chuckled, rasped again: "One finds it easy to speculate what could happen down here."

VAL SAW why as he was shoved along the passage. On the left they passed cell after cell, dark noisome little cubicles, closed by rusty handwrought doors of barred iron. What men had been imprisoned there? In those far off days before and during the Civil War, what sinister scenes had been enacted down here? What men had seen hopes flicker and die? There was no answer to the questions; but the ghosts of those deeds seemed to linger yet.

The scar-cheeked giant strode ahead and opened a door of heavy planks on old strap hinges. And they stepped into a long, low-ceilinged room, startling in contrast to the dismal passage. It had been cleaned spick and span. Thick comfortable carpets were spread on the cold stone floor. Tapestries had been hung on the walls. A luxurious divan sat against the wall. Comfortable chairs stood about. Magazines and books, cigars and cigarettes were on a mahogany table in the center of the room. A small old-fashioned spinet desk stood against the opposite wall.

There was no trace of the Orient about this subterranean chamber.

Carl Zaken noticed the inquiring look Val cast around. "My private den, Easton."

"Very comfortable."

A wave of one clawlike hand sent the two Chinese from the room, closing the heavy plank door behind them. Scarcheek remained.

The Black Doctor shuffled to the table, lighted one of the cigarettes, surveyed Val as he inhaled. The damp sheen of pain was still on his forehead. His face seemed more like a ghastly, cadaverous mask than ever. His voice had a labored rasping sound, overlaid with malevolent triumph.

"I have waited for this night, Easton waited while the doctors thought I would die, and admired when I lived."

Carl Zaken inhaled, and watched Val unblinkingly. Scarcheek stood watchfully, with folded arms, near the door. A pocket of his coat bulged. The dull handle of a gun was visible there. Carl Zaken noticed Val's glance, and said abruptly: "He will shoot you at the first resistance."

"I don't doubt it," Val agreed shortly. "And now that I'm here—what?"

Carl Zaken inhaled again. He was coldly deliberate.

"Upstairs," said Carl Zaken, "are two women who will die in twenty-four hours if the Harmite formula is not delivered. With your assistance we will save them."

"How?" Val asked curiously.

"You will write a letter," said Carl Zaken, nodding at the spinet desk. "In it you will tell Harmsworth that you can guarantee the safe return of his daughter at once, if he brings the formula to Washington immediately—and secretly. You will make an appointment with him at the

Willard Hotel. You will warn him to say nothing to anyone until you see him at the Willard. And you will tell him to deposit the formula immediately in the hotel safe as soon as he registers. His attachment to his daughter will bring him to the Willard as quickly as he can get from Philadelphia."

Val shrugged, wondering if Carl Zaken were as simple as his plan indicated.

"You won't stand much chance of getting it out of the Willard Hotel safe," he pointed out.

"That is up to us, my friend. Pen and stationery are on, the desk. Will you write?"

Val shook his head. "I don't think so."

CARL ZAKEN'S teeth bared. He turned, stepped to the desk, pulled out a drawer. His hands were opening a small leather instrument case when he returned to the table. A cold creepy feeling crawled down Val's back as the talonlike fingers opened it on the table. He knew what it contained before the bright light overhead glinted on the shining steel instruments inside. It was a surgeon's emergency kit.

Carl Zaken lifted out a slender steel scalpel, razor sharp. "I anticipated refusal," he said. "I have a way of dealing with stubbornness, my quixotic young friend."

Tales of the past gleaned along the shadowy paths of espionage flashed through Val's mind. Vague whispered rumors of terror and torture. Carl Zaken, they said, had once been a doctor. And men spoke with white-lipped rage of the use to which that knowledge had been put. Ruthless, fiendish torture on the bodies of helpless men....

Those ghoulish rumors had given to Carl Zaken, the master spy, his name of the Black Doctor.

Carl Zaken pulled up one sleeve and sliced hairs from the matted growth on the back of his arm. His grinning face was like a ghastly, cadaverous death's head; his voice held unholy mockery.

"I dislike violence, Easton. A few cuts here and there. Did you ever see a man without a tongue? Without eyes? Did you ever feel the tortures of the damned? Ever think how it might feel to lie helpless, paralyzed for life because of severed nerve cables?"

Val's throat suddenly felt dry, tight, and cold perspiration crawled out on his forehead. The keen little scalpel winked and blinked in the light as Carl Zaken gestured toward the desk with it.

"In a few seconds you can save those girls and make all that unnecessary."

Locked in the hotel safe the formula would still be out of reach. "All right," said Val briefly.

Following Carl Zaken's dictation, he penned the letter, addressed the envelope and sealed it.

"Good!" said Zaken, slipping it in his pocket. "It will be delivered as fast as an automobile can get it to Philadelphia." Zaken laughed harshly. "And before Harmsworth reaches Baltimore we will have the formula. Thank you, Easton—I will settle our little account later."

And as he looked into that grinning death's face, Val knew he had been tricked. Harmsworth would be followed; the formula taken. Nancy Fraser and Trudie Harmsworth were no nearer safety than before. And for himself—all the tortures of the damned still waited. The Black Doctor still meant to settle his score.

The red fury of hopeless despair exploded in Val's mind, blotting out everything but that grinning face before him.

He leaped for Carl Zaken's throat. Leaped with murder in his heart. And reckless disregard of the consequences.

Carl Zaken's shrill cry of warning, his futile stab into Val's arm with the scalpel, availed not. Val's hand closed tight about the scrawny corded neck. He slammed the Black Doctor to the floor, shaking that creature of evil like a dog might a rat.

But it was a hopeless gesture. A moment later the swift rush of the scar-cheeked giant checked him. Val did not see the gun come down on his head. He only knew that the lighted room exploded into confusion—and everything went black....

CHAPTER NINE
TAI SHAN AGAIN

A **SHARP** needlelike jab of pain in his ear was the first thing Val knew. He struck weakly at it. Something live, warm, wriggled away from his hand. Something else scuttled across his face. A rat squealed angrily.

He found himself sitting up an instant later, blinking at gray, grisly shapes scampering out of sight. The past came back. He recognized where he was.

On the other side of an iron-barred door a dim light bulb shed a sickly glow in the narrow corridor. Val staggered to his feet, groped against the damp brick wall. He was in one of the narrow cells, deep underground.

His head ached dully. His exploring fingers found a scalp wound, came away stained crimson. It was easy to reconstruct the blow which had been delivered by the saffron-skinned giant.

Val stepped to the barred door and tried it. It was locked securely. The cell was barren. Not even a chair or box to sit on. He was a helpless prisoner. Carl Zaken had tricked him. The Harmsworth formula was lost.

By his wrist watch he saw he had only been unconscious a few minutes. Nervous tension drove him to pacing the narrow cramped cell. Ten minutes of that passed, each minute an endless stretch of time. And suddenly Val stopped short, listened, and stepped to the barred door. The light pat of footsteps had sounded in the silence.

Tai Shan, the lovely, the deadly, stopped before the cell door. Her glance was anxious, her voice relieved. "They said you were unconscious?"

"I was," said Val.

"Are you hurt?"

"A gash on my head. What do you want?"

Tai Shan's sigh of relief was audible. "Let me see it," she commanded. With a big rusty key she unlocked the cell door and slipped inside.

Val obeyed, wondering. Tai Shan examined his head. "It will be all right," she said. The heady fragrance of strange perfume crept into Val's nostrils.

"You tricked me neatly tonight," he said shortly.

Tai Shan looked up at him. "You are a strange man, Val Easton," she murmured. "I do not understand you. Perhaps if I were not part Chinese…." Tai Shan's hand touched his arm lightly for an instant. "But I must leave you," she said in a low tone. "They do not know I am down here."

Val caught her as she turned away. Tai Shan knew instantly his purpose. Her face blazed with anger as she wheeled back. Her other hand flashed inside her dress, whipped out a slender dagger.

"Get back!" Tai Shan warned.

Their eyes locked for an instant—and Val knew she would kill him if he disobeyed. "Don't make me hurt you!" he begged.

The gleaming blade flicked at him for answer.

A quick dodge, a lunge against her was all that saved him. The knife ripped his coat sleeve. Val knocked her hand down, gripped her wrist before she could stab again, and clapped a hand against the scream which burst to her lips.

Tai Shan fought like an enraged cat while he disarmed her. Slipping the dagger in his pocket, Val panted: "Will you guide me out of here?"

"No!" Tai Shan gasped behind his fingers.

Val looked at her thoughtfully. Lovely and dangerous. "I'm not going to hurt you, of course. But I'm going to lock you in here."

Tai Shan's last words, before Val locked the cell door behind him, were: "Why did I ever want to save you?"

VAL MADE silently for the steps leading up to the cellar above. Tai Shan did not cry out behind him. Too well she probably knew, no sound could be heard down here, deep underground.

And to that quiet Val owed the warning which reached him.

The corridor widened into a small open room where the steps came down. One could not see the steps until almost on them. Val heard the furtive scrape of feet descending. He stopped short, gripping the knife he had taken from Tai Shan.

Only one person, by the sound. Val flattened against the wall, slipped forward. He was within two strides of the bottom of the steps when one of the Chinese who had led him down stepped into sight—and stopped short, jaw dropping.

Val lunged at him, knife ready.

The surprise was complete, his swift onslaught unnerving. The wiry little Chinaman turned and fled. Not up the steps. Perhaps fear rattled him. Perhaps he doubted his ability to escape that way. Into the black shadows behind the bottom of the steps he scuttled—and vanished.

Val would never have thought to look there, would probably never have found the narrow black opening in the brickwork in the far corner behind the steps where the fugitive had vanished. The noise of his scurrying flight sounded somewhere ahead. Val plunged in after him.

He found himself in a low-roofed, narrow-walled tunnel, pitch black. Damp brickwork on each side scraped his shoulders as he plunged ahead.

It was a mad, reckless thing to do. At any instant a shot, a knife stab might greet him. But his hope of surprise, escape, lay in catching that fleeing member of Chang Ch'ien's household.

He crashed suddenly into a blank wall, reeled back bruised, dazed. To his left the running feet sounded plain. Val ignored his bruises and hurled himself after him once more. He wondered why the other did not shout for help, but as the interminable pursuit through the seemingly endless tunnel continued he saw why. No cry could be heard down here either.

The tunnel seemed to slope downward gently. They must be well out from beneath the big house now. And suddenly he heard the short, gasping breathing of his quarry just ahead. The next instant Val collided with him.

A sharp squeal of pain and fear echoed back through the tunnel as they both reeled back from the brick wall against which the other had been crouching. No shots, no stabs followed. The other tried to break away back through the tunnel again.

Val dropped the knife. He wanted a man who could answer questions. His hand found the other's throat as his shoulder struck the wall hard. With a mighty heave Val slammed him against the wall too.

He heard the dull impact of bone against brick as the head above his hands snapped against the wall. The wiry little Chinaman went limp, sagged down a dead weight.

A clip of matches was in his coat pocket. The yellow flare Val struck showed his victim in a huddled heap, still, motionless. He recovered the knife, pocketed it. A second match showed a strange sight. The tunnel ended abruptly at this point, but the brick end wall had opened out slightly at one side. A draught of cold fresh air was blowing through it.

Val pushed. The wall moved on out like a door. He stepped through cautiously, struck a third match. A few feet away the sheen of black automobile enamel gleamed back at him.

Swift examination with more matches showed him to be in the interior of an old carriage house, remodeled into a garage. The automobile was the black limousine—the one that followed Nancy Fraser earlier in the night. The tunnel connected this garage with the house.

Here was the means of escape and quick action. Alone he could do little to help Nancy Fraser and her companion. Word must be gotten to Harmsworth immediately, before he was tricked into the loss of the Harmite formula.

Val went back into the tunnel, dragged out the limp form, closed the section of the brick wall. The garage doors were unlocked. The ignition key was in the car lock. He opened the rear car door, shoved the unconscious figure in, and climbed inside to arrange it. In the middle of that operation Val suddenly went rigid.

The garage doors in front of the car had started to rumble back. The beam of an electric torch flashed inside.

VAL BARELY had time to close the car door quietly when shoes tramped in on the cement floor. A front door of the car was opened as Val ducked down behind the seat, drawing the keen steel blade from his pocket. He would have been a perfect target for a gun, had he charged into the glare of that electric torch.

The front seat creaked as a man slipped behind the wheel. The door slammed, the starter whirred, the motor caught. A moment later they were rolling out of the garage.

Val crouched, waiting. He wanted no trouble until they were well away from the house and Chang Ch'ien.

The car seemed to coast down a grade. They swung out of a driveway into a street where corner lights began to flash past. A full mile had fallen behind when Val cautiously raised up.

The driver was intent on the street ahead, oblivious of his presence.

A quick jerk slid the glass panel separating them. Before the driver was aware what was happening, Val's arm was about his neck, the knife at his throat. A startled cry—the car swerved as the driver froze.

"Keep driving!" Val rapped out.

The order was followed. A street light showed the driver to be an Oriental, one Val did not remember seeing before. Keeping the knife at the other's neck, Val leaned over, frisking him. He found a revolver in a coat pocket. Substituting it for the knife, he ordered the man to drive to Gregg's office.

When they stopped in front of the building the limp form at his feet was still unconscious. His fingers found a steady pulse, however. Val took the driver up with him.

Gregg was in his office. Hilaire Garre was seated against the wall. Nathaniel Harmsworth was pacing the floor restlessly when they walked in. All three stared. Gregg demanded gruffly: "Who have you got there?"

Val smiled thinly. "The man who will take us to Chang Ch'ien and the Black Doctor."

The simple statement was the sensation he had anticipated. Hilaire Garre came to his feet with a bound. Gregg shoved back his chair and stood up. And Harmsworth was the most affected.

"Do you mean that?" he cried feverishly. "Is there a chance of getting to my daughter?"

Harmsworth's face was drawn, haggard. He had aged noticeably since Val last saw him. Dark circles of nervous exhaustion were under his eyes, and the eyes themselves were feverish and determined.

"Yes," Val told him.

Harmsworth drew a deep breath of relief. "Thank God!" he said huskily. "I couldn't wait any longer. I drove down here with the formula. I have just told Mr. Gregg that I will give up anything to get Trudie back. They must want the formula, of course—and they can have it if there is no other way."

Gregg demanded gruffly: "Where have you been, Easton? I called your apartment and you weren't there. Where did you get this man?"

In brief words Val described his astounding experience.

"Garre and I thought something like that must have happened," Gregg nodded. "He came over again and insisted on staying until you turned up."

"Good," Val nodded curtly. "It's Garre's business as much as ours. I can't emphasize the danger too strongly. It's fantastic, impossible—but true. We've got to handle it ourselves, and quick. If the newspapers get ahold of this—well—"

"*Oui,*" Hilaire Garre nodded vigorously. "I agree. Name of a name—we must act at once!"

Gregg was grim, serious. He stood silent for a moment behind the big desk. "You're right," said Gregg slowly. "This must not get out. We have great responsibility. But can you find the way back there?"

"We were on Massachusetts Avenue when I got my first look. But this man will take us back. I think I'll search him."

Eyes on the floor, the slender saffron-skinned driver gave no resistance as Val did that quickly. Val grunted with satisfaction as he took an envelope from the inside coat pocket.

"The letter I wrote," he said. "He must have been starting up to Philadelphia with it."

Still the driver said nothing.

"We've got to hurry!" Val snapped. "There's just a chance my escape hasn't been discovered. In that case they'll still be there. If not, we may be too late. How much help can we get, Gregg?"

"In half an hour I can have several."

"Too late."

"Messieurs, I ask to assist in this," Hilaire Garre cried vehemently.

"Count me in too," Harmsworth snapped.

Gregg regarded the two men and shrugged. "A trifle unusual, gentlemen—but I am glad to have you."

CHAPTER TEN
STOLEN DEATH

IN THAT subworld loosely called Secret Service where spy and counter-spy must work in secrecy, the most ruthless live longest. Men learn early that theirs is a grim trade, without the usual rules. Judge, jury and executioner must often be their lot. Something of that hovered over the men who left Gregg's office.

The man in the back was still unconscious. He would have to wait. Val took the front seat beside the silent, saffron-skinned driver, his hands secured by small steel thumbcuffs now.

"I'll shift gears for you," Val said. He drew the revolver and shoved it against the man's side. "Now take us to Chang Ch'ien. Go wrong—and I'll empty this in you."

Any thoughts behind that yellow face were hidden. The slant eyes looked down at the gun for a moment—and then the foot pressed the starter and they were off.

Through deserted streets in the before-dawn hush they rolled to Massachusetts Avenue. And along it through one of the most wealthy and aristocratic sections of Washington.

The winding grade of Massachusetts Avenue hill finally appeared before them. Here the houses were scattered, set well back from the street in large tree-filled grounds. It was a small, sparsely inhabited island of loneliness in the midst of a great city.

And here, part way up the hill, the driver suddenly slowed and swung into a winding driveway, in which the boring headlights lighted great, wide branching trees. They made a turn, passed an old two-story brick building in which garage doors were open wide.

"This is the place," said Val.

Gregg uttered a soft oath. "What a nerve that Chink's got—setting up right under our noses!"

Abruptly they swept out of the trees. The headlights glanced over a huge red brick structure, old, stately. It must have dated from before slave days when nearby George-town was the real capitol of the country, and Washington City was a rude collection of buildings on the swamp land along the Potomac.

Not a light showed about the place as they stopped behind a smaller car standing under a porte-cochère at one end of the house.

Val reached over and snapped off the lights. "We'll go first," he husked over his shoulder.

Gripping the driver's arm, he slid past the wheel and followed around the front of the car to the door opposite them. There were the steps he remembered. But still not a light had appeared. The big house loomed quiet, still— ominously still.

"Get that door open!" Val whispered harshly to his pris-oner.

And as if his words had been overheard, the door opened, revealing a long, dimly lighted hall inside. A gong boomed somewhere beyond—and the familiar odor of musk and sandalwood and opium fumes met him as he pushed the driver in and stepped quickly after.

"*Hola!*" a startled voice beside the door greeted shrilly. A blue-garbed Celestial standing there took one look at the thumb-cuffed driver, at Val, and snatched for his coat pocket.

Val stepped in quickly and struck from the waist, driving hard to the jaw. The doorkeeper bounced back against the wall, swayed a moment and crumpled to the floor with a dull, vacant look on his face.

Val bent, grabbed at the pocket, finding a revolver there as he had expected. A rush of steps jerked his head up. The driver had fled along the hall, reckless at this chance of escape. His shout of alarm rang through the house.

Gregg and Hilaire Garre dashed in through the door. Gregg's gun was raised. Val knocked it up.

"Let him go!" he snapped. "He's helpless—and he's warned them anyway."

The driver dodged aside, midway down the passage.

HILAIRE GARRE was suddenly not the dapper little Frenchman. His face was an icy mask in which his eyes were two narrowed, alert points.

Harmsworth was flushed, excited. And the gun in his hand shook from emotion. "Quick—to those girls!" he begged thickly.

They had halted at the door only a moment. Val ran lightly ahead along the hall, both guns ready in his hands. He slid warily through the curtained archway where the driver had vanished, and found himself in the big gold-tapestried room where he had faced Chang Ch'ien.

Face down, under the flood of silver light still pouring from the ceiling, was the limp body of the driver. Protruding from his back was the haft of a long knife.

Gregg stopped short behind Val, exclaiming: "What the devil!"

A bell-like purring voice suddenly filled the room. "He should have died before leading you here, gentlemen."

It was Chang Ch'ien addressing them, slightly mocking again. And yet Chang Ch'ien himself was invisible. The voice seemed to come from overhead, from all sides where the folded golden tapestries hung limp.

Chang Ch'ien spoke again. "Tai Shan was released but a moment ago. A clever man, Valentine Easton. Zaken was right. You will have to die."

The light went out.

From the other side of the room the metallic clash of the gong reverberated loudly.

Val pumped three shots toward it instantly.

And with the smell of powder smoke strong in their faces and the crash of the shots ringing in their ears they heard a purring, mocking laugh.

"Now," said Chang Ch'ien, "I shall have to take forfeit of those two charming young ladies. They are so young to die...."

And as Chang Ch'ien's voice died away Val lost all sense of caution in the blinding anger that swept over him. Nathaniel Harmsworth's anguished cry, "Stop him before he can do that!" hardly registered. Val plunged through the blackness toward the spot where the gong had sounded, the spot where Chang Ch'ien had stepped before. And Carl Zaken had entered.

His shoulder struck the gong and its muted protest vibrated as he plunged past. His hand caught the golden tapestry and clawed it aside. He found the wall on the other side—and found a door a few inches over that opened to his touch. Val lunged through into darkness.

Perhaps it was the very violence of his rush that saved him. For close beside him, at his right, a gun blasted the peace of that pitch blackness, tore and spit fiery powder sparks into the back of his coat. He felt the drag of two bullets slashing through, felt the burn of the powder reach under to his skin—so close was death in that frantic split second of time.

Whirling as momentum carried him on, Val emptied both revolvers in one thundering fusillade.

Gregg's voice yelled from the other side of the doorway: "Easton—are you there?"

Crouching low against the wall, Val said nothing for an instant. And that instant something dropped heavily on the floor. A gasping groan came out of the blackness. Then the dull heavy thud of a body falling inertly.

"Easton!" Gregg called again.

"All right!" Val answered.

He fumbled for a match, lit it. The yellow flare shone on the limp form lying across the hall in which they were standing, face turned up, blood trickling from bullet wounds. He recognized the other of the two men who had led him down to that sub-cellar. The man twitched feebly, lay still. The match flickered out as Gregg pushed into the hall.

"What was it?" Gregg snapped.

"A reception committee with the compliments of Chang Ch'ien," Val said grimly. "Almost got me, too. He's done for, I guess. Can't attend to him now. Chang Ch'ien went this way, I think. Watch sharp. There may be some more of them planted along. Got a flash?"

"I forgot to bring one," Gregg confessed.

VAL WAS already pushing along the hall, listening, trying to read the riddle of the darkness before him. His hand reached into emptiness at his right. His foot struck a step there. Another match showed a narrow boxed stair-case going sharply up to a turn.

And while he hesitated, wondering which way to go, a woman's cry sounded faintly overhead.

"Val! Val!"

"Upstairs here!" Val shouted back to Gregg—and took the stairs two at a time, wary for a possible ambush at the top.

But there was no ambush. And near the end of an upstairs hall he located Nancy Fraser behind a locked door. A key was in the lock. A moment later Nancy was against him, demanding anxiously: "What was that shooting?"

"Tried to get one of us," Val said lightly. "It's all right."

"I knew you were here when I heard the shots," Nancy said unsteadily. "I—I was afraid you were too late. They tried to get in here."

Trudie Harmsworth spoke in the darkness. "It had me frightened green. I don't know what would have happened if Nancy hadn't taken her door key and blocked that other key in the lock so they couldn't turn it when they tried."

Gregg pounded heavily along the dark hall, asked hurriedly: "Are they all right?"

"Miss Fraser saved us," Trudie Harmsworth said sincerely. "She's a brick!"

"So I've heard before," Gregg said drily. "Easton, I wonder if they haven't gotten away. I haven't heard another sound. We'd better get these young women down and out while they're safe. Your father is down there, Miss Harmsworth."

"Dad!" Trudie Harmsworth squealed. "Where? I want to see him!"

Gregg led the way this time. And when they got down-stairs the voice of Hilaire Garre called them back into the golden-tapestried room. Garre was on his knees, a lighted match in his hand. Sitting up beside him Nathaniel Harmsworth was gasping and swearing under his breath.

"I heard a choked cry, messieurs, and when I turned back, Monsieur Harmsworth was not there," Garre explained. "*Sacré*—I stumbled over him on the floor and think I have found a dead man. But, no—he is breathing a little."

"Someone attacked me from behind," Harmsworth groaned. "Threw something around my neck and choked me. I—I guess I lost consciousness. They took everything out of my pockets."

"He had," Garre said briskly, "one formula in his pocket, gentlemen."

"Good God!" Val exploded. "You didn't bring that here with you, did you?"

"Yes," Harmsworth admitted. "And it was taken. I guess that's why I was attacked."

A sickening silence fell over the dark room as the match in Garre's hand died out.

"That's what Chang Ch'ien was egging us on for," Val said heavily. "He handled us like pawns on a chessboard—to get us away from Harmsworth. No wonder the house is empty. They've got what they wanted and flown the coop."

"Help me up," said Nathaniel Harmsworth—and when he was on his feet he cleared his throat without regard for the heavy silence around him.

Trudie Harmsworth said stoutly: "Never mind what they got, Dad. It's enough for me that they didn't get you."

"But that formula," Gregg said hoarsely. "We've got to get it back."

Nathaniel Harmsworth cleared his throat again. "Let them go with it," he said carelessly. "They got the formula that I brought. But I am not such a fool as the facts would indicate, gentlemen. I brought the formula, it is true—but I left out one element, and changed the chlorine radical in another compound. The man who puts that formula together will have a dangerous explosive on his hands— and will be lucky if he doesn't blow himself and laboratory into bits."

"Mon Dieu!" Hilaire Garre burst out in Gallic enthusiasm. "What a brain, messieurs! Let us hope this master of death, Chang Ch'ien, has stolen a little bit of death for himself. Is it not so?"

THE JADE JOSS

IT WAS ONLY A CHUNK OF GREEN
TOMB JADE, BUT CARL ZAKEN—
THE DREAD BLACK DOCTOR—WAS
EAGER TO COMMIT MURDER FOR
IT. AND VAL EASTON—ACE SECRET
SERVICE OP—WENT WILLINGLY
INTO THE GRISLY TORTURE
CHAMBERS OF CHINATOWN
TO STEAL IT BACK. FOR ON IT
DEPENDED THE SUCCESS OR
FAILURE OF THE DOCTOR'S
GHASTLY PLAN. ITS POSSESSION
COULD EITHER KINDLE OR
QUENCH A WORLD-WIDE HORROR
BLAZE.

CHAPTER ONE
THE WOMAN IN BLACK

THE DRONING din of predinner traffic was loud in Herald Square, ten stories below, when Val Easton straightened from his traveling bag and said: "That's that, Bradshaw. I'll reserve a berth on the night train before we dine."

His companion, tilted in a chair against the wall, ran a palm over a gray blaze in otherwise black hair, and grunted: "You chaps are always on the move. Might as well be traveling salesmen."

Bradshaw snorted as Easton turned to the telephone. He was faultlessly dressed, without an ounce of spare flesh on his angular frame. His trim mustache was as black as his hair. He looked like a clubman in the middle thirties, without a care in the world, But Bradshaw was forty-eight, a deputy police commissioner, up from the ranks, at home in all the shady corners of the underworld.

Val Easton was harmless looking, seldom hurried, amiable. His slender figure was not one to attract attention. Few people were aware that behind that amiable face was the full power of the American Intelligence Service, sometimes loosely called the Secret Service.

Having reserved a berth on the midnight train to Washington, Easton turned to Bradshaw. "First spare evening I've had to myself in weeks," he commented. "Dinner's on me, and a thousand thanks for the help you've given me."

Bradshaw raised a deprecating hand. "Not at all," he protested. "It's been a pleasure. Fact is, I'm damned envious of your work. I'm looking forward to future contacts with you."

Val Easton chuckled. "Never can tell what's around the corner," he said.

At that moment the phone rang.

"Pardon," Val murmured, and answered it.... "Yes, this is Easton," he said.... "Put him on."

HIS FACE settled into an expressionless mask as a gruff voice came over the wire. It was Gregg, talking from Washington. Gregg, that heavy-set, saturnine man who stood at the right elbow of the State Department, as unknown and overlooked by the public

Val leaped up on a chair, shouted,
"Keep away from that man!"

as the actions of that subtle force which he controlled. Gregg—the Chief.

Gregg's voice rasped out: "I was afraid I wouldn't catch you. Got something for you to do: Go to the home of Cartier Beurket on Fifth Avenue. They're having a reception tonight. Formal, I'd say. See Beurket himself. Show him your identification badge. Get from him a sealed envelope—and any personal comments he may make—and bring them here to me in Washington. Want it all the first thing in the morning. It's important. Got it?"

"Yes," said Val. "Who is he?"

"Cartier Beurket," said Gregg gruffly, "is an antiquarian, a collector. Specializes in Oriental art. He's just back from a six months' collecting trip in China. Been doing some special work for me. I want his report. Come straight to the office from the train."

Val hung up. He was smiling wryly as he turned to Bradshaw. "Sorry," he said. "The dinner's off. Got an evening's work before I make the train."

Bradshaw threw up his hands. "I was afraid of it. Any help I can give?"

"Guess not. Know anything about a Cartier Beurket, on upper Fifth Avenue?"

Bradshaw nodded immediately. "Who doesn't?" he said. "The Beurkets are an old New York family. Filthy with money. He's a bachelor. Used to be rated a great catch, if I remember correctly. Fooled the women. Only interested in his collection, I understand. He's on the board of the Metropolitan museum, and all that.

"I'm familiar with him because his place is one of the danger spots we keep an eye on. He has a collection worth several millions in a private museum built into his house. Beurket's gone half the time; and the place is an open invitation to all the big time crooks who hit town. He takes all the precautions, of course. Special wing built on the house—iron bars, steel shutters, latest in burglar-alarm systems. I've inspected the place."

"Seems to be safe enough," Val agreed.

"More or less," Bradshaw stated. "The house is wired also. Special guards are on duty day and night. It's harder to get into than the Sub-Treasury. But it's a bet that some day some smart crooks will crash through and make a clean-up. And then we'll have Beurket and the insurance people on our necks to settle the thing. The department's detailed a couple of plain-clothesmen for the evening. Well—"

Bradshaw shook hands and departed.

THE FALL evening was crisp, cool, bracing when Val came out on the street. He shook his head at the carriage starter's lifted hand, and walked over to Fifth Avenue, turned north with long strides. Always, when there was time he walked. His best thinking was done then; and there was much to think about.

Carl Zaken, the Black Doctor, was on his mind now. And Chang Ch'ien, that tall, golden-skinned Oriental. Through the shadowy paths of international espionage tales of Carl Zaken, the Black Doctor, had for years seeped like fantastic nightmares. Master spy, incredibly clever and ruthless, he had been always a menace to those governments he worked against. And Chang Ch'ien, who had come out of the underworld of France a myth of terror, had proved no less dangerous in company with the Black Doctor.

The Black Doctor and Chang Ch'ien were still at large. American Intelligence had no reason to believe that they were not still plotting. So from high quarters had come orders to hunt them down. And it was this hunt that had brought Val Easton to New York, following a slender thread of information which had petered out when fully investigated. In the morning he would be back in Washington, admitting defeat.

He was almost to Forty-sixth Street when the astonishing thing happened.

A taxicab was parked at the curb, motor idling softly. He was abreast of it, paying no heed, when a woman's arm thrust out, beckoning to him. He heard his name called in a clear, vibrant voice.

"Mr. Easton! Mr. Easton!"

Startled, Val stopped, turned. He saw the small black hat, the heavy black veil swathing her features; and the furred coat, collar turned up around her neck, mantling her figure effectively. Black gloves covered her hands. A woman all in black. And a woman of mystery.

Then her voice metamorphosed into quick, vibrant seriousness. "Mr. Easton—don't go to that house tonight! Go back to your hotel! Go to Washington as you intended!"

There was a haunting familiarity about her voice. Nothing that Val could put his finger on definitely; and yet it was there.

He said: "How do you know who I am, or where I am going? What makes you think I intend to start for Washington tonight? And—pardon me—but how the devil did you know I'd be along here at this time?"

Only one man in New York knew that he was going to Washington tonight. Only one man knew he was going to Cartier Beurket's home.

Only Bradshaw knew that.

But not even Bradshaw knew that Valentine Easton would be walking along here at this time of the evening!

Val himself had not known it twenty minutes before. He had passed through the hotel lobby and come out on the sidewalk, half minded to take a taxi. Not until the bracing night air was on his face had he decided to walk. And now this woman in black was here across his path with full knowledge of his plans!

She laughed again behind the veil, that haunting, vibrant laugh. "It doesn't matter, does it? I know many things about you, Valentine Easton. I know you are going into danger tonight if you go to this house. Turn back. Go to the train. Let someone else carry out this order for you."

Val moved a step nearer, stooped, peered intently at her. But the shadows were thick inside the cab. "You know too much," he said crisply. "You say too little. What house am I going to?"

That was merely to keep her talking while he racked his brains and listened avidly for some slight clue to her identity.

She gave him none. There was no laughter in her voice now. It was sharp, serious. "You know what house. You know I tell the truth. Turn back! One who wishes you well warns you."

THERE WAS a foreign inflection about her voice. It smacked of Russian, and that baffled him still more. He had met many women in many countries; some Russian women. But of all these he could think of none who might be in New York now; who might know his movements as this woman did; who might be waiting here at the curb, mysteriously uttering her tense warnings.

"I'm interested," Val told her. "What else have you to say?"

"I have said enough. Good-bye."

"Not 'good-bye,'" Val informed her curtly. "We'll go into this further." He reached for the door handle—and suddenly stopped, moved back a step. The small blunt snout of an automatic had slid over the windowsill.

"Don't do that!" she warned.

The motor of the cab speeded suddenly. It lurched out from the curb, swept down the outer traffic lane and left him standing there. The tail-light was dark over the license plate and the curb lights gave too little illumination for him to get the number. The cab swung right on Forty-fifth Street—vanished.

And Val Easton, standing there, swore under his breath. The next moment he was exploding: "Follow that cab that just turned on Forty-fifth!"

A second cab had swerved in to the curb, unnoticed, its driver's hand raised inquiringly. Val wrenched open the door, leaped inside, the machine started with a jerk.

"Ten dollars if you trail it without being discovered!" Val called.

The man threw up a hand in assent, and swung into Forty-fifth Street.

Only one cab was before them. The drawn rear curtain marked it as the machine they wanted. It whirled to the left under the elevated on Sixth Avenue.

Val's driver swung in under the El pillars too. The two machines zig-zagged across town, swung south on Third Avenue.

Through the gray-black shadows they sped downtown. The cross streets fell back in swift succession. Twenty-third—Fourteenth—Cooper Square—and then into the Bowery. Other machines shifted in and out ahead of them as they rolled along the Bowery. And ahead of them, beyond Bayard Street, the cab they followed turned sharply to the right and vanished.

Val knew this district. That cab had turned into Pell Street, into the compact, warrenlike area of Chinatown, lying just off the Bowery.

Val suddenly exclaimed angrily: "What are you doing? Follow that cab!"

The driver had whirled to the right on Bayard in seeming disregard of the machine they followed. He threw over his shoulder now: "Got a hunch, mister. It woulda been too raw, tearin' into Chinatown after them. If they ain't wise yet we're tailin' they'd be plenty quick after we did that."

"Something in that," Val admitted.

The driver shot to the second block with his accelerator down on the floor boards, and with a reckless swerve headed south again, turned and doubled into Pell, slowing to an idling pace. And they rolled sedately into the heart of Chinatown.

To right and left the balconied fronts of the grimy old buildings rose five and six stories. Lighted windows gleamed. Leisurely figures padded along the sidewalk. An elevated train thundered past on the Bowery straight ahead of them. They were approaching the head of Doyers Street.

"Looks like they've turned into Doyers!" he threw over his shoulder; but the next moment broke out. "That's the hack over there, ain't it?"

They rolled past a taxi pulling out from the opposite curb. Its driver glanced at them without interest. Across the sidewalk a woman was just entering a dimly lit door. A slender woman swathed in a fur coat, with a small, perky black hat visible above the upturned collar. The door closed behind her.

A sign on the window at the left of the door said—*Li Fui Shan, Importer.*

"How about it?" the driver asked over his shoulder.

Val relaxed in the seat and reached for a cigarette. "You win the ten," he declared. "Drive me back uptown."

CHAPTER TWO
THE FACE AT
THE WINDOW

THE HOME of Cartier Beurket was on Fifth Avenue opposite the southeast end of the Park. It was of substantial brick, three stories high, imposing in its disregard of the modern world which had grown up about it.

A new wing, of brick also, had been built on one side, two stories high. The windows of the new wing were set high above the street level, barred on the outside, curtained inside.

It was well after nine o'clock when Val Easton settled with his driver, and sauntered across the sidewalk. Two machines had just pulled away as they drove up.

A man loitered beside the steps, hands in his topcoat pockets. His glance slid over Val unobtrusively, went on to a machine at the curb. Val grinned to himself as he crossed the small portico to metal-grilled gates standing open. That plainclothesman had paid little attention to this arriving guest.

The door swung open and Val entered a spacious hall, octagonal in shape, floored in ebony parquet. At the back a sweeping staircase curved up to the second floor. In the next room a string orchestra was playing. He glimpsed couples dancing. Guests in evening clothes were eddying through the hall. Through an undertone of laughter, animated conversation, a black-clad manservant said blandly: "Your name, sir?"

He was all of six feet tall, this manservant. His shoulders were broad, his face lean, hard. His firm, bald politeness held no trace of servility, and his eyes were direct as he waited.

A small table beside the man held a sheet of typed names.

Beurket, Val thought fleetingly, was amply protected here. This man was a guard, probably a detective, sifting the guests carefully.

"I'm not on your list," Val told him. "I'd like a word with Mr. Beurket, please. I'm Valentine Easton."

A tall man, with a snowy mop of white hair, talking with some guests a few feet away, turned. A murmured word to the others and he stepped across.

"I am Cartier Beurket," he said.

For an instant Val's palm held a small gold badge so that only Beurket's eyes could see it. The other nodded. "I've been expecting you, Mr. Easton. The men's cloak room is at the front of the hall upstairs. I will join you there in a few moments."

Val left his topcoat and hat in the upstairs room, lighted a cigarette and strolled out. Cartier Beurket met him at the head of the stairs. Beurket was half a head taller, thirty or forty pounds heavier. His face was tanned mahogany color, bespeaking long periods spent outdoors in all kinds of weather. He had a hard, fit look, with his aquiline nose, high forehead and steady blue eyes.

Unspoken liking leaped between the two, hinted at only by mutual smiles.

Val said: "I'm a bit foggy about all this. I was ready to push off to Washington tonight when Gregg called me."

Beurket nodded. "I was to go down there myself, but I find I can't make it for a few days. Gregg doesn't care to wait. The papers I am sending to Gregg aren't quite ready. I'll slip up to my study shortly and finish them. Can you spare an hour or so?"

"With pleasure," Val assured him. "Just so I make the night train."

"No trouble about that," Beurket replied. "While you're waiting, join the guests. I am going to open the gallery shortly. You may find it interesting."

AS THEY turned to the stairs Val said: "Have you any reason to anticipate trouble tonight, Mr. Beurket? I was warned not to come here."

Beurket glanced at him from eyes suddenly frosty, alert. "Who warned you?" he asked.

"I don't know. A veiled woman. I can't place her. I understand you're just back from the Orient. You've evidently been doing some intelligence work for the department. Did you bring back any enmities that might come to a head here tonight?"

"No," Beurket said positively. "I'm certain of that. In China I kept my eyes open for certain things Gregg was interested in. But no one over there had any reason to suspect such was the case. You weren't told what trouble to expect?"

Val shrugged. "Sorry—no. But the circumstances were so unusual I have no reason to believe the warning was not given in good faith."

They were halfway down the staircase now. Beurket's laugh was that of a man without nerves.

"I doubt if there's any cause for alarm, Mr. Easton. The place is well guarded. This is not an elaborate evening. There are no jewels or valuables among the guests worth stealing, I'm certain. My collection has never been bothered. The most valuable pieces are kept in a special vault to which my sister and I alone have the combination. It would take at least twenty-four hours for the best equipped cracksman to penetrate it. It is impossible to short circuit the alarm system or circumvent it."

Beurket chuckled. "Enjoy yourself while you're waiting. Ah, here's my sister, Adelaide. May I present Mr. Easton, who is going to save me a trip to Washington, Adelaide?"

Swift comprehension flickered in Adelaide Beurket's eyes. She was almost as tanned as her much older brother. Not more than twenty-four or -five, this girl. She was tall, slender in a sheathlike evening gown of wine-colored velvet. Brown tints made her eyes deep and shadowy. Her hair was waved close along her head and caught low in a knot at the base of her neck. A wide, generous mouth, a direct look, and a healthy, alert manner made her as likeable as Cartier Beurket himself.

For all of ten minutes he was with her, strolling about, meeting the guests, chatting briefly. Adelaide Beurket apparently knew who he was, why he was there. She mentioned that she had been to China with her brother, acting as secretary.

Val told her of the warning, watched her reaction. Adelaide Beurket quirked her lips, frowned, shook her head. "It's Greek to me," she stated. "But if Cart says there's no reason to worry, I suppose there isn't. We're rather well guarded here."

She left him presently. Val moved about alone, thinking. He could not rid his mind of that black-veiled woman who had vanished into the shadowy shop of Li Fui Shan. The name of Li Fui Shan was not familiar. But it sharpened memories, released a flood of conjectures. A vague, disquieting sense of impending disaster was taking possession of him.

CARTIER BEURKET had vanished, in his study, probably, finishing his report to Gregg. Now and then Val caught a glimpse of Adelaide Beurket playing the perfect hostess, smiling, animated. The guests had about all arrived. Shortly they would be admitted to the *piece de resistance* of the evening—Cartier Beurket's latest acquisitions.

Then with no more warning than that, Val's premonitions were borne out.

Val was standing at the foot of the staircase in the big octagonal hall when the girl descended rapidly and stopped before him. He had met her—a Miss Elston. She had a dry, dusty, bookish look about her, despite the soft white evening gown she wore. Shell-rimmed glasses seemed to belong on the face.

"Where," she gasped, "is Mr. Beurket?"

Her face was chalk-white. Her eyes wide and frightened. Her fingers were crumpling and uncrumpling a handkerchief, and she gave every indication of an unnerved, terrified woman.

"I can't say exactly," Val told her. "I think he's busy. Is something wrong?"

"I saw a face!" she told him breathlessly. "It was near the window when it appeared. Horrible, ghastly! It looked in, saw me and vanished!"

Val put a reassuring hand on her cold fingers. "What did it look like?"

Miss Elston gulped. "I can't tell you," she replied uncertainly. "It—it was ghastly! He wore black, I saw that. A hat was pulled low over his face. The face was grinning as it looked in. I could see teeth in the horrible mouth. And the eyes seemed to glitter. When they saw me the face was gone instantly."

Val said to Miss Elston calmly: "What room were you in?"

"The back bedroom on the right side of the hall," she babbled. "I stepped in there to see how it was furnished. The light was on when I entered."

"Quite so," Val said calmly. "I'll attend to this, Miss Elston. I suggest you mingle with the guests and forget it."

She shuddered, forced a smile tinged with relief. "I will," she agreed.

"And don't say anything about it," Val cautioned.

"No," she promised, "not a word."

ADELAIDE BEURKET had gone into the next room where they were dancing. Val found her in there, at the back, talking to an elderly man with a Vandyke and glistening prince nez. She looked up as Val approached, caught his eye, came toward him with a questioning smile.

"Where is your brother?" asked Val.

"In his study. Why?"

"Miss Elston saw a face at one of the back bedroom windows. The room at the right of the hall, I believe."

She became grave instantly. "Impossible! Unless some-one had a ladder—"

"Perhaps someone has."

She shook her head. "No—I can't see how. The outside of the house is guarded. It always is at night."

"Queer," Val admitted. "But she seems positive that she saw something outside the window. I say—would you mind showing me the back of the house before you disturb your brother?"

She took him through French doors at the rear of the room, through a big dining room where a white-aproned maid was busy at a sideboard; and on back to a butler's pantry, and a spotless green-and-white kitchen where other servants were working. She closed the back door behind them.

It took some moments for their eyes to get accustomed to the darkness. She said under her breath: "One of the watchmen should be back here somewhere."

A tiny formal garden lay behind the house, L-shaped. The newer wing built to hold Cartier Beurket's collection did not extend back as far as the house itself. On the right an apartment house towered high; on the left were the higher walls of another great building. Inexorably the city had closed in, until now this old mansion with its tiny walled back yard was an oasis in a wilderness of stone, brick, steel. The traffic out on Fifth Avenue sounded muted, far away.

"I'll look them up while you go back in," Val suggested. "It's a bit cold out here, and you're not wearing a wrap."

"No. I'd better go too," she decided. "The men won't know you."

So they went together along a flagstone walk; and as they went Val looked up at the back of the house, rising three stories above them. There was no back porch. Just the house wall, three sheer stories. Windows on the second floor glowed with light. Those on the third floor were dark. Along the whole back of the house was no spot where a man might peer into one of the windows.

They turned the house corner along a fringe of low-trimmed bushes in the shadowy ell behind the annex. Adelaide Beurket walked slightly ahead, confident, unhurried.

But suddenly she wavered, lurched forward. A sharp little cry burst from her.

Val jumped forward, exclaiming: "What is it?"

"Look out! Don't step on it!"

But her warning was too late.

CHAPTER THREE
THE CRIMSON LOTUS

VAL'S FOOT struck something soft, yielding. He recoiled from the feel of it, caught in his pocket for matches.

A man was lying there on the flagstones. Lying face down, arms stretched out limply above his head.

Adelaide Beurket uttered a low exclamation of dismay. "It's one of the guards!" she cried under her breath.

Val held the flaring matches close as he bent, and turned the figure over. It came limply, slack dead weight. Curly black hair lay damp and close to a bare head. A pallid face turned up to them, ghastly in the matchlight. The open eyes gleamed white in a fixed stare.

"He's dead," Val said, straightening.

Val bent again, looked; frowned. "He seems unmarked. It's queer... wait."

As the matches died out Val hastily lighted others. He held them close to the coat front, and the yellow glow limned a damp, darker stain against the dark fabric of the coat. In that stain a half inch slit through the woolen threads was barely visible.

"Better not look," Val urged quietly.

He lifted the coat collar and looked beneath. The tiny slit was over the heart. A crimson stain, splotched the shirt. And the shirt was slit too, where a thin, keen blade had driven through to the flesh beneath.

"He was stabbed!" Val told her. "We want the police. Take me in to your brother. Can we go around by the front and notify the detective on duty there?"

She did not question his decision. "This walk leads to the front. But—but there should be another man on duty back here."

"I'll have the man out front look for him. Don't want to waste any time."

They were already skirting the side of the annex. As they went Val noticed it had no windows in the back or on the side. They walked on cement beside it, and a high brick wall rose at their right. Beyond the wall towered the big apartment house.

They came out through a stout iron gate into the semi-glow of Fifth Avenue, where pedestrians trod the side-walks, and automobiles and lumbering busses passed.

Automobiles were parked along the curb; chauffeurs idling in some of them. And near his post at the foot of the house steps the detective still loitered unobtrusively.

"There's a dead man at the back of the house," said Val. "One of the guards. May be another back there also. A guest claims she saw a face outside one of the second-story windows."

The transformation in the other was amazing. His leth-argy left him like a discarded coat. "My partner went back there a few minutes ago!" he jerked out. "I've been waiting for him. Lord! I'd better telephone the precinct station."

"I'll do that," Val said. "You search the back yard and look for that man who was outside that window."

He spoke more crisply than he should. He knew it at the quick stiffening of the other; but there was no time to explain. He turned to the steps before the detective had time to reply.

THE BIG octagonal hall inside was strangely deserted. The orchestra was playing softly, but the guests were no longer dancing. A faint hum of voices over the music in the next room marked where they were.

Adelaide Beurket said to the guard at the door, "Has Mr. Beurket taken them into the wing?"

The guard looked down at her alertly. Despite her remarkable control one could see that she was under a strain.

Val spoke: "Where's Mr. Beurket?"

A shrug answered him. "I can't say, sir. I have not left the door here. I heard Jennings, the butler, announcing that Mr. Beurket wished everyone to come into the gallery."

Adelaide Beurket said quickly: "We'll find him in there."

"Watch this front door carefully," Val instructed the guard. "Let no one in or out until you are sure who they are. A man has been killed at the back of the house."

He left the doorman gaping after him, and followed Adelaide Beurket inside. A number of the guests were bunched at one side of the room.

On the wall there, a long, silver-embroidered tapestry curtain had been drawn aside, revealing a low doorway. By standing on tiptoe when he reached the edge of the jostling group Val was able to see the massive steel edging of the door Bradshaw had mentioned.

It was open now, and through the entrance the guests were filing slowly. Soft, shaded light was visible in the annex which housed Cartier Beurket's treasures.

Short of shoving rudely there was no way to get through the jam in the vault doorway. Adelaide Beurket raised her voice. "If Mr. Beurket is in the gallery, will someone please ask him to step out here?" She took Val's arm and drew him back where her words could not be overheard. "I don't believe Cart is in there!" she exclaimed under her breath. "If he had been down here he certainly would not have asked the butler to invite them into the gallery. Cart would have done it himself."

"Probably busy in his study," Val suggested. "He promised to finish the report I came for as soon as possible."

She caught his arm, said with an apprehensive catch in her voice: "I—I'm afraid. It isn't like Cart to do a thing like this. Will you come up to the study with me?"

"Of course."

SHE LED him to the front hall where the black-clad door man was standing flat-footed at his post, shoulders hunched and one big fist clenched as if expecting trouble momentarily. He spoke to them with suppressed excitement. "D'you need any help, Miss Beurket?"

"None, thank you, Wilkins," she refused.

She tapped swiftly up the stairs ahead of Val. She hurried to the front of the hall, opened a door. The room was pitch black. Val was at her shoulder when she clicked the light switch.

For the space of half a dozen heart beats she stood there staring, while Val moved in beside her. On all four sides shelves of books reached clear to the ceiling. In the opposite wall a fireplace was topped by a carved mantel on which sat three slender, graceful Chinese vases. To the left of the fireplace, before the drawn drapes of a window, was a small, flat-topped desk and a chair. Before the fireplace, was a massive, leather-covered easy chair; and on the other side of the chair was a low mahogany table, stacked with books, periodicals, smoking jar, pipes and an ash tray. Those were the physical details of Cartier Beurket's study—but Cartier Beurket himself was not there.

Then Val saw what she saw; was already starting across the room when she exclaimed: "Those papers on the floor! Cart never left them like that!"

The desk top had been swept clean of all papers. They littered the floor around the chair. Envelopes, typewritten sheets, bills, documents, scattered in confusion.

Adelaide Beurket stopped at the corner of the desk. "These were all in order on the desk two hours ago!" she burst out. "I saw them! Cart's mail had accumulated. He hadn't had time to go through it yet. And now—and now, look at that!" She pointed.

The desk drawers had been opened and closed carelessly. Val looked in one and found it looted. The aroma of tobacco smoke was still strong on the air. A pipe lay on the green desk blotter with a scattering of ashes at the mouth of the bowl, as if the pipe had been dropped hastily, Val bent, blew the ashes and uncovered two charred spots on the blotter, touched the pipe bowl and found it still warm. He scowled at the jumbled mass of papers on the floor as he lifted the telephone receiver off the cradle and dialed police headquarters.

A few crisp words to headquarters sketched what had happened, and Val turned away from the telephone.

"Your brother was here a few minutes ago," he said. He didn't make this mess, of course. He probably went down to the gallery after all, and someone went through his desk after he left. You go down," Val urged, "and look for him in the gallery. I'll poke around up here before the police come."

"No!" she refused flatly. "I don't think he's down there. I'll stay up here."

Silently Val turned and scanned the room.

TWO WINDOWS were set in the bookcase at their right. They looked down on Fifth Avenue, he saw, when he pulled the drapes. Both windows were locked on the inside. No hiding place in here. Val's eyes dropped to the great blue-and-white rug covering the floor. It was a beautiful lotus-flower design.

Val lifted his head, nodded at a single door set in the wall opposite. "I'll have a look in there," he said casually. "Be out in a minute."

He walked to the door without looking at the rug again. He did not want her to see what he had seen. It was plain enough, and yet the design of the rug masked it from the casual glance. Two tiny dark stains by one of the lotus flowers. Two little stains, red against the white, where there was no red in the design.

There was another drop, and another, and another, widely spaced across the soft background of the rug, drawing a gruesome trail to that single door set in the bookshelves. Adelaide Beurket moved toward the door as Val did. She obviously intended to enter the room also. Val did not try to stop her. She sensed something was wrong; and to tell her might anticipate more than the truth.

The door opened to his touch. The switch clicked. The room was flooded with light; a bedroom masculine, severer with dark, hand rubbed furniture, a few Chinese prints on the walls.

"He's not in there," she said, and there was sudden relief in her voice.

A gruesome trail was on this side of the door also. One drop—another drop—and still another, leading inexorably to a second door across the room.

Val said: "What door is that?"

"The closet."

"I think," said Val, "you'd better go back."

"Why? Why do you think so?"

Their mutual restraint made the growing tension more electric. Val drew and expelled a regretful breath. "I'll tell you in a moment," he replied—and stepped to that closet door, whipping out his handkerchief as he went. He laid the white linen square over the knob and opened the door. At his shoulder Adelaide Beurket whimpered suddenly.

"It's Cart! Oh dear Lord! He too!"

IT WAS there almost as Val had expected to find it. A huddled form on the floor of the closet. A motionless form as lax and still as that lifeless body in the night behind the house. The shining patent-leather shoes, the formal evening clothes, and, dimly, the shock of white hair back in the closet marked Cartier Beurket at first glance.

He used scanty ceremony in dragging Cartier Beurket out of that cramped hideaway into which he had been thrust. Val was red-faced, panting as he lay Beurket face up on the bed and examined him swiftly.

Adelaide Beurket cried fiercely: "He's been murdered!"

"No," Val objected. "No, I don't think so." For when his fingers settled on Beurket's wrist they detected the faintest beat of a pulse.

Val rapped: "Get an ambulance at once!"

She fairly flew into the next room. As he bent over Beurket again, he heard her sharp, imperative tones at the telephone.

Beurket's shirt front and waistcoat were bloody. The same tiny, familiar slit was visible in the cloth. Beurket too had been stabbed over the heart with a long, slender blade. But this stroke had not gone true.

Nothing could be done now. Skilled medical attention was needed. Val went into the next room.

"Is there a gun up here?" he asked Adelaide Beurket.

"No… what are you going to do?"

He was already leaving the room, grim-faced, quick-moving. "Keep an eye on him," Val directed from the door. "Better lock yourself in."

He ran to the stairs. Short minutes had elapsed since they had hurried up with foreboding; now, as he ran down two steps at a time, more foreboding gripped Val. He barked to the big guard at the door: "Has anyone come down since we went up?"

"No. What's the matter?"

"Plenty. Beurket has been stabbed. Police and ambulance are on their way. Collar anyone who comes down."

Wilkins' hard face set. He dropped his perfect grammar. "Won't do me a hell of a lot of good to watch these steps. There's a back flight too."

"Damn!" Val exploded. "I didn't know about them. Try to watch both stairs."

CHAPTER FOUR
THE BLACK DOCTOR

VAL WENT swiftly across the polished floor to the vaultlike door of the treasure gallery. The orchestra was still playing softly behind the palms. Val smiled mirthlessly, stepped into the humming life that filled the gallery.

Two stories high the vaulted roof swept overhead. Great bronze chandeliers hung from the ceiling, and through intricate frill work backed by colored glass the light dropped in a soft, even glow.

Cartier Beurket's wealth had drained every corner of the Orient. Marvelous old tapestries hid the entire expanse of wall space. Great glass cases held the beauty of long dead dynasties. There was pottery and porcelain, enamel ware and glass, bronze, lacquer ware, and marvelous carvings in wood and ivory and jade. There were textiles of beautiful silks and embroideries.

Val pushed in among the well-dressed guests, grouped about half a dozen big glass cases in a single row.

He glimpsed the contents of one case. Jade. Dozens of pieces, intricately carved, superbly colored. Mutton-fat jade, milky and opaque; and light-green jade, and lavender jade; bright apple-green jade and white jade, spotted with the same green. Bowls, vases, bells, amulets, necklaces....

Moving through the crowd Val looked to right and left sharply. He saw a tall, portly butler standing apart, and went to the man. "Are you Jennings?"

"I am, sir?"

"Did you let these people in here?"

"I did, at Mr. Beurket's request, sir," the butler answered with growing frostiness.

"You saw him in his study?"

The butler shook his head. "Mr. Beurket sent word by one of the maids. He was busy and requested me to open the gallery door and admit the guests."

"I see," said Val—and suddenly whirled around as a woman cried out: "What is this man doing?"

Her voice had come from the end of the row of cases. At that spot the people suddenly began to mill in confusion, jostling together. Some were trying to get away from the case, some pressing in toward it.

Standing on tiptoe, Val could see over the heads to where that cry had been uttered. He saw a figure straighten beside the end case, a tall figure dressed in formal black evening clothes. The man stepped from the case, snarling.

For an instant, over the milling heads, he and Val looked at each other. And for the first time that night Valentine Easton felt his blood run cold. In all the world only one man could be that tall, stooped figure with the pale, bony, cadaverous face and blazing eyes. Only one man could have penetrated among two score carefully sifted people within this guarded domain of Cartier Beurket. There had been some attempt at disguise, a little padding of the cheeks from inside, a few lines carefully changed on the face by clever shading; but Val would have known that face anywhere.

It was Carl Zaken, the Black Doctor!

VAL EASTON was perhaps the only man in that softly lighted gallery who realized the terror among them. Master spy, incredibly clever, cold blooded and ruthless, the Black Doctor killed without the slightest hesitation. Clear now was that dead body of the guard; the savage knife thrust dealt Cartier Beurket. How Carl Zaken had entered, what his purpose was did not matter. It was enough that he was here.

Val was unarmed. He reached for an ebony pedestal on which sat the small bronze figure of some Chinese god. He caught it up, leaped from his perch and started for the crowd of milling guests. The heavy bronze weight was comforting.

He caught a glimpse of the Black Doctor still backing away; grinning now that pale, ghastly grin that could be so terrifying, serving as it did as a window for the soul beneath. Zaken carried something in one hand and with the other was reaching inside his coat.

"Get back from that man!" Val cried out. "He's dangerous!"

But in the confusion ahead of him his words were lost. He passed the end case where the Black Doctor had been standing. A small powerful instrument had ripped the lock and hasp clear out of the wood. On a bed of soft black velvet in the case one single object had been displayed. It was gone now. The confusion was increasing.

"Let me through!" Val shouted, as he pulled and shoved.

And suddenly without warning the lights went out.

An instant later in the pitch blackness a woman cried out, choking. Men strangled, gasped. Val felt a sudden smarting in his eyes and nostrils.

Tear gas had been loosed. Already he could feel the burning sensation in his eyes, the sudden flood of tears; and he started to gasp and strangle.

Val won past the last staggering figure, careened off a case and went forward three paces before he opened his eyes. The big gallery was still in tomblike blackness.

Wild confusion lay behind him as he plunged forward. As he had guessed, there was no gas here back of where the Black Doctor had been standing. The weapon, a small fountain-pen gas gun, had shot the deadly fumes into the crowd of guests; and for some moments it would not drift back of its point of origin.

Zaken apparently had vanished.

Val lost his way. It was some time before he located the door and passed through, leaving behind mad confusion in which women's screams, men's oaths were lost in general strangling helplessness.

Midway of the polished floor he met another figure coming toward him. A brusk voice barked: "Who's it?" A big hand clapped on his shoulder.

"That you, Wilkins?"

"Yeah. Oh—Mr. Easton!"

"Hell's busted loose! Beurket's collection has been raided. Anyone gone out the front door?"

"Nope. But somebody just lammed upstairs in a hell of a hurry. Didn't stop when I asked who it was."

"Let's have your gun, Wilkins!… Don't argue! I need it! That was the crook going upstairs! He's a killer!"

"Here you are then." Wilkins thrust his automatic into Val's hand.

WILKINS WAS swearing with amazement as Val made for the stairs. He was halfway up when he heard a shrieking siren. The police, long overdue, or the ambulance had arrived.

Panting, Val stopped at the head of the stairs and listened. In the dark close by Adelaide Beurket burst out: "Who is it? What is wrong downstairs?"

"Easton. Trouble in the gallery. A thief used tear gas. Did you hear anyone come up these steps?"

"A few moments ago someone ran up, made no answer when I called, and went on to the third floor."

"What's up there?"

"Bedrooms, bath, guest rooms. The servants who live in have their rooms up there too."

A fist hammered loudly on the front door.

"Better go down and take charge!" Val urged. "If that's the police, tell 'em to surround the house. Have the master light switch investigated. The current must have been cut off there."

The third floor stairs were close. Val took them more slowly, warily. He still had the heavy bronze statue in his left hand, Wilkins' automatic ready in his right.

Zaken must be on that third floor. And it was dark too—still, deserted. The quiet up here was ominous. Val slipped toward the back of the hall, guiding himself by an elbow brushing the wall.

He moved deliberately toward the back room on the right side. The dry, bookish Miss Elston had seen the face just below it. Her description now was understandable and like a guiding signpost.

She had seen the Black Doctor there on the sheer outside wall. How he had gotten there was still a mystery. But Carl Zaken must be leaving by the way he had entered.

The bedroom door was closed, but not locked. It opened to Val's touch. Fresh air blew against his face. Gun ready, he edged into the room.

Something sinuous and snakelike jerked across the window as he looked out.

Val put the bronze statue on the floor and grabbed out the window. His hand closed on a ladder made from thin, strong silk cord and light bamboo cross pieces, not more than six inches wide; a ladder that could be rolled up into a small bundle, carried easily, and yet by which a man could descend and mount a sheer wall like this with no trouble.

He looked up. The ladder was still swaying, jerking. He was in time to see a dark figure clambering over the edge of the roof. Leaning out, Val shot at it—once—twice....

Thundering reverberations crashed on the night and echoed back from the high apartment walls nearby.

He could not tell whether he had hit. The figure disappeared. A moment later the silk and bamboo ladder was jerked up. Val caught it, held on. The drag above ceased instantly. A moment later the ladder fell down about his hands.

Val yanked it in, left it lying across the window sill. From the edge of the roof above a voice spoke.

"That will be you, Valentine Easton."

Without answering, Val shouted from the window: "Anyone in the yard?"

He was not answered.

On the roof Carl Zaken laughed at him. "Good night, Easton. Next time I'll deal with you more thoroughly!"

"You're cornered up there," Val called. "The police are here. The house is surrounded. I'll deal with you myself in a few minutes."

"An incurable optimist," Carl Zaken mocked him. "I was expecting you, Easton. I'm sorry you didn't get in my way. Give my regards to Gregg, in Washington." And the Black Doctor was gone.

Val hauled the ingenious ladder into the room, slammed the window down, locked it, and hurried downstairs.

There was no attic to the house. A man could not leave the roof without a ladder. Zaken's ladder was locked inside. Those were the facts, but Val was not sure of them. That cunning mind on the roof would not walk into a trap.

CANDLES HAD been lighted on the first floor. The suffering guests had fled from the gallery, were overflowing outside. Val saw them milling on the sidewalk, wiping their eyes, choking.

An ambulance stood at the curb. A police patrol car was parked behind it. Patrolmen were pushing among the guests inside the front door. A white-coated interne, flashlight in one hand and black bag in the other, hurried to the stairs with Adelaide Beurket.

Val said to a uniformed officer: "Watch the outside of the house. The killer's up on the roof! He won't be down this way!"

The stalwart patrolman, ignoring a weeping woman who caught at his arm, said: "If he's on the roof, we'll go up after him, mister."

"You can't. He went up on a rope ladder and then cut it at the top and threw it down."

"Ain't that nice? Then he's up there until we grab him."

"I doubt it," said Val through his teeth. "He had to get up there some way before he could fasten a rope ladder, didn't he? He can come down the same way." Val left the puzzled cop wrestling with that idea and shoved outside.

An arm's length from the open gate at the corner of the annex, he found the detective who had been standing guard at the front steps.

"Why the devil aren't you in the rear?" Val snapped at him. Again, without thinking, he used the wrong tone. The man took quick offense.

"What business is it of yours?" he retorted illnaturedly. "I've been back there! My partner's dead and another one has the back of his head caved in. No one else in the yard. No way to get out of it over that high wall. I'm waiting to collar anyone who tries to come out this way."

Val pocketed the automatic which he had carried in his hand from the third floor. "All right," he said. "Come on back with me."

"Nix!" the detective refused sourly. "I'm watching this gate until things clear up some."

Val went alone. The back yard was as he had left it, quiet, still, isolated from the teeming city. The dead body still lay on the flagstone walk. The brick wall surrounding the yard was all of fifteen feet high. A quick circuit of it showed no way a man could have climbed it. The house remained dark. But the back door was open; he heard low excited voices there; and then the harsher tones of authority. "This the back yard? Anybody come in this way?"

Val went toward the rear steps, made his presence known, said to the patrolman who emerged from the house: "Watch the roof."

The patrolman moved out into the yard, looked up, grunted: "If there's a man up there he's still there. No way he can get down."

"Looks that way," Val agreed. "If he does try it, shoot first and talk later. He'll do the same." Leaving the officer there, Val went out front.

CHAPTER FIVE
THE MASK OF KUAN TI

THE SIDEWALK was jammed with guests and a curious crowd. More police arrived. No man could leave that roof without discovery.

The ambulance drove off with a warning twirl of the siren. A second siren swept along Fifth Avenue and swerved in to the curb. It was a hook and ladder truck from the fire department. An extension ladder was placed against the front of the annex. A detective and two patrolmen went up the ladder with guns ready in their hands. Flashlight beams glinted, wavered on the annex roof. A fireman took a scaling ladder up. They were on the house roof a few minutes later. Val pushed through the crowd on the sidewalk to the front steps. He was starting into the house when a hand caught his arm.

It was Bradshaw, deputy police commissioner.

Val said, "Come inside. I want to talk to you." And there, Val hastily outlined what had happened.

Candles were still burning in the big octagonal hall. Bradshaw studied Val shrewdly in their wan, flickering light. "You know who the thief was?"

"Yes. Carl Zaken, the man I've been after for the past week."

"Hell!" Bradshaw exclaimed, startled. "He's not a man to make a play like this."

Bradshaw fingered his trim black mustache, frowning. "How the hell did he get up the roof if all he had was a rope ladder?"

"You tell me," Val suggested.

Bradshaw snorted. "We'll sweat it out of him when they get him."

"I doubt," said Val slowly, "if they get him. I've got a hunch he's not up there on the roof now."

The lights flashed on suddenly. A helmeted and rain-coated fireman carrying an electric lantern tramped out of the rear regions of the house. He recognized Bradshaw, lifted the light in greeting and said: "Somebody snatched a fuse out of the fuse box down in the cellar."

Val grinned wryly at Bradshaw. "A little more mystery for you."

A plainsclothesman bustled in, saw Bradshaw, came to him. "No one up on the roof," he stated.

"What!" Bradshaw exploded.

"Nope. The boys have been all over it with their lights. It's clean."

"Search the house!" Bradshaw snapped. "Every part of it!"

SO FAST had the business moved that the confusion had not quieted yet. The guests were still milling around in bewilderment. Through them came Adelaide Beurket. She was wiping her eyes as Val went to meet her, followed by Bradshaw.

"How is your brother?" said Val.

"The doctor says he will probably be all right. The wound isn't as bad as it looked at first sight. Cart evidently fell against something and was knocked unconscious. I thought I had better stay here."

"What did you find in the gallery?"

She made a wry face; she was hard hit, but trying not to show it. "He got one of the most valuable things we have," she said simply.

"What?"

"Cart managed, by a marvelous piece of luck and the expenditure of a staggering sum, to bring out of China this time a thing so valuable, so revered by millions, that it would undoubtedly have been taken from us by the Chinese government had anyone suspected we had it. The jade death mask of the Emperor Kiang Hsi."

She looked at Val and Bradshaw as if expecting some startling reaction; and when they both only looked blank and questioning, she explained patiently.

"Kiang Hsi was the greatest emperor of the T'ang dynasty, the mightiest China has ever known. Under it the Chinese empire reached its highest state of prosperity. Kiang Hsi was the War Emperor, following in the footsteps of Kuan Ti, the War God. Objects of great value are buried in the tombs of the Chinese emperors. Kiang Hsi, among other things, was buried with a jade mask of Kuan Ti on his face. It has become legendary as a source of mighty deeds and power."

"I suppose," Bradshaw commented politely, "it must be valuable."

"Valuable!" she flashed in indignation. "Priceless!" In the first place, han yu, ancient jade or tomb jade, has an appeal all its own to the Chinese. The mask of Kuan Ti was carved from a flawless block of mutton-fat jade, speckled with emerald green, the most precious jade of all. It is darker now, as tomb jade becomes from contact with the body."

Bradshaw asked: "What's it worth today?"

Her eyes looked past them, through them to far things. "Rivers of blood," said Adelaide Beurket slowly. "Thousands of lives. No money could buy the death mask of Kiang Hsi—unless it was purchased from a thief who was also under great obligation, as happened in this case. Kiang

Hsi's memory is revered by millions. His jade death mask of the War God, recovered from the tomb long ago, has become a god-thing in itself. The superstition has grown up about it that some day a man will come to fill the shoes of Kiang Hsi and wear the jade mask of the War God, and bring back to China the glory and power of his reign."

"You mean," Val said shrewdly, "that the mask is worshipped as a joss?"

"Joss," she said, "is the name for any of the gods to whom prayer sticks and prayer papers are burned, and prayers are said. The jade mask is like any other statue of Kuan Ti, the War God; only ranking far above mere statues because of its association with the Emperor Kiang Hsi. It was one of the treasures of the Forbidden City. During the looting that followed the Boxer rebellion it disappeared. It has been lost to the world since, until, Cart, who had been running down rumors of it for years finally got it on this trip."

Bradshaw looked at Val inquiringly. "Will you tell me," he asked with asperity, "what Zaken wants with that mask? It's no good to him. He couldn't dispose of it in this country or on the continent. Besides," queried Bradshaw, "since when has Zaken taken to anything like this? According to you, he's playing for far greater stakes than larceny could bring."

"The mask is associated with the War God," Val said under his breath. "That right, Miss Beurket?"

"Exactly, Mr. Easton. Millions believe the mask carries the power of Kuan Ti."

"And if a leader turned up with the jade mask?"

"It would depend on the man."

"I think," said Val slowly to Bradshaw, "I understand now why Zaken came tonight for the jade mask."

LESS THAN half an hour had elapsed since that first tragic moment in the back yard. Val looked at his watch, slipped it back, said to Bradshaw: "I'm going up to Beurket's study. The butler let the guests into the gallery under mighty suspicious circumstances. He told me one of the maids brought orders from Beurket to do it. It sounds fishy. How about checking it while I'm upstairs?"

Bradshaw agreed grimly. "I'll see him. If he's holding out, he'll come through to me."

In Cartier Beurket's study Val went at once to the scattered papers on the floor. "Perhaps you'd rather look through these yourself," he suggested to Adelaide Beurket. "I want to see if any of that report is here."

She shook her head. "Go ahead. I'm keen to know. Cart was secretive about this. I haven't the slightest idea what he was doing."

Val picked up a double handful of the papers and laid them on the desk. "Your brother is just the type of man we need. Most people talk too much."

Val leafed rapidly through the papers. "Don't know myself exactly what he was doing for the government," he admitted. "But it was all to be in his report."

Ten minutes later they looked at one another. Cartier Beurket's papers had yielded no sign of a report.

"Stolen?" she asked helplessly.

Val nodded glumly; then suddenly snapped his fingers. "The wastebasket! Should have thought of it before!"

He lifted the small metal basket to the desk chair. Discarded paper filled it almost to the brim.

Val opened the crumpled sheets, putting them on the desk. Out of the first dozen he put two aside. Numbered three and seven, they were written in bold, heavy strokes.

Page three—

> … most of the inland provinces I found a strong undercurrent of dissatisfaction. Different from anything I have encountered in twenty-seven years' contact with the country. Distinctly different from the old hatred of the foreigner. Incoherent in most cases unless one probes carefully and deeply. Distinctly ominous. In the province of Shensi.…

Page three had been stopped at that point, crumpled, thrown away.

Page seven—

> … the same condition existed. Little realization of it among the western population there. They all considered Shanghai guarded and docile, as a standard. But they're a stiff necked lot for the most part, unable, or unwilling, to see much beyond their own corner. From sources in Shanghai I checked further. Much money is available to influence native feeling. Heard again and again of a certain Chang Ch'ien, whose prestige seems great among those who spoke of him. The man is not now in China, I gather, and could not discover where he is. Secret bases mentioned in the Marshall Islands, now under.…

Adelaide Beurket returned the papers. Her tanned, frank face was a study. "I see," she said simply.

Val put them in his pocket. "I wish everyone saw as well," he said briefly. "Shall we go down?"

They were both silent as they left the study and descended to the first floor. The shadow of things apart, beyond the evening's happenings, lay over them.

A DEGREE of order had been restored in the house. Patrolmen and detectives were everywhere, taking names and addresses, searching, standing watchful and ready. A word to one of the officers guided Val to the big dining room. Bradshaw was in there, facing a perspiring and distinctly uncomfortable butler, and a chic little maid, now flushed, defiant, and slightly frightened underneath.

"It's the truth!" the maid was insisting as Val entered. "You can do anything you please, but I didn't know about it! I delivered the message, and that's what I'm paid to do! And I'll go into court with the same story! My references are good and I've never had any trouble before."

"That's right, sir," the butler seconded hastily. "She came here with the best of references."

"Blast her references!" Bradshaw grunted. "Oh—hello, Easton." He turned disgustedly. "This girl admits bringing the message from Beurket. She claims she was at the head of the stairs when Beurket's study door opened and a man, one of the guests she thought, looked out and told her Beurket wished her to tell the butler to open the gallery. The man went back in the study. She delivered the message; Jennings here opened the gallery—and that's all these two claim to know."

Val eyed the flushed girl thoughtfully. "What did he look like?" he asked her.

"Why—why, tall, and—and stoop-shouldered. He was in evening clothes like all the guests, sir. His face was thin, and—and ugly. I felt queer when he looked at me. But I knew Mr. Beurket was in there, so I took the order to Jennings at once, sir."

"Let them go," Val said under his breath. And when Bradshaw dismissed them, and they were out of earshot, Val said: "She's telling the truth. Zaken gave her that order. He came in through that upstairs window, finished with Beurket, and entered the gallery with the guests. Everything planned and carried out methodically. Even to his escape—he knew what he wanted, came for it, and he got away with it. Your men can question the guests and search all night and they won't find much else.

"Zaken is one of the most dangerous men in the world today. He has been a professional spy for years. More than one government has tottered because of state secrets he has stolen."

"The devil!" Bradshaw exclaimed.

"Quite. And now Zaken is starting something so monstrous and incredible that if he is not stopped he'll throw the world into chaos."

Bradshaw's hand poised at his mustache. He stared.

"Asia," Val said, "is a heap of powder waiting for the spark. And Carl Zaken," in grim conclusion, "is that spark!"

BRADSHAW THREW up his hands. "I know you people have information the public doesn't get. And I can understand the possibility of an international angle. But the jade mask? Where does it come in? Why is he wasting his time on a small thing like that?"

"Zaken knows what he's up to—and I think I do, too. We've got to get it, Bradshaw. And get those papers stolen off Beurket's desk. Without delay, too."

Bradshaw protested quickly: "You don't want much. You've been looking for some trace of this man for a week, with all the assistance we could give you. And now you say he's got to be found in a few hours. He'll duck for cover."

"Naturally," Val agreed. "We'll have to smoke him out. Suppose you leave orders for fingerprints to be taken off the doors in Beurket's study and bedroom, and come along with me. Zaken's through with this house. And I think I know where he's gone. Where we can pick up his trail anyway. In Chinatown!"

"Then I'll throw men into Chinatown and search every rat hole along Pell, Doyers and Mott Streets!" Bradshaw burst out.

"Then you can't go with me," Val told him flatly. "No more publicity on this, if you please. If Zaken has gone there you'll frighten him away. He won't be expecting me. Come along if you care to, but just we two go."

Bradshaw considered and then shrugged reluctantly. "All right," he assented. "I'm taking it for granted you know what we're doing. But don't forget we have the responsibility of clearing all this up."

"I," said Val Easton grimly, "have something a damn sight bigger to clear up. Got a gun?"

"I'll get one from a dick."

"Get two. I don't want to have to go to the hotel and dig into my bag. And Bradshaw—no publicity about the mask."

"Right," Bradshaw agreed.

Val had a brief word with Adelaide Beurket while Bradshaw was getting the weapons. She looked less grief-stricken; told him that the hospital reported her brother would recover. He had gained consciousness for a short time and was now sleeping easily.

"That's great!" Val said with relief. Then to her he made the same request he had of Bradshaw. "Don't give out any information about the mask," he begged. "Newspaper reporters are out there already. They'll question the guests, get to you without doubt. Tell them a valuable piece was stolen from the collection. Say it was jade if you must. But nothing about the history of the mask, or the missing report."

"Of course," she agreed, "if it will help you any."

CHAPTER SIX
FOG NIGHT

A **THICK** fog had descended on Chinatown. It swirled before the headlights in gray opaque waves, poured cold and damp into Bradshaw's car as it raced down the Bowery.

"I haven't the slightest idea what we're running into," Val admitted. "But I know Carl Zaken. I assure you he'd like nothing better than to see me out of the way."

They rolled slowly, carefully into Pell Street through muggy soup that all but blotted out a big banner in Chinese characters swung above the street. The old iron balconies on the dingy building fronts, the few parked machines at the curbs, the lighted windows in the very street before them were barely visible.

They crawled past the shop of Li Fui Shan. A light glowed dimly inside the window. Pedestrians were few.

Bradshaw parked the car half a block beyond the shop and they got out. "Now what?" he demanded.

"I'm hoping a young woman will be in the shop of Li Fui Shan. Where she is, Zaken should be tonight. If he isn't, she'll know where he is."

"Is that all? We've got a man down here who knows every corner of this district. Charlie Gong. Born in Frisco; been on the department here in New York for ten years. He's just the man to help on this. I can call the precinct from the nearest corner box and find out where he is."

"Good idea. Go ahead. But no cordons. Intelligence has to be sub rosa. And a whole squad out tonight couldn't escape notice. Carl Zaken isn't worried about the police.

He's proven that. He's slippery, and the only way we can nab him is by being just twice as slippery."

"Slippery it is then," Bradshaw agreed as they came into Doyers Street and the police box.

Bradshaw unlocked it with his key, rang in, said into the mouthpiece. "Commissioner Bradshaw talking… hello, that you, Garrity? Where is Charlie Gong?… Gone to Li Fat's restaurant?… Call Li Fat's, Garrity, and tell Charlie Gong to hustle over here to the box… no nothing wrong. Just need him, and I want him quick."

Bradshaw hung up, closed the box. "Charlie'll be here in a few minutes," he said. "Nice boy. Smart. And knows how to keep his mouth shut. You can tell him anything and not be afraid it'll leak all over this district."

They waited less than five minutes near the call box. A short, slender figure, with topcoat collar turned up and slouch hat brim turned down, materialized suddenly out of the fog. Grinning, he shook hands with Bradshaw.

"Regret ten thousand times keeping honorable commissioner waiting," Charlie Gong said in smiling apology. "My unworthy head bows low in shame, while pride swells me near to burst at this chance to shake one commissioner's honorable hand."

"Still the little humorist, I see," Bradshaw chuckled. "He speaks better English than either of us, Easton. And with a Harvard accent when he forgets. I can never quite forgive him that. Charlie, this is Mr. Easton. We've got a bit of delicate work on tonight. Want your help and all the smart thinking you can give. And it may be dangerous; got your gun?"

"Delighted, Mr. Easton," Charlie Gong said, shaking hands. "I am at your service, gentlemen. And I always go armed at night, commissioner. Too many in this district resent my being a member of the police, and my humble efforts on behalf of the law. My tong had made it plain that they cannot take up quarrels incurred while working at my job. That rather makes an open season for me, you see. I shall probably get a knife in the back one of these days," he finished quite cheerfully.

CHARLIE GONG came only about to Val's shoulder. He had the usual high cheek bones, the slant eyes, the general conformation of his Canton countrymen from the south of China. His lips were full, his nose broad, his eyebrows black and heavy beneath the down-turned hat brim; but his eyes, twinkling, direct and shrewd, coupled with a distinct firmness of his mouth and chin, marked him as a man to be depended on.

"There has been robbery and murder uptown, Charlie," Bradshaw stated. "Mr. Easton has reason to believe the man who did it can be found here in Chinatown. Or at least some trace of him. It's vitally important we get him tonight if possible. And there must be no publicity if we can help it. Not a word to anyone."

"I understand," Charlie Gong nodded. "Who is this man, and what reason have you for believing he may be found in Chinatown?"

"The name is Zaken," Val said. "Carl Zaken—sometimes known as the Black Doctor."

No recognition appeared on Charlie Gong's face. "I'm sorry, gentlemen; if he's here I have not heard of him. Will you describe him?"

Val did so.

"No," said Charlie Gong. "I don't believe I've seen him."

"Have you heard of a man called Chang Ch'ien?" Val asked quickly and bluntly. And he watched the other's face closely.

No expression appeared on Charlie Gong's face. He returned Val's gaze unblinkingly, gravely.

"I have heard of Chang Ch'ien, Mr. Easton. Just a word here and there. Those who speak of him do so furtively. He is not a topic of public conversation. What he is or who he is I am unable to tell you. I gather that he has power and wealth; that those who mention him are afraid of him. But if a man by that name is here in Chinatown, I don't know it."

"Do you know anything about a man named Li Fui Shan, who owns the shop back there along Pell Street?" Val asked then.

Charlie Gong's face lighted up. "Li Fui Shan, eh? Can do, Mr. Easton. I know Li well. He's been here in China-town for over twenty years. One of our most respected merchants. He is a man who has prospered by hard work and honesty. His gifts to charity are extensive. He sits high in the councils of the On Leong Tong. I cannot speak too highly of him."

"Is he married? Does he have any daughters?"

"His family is in Kwangtung Province in China," Charlie Gong smiled. "His sons are being educated in Canton, I believe. Like many Chinese in this country he does not see his family for years at a time."

"No women at all?" Val insisted.

"There is, I believe, a niece, Mr. Easton. She does not live with Li Fui Shan, but she has been there frequently of late. I have seen her one or twice entering or leaving; and I have heard her mentioned. Things like that get around. A very beautiful girl, as I recall her."

"I thought so. I want her. She entered Li Fui Shan's shop several hours ago. If she knows she's wanted she'll escape or hide. Have you any way of gaining access to Li Fui Shan's living quarters?"

"I'm afraid not," Charlie Gong said. "Without a search warrant I couldn't go back. And if Li Fui Shan is hiding someone, he would not be apt to invite me into the rear."

"All right," said Val. "We'll go in. You watch the rear of the house. Collar anyone who tries to leave. And watch out you don't get a knife or a bullet in your ribs."

As the three of them talked they had moved over in the shelter of the nearest doorway. Now, as they stood there, one of the infrequent pedestrians came along the sidewalk, materializing out of the fog. His head turned, staring, as he came abreast. Val saw a man of about his own size, stooped, thin-chested, with a head too big for his body. There was something about that head that caught the eye. It seemed to move, hunched forward, like a disembodied member, detached from the slighter body beneath. It had a prognathous jaw, a wide, cruel slit of a mouth, a great hooked nose and staring, burning eyes. Certainly one would not be apt to forget it in a long time.

Recognition glinted in those burning eyes. A dry, harsh voice threw out, "Hello, Gong," and the furtive figure went on without slackening its pace, vanishing in the swirling fog as suddenly as it had appeared.

"Sweet-looking customer," Bradshaw commented. "Who is he, Charlie?" Charlie Gong, who had not answered the other's greeting, said impassively: "That is Emile."

"The devil! I heard of him."

"The honorable devil would be ashamed of his company," said Charlie Gong blandly. "Emile is a dangerous man. I've had my qualms about crossing him."

"Creepy fellow," said Val. "Who is he? What's his last name?"

"Just Emile. That is all anyone knows him by. We are certain he is a leader in one of the biggest dope rings, with ramifications in England and on the Continent; but so far none of his activities here in Chinatown has given us proof of that. He lived," said Charlie Gong, "in China for some time, and all over the East, I believe. He speaks the Mandarin dialect of the north, and has a fair smattering of Cantonese. Ostensibly he is an importer, and I've never been able to prove anything else.

"Queer," continued Charlie Gong reflectively, "that he should be walking on a night like this. He has a ten-thousand-dollar car if he chooses to ride in it."

"Look into that some other time," Bradshaw suggested. "Right now we have other business."

"Give me ten minutes to get behind Li Fui Shan's building, commissioner, and then deal with the venerable Li as you see fit."

PELL STREET was oddly quiet, deserted. But in the shop of Li Fui Shan there was still a light. The door was locked.

"Hell!" said Bradshaw. "But we're going in!" He knocked.

Curtains parted at the back of the shop and an elderly man shuffled to the door as Bradshaw knocked again. He peered through the glass at them, and then unlocked the door with obvious reluctance as Bradshaw gestured.

Looking out, he said severely: "My shop closed till tomollow, gentlemen. You come back then."

"We're in a hurry," said Bradshaw. "We won't be here tomorrow. Are you Li Fui Shan?" And Bradshaw pushed inside as he asked that.

His abrupt entrance was met with composure. "I am Li Fui Shan," the old man said with dignity. "What you want, gentlemen?"

With Charlie Gong's words still fresh in his mind, and Li Fui Shan, the man, there before him, Val found it hard to believe that there could be anything wrong in this modest shop. Li was indeed a venerable man. His scanty hair was snow white. Whatever garb he wore during the business day had been set aside for the dignified comfort of a long black silk coat, swathing silk trousers and thick-soled felt slippers. An old man, but not wrinkled, emaciated, as so many of his countrymen became. Li Fui Shan's face was plump, kindly, dignified. One could visualize him smiling often, always courteous.

He was courteous now as he bent his head after Bradshaw said: "We'd like to look at some pottery."

"You catchee," said Li Fui Shan, dropping into pidgin English. "I give you light." He gave them the freedom of his shop with a gesture and padded leisurely three steps to a light cord hanging from the ceiling.

The shop was filled with a heterogeneous collection of Chinese craftsmanship. Pottery, bronzes, rugs, silks, porcelain ware, statuary, and trinkets of all kinds. Some of the stuff was good and some obviously bad, for the tourist trade. Li shuffled behind one of the cases and began to take down samples of pottery from the wall shelves. He ranged half a dozen on the case and looked at them inquiringly.

Bradshaw examined them with a show of interest.

Val looked about, listening.

The smell of the Orient was strong in here—musk, sandalwood, incense. The shop was very quiet. The faint roar of the Elevated over on the Bowery sounded, died away. Then, fainter still, far off, a fog whistle on the river moaned rhythmically. Beyond the heavy tapestry curtains at the back of the shop no sound was audible. If anyone was in there they were keeping very quiet.

Li Fui Shan waited behind the counter like an impassive Buddha.

"Show me some more," Bradshaw requested. "I'm afraid these aren't suitable."

Li inclined his head and turned back to the shelves. "You wanchee numbah-one vase, eh?" he inquired over his shoulder.

"I suppose so," Bradshaw grunted. Then he turned his head and shot a look of inquiry at Val; a slightly baffled look as if he were beginning to be convinced that this was wasted time.

Val himself was wondering. If he had not so plainly seen that veiled woman in the black fur coat enter here, he would have given this Li Fui Shan a clean bill of health. But she had come in here. She was known to Charlie Gong, if only by heresay. Li Fui Shan, for all his kindly venerable appearance traced directly to Carl Zaken, the Black Doctor.

And where Carl Zaken's influence reached there was danger.

Thinking so, Val swung about suddenly—and caught the barest flutter of the tapestry curtains at the back of the room.

Someone was standing behind them looking into the shop!

And suddenly the quiet and peace took on the ominous look of watchful waiting. Li Fui Shan's kindly Buddha-like face became a mask, hiding breathless tension. Val went to the counter, picked up one of the vases and examined it. He caught the old man behind the counter sliding an imperceptible glance toward the back. Old Li knew there was someone back there.

"It's up to you, Bradshaw," Val said casually. Maybe I can find something else back here that will do." He idled slowly back along the counter, inspecting the contents within.

Li watched him for a moment and then, hurried back. You likee see nice silk?" he questioned. "You come up front; I show."

The curtains had not moved again.

"All right. Get out your silk," Val said—and as Li started back toward the front Val turned away from the counter— and made a quick jump for the curtains.

He was certain that he heard a quick scurry of movement beyond, and the soft click of a latch. But when he jerked the curtains back he found only a small alcove, backed by a door, closed now.

Li Fui Shan's indignant cry filled the shop. "What you do? You come away!"

CHAPTER SEVEN

TAI SHAN

VAL TRIED the door. It did not open, bolted inside apparently. He drew back two steps and lunged at it. The bolt was not strong, nor the door either; it shivered, cracked, gave. Val drew back and struck it again.

Li Fui Shan's rising crescendo of indignant cries broke off suddenly. Bradshaw's cold voice said: "Steady, old-timer. We're from police headquarters. Get violent and I'll call the wagon!"

And Val struck the door a third time, driving it in with a rending of screws from wood. He staggered through the open doorway, peering intently. There was a hall beyond; a dark hall, seemingly deserted. But no—

The light striking past him through the doorway showed a thick-set, black-shirted Chinese crouched against the wall. He sprang out as Val saw him, crouched in the middle of the hall, a short knife glinting in his hand. Still crouching, he moved a step forward, holding the knife ready for a slashing up-stroke. And somewhere in the darkness at the back feet pattered hastily; a door closed furtively.

In the shop Li Fui Shan expostulated shrilly: "What for you bleak in my house this way?"

And Bradshaw said gruffly: "Shut up or I'll crown you! What is it, Easton?"

Val dragged his automatic from his coat pocket. And, as if realizing quick action was the only thing to meet a gun, the crouching figure before uncoiled in a swift rush, slashing up with the knife.

Val stepped back, whirling aside before the silent savagery of that rush. The gleaming blade struck a button on his coat, slid off, and ripped through the cloth, slashing deep, at an angle. He felt the cold slither of it clear through to the skin as he struck the wall. And then, as the knife flashed out from under his upraised arm for another stroke, Val chopped down hard with the gun barrel.

The crunch of steel against bone was the loudest thing about that brief, silent scuffle. The stocky Chinese lurched over against the side of the passage, sank to his knees, crumpled in a limp little heap.

Val witnessed this with relief. He wanted no gunfire, no killing if it could possibly be avoided. For the plain facts were, he and Bradshaw were in this building without a search warrant. A shooting might make it awkward.

Bradshaw yanked the curtains clear back and snapped through the alcove: "Everything all right?"

"So far," said Val shortly. "I had to slug this fellow, but he'll come out of it. Nasty beggar. He slid that knife along my ribs. Would have put it in my stomach if I hadn't jumped quick. Watch him and the old man, Bradshaw. I think someone we want it back here. We were being watched from behind the curtain when I made a jump for it."

"Go ahead," said Bradshaw. "I'll back you up. When they start drawing knives, rough 'em."

Val went back along the hall into thickening blackness. Doors opened to right and left. It was a squalid, grimy hall.

The worn floor squeaked miserably under foot. A staircase, starting from the back of the hall, slanted to black silent regions above. A door on the left showed light underneath and through the keyhole.

Val opened it, blinked with amazement.

He looked from the sordid hall into beauty, richness and excellent taste. The furniture was carved hardwood, dark, polished, intricately inlaid with mother-of-pearl. Heavy silk covered the windows. Gold-embroidered tapestries hung on the walls. Several beautifully carved and painted screens cut off corners of the room.

It was empty now; but it had been occupied short moments before. Blue hazy smoke drifted before a silk-shaded floor lamp. A hammered brass ash tray on a small red-lacquered table held several cigarette ends and one still sent up a faint curl of smoke.

VAL STEPPED in swiftly, gun ready in his hand. He made a circuit of the room, looking behind the screens. They hid no one. There was a door in each end of the room, but before he could try either a commotion in the hall drew him quickly. There was enough light in the hall now to see a strange and welcome sight.

Charlie Gong, short and placid, was shepherding two figures in from the back. A man and a woman. Charlie saw him, and panted: "Here's two who came flying out. I don't think there were any more."

The man was Emile, that grotesque-faced figure who had passed furtively in the fog.

And the woman—in all the world there could be only one such pale, soft, beautiful face framed in jet-black hair, like an alabaster cameo. Her mouth was a vivid red; red as the color of an East Indian flame tree, and her strange, striking beauty had all the lure of a lotus flower in full bloom.

Bradshaw had come into the hall, bringing the now uneasy Li Fui Shan. He whistled softly between his teeth. "Some catch, Charlie. What have we here?"

Emile hunched there, his wide-slit mouth snarling. His big head swayed about as he looked at them. "I'll make somebody sweat for this!" he threatened furiously. "When a citizen can't call on friends without a bunch of cops surrounding the house and crashing in this way, it's time to go high up about it! I'll have Gong's shield before I'm through! Who are you two?" he barked at Val and Bradshaw.

Charlie Gong clucked regretfully, and succeeded in looking very much like a mischievous youngster. "Honorable Emile makee run Horn doah, likee dragon chop-chop his pants seat; so me catch'm and ask how come."

"Lay off that pidgin talk!" Emile snarled malevolently. "I know you can speak as well as I can!"

Charlie Gong chuckled. "Better, old chap," he agreed. "But I'll wager five to one I can't get out of a house half as fast as you left this one. You went down those steps as if you had greased shoes."

Val faced the girl. She was furious, scornful. But even in anger her voice was oddly musical, vibrant. "You—you do this to me, Val Easton! After—after…." She broke off, bit her lip.

Bradshaw stared. "You know her?" he asked Val in astonishment.

"This," said Val, "is the lovely Tai Shan, sister of Chang Ch'ien. Tai Shan, may I present Deputy Commissioner Bradshaw?"

She ignored Bradshaw. "I am not interested in the police," she said indifferently, and again her voice was clear and musical in that dim, dark hall.

"I haven't thanked you for that warning tonight, Tai Shan. You had me fooled for a time. That Russian accent—I'm still wondering how you knew where to find me on Fifth Avenue."

"I would not lift a finger to save you from anything!" said Tai Shan scornfully. "You are not worth it. But if I wanted to know where to find you, I would have someone sit in a hotel room next to yours and listen to your talk."

"We live and learn," Val sighed. "I should have been watching for that."

"What do you want with me?" Tai Shan demanded.

"Where is Carl Zaken?"

"Ah—so?" Her anger left suddenly. She smiled faintly. And in that dim, sordid hall she was like a figure in some lovely old Chinese print. Her exotic beauty was a flame, heightened if anything by the grotesque ugliness of the snarling Emile.

"You want Carl Zaken?" Tai Shan mocked. "Why come to me, Val Easton?"

"We might search the place," Val mused, watching her.

Tai Shan shrugged indifferently.

Li Fui Shan had been standing beside Bradshaw in dignified silence. He burst into shrill protests. "This my place! You no search without paper!"

"Don't waste your breath," Bradshaw counseled the old man curtly. "We're in now and we'll do what we blasted please! And if you're hiding this Zaken, you're in for a rough time."

TAI SHAN melted suddenly. "He can tell you nothing," she said to Bradshaw. "No one you want is in this house. I know. I've been here all evening. I pledge you my word. Li Fui Shan is merely an old friend who has been repaying an obligation two centuries old by giving me a roof when I need it. Don't bother him. His hospitality has been abused enough tonight. Let me get my coat and hat. Take me out of here. I will talk to you some other place."

Li Fui Shan's face softened. He made a slight graceful bow. "My daughter," he said, "this humble house is yours."

Charlie Gong spoke to him in Chinese. Li Fui Shan answered. Charlie said to Val and Bradshaw: "This is not his niece. There is a blood debt between the families dating back eight generations. She is more than a niece to him; she is his blood, his daughter. Such things are done among my people. He assures me there is no one else in the house. I believe him."

"Take us out of here," Tai Shan insisted. "To the police station if you will. I will talk to you there. You see," and her smile at Val was suddenly dazzling, "I am a tractable prisoner."

Val studied her a moment, and smiled thinly. "Too tractable, Tai Shan; too very tractable. You're beautiful, you're lovely—and you've got the heart of a tiger back of it. But there is no hurry. Let us first speak about this Emile, who, I understand, is in the dope game. What business has he with you, Tai Shan? I've thought hard things about you, and I've fought you—but I always supposed you were clean. I've admired you. I never thought you were mixed up with dope."

A slow red flush crept up to her high cheek bones. "Dope!" Tai Shan repeated, and her musical voice was suddenly off key, harsh. "This man a seller of drugs?"

"Yes."

Emile raised a hand whose fingers were short, thick, and rubbed his bulging jaw. He was in no way disturbed. His wide slit of a mouth grinned at them. "Prove it," said Emile comfortably. "Just try to prove it." He acted like a man who had been accused often before and rested secure in the knowledge that he could not be reached.

Tai Shan's dark eyes rested on him inscrutably. "Then it is true?" she said in a dull, metallic voice.

Emile shrugged. "I told him to prove it. My private life has nothing to do with this. I didn't come talking dope to you, young woman. Forget it."

And Val was suddenly sure that this lovely Tai Shan had had no inkling of her visitor's profession. Yet that was no help to the mystery of Emile's presence here with her.

Emile had come alone, afoot when he might have ridden in his expensive car; he had come late and clandestinely; and both of them, at knowledge that the police were in the front shop, had thought of nothing but escape.

"It might be better," Val said to her, "to tell what his business is here."

She bent her head thoughtfully, looked disturbed, seemed to weaken. "I—I will," she nodded. "Take me to the police station, Val Easton. I'll get my coat." She wore a black dress, tight-fitting, sheathing her slender figure closely. She was lovely, exotic, touching in her surrender.

But Val said to her cynically: "You should be an actress, Tai Shan. Before we leave here I'm going to find out why you're so anxious to go to the police station, to get away."

And the words had hardly left his mouth when a telephone rang sharply in the room behind him.

TAI SHAN started; her head came up. It struck Val then that she had been listening for something ever since Charlie Gong had brought her back into the hall. He grinned as the telephone rang again and Tai Shan offered hastily: "I'll answer it."

"You'll stay right here," Val told her gently. "Charlie Gong will answer it. It may be someone who speaks Chinese."

Her meek submission vanished in a breath. "You have no right to take that telephone call!" she burst out angrily. "We are entitled to some privacy!"

"You're getting all you're entitled to, Tai Shan. And if it's an important message you shall hear all about it."

Charlie Gong was already in the room. They could hear him answering the call in English—which shifted to Chinese a moment later. Tai Shan was pale, tense. Her little fist clenched at her side. She was straining to hear. The grotesque Emile was standing taut also, listening. In contrast Li Fui Shan seemed little interested in who answered the telephone.

Charlie Gong spoke in the sing-song cadences of his native tongue—listened—spoke again; and a few seconds later hung up and returned to the hall. He glanced at a wrist watch.

"It is now seventeen minutes after eleven," Charlie Gong said. "At five minutes to twelve an automobile will call for Tai Shan and her friend. Everything, I am informed over the telephone, is all right. And she is not to fail to bring the foreign devil."

Tai Shan bit her lip; her eyes were blazing, but she said nothing. Emile looked uneasy. His burning eyes went from Charlie Gong to Bradshaw, to Val as if trying to read their minds.

"Who was it?" Val asked the little Chinese detective.

Charlie Gong shrugged. "I don't know. I was afraid to ask questions. I merely said that the high born lady was busy. It was evidently taken for granted that since I was here in the venerable Li Fui Shan's home I spoke with authority. I should not be surprised," said Charlie Gong, "if I was not mistaken for that pig lying on the floor inside the door; who is stirring now by the way. I will get him."

Bradshaw smoothed the end of his small black mustache and smiled with satisfaction. "If there's a car coming for these two, we'll grab it, Easton. It should give us something to work on."

Val had been standing, frowning to himself. The frown passed as suddenly as it had come. He grinned. "The car was going to take them somewhere. I'll slip into Emile's coat and hat and take his place."

"But the woman?" Bradshaw objected. "You can't get by with it with this girl."

"No," Val agreed. "But I know one who can take her place—if she is still in town. I haven't seen her for a couple of days. Just a minute—while I telephone."

The telephone was on a lacquered stand in the corner of the big room he had searched. The directory was underneath. He leafed through it, found a number, gave it. It was answered almost at once. He spoke rapidly, finished: "Hurry up! There's no time to lose!"

And back in the hall to Bradshaw, Val said: "She's coming. Nancy Fraser who's worked with me a lot. She's the one woman in the country who could go through with this. I hate to drag her into it—but I can't pass up this chance."

TAI SHAN looked suddenly like an enraged cat; a beautiful cat, but dangerous. Her hand flicked out without warning inside the bodice of her dress, came out with a tiny gleaming blade. Val's hand shot to her wrist. He had the knife, had her subdued a moment later. "I was looking for something like this," he said reproachfully. "It's no use. We're going. Take it sporting."

"Go then!" said Tai Shan breathlessly. "Go with my blessings, Val Easton. And remember—my blessings." She began to laugh.

"Over-wrought," said Val to Bradshaw. "She'll have to be handled carefully. I suggest you get several plainclothesmen here to watch these people. No use taking them to the station house. I'm sure Li Fui Shan would rather have it that way."

The old man nodded in silent agreement.

"I'll do that," said Bradshaw briskly. "And Charlie and I will tail you in another car."

"Good. But you'll have to work fast."

Bradshaw used the telephone hurriedly. And in an incredibly short time three plainclothesmen entered the shop. Bradshaw gave them directions; they took Tai Shan, the grotesque Emile and the browny native who had stood guard in the hall; took them into the big lighted room, handcuffed the man, put Tai Shan in a chair firmly despite her indignation.

Then Nancy Fraser came into the shop, breathlessly, her cheeks pink from cold and haste. Nancy Fraser, whose daring and ingenuity was known all through the Intelligence. In spite of that she stood there inside the door, softly feminine, a little beauty with fine, clean cut features, sun-tanned, chin firm, and mouth wide and quirked humorously at the corners.

Val thought again with admiration that she had the deepest and bluest eyes he had ever seen; and her platinum hair cut short and waved close to her head was as beautiful as ever when she stripped off her little felt hat and smiled at him.

"Here I am, Val. What's the bad news?"

Swiftly as they went back into the hall he gave it to her.

"Exciting," said Nancy gaily. "I've been famishing for something like this." She met Bradshaw and Charlie Gong composedly.

"Are you sure it's all right to take her, Easton?" Bradshaw queried doubtfully.

"Have to," said Val. "She understands. It's part of the game. I'd rather have her than most men. I'll get Tai Shan's coat and hat, Nancy. They'll be a little big, but I guess you can manage them."

In a few moments more they were both ready, Val in Emile's coat and hat; Nancy in Tai Shan's.

"Got your gun?" Val asked.

"Never go out without it at night," said Nancy airily. "We girls are fragile, you know."

Bradshaw and Charlie Gong left the shop for the police car parked down the street. Val and Nancy waited in the front. The hands of Val's watch crept toward twelve—and suddenly there was a soft purring motor outside, headlights gleaming dimly through the fog. A horn blew once.

"Here we go," said Val. "Chin up and keep your hand on your gun."

Coat collars turned up, hats shading their faces as much as possible, they left the shop of Li Fui Shan and walked out into the damp swirling fog.

CHAPTER EIGHT

HOUSE OF HOODED MEN

A LIMOUSINE stood at the curb, big, black, powerful, fast. Two figures were in the front seat, and as Val and Nancy came out of the shop of Li Fui Shan one of the men leaped out, opened the rear door and stood stiffly at attention. He was a short, slender Oriental, wearing a chauffeur's uniform. As Nancy came abreast of him he said something to her in rapid singsong Chinese, finishing his speech with a rising interrogation.

Val stiffened; his hand in his coat pocket clutched tight on the automatic. Was their masquerade to be penetrated at the very start of this mysterious journey?

But Nancy acted quickly, as she always did in moments of stress. Her little gloved hand came up in a careless gesture of assent. She stepped into the limousine without speaking.

It was evidently enough. When Val sank into the deep luxurious seat beside her the door closed, the fellow entered the front, and the driver pulled away from the curb at once.

Val reached out and touched Nancy's hand. He had to grope to find it; for the rear inside windows were curtained, and there was even a curtain lowered behind the two men in the front seat. They were in complete blackness, unable to see where they were going.

"Emile was slated for a blind ride," Nancy said under her breath.

"But I am not Emile—and you are not Tai Shan to keep an eye on him. We'll cheat a little."

Val lifted the curtain at his side and looked out. They were rolling swiftly out of the fog-filled tangle of China-town. They passed under the forest of Elevated pillars, criscrossing Chatham Square, rolled along Division Street under the Elevated and turned north with it. In a few minutes they were on First Avenue, speeding north. They crossed the Harlem River on the Willis Avenue bridge, turned on the Westchester road.

The fog thinned out but as they neared Westchester it began to thicken again. The limousine rolled faster toward its mysterious destination. Nancy peered out for some moments. "I wonder where we're going," she whispered.

Val had sketched to her the evening's happenings in a low tone; he said now, "I wish I knew. I don't like it. I had no idea we were going so far out." He lifted the rear curtain, looked behind. The headlights of several cars were visible. Back there somewhere were Bradshaw and Charlie Gong.

"At least," said Val, "Bradshaw and Charlie Gong are our ace in the hole."

"Makes me feel better," Nancy confessed. "I'm not afraid—but Carl Zaken is a horrible person. I can't forget him as he was in Washington."

They turned off the Avenue. Val lost track of the streets and directions there. He was in unfamiliar territory, and the still thickening fog was no help.

Nancy lifted the rear curtain, looked back. "I don't see anyone following us, Val."

In the swirling mist behind, no car was in evidence.

Val tapped a cigarette on the back of his hand and lit it. "We're in for it now," he said slowly. "We're on our own."

"I've been that way before," Nancy said philosophically. But her voice had a slight tremble.

And suddenly they were there....

FOR SOME minutes there had been no street lights, no sign of houses, and the wheels had left the pavement. The limousine made a sharp turn. Looking out they could see bare, ghostlike tree trunks looming eerily through the fog. The car stopped; the motor died. The man who had let them into the car opened the door and the cold night air swept into their faces as they got out. Fresh air, tangy with the salt and fish smell of the open sea. The hoarse blast of a fog whistle vibrated through the night at no great distance away.

The car door closed. The little Chinaman spoke again in his native tongue to Nancy. And again she did not reply. There was not even light now to gesture. They stood in blackness, complete and abysmal, except for the dim cowl lights, fog-smothered before their glow reached the front bumper.

But again luck saved them. A powerful flashlight in the hands of the saffron-skinned footman glowed out before them and swept ahead, piercing the fog. It shone on steps of stone, and piercing on beyond brought up against a house wall covered thickly with ivy. It picked out a shuttered window, stark, forbidding. And then the footman walked up the stone steps, keeping the light down so they could see as they followed.

There was nothing else to do but follow. Where they were, what this place was, what was expected of them, was mystery, dark, sinister. They mounted five steps—Val counted them—and crossed the porch to a boarded door. The flashlight showed it clearly, dark, weathered boards, guarding a deserted house against intruders.

And the house seemed deserted. Their steps scraped loud, harsh; there were no sounds, no lights, no signs of life. And yet, when, stopping before those weathered boards, their guide said in a voice that sounded startling loud:

"Hola!" The weathered storm door swung out silently on oiled hinges.

A second door of heavy bolted planks stoop open inside it, and beyond, in a high-ceilinged reception hall, a faint red glow streamed out to meet them.

Their guide stepped back as a second figure materialized in that dim ghastly glow, bowing welcome. This was another Chinese, bland, inscrutable, wearing black trousers and silk jacket. He bowed a second time as they entered.

The dim red light came from an inverted globe high up against the ceiling. It was so faint that what small part of their faces was visible could hardly be seen.

The doors were closed behind them. This second man bowed a third time and padded ahead of them on noiseless felt soles. He stopped at a table against the side wall, picked up a piece of black cloth, and said something to Nancy in Chinese, at the same time moving behind her for her coat.

Val watched, slit eyed, his hand on the gun in his pocket. Nancy shook her head.

Her wish seemed to carry weight. Muttering a singsong something, the fellow lifted his hands and brought the black cloth down over her head.

Nancy's hand was in her coat pocket also. And for a moment Val thought she was going to step from under the cloth and bring her gun out. Then he saw, with a foolish surge of relief, that a black mask with eyeholes and a place to breathe had been placed over Nancy's head.

A second mask was handed him from the table. Val slipped it on, pushing his hat off as it went on, so that at no moment was his face entirely visible. He too refused the offer to take off his coat.

The hood felt close and warm about his face. Through the eyeholes he could see Nancy, grotesque and rather horrible in the ghastly red glow. But for all the eeriness of this little bit of stage play there was relief too. Their faces were hidden.

THEIR YELLOW-SKINNED attendant bowed, walked noiselessly to the rear of the hall and opened a door, going through ahead of them. They were taken to the left along a second hall, through profound quiet. They came to a door. Their guide knocked. It was opened. Incense, thick, heavy, cloying, rolled out to meet them. And behind his mask Val almost uttered an exclamation.

A great hall-like room opened before them.

Here was Asia, mysterious, inscrutable, beautiful. The high ceiling was vaulted, braced by great carved timbers. And from those timbers, hung silken lanterns, their gay colors dimly visible.

A dais at the far end of the room was backed by a marvelous tapestry covering half the wall. One single throne-like chair rested on the dais. And in each corner of the dais a bundle of joss sticks in brass containers sent up thin wavering spirals of smoke. Nancy's fingers dug into Val's arm again as the scene burst on them; and it was not the room but the two score figures in it that were so startling. Figures masked like themselves in black, some seated on the chairs against the wall, some standing and moving slowly about. A very few were engaged in conversation. The most of them were sitting silently.

It was a strange, uncanny scene. The eyeholes in those loose enveloping hoods gave the impression of life without emotion through the eery red glow of the lanterns. Such voices as were speaking were low, muffled. They were all men, all but Nancy. Further than that one could see nothing. What manner of men they were, what nationality, what they were doing here, was all a mystery.

Their guide had closed the door behind them, leaving them on their own. Nancy spoke from behind her mask in a muffled whisper. "Val, what is this?"

"Your guess is as good as mine," Val husked back.

Black-shrouded heads turned, stared at them as they entered. Some turned away after a moment, others continued watching them. The thick cloying atmosphere, of the room, for all its silence, was electric with an undercurrent of tension.

No one came forward to greet them, no one spoke to them. And after a moment, Val sensed that the gathered company had no cohesion. Each man was apart from the others. No man could tell what lay behind the shrouding hood next to him. Val Easton had been many places in a somewhat hectic career, but never had he been a part of anything like this. He kept in mind that he was Emile, a power in the big dope rings, and that besides him should be the lovely Tai Shan. It still did not make sense.

And the next moment his pulses leaped; he went tense and watchful. The crashing notes of a great gong vibrated through the room. The seated figures came to their feet abruptly, turning toward the dais behind which the gong was booming. And before the last vibrant note died away, the great gold and silver tapestry curtain parted in the middle—and Carl Zaken, the Black Doctor, stepped out on the dais....

THERE WAS no applause or greeting. The Black Doctor was not masked. He still wore the evening clothes in which he had appeared at Cartier Beurket's.

The notes of the gong seemed to echo and re-echo, farther and fainter into the distance, until finally they were vibrant no more. And in those long seconds the tall stooped figure on the dais was imperceptibly bathed in a brighter red glow, while the rest of the room grew dimmer, darker. The pale, ghastly, cadaverous face of the Black Doctor stood out in blood-red relief until it and only it, was a focal point for all eyes. The emanations of that silent figure reached out and dominated the room. And then:

"Voila, you are here!" His dry grating voice reached into every corner of the room.

"You are here," the Black Doctor repeated, looking slowly about. "From Europe, from China, from India, from this country. You have been called here for your reports, and they are pleasing. No man among you knows his neighbor. Your identities are safe tonight. But all of you know toward what you have been working. Your rewards will be magnificent, your power unlimited. Once in a thousand years the current of history is reversed and one part of the world rises to master the other. That time is here. Asia, so long eclipsed by the white man, is ready for the spark...."

Carl Zaken paused; and his flaming malevolent eyes stared through the blood red halo about him. He smiled; and to Val Easton who knew the man, it was the smile of a monster, indescribably vicious and dangerous.

"*You* will be the spark," Carl Zaken's dry grating voice told those standing hooded figures. "Tonight you will see that which will put the power into your hands. Gentlemen...."

Carl Zaken lifted a hand, half turned to the great silver and gold tapestry curtain at the back of the dais.

Crash....

The hidden gong thundered its blood chilling reverberations through the silence of the room.

The curtains parted—and a gasp ran through the room. Standing there, stiff, erect, was a great tall figure clad in a magnificent dragon robe of Imperial yellow; an Oriental, a member of the Celestial Kingdom unmistakably. A round silk hat with a yellow button on the crown topped the giant figure's head. But not that brought the gasp, not that sent Val Easton's pulses hammering and brought Nancy Fraser closer to his side. For covering the face of the figure was a life size dull amber mask of jade.

Life size and lifelike, that jade mask shaped in the perfect lineaments of a man that had never lived; The features of a god, stem, haughty, with a small beard cunningly carved on the chin.

"Is that it?" Nancy whispered.

"That's it," Val said through his teeth.

And though he had never seen a jade mask before he knew it for what it was. The death mask of the great

Emperor Kiang Hsi. The mask of Kuan Ti, the War God. Once beautiful mutton fat jade speckled with emerald green, it had darkened to its present colors, in the tomb, where, for centuries, it had covered the face of an emperor who had made his power felt over most of his known world. By the hundred thousands men had died in the name of Kuan Ti. By the millions men would die in the name of that cold jade mask, given life and meaning by the deeds of one man thirteen centuries dead.

Already, tonight, blood had stained that beautiful jade. The future promised rivers of it in the name of hatred, greed and lust for power.

AND NOW the great golden figure in the Imperial dragon robe paced sedately to the gilded, carved throne chair and seated himself, hands palm down on his knees, erect, stiff, regal.

Carl Zaken's voice rang through the great vaulted room.

"Gentlemen, the death mask of the great Emperor, Kiang Hsi. The god mask of the War God Kuan Ti. A joss that will make its wearer infallible. Gentlemen, Chang Ch'ien, the war leader who will inflame all China, will lead the yellow race as conquerors of the world. With this mask he cannot fail."

The great gong crashed out about them once more. And Chang Ch'ien sat there, stiff, immovable, hands on his knees and the god mask staring at them without expression, as it had stared for thirteen centuries. And the golden robe on that golden figure seemed to take on some of the blood tinge of the ghastly light which drenched it from above.

It was high drama, cunningly staged. And yet Val Easton's palm was damp about the handle of his gun as he witnessed it from among those black-hooded figures. For there was menace here too. Menace, danger and death for Nancy Fraser and himself. And for scores of thousands of unsuspecting people who tonight were sleeping peacefully in well-sheltered homes. Here, all about them, in the great room was something so vicious and threatening to the peace of mankind that it must be stamped out quickly, as one would destroy a venomous snake. And Val realized with a sickening feeling of helplessness that he could do nothing against this mad man who desired to rule a world. His own life, Nancy Fraser's life, hung by threads—the thickness of the threads forming the black cloth over their faces. If they were discovered it meant the end.

Something of that must have been running through Nancy's mind also. For she crept close to Val. He could feel her arm rigid against his. Silently he berated himself for drawing her into a thing like this. And his eyes riveted on that gilded throne chair; for Chang Ch'ien spoke from behind the jade mask....

"Go back and whisper what you have seen. Tell all your people that the spirit of the great Kiang Hsi has returned again. Tell them to make ready. Plans of which you know nothing are maturing. A few more moves, a little patience, and we shall be masters of the world—'For he who aims the bow that kills is master!'"

The calm, clear voice speaking in perfect English had an uncanny rhythmic purring quality that was half hypnotizing. One felt that the mind behind it was a mighty thing, projecting out, enfolding the will to which it was addressed. One felt that here were depths beneath depths, and a man whose power, ruthlessness, and cunning could sway a multitude, set a world at war. Val felt it. And those motionless black hooded figures about him felt it too. They stood like statues, spellbound.

Chang Ch'ien spoke again. "There is among you one whose beauty is no less than her sagacity. She has guided here tonight a man whose power reaches into strange and vital places. A man unknown by the world. A man who can bring disgrace and fear to those high in government circles in half a dozen countries. By his connections and his knowledge he can help us undermine where other men would fail. A dealer in drugs, gentlemen, whose victims are his slaves. His face you shall not see until his work is done and Asia rules the world. But she who brought him here shall be known to you all."

Val heard the uncanny purring voice with quick horror. Unexpected disaster had fallen on them. He sensed what was coming, even before the great golden Chang Ch'ien said distinctly:

"Tai Shan, my sister, come forward and show yourself...."

NANCY STOOD breathless and unmoving by Val's side.

A hush of expectancy held the room. The black hooded heads turned toward them. All eyes were on Nancy, waiting, waiting....

Chang Ch'ien spoke again with a sharper note of authority, "Tai Shan, come forward!"

"What shall I do?" Nancy's tight whisper came from beneath her mask.

There was nothing she could do; nothing. If she went forward and removed that black hood she was doomed. If she refused to obey she was lost. The real and lovely Tai Shan would never have refused. The brief fleeting seconds seemed endless. Carl Zaken, on the edge of the dais, bent his head forward and stared through the blood-red glow suspiciously. A queer ripple of tension stirred the hooded figures about them.

Chang Ch'ien's voice cracked like a lash. "Tai Shan!"

"Val!" That was Nancy, whispering her helplessness through the black cloth.

"I'm sorry," Val whispered back.

And even as the words passed his lips Chang Ch'ien came out of the gilded throne chair in one catlike movement. His hand lifted, pointed. His purring voice rang out from behind the mask. "Hold her! Hold that man with her! My sister would never disobey my order like this!"

"We're on our own, Nancy! Do what you can!" Val threw that at her as he jerked the automatic from his coat pocket. They had no hope of escaping. Their lives at this moment were running out as fast and surely as the last grains in an hour glass.

"Stand back!" Val cried out to those black-hooded figures about him.

Carl Zaken's harsh voice cried from the dais, "Stop him!"

They were dangerous, desperate men hand-picked by the Black Doctor and the golden Chang Ch'ien. They closed in from every side. Val pumped the automatic twice savagely; and heard Nancy's gun bark at his side. They both would die—but they would die dearly....

A man staggered, fell; another lurched—but still they came in. Hands caught at him from behind. Val's next shot struck the floor as his arm was knocked down. He heard Nancy cry out. And then, struggling futilely, he was jerked back and borne to the floor. The black hood was tightened about his face, his neck. Fingers choked. The weight of many bodies crushed him against the floor—and a red haze dosed in. Red, blood-red, like that halo bathing Chang Ch'ien and the Black Doctor on the dais.

And then the blackness of death....

LIGHT STRUCK into Val's eyes. Bright light, coming from a floor lamp somewhere to the left of him. His throat was dry, sore, painful. He felt sickish, dizzy. Then memory of all that had happened flashed over him. The Black Doctor—Chang Ch'ien—Nancy Fraser.

He was on his back, looking up at the ceiling as thought of Nancy cleared his head like a dash of cold water. He tried to sit up—and couldn't. He was held rigid by a strap over his throat. His wrists and ankles were strapped down tight. Rolling his eyes, Val saw that he was on some sort of table raised above the floor. He could lift his head an inch or so, turn it from side to side. He was in a small room whose walls were hung with black silk embroidered at intervals with writhing golden dragons. With difficulty he made out, a cabinet, a couch, and over against one wall a bookcase about the height of a man's head.

Under the table on which Val lay suddenly sounded the shrill hungry squeal of a rat, the rapid chattering of tiny, sharp teeth.

Val's heart beat faster at the sound. Alone, rats in the room! His coat was off, shirt sleeves loose. Helpless, defenceless—and rats in the room! The rat squealed again, but remained tinder the table. And in the minutes that followed Val heard it again and again, always directly beneath him. He puzzled for a little and then ignored it, thinking of Nancy Fraser. Where was she? What had happened to her?

Movement beyond his feet caught his eye. Neck strained against the strap across his throat, he saw a bookcase across the room swing out noiselessly on hinges at one end, revealing an opening behind it. And from that opening a tall, powerful figure wearing a green mandarin coat and a round hat with a yellow button, stepped into the room. He closed the bookcase, came to the table where Val lay and looked down at him. The uncanny purring voice of the man called Chang Ch'ien said:

"I have waited for this, Valentine Easton."

Chang Ch'ien's words were without emotion—and chilling and foreboding for the very lack of it.

Without the ancient jade mask Chang Ch'ien was just as impressive. The shades of that golden dragon robe he had worn on the dais seemed still to linger in his golden-tinted skin. His full-lipped mouth, his stabbing slant eyes, with a small sickle shaped scar at the corner of his right eyes, his smooth black hair sweeping back from his forehead as he lifted the hat for a moment gave him the appearance of a tall yellow god. The scar drew his eye up into the slightest sardonic cast. And then he smiled; and cunning lay behind it, and ruthlessness, and cruelty. And one saw how this man had become a myth, a legend, a terror in the underworld of many lands.

Beneath the table the rat squeaked again and chattered its teeth. Chang Ch'ien smiled broadly, without humor, said:

"Where is my sister, Tai Shan, Valentine Easton?"

"Where is Nancy Fraser?" Val countered huskily. His throat was swollen, tight.

"A beautiful girl, Miss Fraser; and spirited. She's been asking for you."

"Damn you!" said Val thickly.

"Where is Tai Shan? Miss Fraser came here wearing Tai Shan's coat and hat, in the car that should have brought Tai Shan. What have you done with her?"

And a fierce joy burned through Val's veins at the sudden break of anguish he caught in Chang Ch'ien's voice. The man was vulnerable in one spot at least.

Val said bluntly: "She's guarded. You can't help her."

Chang Ch'ien looked down at him without moving a face muscle. "I believe she is, Easton. You found her at Li Fui Shan's. How, I don't know, but I would have heard from her by now if she were free."

"Quite," Val agreed. "Suppose we talk business. Nancy Fraser, myself, Cartier Beurket's jade mask, and, say—Carl Zaken, for your sister."

"You fool!" Chang Ch'ien purred. "*You* bargain with me!" One hand with long tapering fingers came out of a coat sleeve and caught the front of Val's shirt. Calmly, methodically, Chang Ch'ien ripped the cloth away until Val lay on the table bare from the waist up.

"You fool!" said Chang Ch'ien again. "Once before you crossed my path and got away. You were a dead man when you entered this house. But before you die, you will tell me where Tai Shan is. You will write the order that will release her."

Val laughed at him. It was all he could do.

"You will scream for the privilege of releasing that girl whose foolish interest in you probably betrayed her this evening," Chang Ch'ien said without emotion.

CHANG CH'IEN stooped, reached under the table, and when he straightened he held a small wire cage in his golden tapering fingers. A wire cage filled with scurrying frantic movements, shrill keening chatters of fright and rage, and a brown furry body that dashed from side to side in the upper half.

At first Val was puzzled. Two straps dangled from the bottom of the cage. It was partitioned in the middle. In the upper half, bounding about on the partition which formed a floor, was the gaunt hungry body of a great savage rat.

"He has been starved for a week," Chang Ch'ien purred. "He is frightened, angry, desperate for escape." Speaking, Chang Ch'ien set the cage on Val's chest, passed one of the straps beneath Val's bare torso and buckled it on the other side, holding the cage firmly in place. There was no wire in the bottom; nothing but space between his flesh and the partition halfway up in the cage.

"When I pull this slide out," Chang Ch'ien said evenly, "he will drop to your chest. There, for a time, fright will keep him busy. But when he begins to think, he will see that the only way out is through your chest. Food and escape in one." Chang Ch'ien smiled lazily, but his eyes were flaming. "Before he has won free," he said, "you will be a madman, Valentine Easton."

And Val knew that it was so. Only an Oriental could devise such ghastly, terrible torture. He shuddered; cold perspiration broke out on his forehead as he visualized those hours of agony in which sharp rodent teeth gnawed through flesh, nerves, bones on their way to freedom and satiated hunger.

The rat had quieted now, was staring nervously about from little beady, blinking eyes. The tapering fingers of Chang Ch'ien's left hand caught the slide and drew it slowly out. The rat balanced precariously on it, and as the opening into the bottom of the cage widened before him he thrust his head down, staring at the bare expanse of flesh below. Rigid, Val waited for the impact of tiny cold feet on his chest—and the horror that would quickly follow.

And suddenly that ghastly taut moment was broken into by the swift slide of books in the bookcase. Raising his head, Val saw volumes falling out of the second shelf from the top; volumes thrust aside by a hand that shoved through, holding a large caliber revolver!

CHAPTER NINE
STASHING BLADES

CHANG CH'IEN started back from the cage, turned as if to flee. But a crackling command in singsong Chinese from behind the bookcase stopped him rigid. The voice of Charlie Gong said: "Good. Now unstrap him. The cage first, and perhaps we'll put it on you. Quick, before I shoot, my friend!"

The sickle-shaped scar at the corner of Chang Ch'ien's right eye flamed with silent passion. Silently he turned to the table, fumbled with the straps, and set the wire cage down on the floor again. Still silently he freed Val's neck, arms, ankles. Val swung to the floor, swayed a moment, and turned to the bookcase. The smiling face of Charlie Gong peered through at him.

"Search him," said Charlie Gong. "Quick!"

Val did so, found a long knife tucked in the waistband of Chang Ch'ien's trousers, but no gun.

"Now watch him!" Charlie Gong directed. "I'm coming in. I would have shot him but I was afraid it would bring the house down on our ears."

Charlie Gong withdrew his gun, pushed open the bookcase and stepped into the room. Chang Ch'ien waited, hands in his sleeves, face impassive once more. He had spoken not a word. Charlie Gong closed the bookcase and stepped toward the table. One step he took on a small Chinese rug lying on the floor—and the rug suddenly dropped beneath his feet and Charlie Gong vanished in a yawning hole in the floor. Vanished silently, his gun flying up above his head, and on his face a look of unutterable amazement.

And as Charlie Gong dropped from sight Chang Ch'ien's hand came out of his sleeve holding a second knife. He whirled on Val like a great golden-skinned cat.

"Now!" Chang Ch'ien said, and the word came like a whip lash as he lunged forward, sweeping the knife up before him.

Val was cornered against the table, hemmed in, unable to dodge. Chang Ch'ien rushed suddenly, his knife upraised. Val did the only possible thing. He countered instantly with the knife he held. His gleaming blade slashed out, down, countering with the skill of one who had fenced much.

The blades dashed metallically. With a quick twist Val threw himself to one side, pivoting his weight on the clashing blades. Chang Ch'ien's knife was deflected, sliding on up past Val's blade at an angle. Its keen point ripped skin and flesh above the elbow of Val's left arm as the blow swept on past into space. The force of Chang Ch'ien's rush brought him hard against the edge of the table, his green mandarin coat brushing against the blood welling from Val's arm. And, catlike, the big Chinese recovered himself and swung about for another stabbing blow.

Val's right arm was free. He reversed his palm and smashed it toward Chang Ch'ien's head. The solid, heavy end of the knife handle caught the big fellow squarely behind the ear. Chang Ch'ien dropped like a poled ox. Dropped and rolled over on the floor, his knife clutched in nerveless fingers. He never moved. The fresh scarlet blood from Val's arm stained the front of the green mandarin coat; and close beside it the great gaunt rat bounced in fright from side to side of the small wire cage.

PANTING, SUDDENLY weak from the nervous reaction, Val laid the knife on the table and picked up the torn fragments of his shirt. He mopped the blood off his arm. He had a gash several inches long and a quarter of an inch deep, bleeding freely. Quickly he wrapped the shirt around it, tied a quick rough knot as best he could and stepped to the square yawning hole in the floor.

"Charlie Gong!" he called down cautiously.

From the black well-like hole Charlie Gong's voice came up, surprisingly cheerful. "Astonishing! I thought you would be dead by now, Easton."

"Still kicking. Our friend is out cold."

"You should have killed him," said Charlie Gong cheerfully. "Sorry I can't help you. Better get out of the house as quickly as you can—if you can. Don't know how many men they've got."

"Where is Bradshaw? How did you get in? I thought you'd lost us. I'd given you up."

"We had a puncture," Charlie Gong explained. "Last we saw of you the car was heading into Westchester. We came on, looked around. No sign of you. Bad business. Bradshaw was stumped. And then we suddenly ran into a string of cars leaving some place hurriedly. We found the drive they were coming out of and walked in to investigate. And bless you," said Charlie Gong in his flawless English, "there was the car we had been following, standing in front of the house. The driver was behind the wheel. I surprised him. We took him off in the fog and I talked Cantonese to him. After I had knocked his front teeth out he talked to me as one brother to another. There was trouble inside, he said. His partner had blundered and would perhaps die for it. Two strangers had been caught in the house."

Charlie Gong's voice floated up out of the darkness, calm and careless, with no hint of the drama and bravery he was recording.

"There was no time to go for help. I doubted if you were alive even then. I slugged the fellow after he had told me all I wanted to know, took his cap and coat and walked to the front door. The man at the door let me in, thinking I was the driver. We Chinese have moments of reason. It wasn't difficult for me to persuade him to bring me upstairs to you. Our friend Chang Ch'ien was talking when I arrived on the other side of the bookcase. I let him finish before I rudely interrupted his modest pleasures. You will find the doorman on the other side of the bookcase on the floor."

"Where is Nancy Fraser?"

"I don't know. I wanted to get you first. Better get out of here quick and send Bradshaw for help. From what Chang Ch'ien said I doubt if she's harmed—yet."

"How about you? Can you get out of there?"

"No," said Charlie Gong casually. "I am underground, I think. The walls are stone, and damp. Leakage from the beach probably. I must be below water level. Besides, my leg is broken." And not until then did Val have the full measure of that little Chinese detective.

VAL LOOKED about. There were no windows in the room. Impossible to try to get Charlie Gong with his broken leg out of the house. He would be safer down there.

"I'm going," said Val. "I'll do the best I can."

"Good luck. And by the way, I understand you're mystified about how that chap got off Beurket's roof. The chauffeur was driving the same car for that job. He kindly told me before I broke his head that your man swung down from the seventh floor window of an apartment they had rented in the building adjoining. The space between it and the roof edge of Beurket's private gallery was two or three yards. By pushing hard this Zaken crossed the gap, stood on the roof. One of his men followed him and slid on down the rope into the back yard. After disposing of the watchmen there, he entered the back door when no one was looking and slipped down into the cellar.

"After putting the lights out he left without discovery in the darkness, climbed up to the roof again and swung across the space into the third-story window of a second apartment they had rented. This Carl Zaken followed in the same way. They walked out of the door of their apartment house, around the corner to their car and drove away. Everything had been planned, I understand, from the moment word had come from China that the mask of Kuan Ti had been smuggled out of the country. Chang Ch'ien's agent had been looking for it there.

"I tell you all this," Charlie Gong's cheerful voice floated up out of the darkness, "in case I am unable to talk when you find me again. Good luck."

Val left him there, that gallant little fellow. And naked to the waist as he was, with blood-stained arm and side, he opened the bookcase and stepped through. He could have asked Charlie Gong to try to throw his revolver up. Deliberately he left that comfort to Charlie Gong.

The bookcase was double, with books facing out on both sides. Val found himself in a bedroom. He stepped over the inert form of the doorman, crossed the room, opened the door into the hall and was greeted by an exclamation of astonishment. Coming toward him two paces away was a blue-clad, saffron-skinned servant, carrying a big leather kit bag in one hand. He dropped the kit bag and turned to scurry along the hall.

Val caught him in the first step, succeeded in throttling most of his squall of fright. With a full armed sweep he shoved the fellow against the wall and smashed him in the jaw. The first blow didn't do it—but the second and third did. He left the fellow there on the floor.

The hall turned at both ends. No stairs were visible. It was impossible to tell which way to go. Val went in the direction from which his victim had been coming.

He made the turn to the left, found steps a short distance beyond—narrow steps that turned at right angles as they went down. Blood was dripping from Val's arm, staining his torso. He still carried the knife in his right hand. Hair rumpled, face set, blood-smeared, he was a startling and savage sight. At the bottom of the stairs he found another hall. This big old stone house seemed to be a tangle of rooms and halls.

Fate decided his direction this time. A door slammed to his left. He went to the right. Another door slammed behind him. He heard steps shuffling in his direction, men talking excitedly in Chinese. Val opened the first door he came to; it happened to be on the left. He stepped through—and stood stock still, nerves tense.

He was in the big vaulted room where he had been throttled unconscious. The dais, the thronelike chair, the great silver and gold tapestry and all the other furnishings were still in place; but the room was empty. His own cautious steps sounded loud.

Val hesitated, stared. He knew now how to get to the front entrance to leave the house. But what would happen while he was gone? Could he get back in the house, find Nancy Fraser....

VAL TURNED his back on the door which led to the open, free night outside; turned his back and went to the dais. Carl Zaken had disappeared from behind that great tapestry. He might still be found beyond there. Val clutched the knife ready as he stepped nimbly upon the dais and approached the tapestry. The Black Doctor would get short shrift if they met—and Val sought that meeting.

Silently, he slipped through the tapestry and found an open door in the alcove behind it. He went down the steps at the back of the dais, through the door, and found himself in another hall. The great brass gong that had been struck hung from two uprights by the wall. The striker leaned beside it. The hall was empty.

Walking carefully along, Val suddenly heard a muffled voice saying: "It will be too late in a few minutes. Too late. It's your last chance to help him. Who knew you were coming here?"

And Nancy's voice, shaken, desperate, denying, saying bravely: "No one knew. Let me think. I—I can't think. Give me time. Don't do anything to him—yet."

"Where is Tai Shan?"

"I don't know."

And Carl Zaken's harsh voice: "I have a way, Miss Fraser, of stimulating memory. Perhaps this will do."

Nancy cried out with pain.

Val sprang into the room through a red haze of anger. There, opposite the door, sat Nancy tied in a chair. And standing over her was the tall, stooped figure of the Black

Doctor, twisting one wrist cold-bloodedly and methodically.

On a table close by them rested the jade mask of the Emperor Kiang Hsi!

Nancy saw Val enter the room. Her eyes widened, her face puckered in astonishment through her pain at sight of his blood-smeared figure. Carl Zaken saw her face and whirled.

One look—and Zaken grabbed under his coat, under his left arm....

Val leaped at him, swinging the knife. The Black Doctor met him with a gun snapped out from a shoulder holster; a gun that roared, caught Val in mid-stride.

Val felt the shock of the bullet striking his shoulder, spinning him off balance, so that he staggered. That saved him from the second hasty shot that roared from Carl Zaken's gun, point blank; for this shot went between Val's arm and side. Val heard Nancy cry out with fear. And then he was on that tall, stooped figure whose pale cadaverous face was snarling like a death mask. Val knocked the gun away as the third shot roared out, slashed across and down with the knife.

The keen edge cut deep to the bone across Carl Zaken's knuckles.

The Black Doctor cried out with the pain of it. His nerveless fingers opened. The gun fell to the floor. Zaken scrambled back away from the menace of that flashing knife. He struck the table, knocked it over. The jade mask fell to the floor with a ringing sound. But such was the quality of that ancient jade that it did not break.

At the moment however Val had no thought for it as he followed that scrambling figure across the room. Carl Zaken caught a chair in passing, swung it around. Val threw up an arm. But the chair struck him heavily, drove him back, stopped him dead for a moment, dizzy with pain.

And in that moment the Black Doctor plunged to the side wall of the room bolted through a second door, slammed it. When Val reached it the door would not open. A bolt had been shot on the other side. The Black Doctor was gone. His voice, shouting, could be heard receding on the other side.

Val swung quickly, shaking his head to clear it. Quickly he cut Nancy loose from the chair.

"You're wounded! You're bleeding!"

"Never mind!" Val panted. "Come with me quick! We've got a chance to get out! A bare chance! God knows how many of them are in the house here!"

On the way to the door he scooped up the jade mask and the gun Zaken had dropped.

The hall was empty as he burst out into it ahead of Nancy.

But somewhere to the back voices were answering the Black Doctor's shouts.

"This way!" Val threw at her.

He led her to the end of the hall, past the great gong, up the steps to the dais, through the tapestry curtain and down across the big room where they had been trapped. Those three roaring shots, the Black Doctor's shouts had brought life to that ominously quiet house. As they neared the door which they had passed through earlier in the night, it opened and two blue clad Orientals, knives in hands, rushed through.

Val shot the first one without slackening his pace. The second one squealed with fright, doubled back through the door, slamming it—but not locking it. Val jerked it open, rushed through. The clamor behind them grew louder as more men joined in the pursuit.

That run to the front door seemed endless. But they made it without further opposition. The guard was gone. Charlie Gong had taken care of him. Val jerked the door in, kicked open the storm door—and suddenly they were both out in the dank, dark, fog-filled night.

The big ivy-covered stone house loomed behind them, black, seemingly deserted—but with the rising cacophony of furious pursuit sounding inside like a hive of bees erupting.

They stumbled down the steps. Headlights suddenly glowed through the fog ahead of them. Val raised the gun, shouting:

"Bradshaw! Bradshaw—where are you?"

And where the headlights were the voice of Bradshaw called: "Here!"

Bradshaw was by the car. It was Bradshaw who took in the situation in a flash, slid behind the wheel, stamped on the starter; and as they tumbled in the back started the big limousine with a lurch. They roared off into the fog just as pandemonium burst out of the house.

And the fog which, had veiled its mystery earlier, now saved them. It blotted out the trouble and pursuit behind. Bradshaw left his own car where he had parked it and drove swiftly to Westchester Avenue, to the first light, the first telephone.

And it ended that way. The house was deserted when the police squad got there. Charlie Gong, broken leg and cheerful grin, was in the well-like prison into which he had fallen. But Chang Ch'ien and Carl Zaken, the Black Doctor, were gone. There was no trace of Cartier Beurket's report. But Beurket was alive, could write another shortly.

And the mask, the precious jade mask of Emperor Kiang Hsi, was safe. No mad leader would incite yellow-skinned millions to follow the god of war!

THE EVIL
BRAND

THERE HE LAY ON A SLAB IN
THE MORGUE WITH THE SIGN
OF THE DRAGON SEARED INTO
HIS BACK. WHAT WAS THIS
INSIGNIA THAT BROUGHT DEATH
TO THOSE WHO WORE IT? WHY
SHOULD THE TRADE-MARK OF A
SAFFRON-SKINNED TERROR TONG
BE STENCILED ON A WHITE MAN'S
BODY?

CHAPTER ONE
THE DRAGON STRIKES

IN WASHINGTON, beside the White House, the ugly stone pile of the State, War and Navy Building dominates that stretch of Pennsylvania Avenue. In the labyrinth of high-ceilinged rooms inside, the mysterious machinery of government creaks slowly and methodically in aloof disdain of the busy streams of passing traffic outside.

Mr. Adolphus Crumpmeyer seemed to hesitate as he trudged up the gray painted wooden treads which had been erected over the wide stone steps. Mr. Crumpmeyer climbed with reluctance—the utter unwillingness of a nervous animal investigating a trap.

This, in a way, was strange when the full facts are known. Into the State, War and Navy Building, this particular afternoon, Adolphus Crumpmeyer was taking the backing of a powerful senator. In his pocket, on the busy senator's letterhead, was a highly praiseworthy recommendation of Mr. Crumpmeyer and an urgent endorsement of his mission.

Nevertheless Crumpmeyer was nervous.

He was short and pudgy and his smooth, finished pepper-and-salt suit was tucked neatly over a comfortable little badge of prosperity. His round face, pinked by the sun and the exertion of walking, was as smooth and

cherubic as a child's. Behind rimless noseglasses, Crumpmeyer's pale-blue eyes were artless and near-sighted. Few
more harmless appearing men had ever entered the State,
War and Navy Building.

At the top of the steps Crumpmeyer looked nervously
over his shoulder, then hurried inside.

A uniformed guard gave him a searching look.

The Sign of the Dragon was
blazoned there to mock us.

Crumpmeyer stopped, spoke to the guard nervously. "Where can I find Mr. Gregg's office?"

The harmless question got Crumpmeyer a second, more searching, scrutiny. The guard seemed suddenly suspicious of him.

"Gregg?" the guard repeated vaguely. "Sure that's the right name?"

Crumpmeyer blinked. "That is the name. He has an office here."

"What's your name?"

"Adolphus Crumpmeyer."

"Wait here," the guard directed.

He stepped to a nearby telephone, held low-voiced conversation while his eyes remained on Crumpmeyer. He was less suspicious when he left the telephone.

"Come with me," he ordered.

Adolphus Crumpmeyer could never have found that room himself. He was guided up an elevator, through endless corridors, past innumerable doors to an unlettered door no different from many others they had passed.

An aged negro sat outside at a little desk. He got to his feet, looked with suspicion at Crumpmeyer.

The guard said: "O.K., Charley. He's expected. The name's Crumpmeyer."

"Wait here, please, suh," the negro requested. He disappeared inside, returned in a moment. "This way, suh."

There was no anteroom. Crumpmeyer stepped directly into a large high-ceilinged room. A filing cabinet, several chairs, a rug and a single desk in a corner were the furnishings. At opposite ends of the room, portraits of Lincoln and Washington looked down upon the desk.

A heavyset, saturnine man stood up behind it, surveyed the visitor with a low-lidded stare, spoke gruffly: "Mr. Crumpmeyer?"

"Uh—yes. Is this—ah—Mr. Gregg?"

"Sit down."

Gregg sat, picked a cork-tipped cigarette from a copper ash tray, said curtly: "The senior senator from your state telephoned me that you had some facts I should hear."

Crumpmeyer nodded hastily. "He—seemed to think so. Uh—he gave me this letter and told me to come here. He—didn't say what department this was."

Gregg scanned the letter, laid it on the desk without enlightening Crumpmeyer.

"One of my men will be here in a moment," Gregg said. "I want him to hear your story. If your senator thinks it's so important, we'll give it every consideration."

Adolphus Crumpmeyer passed a handkerchief over his face as he waited. His nervousness was increasing.

THAT WAS the first thing Valentine Easton saw as he entered Gregg's office; the pudgy, pink-faced little man passing a handkerchief over his face with a nervous gesture.

Gregg said: "Mr. Easton—Mr. Crumpmeyer. Now let's have it, Mr. Crumpmeyer."

Crumpmeyer hesitated, then began his recital. "I—ah—am an import and export broker," he said. "A great deal of my business is done with Chinese scattered from Singapore to Shanghai. My contacts are rather extensive. Uh—at times I obtain information no one else could get."

Crumpmeyer brushed the handkerchief over his face again, looked inquiringly at Gregg. He ignored Valentine Easton. That young man resembled a young college professor, cheerful and harmless. Gregg, gruff and saturnine, was a reassuring force.

Gregg nodded slightly. Crumpmeyer went on. "Some—uh—three months ago, a Chinese gentleman came to this country with letters of introduction to me. He left the boat—and that was the last seen of him. Inquiries by the San Francisco police have turned up nothing so far. But—uh—in San Francisco's Chinatown there are rumors—"

Crumpmeyer's voice trailed off. He swallowed, obviously making heavy weather of it.

"Rumors?" Gregg prompted.

"That—that he was murdered," Crumpmeyer got out.

Valentine Easton asked casually: "Why should he have been murdered?"

Crumpmeyer stared from his pale blue eyes. "I—I'm not sure," he said uncertainly. "Rumors among the Chinese are vague. White men hear little of them. I am, perhaps, the only white man in the country who would hear such a thing."

"And what," Gregg asked impatiently, "did you hear?"

Crumpmeyer blinked, leaned forward, lowered his voice. "Among the Chinese there is an organization called the Sons of the Dragon. Highly secretive, very efficient, it has members on both sides of the Pacific. Each member, at the time of initiation, is branded on the back with the Mandarin character for 'dragon.' He—he is marked for life. And death alone can remove him from membership."

Gregg's face betrayed no emotion as he put the cork-tipped cigarette between his lips and drew slowly on it.

"Never heard of that before," he admitted. "What is the purpose of the organization?"

"Politics and the acquisition of money. Uh—I think I am safe in saying the Sons of the Dragon are the guiding force behind the present Nanking government. You might be surprised to know how many high officials over there carry the dragon symbol on their backs."

"Interesting," Gregg said.

"How do you happen to know so much about them, Mr. Crumpmeyer?" Valentine Easton asked.

Crumpmeyer smiled, a rather sickly smile. "My contacts are extensive. Information comes to me."

Crumpmeyer wet his lips. "Day after tomorrow," he continued, "Li Hung, a prominent member of the Chinese government, will land from the *Shanghai Queen* in San Francisco. He—is branded with the dragon mark. He is coming to the states ostensibly to confer with the State Department. I—uh—am informed that Li Hung will not reach Washington."

Gregg weighed the statement in silence. Valentine Easton said mildly: "What is your interest in this matter, Mr. Crumpmeyer?"

Crumpmeyer's pale blue eyes had a touch of fear this time. He was not as calm as he was trying to appear. "The man who carried letters of introduction to me a month ago was branded with the dragon, Mr. Easton. As—as a citizen I'm doing what I can to help the government. If anything happens to Li Hung it will mean international complications."

"What makes you so certain this Li Hung will run into trouble after he lands?" Gregg questioned bruskly.

CRUMPMEYER'S PLUMP hand shook slightly as he passed his handkerchief over his face again. "I can't tell you," he said. "But while calling on my senator on other matters, I mentioned this to him; and—and he thought it important enough to send me here. Do you think you'll do anything about it?"

Crumpmeyer was unable to conceal his eagerness as he awaited Gregg's reply.

Gregg shrugged. "Perhaps," he said noncommittally. "Is that all you have to tell us?"

"I think so."

"I want your sources of information, Crumpmeyer."

But Crumpmeyer shook his head with a firmness he hitherto had not shown. "I'm sorry," he refused. "That is impossible. It was all confidential."

Gregg made no effort to persuade him. "Thank you for telling us," he said, standing. "Where are you staying?"

"At the Mayflower," Crumpmeyer said as he stood up also. "But I'm taking the train tonight for San Francisco. If you wish to get in touch with me, Crumpmeyer and Company is well known." Crumpmeyer moistened his lips again, hesitated. "I'm very curious," he said, "as to what you intend to do."

"Can't say whether we'll do anything," Gregg told him gruffly. "We'll get in touch with you if it's necessary."

Adolphus Crumpmeyer departed, leaving the impression that he was disappointed.

Gregg sat down, smoked for a moment in silence. His glance at Val Easton had no expression.

"What d'you make of it?" Gregg queried.

"Hard to say, Chief. Rather queer, isn't?"

"Damn queer," Gregg grunted. "If he's right and anything happens to this Li Hung, there'll be a stir in the State Department that will make history. The situation in the Orient is critical enough now without having one of China's statesmen murdered over here."

"Queer we didn't know Li Hung was coming over here," Val Easton mused. "Hasn't the State Department said anything about it?"

"Not a word. Nothing from our agents in China either."

"Sons of the Dragon. Brands on their backs. Sounds like a pipe-dream."

"Live and learn," said Gregg.

Val Easton grinned as he stood up. "At least live. Any orders on this. Chief?"

"Not yet," said Gregg. "I'll have San Francisco check Crumpmeyer at once; and I'll radio the *Shanghai Queen* and see if this Li Hung is aboard under his own name or an assumed one. You might ask the senator from California what he knows about Crumpmeyer and why he thought the man's story important enough to relay to us."

Val Easton was on his way out of the room when the telephone burred sharply on Gregg's desk. He was at the door when Gregg said sharply; "The devil! Thanks for calling me."

Gregg's chair creaked as he sprang to his feet.

"Hell's to pay now, Easton. Crumpmeyer has just been murdered in front of the building! The guard who brought him up saw it and telephoned me! Let's get down there!"

GREGG TOOK the lead down the hall, almost running to the elevator. The guard who had telephoned was at this post. Pale, excited, he said: "I thought you'd want to know about it right away, Mr. Gregg! He had just reached the sidewalk when a taxicab pulled in to the curb. This Crumpmeyer looked into it and started to run back here in the building. A gun muzzle was thrust out of the taxi window. A—a machine gun I think it was. A burst of shots hit Crumpmeyer in the back. He fell there on the sidewalk and—and I ran to telephone you."

"What happened to the taxi?" Val demanded.

"It turned north off the avenue and disappeared by the park there. It was gone before the traffic cop on the corner could leave his post."

Out on the sidewalk a crowd had formed, growing swiftly as others ran up. Gregg stayed there at the door probing for facts. "What kind of a taxi was it?"

"A yellow cab, I think."

"You *think?* Don't you know?"

"I—I was watching Crumpmeyer," the guard explained hastily. "He acted peculiar when he went out. He stopped and hesitated in the doorway, looking up and down the street. He acted like someone might be out there whom he was afraid of. That's why I watched him clear out to the sidewalk."

Gregg said: "Let's have a look at this, Easton."

Adolphus Crumpmeyer had fallen at the inner edge of the sidewalk. The traffic cop from the corner was trying to get the crowd back from the body. Two other policemen ran up, began to clear a space. One of them said loudly: "I'll report it!"

A woman cried with a trace of hysteria: "I saw it! I was right behind him when the shots were fired! I saw him fall! My God, ain't it awful?"

The nearest cop was young, husky, excited. "Did you get the taxi license number lady?"

"Of course not! I thought I was going to faint!"

She was stout, belligerent, excited; and she turned with a challenging manner to a thin little man in a brown suit who said: "I saw it too, officer. I got the license number. Here—I wrote it down."

Pursing his lips with satisfaction, he tore a page from a small note book. The cop snatched it, snapped to his brother officer: "I'll turn this in for a broadcast! Out of the way, you people! Let me through!"

He plowed through the crowd and ran toward the corner.

Adolphus Crumpmeyer would never be deader than he was now. He lay on his face. Half a dozen bullet holes were visible in the blood-stained back of his pepper-and-salt coat.

Gregg eyed the body for a moment, shrugged, spoke to Val out of the corner of his mouth.

"Stick with this and find out what you can."

There was not, at the moment, much to find out. The thing had happened so suddenly that all witnesses had been caught off guard. Their stories added nothing to what the guard had said. The shots had come from a taxicab. A yellow cab. Crumpmeyer had dropped. The taxicab had raced from the spot and vanished.

An ambulance from Emergency Hospital just around the corner, was at the curb in an incredibly short time.

Squad cars from police headquarters arrived just after it. Other policemen had appeared. The crowd was hustled back. Names of witnesses were taken. Newspaper men arrived. A cameraman managed to snap some pictures.

And finally all that was left of Adolphus Crumpmeyer, of San Francisco, was loaded into the ambulance and started toward the morgue.

VAL EASTON taxied to the morgue following the ambulance closely. He wanted several things. Among them a set of Crumpmeyer's fingerprints. That was mere routine. The senior senator from California would not vouch for a man, as he had Crumpmeyer, if there was any doubt about the chap. Gregg would even now be having Crumpmeyer investigated in San Francisco.

But there was a mystery here; everything about Crumpmeyer was mysterious. His visit to Gregg's office could not be laid entirely to anxiety over the fate of Li Hung. Fear had come into Gregg's office with Adolphus Crumpmeyer.

They were hardboiled at the morgue. A redfaced assistant snapped: "Nothing doing on that guy just now! Wait'll the coroner gets through with him!"

Val palmed a small Department of Justice shield. He did not belong to the Department of Justice. But his name was on file there. In emergencies he could pass as a Department of Justice man. Often it smoothed the way. It did so now.

The belligerent attendant waved him inside, grumbling: "Whyn't you say so in the first place? I ain't a mind-reader. You guys all look alike to me."

The coroner was waiting while an attendant removed the clothes from Crumpmeyer's body. As the torso was bared, Val suddenly requested: "Turn his back up. I want to see that mark."

And as Crumpmeyer's back was bared, the morgue assistant swore under his breath. "Geez! Look't that! It's been burned in the skin!"

They gathered close, looking down at the mark which had caught Val's eye. On the white skin between Adolphus Crumpmeyer's shoulders a livid brand stood out starkly.

Val Easton could not read Chinese. It was not necessary. He knew Adolphus Crumpmeyer had been branded with the dragon sign. Crumpmeyer belonged to the Sons of the Dragon; the members of which, by his own words, could not withdraw until death. Now here on the cold morgue slab, Adolphus Crumpmeyer lay dead.

CHAPTER TWO
MARK OF THE RING

IN HIS office Gregg said: "San Francisco just telephoned. They report that Crumpmeyer and Company has been in business for ten years. The firm's rating is excellent. Crumpmeyer is a widower. Has one daughter. Nothing against him."

Val Easton said: "The Bureau of Identification at the Department of Justice is checking his fingerprints. I've just come from the senator's office. He was surprised but not greatly upset by Crumpmeyer's death. Seems he doesn't know a great deal about Crumpmeyer. Crumpmeyer was a campaign contributor. The senator had met him once or twice in San Francisco; that's all. He was able to tell me Crumpmeyer's daughter acted as her father's secretary; and he confessed that he was a bit puzzled himself as to the why of Crumpmeyer's visit to his office. There was some vague talk about using senatorial influence to cut down some import duties; and then the story which Crumpmeyer told us. The senator said Crumpmeyer was visibly agitated. He asked the senator himself as to who could best handle it—and then insisted the senator use his influence to do something about Li Hung. The senator sent him over here because the thing had an international angle. The senator wasn't sure, at the time, that it wasn't all a pipe-dream. But a man who shells out for election expenses has to be humored."

Gregg drummed slowly on the desk with his finger tips. His glance lifted to the portrait of George Washington on the end wall above his desk.

"Hardly a pipe-dream," he said slowly. "Dreams don't mow a man down with a machine gun. The brand on his back is proof he wasn't lying."

"A white man," said Val, "belonging to a Chinese secret society."

Gregg's next remark was a flat statement. "We're going to find more to this than we think."

The telephone rang. Gregg answered it, listened a moment, spoke a few brief words and put the receiver back.

"The Department of Justice reports that the fingerprints you left tally with a set made about twelve years ago in Manhattan. Crumpmeyer was picked up and later released on suspicion of murder. His name was John Brandt. He was suspected of murdering a Chinaman named Wo Hung."

They looked at one another.

"And two years later," Val said thoughtfully, "he was an importer in San Francisco."

Gregg said: "The yellow cab, from which the shots presumably were fired, has been located on upper Connecticut Avenue. The driver who took it out this morning has vanished. It may be days before they get any further with that angle—if they ever do. You'd better take the next plane to San Francisco. You've just about time to get there before the *Shanghai Queen* docks. Her captain reports by radio that a Chinese by the name of Li Hung is traveling first class."

Gregg pulled strings like that. The bare Washington office was the center of a far flung web—a hidden web—unsuspected—unknown. Gregg was not even the man's right name. Gregg was the code word for "chief." The actions of the men he directed were a mystery to all but him. Men acting on Gregg's orders had died before firing squads in foreign countries and the Department of State had blandly denied knowledge of them.

Val Easton, roaring west out of New York before midnight, might have been the young college professor he resembled or an alert young business man. Certainly there was nothing about him to suggest his errand.

A ROUND dozen passengers were Val's companions on the plane. He scanned them all carefully. None looked suspicious; but he was wary—and remained so. The sudden and mysterious death of Adolphus Crumpmeyer was all the proof needed that much was going on under the surface. Crumpmeyer had been followed to Gregg's office. His errand had evidently been known. So the men who had killed Crumpmeyer so boldly and recklessly would not be apt to stop at anything.

At Cleveland, an hour and fifteen minutes after midnight, a man and a woman got off and three men got on. Business men obviously.

At Chicago there was a general shifting of passengers. Seven left the plane and five got on.

The fifth, the last one to enter, was a Chinaman.

Val was alert instantly. But this particular Oriental did nothing to justify suspicion. Small—Cantonese probably from his slight stature—he was somewhere in his middle or late thirties. He wore a neat gray suit, a dark hat, and carried a light traveling case unobtrusively to the front seat across the aisle.

Thereafter, as they flew through the dawn into Omaha, the Oriental displayed no interest in any of the passengers seated behind him. For the most part he dozed. At Omaha, Val, heard him speak to the stewardess in perfect English.

Probably an American-born, certainly an American-educated, Chinaman.

The other new passenger, who caught Val's eye at Chicago, was a young woman. Certainly the youngest and prettiest of the three women in the plane. She was small, almost doll-like, with tiny hands and feet. Her face was pert and impudent. Her red hair had a saucy wave in it. Eager, alert, interested, her eyes were everywhere, and when she tried to read a magazine her interest did not stay with it long. After the gray dawn gave way to sunlight, she watched the ground.

The air was rough for a time. Through one unusually heavy air-pocket, when the plane dropped plummet-like, she gasped and clutched the side of the seat. Her glance turned despairingly across the aisle and met Val's. He smiled reassuringly. She smiled back faintly. At Omaha, as they got out to stretch their legs, Val spoke to her: "A bit rough back there."

She looked up with a saucy tilt of her head and the same faint smile.

"Wasn't it?" she agreed. "The first time it happened I thought we were going to the ground. I was frightened. You see—this is the first time I've ever been in the air."

"You'll get used to it."

"I suppose so," she agreed. "I haven't been sick yet. Everyone told me I would be. Will I?"

Val chuckled. "Everyone hasn't ridden in a plane—and everyone doesn't get sick. Going through to the coast?"

She nodded. "I hope I'm going to like that too. I've never been to San Francisco before. Are you going there?"

She was so doll-like, so pert with her red hair and her sparkling manner that Val smiled indulgently down at her.

"I am," he said. "You'll like it."

She laughed. "Perhaps I'll see you there then. I'm going to see everything—the waterfront, Chinatown, the Golden Gate. I've always wanted to."

Val chuckled. "Perhaps we'll run across each other. If we do, I may have time to show you some sights you've never seen before."

"Oh—I wish you would. Is that a promise?"

"If we run across each other."

She warned: "I'll remember that."

They were soon boring into the west toward Cheyenne. And presently the copilot came back into the cabin with a folded sheet of paper. Bending over, he asked: "Are you Mr. Easton?"

Val nodded.

"Picked up a message for you."

THE CO-PILOT looked curious as he lingered a moment while Val scanned the sheet of paper. It was in code—from Gregg of course. The gibberish must have bewildered the man who picked it off the air.

Long practice in decoding such messages enabled Val to decipher it quickly with his eyes. It read: *Fraser flying from San Diego to assist if needed. S-19, Hopkins, waiting at St. Francis Hotel. Chinese Ambassador expecting Li Hung. Use any measure needed. Signed, Gregg.*

Val folded the paper and slipped it in his pocket. The case was getting more important. Gregg had dispatched Nancy Fraser from San Diego.

The plane dipped, swerved. A flash of light from up front struck Val's eye. It was gone instantly, but Val knew what had made it and why.

The Oriental in that front seat had been holding a small pocket-mirror so that he could look over his shoulder. The plane's swerve had thrown sunlight on the mirror. The beam had reflected back. And Val knew then he had been under observation since leaving Chicago. The message delivered by the co-pilot had undoubtedly inspired this last scrutiny.

Nerves tightening, Val looked out of the window. He had not left Washington and New York unobserved. Orders had been sent ahead for this man to board the plane. It took an organization to work as smoothly as that.

Thinking back, Val could not recall anyone who might have been watching him. But that little pocket mirror, that unobtrusive Oriental flying west with him cried trouble, danger, perhaps death. Crumpmeyer had died.

At the moment, however, there was nothing to do but ride west through the sky.

Noon—Salt Lake City. A fifteen-minute wait, and then the last leg over the dry Utah desert, the towering coast range and San Francisco.

The desert fell behind. The big multi-motored plane began climbing high for the passage over the jagged peaks ahead. The air was rough again when the slender Chinaman left his seat and walked back in the aisle. He lurched, clutched the seat backs as he advanced. His face as he passed Val was a bland, inscrutable mask.

Yet under the prominent cheek bones was the faintest hint of a smile. Val had seen that look before on men certain of their ground, disdainful of an adversary.

In the pass the air grew rougher. The pert little redhead across the aisle gripped her seat often. She looked slightly ill. Her glance finally went despairingly to Val; she leaned over to speak to him. Val bent toward her.

"How long is th-this going to last?" she asked.

"Not very long. Feeling bad?"

She nodded. And in that moment the plane gave a lurch. Someone staggered against Val from behind. A hand slid across his neck. A flick of pain followed.

In his ear a voice spoke in suave apology. "So sorry, my dear sir. I was thrown off balance."

It was the Chinaman, smiling apologetically as he clung to the edge of the seat ahead.

Val put a handkerchief to his neck. The white linen came away with a tiny smear of red.

"What the devil did you cut my neck with?" Val demanded.

The man leaned close. "I beg your pardon?" He was smiling placatingly.

The question repeated brought a regretful shake of the head. "I don't understand you, sir."

"My neck, blast it! you cut my neck. I want to know," said Val, "what did it. Where's the ring which was on your finger?"

A faint red line circled the forefinger of the saffron hand gripping the seat. A ring had been on that finger in the last few minutes, pressing into the flesh. It was gone now. The man was denying it with another shake of his head, speaking low.

"I wear no ring, sir. You are mistaken—mistaken."

The smile was broad; the saffron face was beaming; the beady black eyes dancing a little. Wavering. The whole cabin was wavering—

Val suddenly felt giddy, light-headed. Strength seemed to be draining out of his body. The broad smile on the yellow face so close to his looked more like a leer.

Val stood up—and he made it slowly, painfully, while the cabin whirled, blurred. The mocking smile did not go away. The beady eyes watched his face.

That was the last thing Val remembered—beady eyes fixed on his face as he staggered. He tried to cry out. It stuck in his throat. The plane lurched. His knees buckled. He fell—into yellow arms waiting to receive him. Then blackness.

A MAN'S voice said:

"He's coming out of it. Strangest case I've seen in a long time."

A woman's voice said: "It couldn't be air sickness."

"Not at all. It doesn't get them like this. His heart is sound. Seemingly nothing organically wrong. Very strange."

Val opened his eyes. The crisp, white-clad form of a nurse was bending over him. She was smiling as she asked: "How do you feel?"

Val felt like the devil but did not say so.

A hand—not her hand—lifted his wrist. Turning his head on the pillow, Val saw a white-coated interne taking his pulse. The interne smiled with professional reassurance.

"You're coming out of it fine, old man. Pulse picking up every minute. Ever have this happen to you before?"

"No. What happened?"

He was very weak. It was hard to talk. But his mind—foggy when he first heard them talking—was clearing quickly. Val remembered the beady eyes, the mocking smile, the whirling plane-cabin. He tried to sit up. The nurse helped him and put pillows against his back.

They had taken only his coat and shirt. The coat was on the chair at the foot of the bed. He asked for it. The nurse handed it to him.

"Your billfold and watch are in the office safe," she told him.

Val felt in the coat pocket. Gregg's code message was not there.

"Were any papers taken out and put in the safe?" he demanded.

The nurse said: "I took your watch and billfold. No papers were in your coat."

"Doctor, look at my neck. There's a scratch there."

"Only a slight one. You must have gotten when you collapsed in the plane."

"Would it be possible, doctor, for something to be administered in that scratch which would knock me out in a few minutes?"

The interne frowned slightly, rubbed his chin. "I suppose so, if anyone was interested enough to try it—and had the chance."

"I suppose this is San Francisco?"

"You were brought here from the flying field."

"I'm ready to leave now."

"I wouldn't advise it," said the interne. "Rest up tonight and we'll turn you out fit as a fiddle in the morning."

"I'm leaving now. Call a taxi."

They had to help him into the taxi; but by the time the driver stopped before the St. Francis, Val was feeling strong enough to get out by himself.

His watch showed a little after seven thirty in the evening. He had been unconscious for some hours. Ordering the desk clerk to get his bag from the airport, Val went up to his room and telephoned Hopkins in the latter's room.

"This is Easton," Val said. "I'm in Six-ten. Is Miss Fraser here yet?"

"She flew in today."

"Bring her along."

In a few minutes they knocked. Val opened the door. Nancy Fraser came in first. And Val felt better at sight of her.

In all the world there was hardly a girl to equal Nancy Fraser. Tales of Nancy Fraser's daring ingenuity had become classics of the service.

But with all that she was Nancy Fraser—a little beauty, softly feminine, with clean-cut features, sun-tanned, a fairly wide mouth which quirked humorously at the corners. Nancy's silky platinum-blond hair was cut short and waved to her head in a style almost mannish. And Nancy had a pair of the deepest and bluest eyes Val had ever seen.

Those blue eyes now showed quick concern as Nancy faced him in the room.

"Val Easton. What is it? You look pale and shaky, as if you've been terribly ill."

"Tell you about it in a minute. Hello, Hopkins. I've heard about you."

They looked at one another curiously, these two whose orders came from Gregg's office in Washington—and yet who might never have seen one another if Adolphus Crumpmeyer had not been riddled with machine gun bullets.

Hopkins was a tall, bony young man, solemn and quiet. His big hand engulfed Val's.

"I've been wondering what happened to you," Hopkins said. "Knew you were due in on the afternoon plane. When you didn't show up I thought you'd probably stopped off on some business before you registered here."

Nancy Fraser dropped on the edge of the bed. Val sat beside her. Hopkins took a chair, saying: "I'm curious. Washington ordered arrangements made to take you out on the pilot boat to meet the *Shanghai Queen* in the morning. Nothing more, except that I'm to take orders from you."

"And I," said Nancy Fraser, "don't know a darn thing either—except I'm here to take orders. It's all very curious, Val. I had my hands full down in San Diego."

Val offered them cigarettes, held a match to Nancy's and to his own.

"A bit of mystery," he said. "One man dead already. I think murder was attempted on me in the plane this afternoon. Almost got me too."

He told them what he knew, what had happened since Crumpmeyer's visit to Gregg's office.

"Gregg's code message is gone," Val said. "That Chinaman got it. No use trying to locate him now. He's gone underground in the Chinese colony here. That's that. He must have been certain I was done for. I don't think anyone tailed me from the hospital."

Nancy Fraser put her finger unerringly on the kernel of the matter. "If they tried to kill you before you got here, that means, they're planning something. They want you out of the way before you cause them any trouble."

"Exactly."

Nancy crinkled her nose thoughtfully.

"I've never heard of anything so fantastic and gruesome as these Sons of the Dragon. That brand on the back.

Ugggh! I wouldn't believe it if you hadn't seen the mark with your own eyes."

"Neither would I," Val admitted. "But I saw it on Crump-meyer's back. It's so." Hopkins leaned forward, elbows on his knees, speaking seriously.

"I've spent eight years here on the Pacific coast. Where the Chinese are concerned, anything can happen. You dig under one layer and you find another; and under that another. They're clannish, they're secretive, they can be dangerous. If you had any idea who was behind this—"

Nancy was grave too; but her mind did not seem to be on what Hopkins was saying. A faint dread was stirring back of her face. Her voice dropped, as if she was fearful that even here in the room words might be overheard.

"Val—do you suppose it could be—the Black Doctor? And—and Chang Ch'ien?"

CHAPTER THREE
TAI SHAN

THEIR EYES met. The dread was there. Val felt a slight chill crawl between his shoulder blades. Carl Zaken, the Black Doctor, whose fame had seeped for years through the shady channels of international espionage like a dark miasma. And Chang Ch'ien, the huge, gold-en-skinned Oriental who had cast his lot in with the Black Doctor's in a series of wild, fantastic plans which could have sprung only from the brains of men drunk with power and half mad with fantastic visions.

The very mention of the names seemed to spread a chill.

"They've been quiet for months," Val said. "They were both injured. For all we know one or both is dead."

"And—if they're not, Val?"

"Then—it could be—"

Nancy drew a deep breath. She was not frightened. Val knew her too well to believe that. But—the Black Doctor and Chang Ch'ien. Nancy drew that deep breath—

"If either of them have anything to do with this, we'll know it soon," Nancy said. "Carl Zaken hates you—hates me. He'll strike—and strike to kill at the first chance. What is the first thing, Val?"

Hopkins had been watching them closely, listening intently. He started as the telephone rang. It rang again as Val and Nancy looked at it, and then at each other.

"No one knows I'm here," Val said, getting up. "I left no address at the hospital. My call to Hopkins' room is the only contact I've made."

The telephone rang a third time, sharply, insistently as he picked it up.

A woman's voice said: "Is this Mr. Easton?"

"Who is talking?"

She said: "This is Susan Crumpmeyer, Mr. Easton. I must see you. Can you come out here to the house?"

"How did you get my name, Miss Crumpmeyer?"

"A Mr. Gregg telephoned from Washington. He told me you would be at the St. Francis and asked me to call you."

Her voice was clear, distinct, controlled and rather sad. That was understandable.

"You know about your father, I suppose?" Val asked her.

He thought she sobbed then—just once—as an admirable self control gave way. But only for a moment. She spoke steadily again.

"Yes—I know. The newspaper men have been here. Washington wired and Mr. Gregg telephoned. I must see you this evening, Mr. Easton."

"You're at home now, Miss Crumpmeyer?"

"Yes."

"Wait there by the telephone a moment. I'll call you back."

Val hung up, opened the telephone directory.

Nancy Fraser stood up, concern on her face. "Was that Crumpmeyer's daughter, Val?"

"Yes. I'm going to call her back as a matter of precaution."

"How did she know you were here at the hotel?"

"Gregg telephoned her. Asked her to look me up here at the hotel."

"But—but he sent you no word of it?"

"Probably didn't think it necessary." Val ran his finger down the "C's."

"Here it is—Waller Street."

He gave the number. In a moment the clear, controlled voice answered.

"Good evening again, Mr. Easton."

"I merely wanted to make certain, Miss Crumpmeyer. I'll see you shortly."

As he turned away from the telephone, Nancy said dubiously: "It's queer Gregg would telephone her and not send you word."

"He may have forgotten it, or may have sent a second message to the plane which arrived after I lost consciousness. Since I slipped out of the hospital and came straight here without a word to anyone, there'd be no chance to deliver it. Hopkins, what kind of neighborhood is Waller Street?"

"Fair," Hopkins replied. "It's out toward Golden Gate Park."

"Got a car?"

"At the garage."

"Run me out there, please. She was her father's secretary. She must know something about this. He couldn't have hidden everything from her."

Nancy said: "I'd like to go along."

"No need for it," Val told her. "You've had a hard day. Turn in early and get some rest. You'll be busy enough when Li Hung leaves the boat tomorrow."

Nancy made a *moue*, said: "I'm not sleepy. I'll wait here until you return."

VAL WAS himself again as he walked to the garage with Hopkins. The scratch on his neck was inflamed, sore under the gauze and tape the interne had put over it. But his strength was back, his mind clear.

Hopkins drove up brightly lighted Market Street, turned into Waller, skirted Buena Vista Park and came, finally, to the address they sought.

The hour was nine thirty. Few automobiles were on the street in this residential neighborhood. Crumpmeyer's home was a two-story, tapestry-brick house.

The owner of a successful importing business could have lived in a larger, more expensive place. But, like Crumpmeyer himself, the house looked comfortable, respectable, modest.

The front windows downstairs were lighted. An automobile stood at the curb.

"Friends in with her," Hopkins guessed as he stopped behind the other car. "Shall I go in?"

"Might be best to wait out here," Val suggested, getting out. "She'll probably talk more freely if she's alone with me."

The front doorbell was promptly answered by a Chinese houseboy wearing a white coat and black alpaca trousers. He stared without speaking.

"Miss Crumpmeyer."

The boy stepped back, opening the door wide as he bowed. "You come in, please. I tell Miss Clumpmeyah."

The inside was severely ultra-modern. No suggestion of the orient, other than the China boy; and here in San Francisco his type was common. He ushered Val into a large living room, dimly lighted by one floor lamp in a corner.

"I tell Miss Clumpmeyah," he said again, and vanished.

Val remained standing, wondering if she would resemble her father. Wondering too if she would talk freely. There was so much to learn, and quickly too. If she could tell him what contacts her father had maintained among the local Chinese colony, there would be something to work on. For there was no doubt that Crumpmeyer's death had a direct connection with that livid brand on his back.

And as her father's secretary, she might make suggestions which would connect this business with the infamous Carl Zaken.

If the car outside had brought guests, they were in another part of the house. The quiet was intense. The second hand of a chromium-finished electric clock on a mantel moved steadily, noiselessly around the dial. Val caught himself staring at it, and a black glass panel behind it, knowing that furtive, hidden moves in this matter were going on as steadily and unobtrusively as the progress of that second hand.

At the back of the room was a curtained doorway. In the semi-gloom, the black glass panel acted as an excellent mirror. Reflected there Val could just see the curtains at the back of the room. They parted noiselessly. A white face stared through at him.

Whistling softly between his teeth, Val stared past the clock at the glass—and the reflected face. A woman's face. A woman who did not want her presence known as she surveyed him.

In the black glass the dark curtains were invisible. The white face swam there in a small ghostly blur, pale and beautiful. But there was enough form to it to show the high cheekbones, the dark vivid mouth, the strange lurking beauty. Expressionless as the features of Buddha, the blurred beauty was as striking as that of a lotus flower in full bloom.

Through the room—or it might only have been through Val alone—crept a new, sudden feeling of danger. Without a move being made, a sound audible, the danger was there. Out of the past, memories of that face swept back over Val Easton's mind.

This was not the daughter of Adolphus Crumpmeyer. This woman had no business in the house. Her presence meant danger greater than he thought existed this night.

Val spoke without turning his head. "Good evening, Tai Shan."

In the glass the blurred face remained motionless for a moment; then it swam slowly toward him. Val turned to meet it.

IN SPITE of himself he drew a breath of startled appreciation. She was lovelier, if possible, than she had ever been before, this strange, exotic woman from the East. This Tai Shan, sister of Chang Ch'ien.

Tonight she wore smooth black satin which sheathed every soft curve of her slender little figure. Jet black hair framed the creamy skin of her face. Her mouth was red and vivid. She was, Val thought again—as he had in the past—like a figure out of an old Chinese print, mysterious, inscrutable, incredibly lovely as she came slowly and noiselessly across the rug toward him.

"Good evening, Val Easton," she said.

Her voice was low, clear, musical, as striking as the rest of her. She was not smiling. Grave and self-possessed she stopped and looked at him.

Val smiled with a twist of his lips which had little humor.

"I hardly looked for you here, Tai Shan. But I might have known. I thought there was something familiar about that voice over the telephone. You were calling for Miss Crumpmeyer."

She nodded assent. Her grave musical voice told him. "Miss Crumpmeyer is indisposed."

"I have no doubt of it," Val assented. "Is she—er—still alive?"

Tai Shan looked at him with brooding, inscrutable eyes. "She is alive."

Tai Shan never lied. If she said Susan Crumpmeyer was alive, it was so.

Val smiled again, crookedly. "That's something. She's having a little better luck than her father—so far. I was wondering if your brother and Carl Zaken weren't mixed up in this. Thanks for making it certain."

Inside Val felt no gratitude. He had been summoned here. Tai Shan had called him. He had walked into as neat a trap as could be devised. Even a bulge of the small automatic under his left arm was not too reassuring.

Near Tai Shan was always her brother, Chang Ch'ien. And where Chang Ch'ien was, there would be Carl Zaken, the Black Doctor. And stalking at the heels of that pair was always—death.

She stood there in the semi-gloom, slender, lovely—and sad-seeming. Her musical voice was sorrowful.

"You are young, Val Easton," Tai Shan said. "And brave and reckless. I think I am wasting my breath— Here in San Francisco you are going to die."

Tai Shan paused. Her small rounded bosom lifted and fell as she drew and exhaled a slight, inaudible breath. Almost a sigh.

"That," Val told her smiling, "is a moot question. I seem to recall other times when I was due to die."

Her glance was brooding.

"This time it will be different," Tai Shan said with a lack of emotion which carried conviction. "You have intruded into something this time which will destroy you. You were summoned here to this house to—die."

"I can't think of a lovelier decoy, Tai Shan."

She closed her eyes for an instant. A faint quiver was visible in her creamy throat. Behind that lovely, emotionless face Tai Shan was fighting emotion. Her voice could not entirely hide it when she opened her eyes and spoke.

"I did not want to do this—no!" said Tai Shan abruptly. "I did want to do it. I wanted to see you, Val Easton. I wanted to talk to you face to face. Perhaps you will listen to me here. Perhaps I can make you see. Take the first plane or boat out of San Francisco and—and forget this. You will be safe then. I will see that you are allowed to go."

This lovely creature wished to protect him. She had saved his life before. She was willing to do it again—if he turned his back on all that he had been ordered to do.

"And if I don't, Tai Shan?"

"You will die," said Tai Shan. "Die here—tonight—in this house. I can't save you. I can't...."

HER WHISPER trailed away. The room was silent about them. In the shadows her strange, exotic beauty was like a flame dwarfing the memory of every other woman Val had ever known; and, as in the sinister beauty of flame, there was also the threat of danger, of pain and cruel hurt.

Tai Shan was incredibly lovely. Tai Shan was incredibly dangerous. That danger was here in the room about her, about them both.

Val felt its presence. He could throttle her with his hands. He could send a bullet smashing into her slender body. He could break for the door and safety. Yet he knew he could do none of those things—because none of them were possible. Tai Shan would not be here in the room, seemingly alone with him, if escape were possible.

He could lie to her also—and he did not consider it.

"I think you know," Val said gently, "that I am not going to run out of town."

Tai Shan sighed. She seemed to droop, nodding slowly.

"I know," she said almost inaudibly. "I knew it when you came. I'm sorry—Goodby."

Val slid a hand under his left arm. The cool grip of the automatic was reassuring. "Stand still, Tai Shan," he ordered.

She made no move to depart. Relaxed, drooping, she watched him. Her regard was sorrowful, distant, as if already a great gulf had opened between them.

Without moving Tai Shan uttered one high, musical word in Chinese.

And the single floorlamp went out. The hall light—all the visible lights on the lower floor were extinguished. Thick, velvety blackness engulfed them.

And when Val jumped to the spot where Tai Shan had been standing, she was not there.

CHAPTER FOUR

THE BLACK DOCTOR

WHEN HIS hands found empty space, Val had the choked feeling of suffocation. The blackness, the silence was the trap. Tai Shan had vanished without a sound.

Val's rush carried him to the curtains. They hung without movement. He turned, rigid, listening, gun gripped in his hand.

Inside the room and outside it no movement was audible. But movement there was—an unseen presence. On his toes, noiselessly, Val started toward the center of the room, damning himself silently as he did so. He should have brought Hopkins in with him. Outside Hopkins was waiting patiently—as useless as if he were miles away. Now that he thought of it, Hopkins had probably not even brought a gun. Before Hopkins could get into the house, the death Tai Shan had promised could strike. And Hopkins, if called now, would only blunder into the same peril.

Slowly Val crept toward the front of the room. The nerves of his skin crawled as he thought of the single slight scratch which had almost caused his death that afternoon. Another one here in the dark, deeper, more certain, would succeed this time.

He came to the hall door. He listened. The blackness pressed in like fluid pitch. Three steps away the front door waited—and beyond it the open night and safety. Perhaps Tai Shan had exaggerated. Perhaps the way was open.

Val lunged for the door. His hand found the knob, turned it—

Then, over him dropped folds of heavy woolen cloth. He never heard the naked feet which suddenly were all about him. Hands pawed at him, caught at him. Fold after fold of cloth wrapped him about, smothering, enveloping....

His shoe trod heavily on bare toes, bringing a grunt of pain beside him. He got the automatic around and fired through the cloth.

The crash of the sound deafened him. The biting powder fumes came up to choke him. He felt a hand release him. Heard dimly the groan of a wounded man. But there were others.

Hands caught the gun through the cloth, bearing the muzzle down toward the floor. A sinewy arm went around his neck. A heavy object struck his head. A leg tripped him.

Smothering, groggy, helpless, Val went to the floor there inside the door, only a step from safety.

He went down wondering whether Hopkins had heard the shot and would know what to do.

Silently Val was rolled tightly in the heavy folds. Helpless and inarticulate he was lifted, carried back through the house hurriedly.

Two doorways was passed. He was bundled down steps. The grateful tang of fresh night air seeped through the cloth. He was cramped, crowded, pushed into an automobile and left lying on another squirming object easily recognizable as a body.

The body emitted furious muffled oaths near Val's ear as the automobile started with a jerk. Distorted though they were, the oaths were plainly coming from Hopkins.

The woolen cloth was scorching around the bullet hole where it had ignited. The rank smell came up around Val's face, making breathing almost impossible. A hand slapped hard at the charring fibers and put them out.

Gasping for breath, Val called: "Hopkins?"

"Yes!"

"How are you?"

And, under him, Hopkins answered bitterly: "All right, I guess, if you'll get off my face! I thought the mugs had killed you!"

Val squirmed over. They were in the back of the automobile, half on the seat, half crammed down into the foot space. Other men were back there with them; two, Val thought. For the moment the two seemed satisfied to let the prisoners adjust themselves.

"I don't seem to be dead yet," Val said through the cloth.

Hopkins was still bitter. "You probably will be soon enough. They're quite business like. Two of them popped up at my car doors and shoved guns under my nose. I didn't have a chance. I hope the gentle little lady said more to you than those two Chinks did to me."

"I didn't see Crumpmeyer's daughter."

"I didn't think so," Hopkins admitted, trying to wiggle into a more comfortable position. "Where was she?"

"God knows."

"When Gregg hears about this," Hopkins groaned, "he'll hit the ceiling." Despite pain in the head from the blow which had been dealt him, and the gravity of their position, Val had to chuckle.

"If you're right, it won't matter much to us what Gregg does," he said.

AT THE moment they could do nothing. After turning several corners the automobile rolled at a slower pace. Taking no chances, Val guessed, on being stopped by a speed cop.

He was sure Tai Shan was not in the car. She had warned him; had given him a chance; and then she had abandoned him. He felt no resentment. Her regret had been too genuine.

That ride seemed endless. Val heard the clang of streetcar bells, the scrambled noises of traffic in the business district. It died away. Shortly the machine stopped, turned sharply, went a short distance.

The doors opened. Hands caught them, carried them out. Val was lifted, carried. The footing underneath creaked, gave for a moment. He was bumped roughly against the narrow side of a door; then dropped heavily.

Strangely, for the first time that made him angry.

Scuffing steps came after him. An object was dropped heavily beside him. Hopkins swore luridly.

A rasping voice advised Hopkins: "Save your breath. You'll need it."

Chill, malevolent, that voice. A moment after it spoke, an engine began to throb. Val had suspected it; he knew it now. They had been taken to some point along the Embaracadero and put on a boat.

"Free them," the voice said.

The smothering folds were stripped away. Val was hoisted to his feet.

Blinking, he staggered for a moment, breathing deep of the fresh air. He was standing in the low, crude cabin of a fishing boat. The steady chug of the engine and the strong smell of fish left no doubt as to the kind of craft they were riding.

Two men held Val's arms. Yellow men, impassive as they looked past him for orders. Two more were freeing Hopkins.

But it was not at those four men Val looked. In front of him, under a small glaring electric light bulb stood a tall, stooped figure. Green-flecked eyes in a long, pale, cadaverous face were surveying him malevolently. Revulsion swept Val as he looked into that pale, ghastly face. Carl Zaken looked more like a corpse than a living man; for this was Carl Zaken—the dread Black Doctor of international espionage.

The shabby, secret channels of espionage had long carried tales of the Black Doctor. Tales like fantastic nightmares. A wizard at disguise, utterly ruthless; clever and cold-blooded, Zaken's favorite role had been that of a doctor. Rumor had it he once had been a doctor. That rumor had won him the title of the Black Doctor.

Without disguise, now wearing a dark suit, dark hat with the brim turned down in front, Zaken stared from greenish eyes which seemed to blaze and glare with inward passion. White teeth showed momentarily in the long pale face. Talonlike fingers caressed a bony chin.

"This is a pleasure, Easton."

"I can understand it," Val said coolly. "I wondered if you weren't behind this."

"Your ideas are prolific, Easton."

Hopkins was hoisted to his feet, spluttering. Like Val, he blinked for a moment and then looked at the tall, stooped figure confronting him. Hopkins' jaw clenched. Challenge came into his manner.

"So this," said Carl Zaken, "is Hopkins."

Hopkins retorted explosively: "Who the devil are *you?*"

"The name," said Val, "is Zaken. Carl Zaken. Sometimes called the Black Doctor. His name was mentioned this evening. He had Crumpmeyer killed."

Hopkins said softly, "Oh." His hands clenched slightly.

ZAKEN'S SMILE was a grimace. The white teeth that showed were more like tusks. His rasping voice was bitter.

"Unfortunately Crumpmeyer died too late to prevent this mischief. He was a weakling; and like all weaklings his destruction was inevitable."

"You picked the wrong place to do it," Val said cooly. "You tipped your hand to Gregg."

Zaken shrugged carelessly—but his eyes were not careless. Suppressed fury showed in them. "Gregg is a fool! A political cypher who fumbles like an amateur on a chess board."

Through his teeth Hopkins said: "What the devil's the idea of all this? What do you think you're going to do?"

Val spoke before Zaken, grinning faintly. "He's going to kill us, Hopkins. Never expect anything else from him when he catches one of Gregg's men. And if you ever get a chance, kill him like a snake without waiting for words. He was behind that little bit of business on the plane this afternoon. Shall we say accident, Zaken? Gregg's message was passed on to him and decoded. That's how he knows your name and knew where to find us."

"At times," Val said judiciously, "you show a flash of inspiration, Zaken. Would you mind telling us just how we're to leave this delightful world?"

Zaken smiled again.

"If your bodies were found ashore there would be an investigation. But if you vanish, who can say? Iron weights will take you both to the bottom of the bay. The water is deep. The bay is large. You'll both stay there in the mud."

Hopkins licked his lips. "By God," he said huskily, "no wonder you rate being killed like a snake. I wish I'd had the chance!"

Val smiled faintly. "I've tried it, Hopkins. Almost succeeded more than once. If there's another time, I'll try to be more careful. Zaken, would you mind gratifying a mild curiosity before you lay me away in the mud. Just why did you kill Crumpmeyer? What's behind all this?"

The claw-like fingers moved about the bony chin again. Zaken's smile was vicious. No other word would have described it. Vicious.

"It will give me a bit more pleasure when you sink," Zaken said, "to know that you're going down wondering what you failed to check. Are there any last messages you wish to send to Gregg?"

"None."

"Or—the charming Miss Fraser?"

Val had been waiting for that. Thought of Nancy Fraser had been in the back of his mind from the moment he had gone in Crumpmeyer's house. Zaken's hatred for her was no less. Even the lovely Tai Shan hated Nancy.

And Nancy, waiting in the hotel, would be an easy victim. The cards were stacked against her.

"What about Miss Fraser, Zaken?"

"It is too bad," said Zaken, "that it was necessary to—er—eliminate her also."

Through stiff lips, Val said: "*Was* necessary?"

The man was venomous when he answered. "I have her too. She is going to the bottom also."

In Val's neck the muscles went stiff, taut. Blood rushed to his face. For a moment the cramped cabin swam dizzily. Only Zaken's face remained in his sight—floating there under the light—within reach of his hands if they were free.

Zaken saw it, knew; his quick chuckle rasped through the red haze.

"A last charming thought to take with you," Zaken said. "I'll have the iron weights sent down. We should be getting to where you can go over the side. These men understand only a word or so of English. They can't be bribed."

Zaken went out, stooping through the low doorway.

HOPKINS DREW a deep breath, groaned faintly. His solemn face was haggard.

"What the devil," said Hopkins, "are we going to do?"

Val grinned crookedly. "Doesn't look as if we can do anything, old man. They got your gun, I suppose."

"Yes."

"Not much chance of walking ashore."

Hopkins moistened his lips. "This isn't any time to be funny. I can swim."

"How far d'you think you'd get in these bay currents with a boat full of men here to run you down?"

"Damn his rotten, murderous heart!" Hopkins blurted out with the utter rage of helplessness.

His tone told as much as his words. The two men holding him grinned. One of them said something in Chinese. The other chuckled.

Val said nothing. He was thinking. His silence seemed to irritate Hopkins.

The door opened. Zaken returned, followed by a fifth yellow man straining under the weight of two round iron bars and a coil of wire.

"In a few minutes," Zaken said, "we will be passing some of the United States Battle Fleet which is anchored here in the harbor. It will be a poetic end to send you to the bottom near them." His smile was another ghastly grimace. "The little touches give me the greatest satisfaction," Zaken said.

He shifted into Chinese, speaking curtly, and then turned on his heel and went out.

The iron bars and wire were dropped on the floor noisily. The bearer gestured at Hopkins, spoke in Chinese—and Hopkins was tripped without warning and thrown to the floor. He lit swearing and struggling.

And then Val, who had been standing passive and downcast in the grip of his two guards, exploded into action.

Val's body, so deceptive to the casual glance, was lean, corded with muscle. His right arm crooked forward, jerking the man on that side off balance. His leg tripped the fellow. A savage pull freed the arm. Val whirled on the man holding his other arm.

Paralyzed amazement showed on the saffron face. Val's fist smashed it in. The clutching fingers let go. The man spun back dazedly.

Catching an iron bar off the floor, Val turned. Two men had left Hopkins and were coming at him. The first one tried to dodge the down-chopping swing of the bar. He failed. The bar caught him on the shoulder at the base of the neck.

He screamed once as bone and flesh crushed in and the iron bar beat him to the floor.

Hopkins came to his feet, shaking off the man who was trying to hold him down. A knife flashed. Out of the corner of his eye Val glimpsed the knife; then saw a second knife flash as the man before him dodged back and lifted his hand to throw the long, sharp blade.

No time to retreat, to strike with the bar. An instant more and the knife would be in him. Val snapped the bar straight out with his wrists. A parrying hand stopped it only for a moment. Whirling around that hand, the flying iron slammed into the face behind it. The knife missed by inches. Gurgling in his throat, the thrower dropped with his cheekbone smashed in.

Hopkins, bleeding from a slashed hand, was beating his man to the floor in berserk rage. He would have killed the man with his bare hands if Val hadn't caught his arm, snapping: "Get out of here quick! They'll be on us with guns in a moment!"

THE WHOLE thing had been done in seconds. But one of the wounded had cried out loud enough to be heard on deck. Val caught the other iron bar off the floor and jumped for the low doorway.

The door opened as he came in it. A yellow man gave one look and darted back, squealing alarm. Val followed him out on deck swinging the bar.

All portholes were covered. The night lay thick. The squealing Oriental was running toward the wheelhouse. A flashlight was already bobbing out of the wheelhouse, flicking back along the deck.

Val looked out across the water. Many lights were twinkling a short distance away. They outlined the low squat bulk of a warship. Beyond them were other lights, and still more lights. Carl Zaken's monstrous vanity had caused him to pass close to the fleet anchorage.

From the moment Zaken had mentioned that intention, Val had counted on it.

The flashlight centered on him.

Zaken's rasping cry of rage came along the deck: "Get back there, Easton!"

A waste of words. Zaken must have known it. Before there was a chance of the order being obeyed a gun crashed back of the light. The bullet struck the deck at Val's feet. He dodged as a second shot blasted on the night. The bullet whined past his head.

Hopkins ran out and joined him.

"Over the side!" Val yelled. "Swim toward the battleship. We've got a slim chance of making it! Keep clear of the propeller!"

The last words floated back over Val's shoulder as he dove overside. He plunged into the cold water, came up swimming hard away from any suction which might drag him back into the whirling propeller blades.

There was some suction—but he won clear of it, buffeted by the wake. Zaken ran back to the stern with the flashlight. The beam searched over the water, found Val. Zaken's gun spat loudly in the night, again and again as he emptied it.

Bullets spatted in the water as Val ducked under to escape them. And when he came up again the whole night had changed. From the low bulk of the battleship a blinding white searchlight beam had flung out over the water, blazing into his eyes.

Looking over his shoulder, Val saw the grimy fishing boat sheering off sharply, heading toward shore. The beam pursued it.

Hopkins was threshing water near him. Val swam over to him, called: "All right?"

"Fine!" Hopkins panted. "I'm going to shed my clothes. They're dragging me down."

"Hold it!"

The searchlight had wavered, fixed on them. Faintly they could hear a whistle piping on the battleship. Lights began to gleam on the side.

"They see us!" Val panted. A wave swept into his mouth. He spat out the salt water, gasped: "I th-think they'll send a boat after us!"

HE WAS right. In a few minutes the hard sharp exhaust of a speeding motor-boat drifted over the water. The searchlight continued to bathe them in a blinding glare.

They were treading water side by side when a trim, gleaming launch manned by uniformed sailors swung smartly around and stopped beside them.

Hands dragged them over the side. Flashlights played over them. A young officer spoke with a touch of asperity: "What's the idea of a private little war on our anchorage?"

Streaming water and feeling like a half drowned cat, Val replied. "Get after that boat we were on! Stop it!"

The reply was more than a bit sarcastic. "Name your chestnuts and we'll pull them out of the fire. Like hell. We're not a harbor patrol. I haven't any authority to go after that boat and stop it. Haven't any guns along, as a matter of fact, to stop them if they got nasty."

"You don't understand," Val panted. "It's official business. Here—have a look!"

Val dragged out a soggy billfold, abstracted a pulpy card on which the ink was running badly. The young officer brought it under his flashlight, whistled softly.

"Makes it a bit different," he admitted. "But I still haven't any authority to go after that boat. We were sent to pick you out of the water."

"You've got a chance now," Val urged. "If you go back to the ship for orders, that boat will be ashore."

The searchlight beam had shifted, thrusting on past them after the fishing boat. It was headed directly in to shore, running as fast as its engine could kick over.

The naval man looked after it, decided abruptly. "I'll take a sporting chance. Henderson, see if you can catch that scow."

"Aye, sir."

The sleek little launch shook as the motor roared wide open. It swung in a sharp semi-circle and headed after Zaken's larger, slower craft, throwing a creamy bow wave and spray as it drove through the harbor swells.

They overhauled the other craft quickly. But the fishing boat had a long start. The shore was near. The launch was still some two hundred yards behind as the fishing boat headed into a dark slip.

The searchlight followed to the head of the slip, lost it there. The launch roared into the slip. The officer's searchlight located the fishing boat nosing against the piling at the shore end of the slip.

No signs of life were visible on it when they drew up alongside.

Val led the way up on deck, jumped over to the pier and ran out to the Embarcadero. But on that dark and gloomy way no fleeing men were visible. He returned to the boat, found the naval officer, Hopkins and two enlisted men on deck.

They followed him into the cabin. The man Val had first struck down with the iron bar was lying unconscious on the floor. The others had recovered enough to escape.

The naval man looked at the blood-spots on the floor, at the long bleeding cut on Hopkins hand, whistled softly.

"Must have had a little excitement," he said. "Care to tell me about it?"

"Nothing to tell," Val said absently.

He was bending over the unconscious man, stripping away coat and the shirt beneath. On the saffron back, which he bared, the livid brand of the dragon looked up at him.

CHAPTER FIVE

INFORMER'S REWARD

H ALF AN hour later, a taxi let Val and Hopkins out at the hotel. Police had arrived at the pier, attracted by the battleship's searchlight. The injured man had been sent to the hospital with a formal charge of kidnapping against him. The machinery of the police department was investigating the fishing boat, spreading a net for a man of Carl Zaken's description on a kidnapping charge. Val had made no other charges.

Val paid off the taxi with a soggy bill. They ran a gauntlet of curious stares in the hotel lobby as they hurried to the elevator.

He was sick at heart as the elevator bore them up. He had searched the fishing boat and found no trace of Nancy Fraser. Zaken had taken her ashore somewhere. She was probably dead by now. Locating her in the maze of streets and buildings would be more difficult than hunting the proverbial needle in the haystack.

Granting that Nancy was still alive, the entire force of the local police would not be able to locate her in time.

As they hurried to Val's room, Hopkins said: "I know a man in Chinatown who may give us a lead on this. Old Sam Hop. If there's anything going on under the surface, he'll know something about it—and he may talk—to me."

Val had left the door of his room unlocked. It was still unlocked. He walked in—and swore aloud with relief as Nancy Fraser came out of a chair to meet him.

"God be praised," said Nancy thankfully—and she meant it. "I was just on the point of turning out headquarters to look for you two. What on earth has happened? You both look as if you've fallen into the bay."

Val grinned from sheer relief. "We jumped in the bay," he said. "I—I— damn it, I thought you were dead. Carl Zaken told me he had you."

"So!" said Nancy softly. "Carl Zaken! I was afraid so. I'll bet you didn't find the Crumpmeyer girl. I've telephoned her house several times and no one answered."

"Zaken was there first."

"I wondered," said Nancy. She was still pale, shaken. "I went to my room after you left," Nancy said. "And while I was there Miss Crumpmeyer telephoned me. She said she was delivering a message for you, Val, and that you wanted me to take a taxi to the house right away. I asked to speak to you. She said you were downstairs and couldn't come to the telephone. I told her I'd have to hear from you before I left the hotel; and that if I didn't hear inside of five minutes I was going to call the police. She hung up. I waited the five minutes and then called headquarters. They sent a squad car out there and found no one in the house or no automobiles around it."

Nancy drew a deep breath. "I knew something must have happened. I didn't know what. I was afraid to make too much fuss over it. I couldn't give them any information as to where you two might be, other than Crumpmeyer's house, so I gave them your description and decided to wait here by the telephone another hour before I turned out the entire police department."

Nancy looked at her wrist watch. "Three minutes more and the hour would have been up. Mr. Hopkins—your hand! What happened?"

So Val told her—and Nancy listened attentively, and shook her head at the finish.

"It's big," she said. "And important, Val, or Zaken would not be going to such pains to get you out of the way. It—it makes me shiver at how near he came to succeeding."

Val grinned at her. "All he really did was let us know what we're up against. Far better to know it now than later. Hopkins, get into some dry clothes. I'll have a doctor come to your room and dress that hand. Nancy, skip out until I change. I want to see this Sam Hop."

CHINATOWN HAD not changed. The same smell hung before the little shop windows—dried duck, fish, ginger, incense; the indescribable odor of the Orient, blended from a thousand mysterious sources.

It was not yet midnight. Some shop windows were still lighted. Saffron-skinned figures were chattering behind open doors, slipping through the shadows. Music blared down a fight of brass-treaded stairs from a garish chop suey palace catering to the tourist trade.

And Hopkins, his hand swathed in white bandages, opened a door, walked back through a dark passage into a little open courtyard lighted by one dim bulb. He crossed it to another dim hallway, walked up a narrow flight of steps to the third floor and knocked on a door there.

A crack of light showed under the door. But Hopkins had to knock a second time before shuffling steps came to the other side. The door was opened an inch or so against a chain.

An eye peered out at them.

"Sam Hop," Hopkins said.

"What you want Sam Hop?"

"Tell him—Hopkins. I've some business with him."

The door closed again. A bolt was shot on the other side. The feet shuffled away.

Val grinned. "Sam Hop isn't taking any chances."

"Habit more than anything else, I suppose," Hopkins stated. "The old boy's had his share of enemies. Still has, I guess. His tong connections aren't infallible protection. He's rich and fat and wants to stay that way. Made a chunk of it out of opium in the old days. But I've done him a favor or so. He likes me; I like him—and there's a chance he may be able to help us."

"A Chinaman's chance," Val chuckled. "But, in this town, that can mean a good chance."

The shuffling steps returned to the door. The bolt was shot back, the chain unhooked and the door was opened wide. A little old wizened Chinaman, wearing felt slippers and a black shirt outside his trousers, bowed low before them.

"Sam Hop say come," he stated.

When they entered, he chained and bolted the door behind them and shuffled ahead of them across the cheap bare room. He passed through another door, along a dark little hall. At the end of the hall he opened still another door and bowed them through.

And Val looked around with amazed appreciation at the large room into which they walked.

The polished floor was inlaid with intricate patterns in wood. Ebony furniture was inlaid with gleaming mother-of-pearl. Gorgeously painted screens stood in several of the corners. A priceless Chinese rug lay in the center of the floor. Gold-thread tapestries were on the walls.

And in a great carved chair at the other end of the room sat a massive figure. The chair was large. The man who sat in it was larger. He seemed to overflow into space. His face was a vast placid moon, topped by a thatch of coal-black hair.

On that face not a wrinkle was visible. In the black hair there was no gray; and yet about the man hovered an air of age, of experience, of accumulated wisdom.

As they came toward him, the vast figure twisted in the chair and put a little round teacup on a low inlaid table beside the chair. His face was one bland beam as he came to his feet with a mighty effort and bowed.

"Much honor comes to my house tonight," he said in perfect English.

The formality was old country Chinese. Val was introduced. They were waved to chairs. The wizened servant brought in fresh tea. Little cups of the steaming beverage were pressed into their hands. Polite inquiries were made. Hopkins more than held his own in the exchange of courtesies. Finally when it seemed that he was never coming to the point, he asked casually: "Have you heard of a man named Carl Zaken?"

Sam Hop smilingly shook his head in denial.

"He will be found near a man named Chang Ch'ien," Val suggested.

The moonlike smile on Sam Hop's face did not alter. But, quickly veiled though it was with drooping lids, a gleam of intelligence appeared in his eyes.

With both hands, Sam Hop lifted his teacup and sipped noisily. And said nothing.

Hopkins looked at him solemnly. "It's rather important that we get track of them, Sam."

Sam Hop nodded, smiled at them over the top of his teacup—and gave no indication of knowing anything.

Val leaned forward. "These men will be connected with the Sons of the Dragon," he said.

So sudden was Sam Hop's slight start that a bit of tea slopped over on his fingers.

Behind Val a cup shattered on the floor.

The wizened little servant stooped quickly, gathered up the broken bits and shuffled from the room without a backward glance.

FOR A moment silence held the large room. Sam Hop stared over the top of his teacup like a musing Budda. That one slight start was all the indication that he had heard anything out of the ordinary.

But Val, watching closely, sensed rather than saw a tautness, a wariness and an alertness behind the fat placid face.

"The Sons of the Dragon," Val repeated softly.

Sam Hop sighed. Slowly he put the teacup on the low table beside his chair, straightened, laid his soft white hands on his knees, blinked at Val. "You ask about things which are best left alone, my friend," he said heavily.

"Some things cannot be left alone."

Sam Hop considered that. Slowly inclined his head in assent. "Even among the Chinese the Dragon men are seldom mentioned, Mr. Easton."

"I am not Chinese."

"The more reason for not prying into matters you do not understand."

"This matter is going to be pried into," said Val grimly. "We want this man Carl Zaken—and Chang Ch'ien."

The last name caused a visible shiver in the huge figure of Sam Hop.

"You know—Chang Ch'ien?" he asked.

"Yes."

Fear had come into that placid room. Fear was on Sam Hop as he leaned forward, lowering his voice. "This man—Chang Ch'ien—you will not find in Chinatown, Mr. Easton. Nor will you find me to speak of him. No— not even among the men of the Dragon will you hear of Chang Ch'ien."

"No?"

"No," said Sam Hop. He closed his eyes for a moment, as if shutting out visions that were not pleasant.

"Why?" Val asked him.

The eyes opened. "They are afraid," said Sam Hop. "The men of the Dragon are afraid. They will not talk—for those who talk, die. I am an old man. I hear things that I do not understand." Sam Hop shrugged. "Things I do not want to understand. But if you look for Chang Ch'ien—do not look in Chinatown. He is not here." Sam Hop closed his eyes, opened them again, sighed. "But think," he added, "that you will find that Chang Ch'ien very close to China-town."

Val looked at Hopkins.

Hopkins nodded. "If Sam says it's that way, then it is. He always tells the truth." Hopkins smiled faintly. "If he talks at all," he said.

Val stood up. He was still grinning as he spoke to the figure in the chair. "Is that all you know?"

Sam Hop looked at him thoughtfully. "All," he said. "In this matter a little is as dangerous as much. If you must know more, find the woman with the flaming hair who has carried messages for Chang Ch'ien."

Val frowned. "Flaming hair? You mean—red hair?"

Sam Hop nodded.

Val's mind flashed back to the girl who had sat across from him on the plane. "I see," he said thoughtfully.

Sam Hop looked at him without expression. "If you cannot find her, ask the daughter of the White Dragon."

"The White Dragon? The White—" Val broke off. "Crumpmeyer," he said. "The White Dragon."

And it seemed to him that Sam Hop relaxed. "I see there is not much I can tell you that you do not know, Mr. Easton. I can tell you no more."

"The White Dragon is dead."

"I have heard it whispered."

"And only Chang Ch'ien knows where his daughter is."

SAM HOP looked startled. He shivered again, spread his ivory hands wordlessly.

"One thing more," Val said. "There is a man coming from China named Li Hung."

"That," said Sam Hop without interest, "I have not heard."

They left a few minutes later—and behind them they left fear and, Val was convinced, a certain relief at their departure.

Outside, Val said: "We didn't get much."

"We got all there is to know in Chinatown," Hopkins stated flatly. "What Sam Hop can't tell us, no one can."

"Li Hung's coming apparently isn't very important."

"It is to someone. Sam can't know everything. What are we going to do about Crumpmeyer's daughter?"

Val said thoughtfully: "If her number has been turned up, she's dead already. If not—there's time enough to look for her. The police can't find her any quicker than we can. Probably not as quick."

Hopkins said gloomily: "A hell of a chance we've got to find her. How would we go about it?"

Val smiled faintly as three Orientals drew aside to let them pass. They were walking on Grant Street, through the heart of Chinatown. "There's no way of searching her out," Val said. "If we were certain she was here in Chinatown, we probably couldn't locate her."

"Probably not."

"But—granting that she's alive—she probably isn't here in the quarter," Val said. "Sam Hop said Chang Ch'ien wouldn't be found here. He seems to know. She'll be near Chang Ch'ien. We can't report it to the police, for that means publicity about Chang Ch'ien, which we don't want. So we find Chang Ch'ien—and we have her. Simple—eh?"

"Very simple," Hopkins said sarcastically. "How do we find Chang Ch'ien?"

"Through Li Hung, who is arriving on the *Shanghai Queen* tomorrow. Crumpmeyer was killed because he talked about Li Hung. Only one answer to that—Chang Ch'ien—Carl Zaken—or someone near him, will contact Li Hung—either to kill him or have speech with him. We'll have our lead there. Have you made arrangements for me to meet the *Shanghai Queen* tomorrow?"

"I have," said Hopkins. "And I'll be at the dock."

"And so will Nancy Fraser," Val said. "With a black wig and a little disguise, now that they know she's on this matter. Get me on that pilot boat in the morning—and I think this thing will begin to clear up, one way or another."

A FIST hammering on the door awoke Val early the next morning. He sat up groggily, rubbing his eyes, and looked at his watch. The hour was fifteen minutes to five. Putting his feet into slippers and belting a dressing gown he went to the door and opened it.

Hopkins pushed in, brandishing a paper. "See this?" Hopkins demanded.

"How the devil could I? I've been asleep."

Hopkins pointed to a morning paper which had been slipped under the door, thrust his own paper into Val's hands. "I rolled out early and took the paper down to read over my coffee. And I found this."

Hopkins' finger indicated a headline.

PROMINENT CHINESE MURDERED
Branded on Back.
Tong War Feared.

The body of Sam Hop, wealthy member of the Chinese colony was found in an alley off Grant Street early this morning by detectives of the Chinatown squad. Marks on the throat indicated the victim was throttled by a rope. Investigation in the rooms occupied by Sam Hop disclosed the body of a servant, with a knife buried in his throat. Detectives stated that robbery was not the motive as a large sum of money was found on the body. An old feud, or tong rivalry, was assigned as the probable cause by members of the Chinatown squad. A peculiar feature of the case was a mark on the back of Sam Hop apparently made a few hours before by a hot iron. A linguistic expert stated that the mark was the Mandarin sign for Dragon.

Fearing an outbreak of tong violence, extra men were posted throughout Chinatown....

Val tossed the paper on the bed, walked to the dresser, lighted a cigarette. "So they got Sam Hop?" he said softly.

Hopkins lighted a cigarette too. He was badly shaken. "Sam was murdered because he talked to us. And branded on the back so the right people would know why he was killed. God, I feel rotten about this! He was my friend— and because he came through when I asked him to, he's dead! He—he was afraid while he was up there—but he talked."

"I saw that," Val nodded. "We must have been followed there. They gathered him in right after we left."

Hopkins blew smoke viciously. "What are we going to do about it? By God, I won't feel right until I get my hands on the man who held that iron!"

"You may have a chance at that, Hopkins. Rather, his hands may be on you. Every move we make seems to be known."

Hopkins growled in his throat. The usually solemn fellow was raging. "Maybe we'd better all get off the case," Hopkins suggested harshly. "Keep them running after us while Gregg puts new people on to do the actual work."

"No time to try that," Val said calmly. "It's a tough break having them spot us before we get started. But I'm not surprised. I've dealt with Carl Zaken and Chang Ch'ien before. They don't come any cleverer than those two. The French, the British, the Germans—most European governments have found that out long ago. You're getting a taste of it now. Zaken and Chang Ch'ien have money and brains. They're fanatically intent on whatever they do—and utterly ruthless. We'll have to take them as we find them and do the best we can. And I'll tell you this— I've proved it—I know what I'm talking about—they do make mistakes. The breaks aren't always with them. We'll get ours."

Hopkins glowered. "I doubt it," he said candidly. "But I'm willing to be convinced. What do we do?"

"What we planned, old man. Give me time for a shower and a cup of coffee and get me to that pilot boat." Val turned toward the bath, stopped, grinned back over his shoulder. "That's one place I don't think they'll follow. And if I know our little Nancy Fraser, I think she'll vanish from sight this morning and they'll be running around in circles looking for her."

CHAPTER SIX

MR. LI

THE FORENOON sun was bright. A dead calm hung over the sea. The long swells sweeping in off the broad Pacific were flat and glassy when the liner finally moved up over the horizon, bore down on the small pilot boat and stopped briefly to take on a pilot. Val went up the ship's side after the pilot, clinging to the wooden-treaded rope ladder. The rail above was lined with curious passengers.

The pilot led the way up through corridors and stairs to the bridge. There, as the ship got under way again, Val faced the master.

Captain MacMurtrie was a spare Scot, weatherbeaten, incurious matter-of-fact as he talked with a Scotch burr.

"This mon you people ha' been sendin' Marconigrams aboot, Mr. Easton, is in the first class, wi' a traveling coompanion. 'Tis no business o' mine what he's done. I ha' my orders from the owners. I weel send ye doon with a steward tae have him pointed oot to you. All I ask, Mr. Easton, is that ye make no disturbance on my ship before the passengers go ashore."

Val smiled slightly. "I don't think you need have any worry on that score, Captain. I'm not here to cause a disturbance. I'm afraid you've been misinformed if you're looking for an arrest."

The captain answered bruskly. "I ha' no care aboot that, sir. I ha' my orders to gi' ye a free hand. I will gi' ye the man's deck steward. He's a white mon."

The captain stepped to a speaking tube, gave a brief order. In a few minutes Val went off the bridge in the company of a bandy-legged Cockney steward wearing a white coat.

"You've had an eye on this man all the way across?" Val asked him.

"That I has, sir. An' a nicer one I ain't never 'ad, sir, if I do say so. Even if 'is blomin' skin is yellow. 'E's a gentleman, 'e is."

"How did he spend the trip? Mix with the passengers much? Have any intimates?"

"Carn't say 'e did, sir. Kept to 'is self, 'e did. 'Im an' that other Chink wot's travelin' with 'im. Kind of a secretary the young one is, 'e is."

"Any other Chinese aboard they were friendly with? Or who seemed to pay any particular attention to them?"

"No, sir. Those two is the only ones travelin's first class this trip. They were walkin' the promenade deck when I went to the bridge."

A moment later Val and the steward were on the broad promenade deck, crowded now with passengers watching the approaching land. The steward led a deft way aft; and amidship spoke out of the corner of his mouth, without turning his head.

"There 'e is, sir. Both of them."

"Thanks. That will be all," Val said.

The steward turned away. Val walked on, paying no attention to the Chinese pair who strolled past him a moment later. Nor did they seem to notice him.

There could be no mistake about Li Hung. He walked a pace in advance, a tall, scholarly-looking figure wearing shell-rimmed nose glasses and a well tailored black suit. His face was thin and aristocratic; the nose rather more hawklike than was usual among his countrymen. A little on the other side of fifty, Val guessed—and it was only a guess. Whatever his years, Li Hung carried an air of authority, of accomplishment, of aloofness with him. His thin-lipped mouth had a firmness which bordered on latent cruelty, if one looked close enough.

The secretary who walked a step behind was much younger, slighter in build. He was intellectual, but not forceful, Val decided after one swift look. The secretary wore horn-rimmed glasses, a gray suit, and looked the incipient diplomat. And he might be at that, if the Chinese Ambassador in Washington was expecting the master.

Without looking behind, Val continued on around the promenade deck. Li Hung had not looked worried, but with his countrymen he undoubtedly shared the faculty—often exaggerated in Western imaginations—of concealing his emotions.

The hardest thing to believe, after seeing the man, was Crumpmeyer's assertion that on Li Hung's back a searing iron had left the livid mark of the Dragon.

Other questions ran through Val's mind on that short walk through the crowd of passengers gay with land-fever; questions which occurred with increasing frequency.

Crumpmeyer, branded with the Dragon, had warned Gregg that Li Hung would be in danger when he landed. Crumpmeyer had been killed because he talked; killed through the influence of those two masters of intrigue Carl Zaken and Chang Ch'ien. Because he was assigned to the case, Val's life had been attempted. Sam Hop had been murdered because he talked of the matter.

Sam Hop had said that the men of the Dragon were terrified. And yet, branded freshly on Sam Hop's back, by the men who had killed him, was the Dragon sign.

Why were those men terrified. Why had Crumpmeyer been killed, when the killers themselves used the Dragon sign?

THE OPPOSITE deck Val met the two men again. He spoke to Li Hung. "A few minutes of your time, please, Mr. Li."

Li Hung stepped back quickly. His secretary slipped a hand in his coat pocket. A bulge there looked suspiciously like a gun.

The two were aware of danger, were watchful, ready for it.

Li Hung frowned through his shell-rimmed glasses. His English was faultless, touched slightly with an Oxford accent as he said; "I have not the pleasure, sir."

"Tell your man he needn't bother with that gun in his pocket. If you'll step over the rail where we can talk alone. I'll explain. My name is Easton."

Li Hung showed no intention of stepping over to the rail. "Just who are you, Mr. Easton? You came aboard with the pilot, I believe."

"Yes—to talk with you about the mark of the Dragon which you carry on your back."

Only master and secretary heard the words—and the young secretary's reaction was startling. He jumped a step, shrinking from Li Hung. He was afraid of Li Hung in that abrupt moment of revelation.

Li Hung was stupefied. No other word for it. He looked at the secretary, spoke sharply in Chinese. The secretary bowed, turned, hurried away. And Li Hung, his face once more composed, but with a strange glitter in his eye, spoke softly.

"You are one of the few men alive who could make that remark, Mr. Easton. Will you enlighten me?"

Li Hung walked to the rail, waited.

Standing beside him, Val met the scrutiny of dark, penetrating eyes. "Your secretary," he said, "evidently does not carry the dragon mark."

The answer was impatient. "No. The man is afraid of me now. For all I know, he will have a knife ready for my back as soon as we are alone. You did me no kindness by making that statement before him, Mr. Easton."

"Sorry. I supposed he knew. Had an idea you both carried it. You're wondering how I know."

"I am," Li Hung admitted coldly. "Only one white man has ever known of the mark of the Dragon. You are not that man. He would die before he would tell."

"He told—and he's dead."

Li Hung regarded Val silently. "Dead," he said. "I had not heard."

"Have you heard," Val said, "of a man named Carl Zaken?"

"No," said Li Hung.

"Perhaps—Chang Ch'ien?"

The penetrating eyes flashed. "That name," said Li Hung, "I have heard." His thin lips pressed tightly together. The latent cruelty leaped out, stark and obvious for an instant. Then Li Hung smiled, a slow, thin-lipped smile. "Yes, I have heard of Chang Ch'ien."

Val said: "You're apt to hear more of him. Why should Chang Ch'ien be interested in your arrival, Mr. Li?"

"Ah—why?" Li Hung said softly. "Is he?"

"Decidedly."

"And why are you interested, Mr. Easton? I'm afraid I don't understand your knowledge and your interest."

"Rather simple. The American government understands that the Chinese Ambassador is expecting to see you in Washington. Your position in China makes it necessary that you arrive safely at the embassy."

"*Ahhhh,*" said Li Hung. "I begin to understand. You are representing the government."

"In a way. When Washington became aware that there might be some danger of your not arriving at the embassy, I was sent here to meet you."

Li Hung smiled, spoke with a touch of irony. "My compliments to the thoroughness with which you have met me—bringing facts which I did not think it was possible to become known."

"Facts," said Val calmly, "which have nothing to do with your visit to the Chinese Ambassador."

LI HUNG tapped the rail with slim finger tips. "I intend to arrive at the embassy. I hardly think there is anything you can do for me, Mr. Easton. I shall be met at the dock by—friends. They have radioed me that certain—disasters—have befallen mutual friends and it will be best if I am adequately protected."

"You're not leaving San Francisco at once?"

"Unfortunately," said Li Hung, "I have several pressing matters to attend to first. I shall be in San Francisco for at least two days. Perhaps more."

"You'd better request protection from the police."

The ironical smile appeared again. "I hardly think that would be wise, Mr. Easton. It seems that I can talk freely with you, since you know so much. Your police, I understand, often let one in for publicity. I do not want that. If it were known that I had to call on them for protection, my prestige in—er—certain quarters would be seriously impaired."

"I see. The men of the Dragon are supposed to take care of themselves, eh?"

"Partly," Li Hung agreed. "And partly that it is not wise that my name be connected with—er—these dangers you have mentioned. You noticed the reactions of my secretary. His knowledge will go no further; no further," Li Hung said softly. "But I must think of others—on both sides of the Pacific. If you do not mind, Mr. Easton, I will land and disappear."

Val grinned. "You may land," he said, "but I doubt if you'll disappear. However, I've done my duty. The rest is up to you."

Li Hung bowed formally. "I shall remember the interest your government has taken in me—and my affairs," he said. And with that rather enigmatic remark he turned back along the deck.

Val watched the tall figure go inside. He lighted a cigarette, smoked it there by the rail, and then went forward and watched the always interesting passage through the Golden Gate.

It was well on in the afternoon when the last hawser was made fast to the dock and the debarkation through the customs began. The pier was crowded with the usual mob of friends, sightseers and, quickly, passengers.

Val waited near the head of the gangway, well back on the deck where watching eyes on the dock would be hard put to see him. He glimpsed Hopkins loitering near the foot of the gangway. Nancy Fraser was not in sight.

But more interesting than Hopkins was a group of half a dozen Chinese clustered at one side of the gangway. Most of them had right hands in their coat pockets. A safe bet, Val thought, that those hands clutched loaded guns. Li Hung was evidently not going to lack for protection.

The debarkation was half over when Li Hung appeared—walking behind his bland young secretary. And, legends of Oriental inscrutability were given the lie as they passed. The secretary looked most unhappy.

Other passengers trooped down the gangway after them. From the deck Val saw Li Hung and his companion surrounded by the waiting group and hurried inside the dock shed.

Hopkins drifted after them.

If there was anyone else about who displayed interest in Li Hung, they were not visible as Val went down the gangway a moment later. He hurried into the dock shed, for Li Hung, as a diplomat, would not be stopped by the customs.

And it was well he hurried. The party was just entering two taxicabs when he came in sight of them again. The taxicabs were driven by Chinese, Val noted. Picked men, evidently, so that there would be not hitch.

Hopkins was nearer to the group, blowing his nose vigorously, without paying any attention to the men he was watching. And as the two cabs drove away Hopkins turned his back on them and lost interest.

A customs guard stopped Val, then motioned him past quickly at sight of the card which Val palmed for his eyes. A moment later Val was at Hopkins' side.

"Why the devil didn't you follow them?" he asked sharply. "That's why you were waiting here."

Hopkins chuckled. "No need for it," he explained. "Miss Fraser was outside in a rented car, waiting for me to signal with my handkerchief. She made a clean exit out of the back of the hotel this morning, headed for a dark wig and a bit of disguise and showed up here to catch my signal. And if anyone spots her, he's a wizard. I could hardly recognize her myself. She's following them. I stayed behind here to see if anyone else trailed them away."

"I didn't see anyone."

"Not a soul," Hopkins said cheerfully. "I rented a room at another hotel without being spotted, too, I'm certain. Miss Fraser is going to telephone there as soon as she knows where our friend goes."

"Did you get the numbers of those cabs?"

"Yes. When they arrived."

"Get over to your hotel then and catch that call," Val said. "I'll go back to the St. Francis and freshen up a bit. Call me at my room. And watch yourself. Zaken hasn't turned into a fool overnight."

CHAPTER SEVEN

THE HOUSE ON RUSSIAN HILL

A TAXI took Val to the St. Francis. If another car was trailing him through the traffic, he was unable to spot it. He paid the driver, entered the lobby and was halfway to the elevator bank when a delighted voice called to him.

"Hello, stranger! Isn't this luck? I didn't think we'd ever meet again."

It was the pert little redhead who had made the trip west on the plane with him. She was as small and doll-like as ever as she came from the chair where she had been sitting. And as eager and alert as she put a small hand in his and smiled up at him.

"How are you feeling?" she asked. "I thought, from the way you collapsed on the plane, that you would be a hospital case for a long time. You frightened us all half to death."

"I'll bet I did," Val chuckled. "Altitude sometimes gets my heart that way. We were just climbing over the mountains, you remember." He smiled down at her.

"I've been having the grandest time. Seeing everything. Are you going to make good that promise to steer me around to places I haven't been?"

Looking down at her, Val found it hard to believe that this vivacious girl could have anything to do with Carl Zaken and Chang Ch'ien. She was too frank, too open, too bubbling with the joy of life. And yet—Sam Hop had been murdered for what he had told. Sam Hop had not been lying.

"The promise still holds," Val told her with a grin. "Have to put it off a little. I'm too busy today. But if you're here long enough we'll see things with a bang. Are you staying here at the hotel?"

"Yes. Don't you want my name, Mr. Easton?"

"We have a detective, I see. How do you know mine?"

She laughed. "I'll break down and confess. I heard the crew use it on the plane while you were unconscious. And since I seem to have met you without your knowledge, I am Martha O'Leary."

"How do you do, Miss O'Leary? This is a pleasure. And now if you don't mind, I'll have to leave you for the time being."

But on the way up to his room Val was not smiling. The watch was still on him. He wondered how much she had to do with Tai Shan's knowledge that he had arrived at the hotel. As he took a quick shower and changed clothes, Val was glad to know she was there. He could watch her now.

He waited by the telephone half an hour—three quarters—and the minute hand of his wrist watch was nearing the hour before the telephone rang.

It was Hopkins, worried, uncertain. "Has Miss Fraser telephoned you?" he asked.

"No. Hasn't she called you?"

"Not a thing from her. It seems to me she's had time to follow them wherever they were going and get word back to me as we agreed."

And Val snapped at Hopkins; snapped because of the sharp fear which swept over him: "She's had time to follow them down to San Mateo and get word back. And there isn't a chance they went that far. Something's happened to her!"

Hopkins spoke heavily. "I'm afraid you're right. I'm stymied, Easton. What do you suggest?"

"Check those taxi numbers. I'll meet you at the license bureau in fifteen minutes."

Thumbing down the hook for a moment, Val called headquarters, asked to be connected with Homicide; and when Homicide was on the wire, asked: "Have there been any gunfights or kidnapings around the city in the last hour?"

"What is this, a gag?"

"No, you idiot!" Val snapped. "I've a reason for wanting to know."

"Who's talking?"

"The district attorney's office. Let's have an intelligent answer quick."

"All right, mister. Calm down. How was I to know? Nothin' new has busted since the bodies of those two Chink hackers were found dead up that alley a little while ago."

"What hackers?"

"Say—the ones we called your office about. The two guys with brands on their backs, like we found on old Sam Hop last night. Only these were old burns. You been asleep over there so you didn't hear about it when the dope went through?"

Val found it hard to keep the excitement out of his voice as he said: "I just got in. Do they know who the two hackers are yet?"

"Sure. George Sun and Foo Lung. Everybody in the quarter knows them. They've been hacking around Chinatown for years. Say, who'n hell are you anyway that you're crackin' so dumb about all this? You people oughta be buzzing about it?"

"I'm the D.A. himself," Val replied. "We're getting ready for election day."

He hung up and left the room.

The red-headed Miss O'Leary was not in the lobby when he went through. He looked about for her, failed to see her, hurried out to a taxi.

LITTLE OF that ride through the busy streets registered as Val hunched in the corner of his seat, thinking. Carl Zaken had scored again. No matter what moves were made in this matter, Zaken always seemed to step ahead. Two dead taxi drivers tossed out into an alley. Men who had piloted taxis through Chinatown for years; who all that time had borne on their backs the Dragon sign. Dead now, tossed into an alley in a brazen gesture of defiance— or was it warning?

Hopkins was just coming out of the license bureau. He was excited as he asked: "Any news of her?"

"None. What luck here?"

"Plenty. I know Charley Snell in there. He gave me quick attention. Those two taxis were owned by a couple of Chinese named Foo Lung and—"

"And George Sun," Val finished. "And headquarters have been checking within the last hour or so to get the license numbers of their cars."

Astonishment spread over Hopkins' face. "How d'you know that?"

Val grinned without mirth, coldly, grimly. "The bodies of those two drivers were found this afternoon. They had the Dragon mark on their backs. Old marks, branded years ago."

Hopkins stuttered. "Then—then—"

"That means strangers were driving those two cabs. And it means further that the men who met Li Hung were not the ones he expected."

Val smiled coldly again. "We stood there, Hopkins, and watched Zaken's men neatly gather in Li Hung and his secretary."

"And Miss Fraser followed them and was gathered in herself," Hopkins groaned.

"Exactly."

Hopkins drew a long breath. "We've got to get her!" he said thickly. "Li Hung—"

"Said he was going to vanish when he stepped ashore. There's no way we can check on him in Chinatown. But we know what happened to him. If we get Nancy Fraser, we'll find Li Hung—alive or dead."

"But how," Hopkins groaned, "are we going to get her? There's nothing to work on. She—she may not even be alive now."

Val said bruskly: "Forget that part of it. We'll do the best we can. I've an idea—one slim chance that may work out. If it doesn't, I'm afraid nothing can be done for Nancy and

Li Hung. I want you to do exactly as I say—no more and no less. Listen...."

Val talked for several minutes.

Hopkin's face grew long. "I don't think it will work," he said. "I think it's wasting time when he should be doing something else."

"What?"

Hopkins threw up his hands. "You've got me," he confessed. "Go ahead."

A TAXI took Val back to the hotel—alone. He went up to his room, took off his coat, hurriedly strapped a second gun harness under his right arm. A second .38 automatic went in it. And then, from his bag, he took a soft leather holder, slipped from it a large plain jackknife. He pressed a button in the handle and a long keen blade flashed out into position.

Smiling thinly, Val closed the blade, returned the knife to its sheath and fastened it behind his belt buckle, inside the waistband of his trousers. A few moments later, whistling tunelessly through his teeth, he stepped from the elevator into the lobby.

One of the first objects which caught his eye was the red-headed Miss O'Leary, reading a newspaper in a nearby chair. She lifted the paper in a gesture of greeting, came toward him.

"I saw you go up," she said. "And wondered if you were coming down to keep your promise. I'm beginning to be bored toddling around by myself. And I don't mind chasing you like an Amazon to tell you so."

"I like having you," Val smiled. "I think you're a mind reader. Where shall we go?"

"That," said Miss O'Leary, "is something you'll have to decide. You promised to show me magic in this here town, mister."

Val chuckled. "I'll show you more than magic," he said. "I'll bring about a miracle. Shall we start now?"

"Lead on," Miss O'Leary invited gaily.

"Chinatown?" Val suggested as they walked to the door.

"That isn't a miracle, sir. I've seen it already."

"The bay front?"

"I've practically worn my feet away trotting along the Embarcadero."

They were on the sidewalk by then. "You make miracles difficult," Val chuckled. "Let's see—it's almost five now. Be getting dark before long. If we move fast we should be able to see the sun set over Seal Rocks on its way down to China. Nothing like it. And then we can have a sea-food dinner and really start working miracles."

"I'm beginning to believe you can produce miracles, Mr. Easton. Have you a car?"

"We'll take a taxi."

"Please—a miracle deserves something better than a taxi. Can't we have a scrumptuous big car to see the sunset from? Or do I sound like a gold digger?"

"On the contrary. Here is a car for rent worthy of any sunset. Does it suit?"

The car was standing behind the rack of taxicabs, a large black limousine with a sign announcing it was for hire by the hour for sightseeing. The neatly uniformed driver who had been leaning against the front fender saw their interest and lifted a hand inquiringly.

Miss O'Leary nodded eagerly. "I can't think of a better one," she confessed.

"Drive out to the Cliff House," Val said to the driver. "And see if you can make it in time for the sunset."

"Yes, sir. Plenty of time."

The driver ushered them in, closed the door, and tooled the big car down the street. Miss O'Leary leaned back in the seat with a sigh of pleasure. "This," she said, "promises to make the day perfect."

Val grinned at her. "I'm sure of it," he said.

Miss O'Leary pulled down the back shade, took from her purse a little gold vanity case and did things to her complexion composedly. She was humming under her breath as she put away the vanity case. And she was still humming as her hand brought from the purse a small .25 automatic pistol. It was against Val's side with a quick movement.

"Please sit very still," Miss O'Leary said with the same composure. "I don't want to shoot you. It's so messy."

VAL SAT still. The little gun, almost concealed by Miss O'Leary's hand, was very firm against his side. Almost in a line with his heart. A slight contraction of her finger and the result would be messy indeed.

He said lightly: "I see I'm not the only one who can work miracles. Be careful or that will go off."

"You be careful, Mr. Easton, or it surely will." She spoke with the same composure, without smiling.

The glass slide behind the driver was open. He heard them, cast a quick look over his shoulder. "Everything all right, Martha?" he asked.

"In the bag, Bill. Get us there quick."

Val scowled. "Say, what is this? D'you know the driver?"

Miss O'Leary was no longer pert. Her jaw was firmer, her manner brisker. "I'm engaged to him," she said. "And for gathering you in this way, we're going to get enough money to be married on. For a government man," said Miss O'Leary with a touch of scorn, "you turned out to be pretty much of a sap."

Val's jaw dropped. "How did you know that?"

"Sucker," said Miss O'Leary. "Why do you think I got on that plane and flew out here with you? When you did a black-out on the plane you were pushed over against me— and I went through your pockets before the stewardess got to you. I was waiting in the hotel lobby when you walked in from the hospital—and I've been waiting around to take you if other ways fell down."

The smile Val gave her was rather sickly. "You must be working for Zaken and Chang Ch'ien then."

"Bill is," said Miss O'Leary. "And I go along with Bill."

Bill's neck was thick, shoulders broad, his young face hard and determined in silhouette.

"Where are you going?" Val asked after a moment.

"Give a guess. Sit still."

Miss O'Leary slipped a hand under Val's left arm, brought out the automatic, said: "Bill, take his rod."

Bill reached back, took the gun. "Let him have it if he squirms," Bill ordered callously.

"You bet I will," said Miss O'Leary.

"Listen," said Val harshly, "do you know that if you take me to Carl Zaken, he'll kill me?"

"That isn't our business," said Miss O'Leary. "Bill and I bring you in and what happens is your own hard luck."

"You don't happen to have the Dragon mark on your back, too?"

"The what? Say, listen," said Miss O'Leary with a touch of indignation. "There's nothing the matter with my back."

"Never mind. Where are we going?"

"Get down on the floor and forget that."

"I'm doing very well here."

The gun prodded his side. "Get down there," said Miss O'Leary, "or I'll have Bill use his blackjack on you."

Val got down. The car was big; it was not too cramped; but he could not see where they were going. In a general north and westerly direction he judged.

Presently the grade grew so steep that second gear had to be used. From the distance and direction they had traveled it might be Russian Hill, Val judged; but he wasn't sure; he wasn't allowed to look; and when the car suddenly slowed, turned in to the curb and gave two short blasts on the horn he had no exact idea where he was.

He heard doors creaking open. The limousine surged slowly up over the sidewalk and was abruptly engulfed in the small dark cavern of a first-floor garage.

It was easy enough to visualize the building clinging to the steep side of the hill, garage on the street level, floors rising above it as the house spread back against the rise of the hill. An old house evidently by the look of the stone walls just beyond the car.

The closing doors cut off the fast-fading daylight. A dim bulb on the right of the car shed sickly light. Miss O'Leary's Bill spoke gruffly over the back of the seat.

"Climb out on the right side."

He was standing there with an automatic in his hand when Val got out. "Through that door," he said. "An' up the steps inside. I'll be right behind you with this rod."

Whoever had opened the doors had vanished. The smaller door was a stout wooden one. The steps beyond it were narrow, steep. Bill not only was behind, but with one big hand he kept a firm grip on Val's collar. Miss O'Leary followed them up—up—up....

CHAPTER EIGHT
BRAND OF THE DRAGON

THERE SEEMED no end to the steps. Several small bulbs gave dim light. They passed one landing with a door, went up to another floor; and above it other steps went on up. Steps, landings creaked under their weight. The air was damp, musty, holding the faint odor of decay.

He had little time to think of that. On the second landing a door opened as he came abreast of it. He was guided through, down a short hall, through another door into a bare room lighted by a single bulb in the ceiling. And as he came into that room Val stopped short, pulses hammering. Muffled, faint, the shrill scream of a man in great pain had seeped through to his ears.

The hand on his collar pushed him into the room. Behind them Miss O'Leary spoke with a burst of emotion. "My God, listen to that! Turn him over, Bill, and let's get out of here! It gives me the creeps!"

Through a small wooden grating in a door opposite them a calm voice answered her. "Such small things do not matter. You hear a man's stubbornness. In a little while he will not be stubborn."

The voice had an uncanny, rhythmic, purring quality which seemed to vibrate through the room. Soft though it was through the grating, it carried an overwhelming sense of latent power, force. And Val Easton, as he heard it, felt his muscles tensing, tightening. Only one man in all the world had a voice like that.

And then the door opened and that one man stepped into the room.

Chang Ch'ien.

He came with the effortless, gliding movement of a great golden-skinned cat; attired like a gorgeous peacock in the stiff silken robes of Old China, with a round hat upon his head.

Tall and powerfully built, Chang Ch'ien overtopped them all by inches. His mouth was wide, full-lipped; cheekbones high, wide; eyes only slightly slanted. A small sickle-shaped scar at the corner of the right eye drew that side of the face up into the slightest sardonic cast. The faint black mustache and goatee had not been there the last time Val looked on that face; but the same cunning was visible in the lazy smile; and ruthlessness and cruelty lay dormant about the man like velvet-sheathed claws.

Lifting sinewy supple fingers, Chang Ch'ien spoke courteously, with a background of mockery. "Welcome again to the shelter of my poor roof, Valentine Easton. I have waited for this honor."

"I have no doubt," Val agreed dryly.

He thought of Chang Ch'ien's history as he looked at the man. Scraps gleaned here and there from the dossiers of foreign countries. Part Chinese, part Burmese, with a dash of English, Chang Ch'ien had come as a young man out of the isolated state of Szechuan, far up above the Yangtse gorges. Had come with Manchu retainers and a junk crammed with family treasure—and had dropped out of sight for years, until recognized by a missionary in Paris.

By that time the name of Chang Ch'ien was a myth, a legend, a terror in the underworlds of the Continent. The Sûreté and the French secret service knew him well.

Chance had thrown Chang Ch'ien with the master spy, Carl Zaken, the dread Black Doctor. The mad and grandiloquent plans of that partnership, led by Carl Zaken, had been transferred to America. And finally to this matter of Adolphus Crumpmeyer, the Brotherhood of the Dragon—and that scream of agony which had sounded a few moments before.

Looking at Chang Ch'ien now, Val thought—as he had often thought before—that never had he seen a man who so personified sheer satanic power and cruelty. That the lovely Tai Shan could be his sister was almost unbelievable.

Chang Ch'ien spoke to the two behind Val. "You have done well. Now leave."

"Do we get that money?" Miss O'Leary asked bluntly.

"What you were promised and more. Leave." The purring voice sent them from the room with no more words.

Chang Ch'ien clapped his sinewy hands as they left. Two Chinese stepped through the other doorway. They carried automatics. One of them Val recognized as the man whose knife had cut Hopkins.

Chang Ch'ien was smiling. "Miss Fraser will be glad to see you," he said.

"So—she's here?"

"Black wig and all. At this moment, I believe, with another charming young woman who is a guest."

"Crumpmeyer's daughter?"

"As astute as ever, Valentine Easton."

"And of course Li Hung and his secretary."

"Most unwillingly," Chan Ch'ien murmured. "You—er—just heard the secretary being persuaded that there are things more to be feared than Li Hung himself."

VAL STUDIED the man. One flaw lay behind that golden-tinted face. Vanity. Dangerous, ruthless and cunning as he was, the vanity of Chang Ch'ien was greater. Carl Zaken was the only man living who could hold it in check. Carl Zaken was the only man Chang Ch'ien feared—and Carl Zaken was not here.

"Why should Li Hung be feared?" Val asked.

Chang Ch'ien slipped his hands into the wide sleeves of his gorgeous coat.

"So there are things you do not know, my dear Easton? Since it cannot matter now, for you will not see the sun rise again, you shall know. Li Hung is the head of the Brotherhood of the Dragon. Not fifty men of all the thousands know that he is. Few of them know who the others are. Each man knows five others—no more. A few know many more. But only one man possesses the records of all who bear the mark of the dragon."

"Li Hung, eh?"

"Li Hung."

"Crumpmeyer knew," Val guessed.

Chang Ch'ien smiled reminiscently.

"Yes. Crumpmeyer knew. Crumpmeyer, who was born in China, and became more Chinese than those of the blood in all things but one. He could not"—Chang Ch'ien smiled—"stand pain like a Chinese. He talked, in that room where Li Hung's man will presently talk; and having named Li Hung to win his freedom, he grew afraid. He could not warn his brotherhood. They would have killed him for his weakness. He could not see Li Hung walk into a trap, for his treachery would still become known and death find him. So he fled to Washington; and before we could find him and stop him, he had talked. And so he died anyway.

"It was too bad, Easton, that he did not die an hour sooner. You would still be safe in Washington."

"Regrettable," Val agreed. "But it seems to me you and Zaken are going to a lot of trouble over a Chinese secret society."

"It would," said Chang Ch'ien. "But when we are through, we shall be masters of the Brotherhood of the Dragon. The vast sums they have been remitting to China will come to us. And through those in high places in China who bear the mark, we will have power otherwise impossible to get. The fifty men—less one—who knew Li Hung, will die, and thousands who obey orders blindly will answer only to us. In this country they know fear now. They will be docile when we know the names of each man."

Val said slowly: "I see. You and Zaken are working more or less in the dark now. You can't make much progress until you can locate the men you want to deal with. And only Li Hung can make that possible."

Chang Ch'ien bowed. "You see clearly. A pity you cannot live with that information."

"Isn't it," Val sighed. "Miss Fraser, I suppose, will get the same?"

"Exactly. And Crumpmeyer's daughter. All of you will be branded with the sign of the Dragon, strangled and left where your bodies will carry the greatest lesson." Chang Ch'ien smiled broadly. "Strangling, my friend, is not too painful a death. A few moments—and then sleep."

"You'd put a branding iron against the backs of those young women?"

The ruthlessness, the cruelty were there now behind the lazy smile.

"It must be done, my dear Easton. Their short-lived pain will bring bewilderment and fear to many men who read of the mark on their backs."

"Damn you!" said Val thickly as his self-control snapped for a moment.

A QUICK step took Chang Ch'ien back from him. The two armed men rushed in. Chang Ch'ien gave a sharp order in Chinese. One held his gun ready; and the other searched under Val's coat and brought forth the second automatic.

Chang Ch'ien frowned at sight of it. "Those two were ordered to disarm you," he said. "They were careless. They will hear of this."

Chang Ch'ien spoke again Chinese to the guards—then said in English: "I must go to Li Hung's man. I will see you again in a few minutes. In the meantime these two will keep you company."

He bowed, politely, smiling, and left the room with the same catlike flow of movement.

The two guards prodded Val through the same doorway with their guns. Val caught a glimpse of Chang Ch'ien mounting a flight of stairs; and then was hustled on past the stairs, through a hall, a doorway, a room, into another room. The house seemed to be a maze of rooms and passages.

A table, two chairs, a cot against the wall comprised the furnishings. A stout wooden shutter was closed outside the one window. The guards motioned him to the cot, dragged the chairs into the middle of the room, sat down facing him, the guns resting across their laps.

And there they sat, watching him.

On the edge of the cot, Val scowled at the floor. He had found Chang Ch'ien. He had reached his goal—and he seemed no better off than before. It was beginning to look as if Hopkins had been right. To use himself for a decoy, to let himself be caught, trapped as had Nancy Fraser and Li Hung was of little use after all.

With two automatics, with one, he might have a chance. With none the odds were high. He had counted on time— hours perhaps. And he had minutes. How long would it be before that hot branding iron was pressed against Nancy Fraser's back?

Thought of that made Val a little sick. Nancy Fraser, smiling, clever, beautiful, to feel the sear of heat against her soft smooth skin. And then die, choking and gasping that her death might further the plans of two men who were half mad with their lust for power.

The minutes fled. Never had the hand of his wrist watch seemed to travel so fast; for time was what Val wanted now, as he had never wanted it before.

The two guards sat watching him.

The house was quiet, ominously quiet. Li Hung's young secretary had not cried out again. He might be dead—or his cries inaudible now. Anything was possible in this old rookery with its maze of passages, rooms and stairs.

Then a woman cried out. Louder, clearer, closer than the cry of Li Hung's secretary had sounded in that first room. Val found himself sitting there on the edge of the cot quivering.

One of the Chinese before him grinned, said something to the other; and the man laughed.

That laugh brought the red mist before Val's eyes, sent his hand to his belt. The knife was out in his hand before either of them noticed what he was doing. His thumb pressed the handle as he lunged to his feet.

The sharp blade flew out. Val hurled the knife without stopping his lunge. Hurled it with the skill of long and constant practice; with the strength of madness.

He saw the sharp blade fly true to one yellow throat and sink out of sight. The awful gurgling gasp of a dying man was in his ears as he reached the second man, hammering one terrible blow in at the startled saffron face with his left fist.

The weight of his rush, his body, his fury were behind that blow. Val felt his knuckles crush, go numb; felt the terrific shock clear back to his shoulders; and staggered as the man catapulted back out of the chair, slid across the floor and lay still with blood gushing from a great gash in his cheek.

The revolver had skittered halfway across the room. Val's left hand was useless. He snatched up the gun with his right and ran out of the room for the narrow stairs up which Chang Ch'ien had vanished.

No one barred his way. A door at the top of the stairs was closed. But as his pounding rush came up to the door it was hastily pulled ajar. Val glimpsed a startled face looking at him. An instant later his shoulder struck the door, knocking it open, knocking the man on the other side staggering—and Val staggered through himself in time to see a knife being drawn.

This time the steel side of the revolver struck above the ear. The man was dead before he hit the floor, the bone of his skull broken by the savage impact.

VAL STEPPED over the body. He was in another hall which, a few feet ahead, turned to the right and ended within two paces at another door.

The door opened freely.

And on the other side the dim, damp ancient feel of the place gave way to a bright light, soft rugs, gay colors. The room was a study, small, sparsely but richly furnished according to Oriental custom.

But it was empty.

Val stood panting in the doorway, looking, listening. Chang Ch'ien had come up those chairs. They led only here. This richly furnished little room fairly cried the presence of Chang Ch'ien. And yet—where was the man? Where had that cry come from?

It came again—not a cry this time. She was groaning, panting, whimpering softly, as a trapped animal might who struggles helplessly.

The sounds seemed to be in the very room where he stood; but the room was empty. Val went across the room on his toes, following the sounds to the opposite corner, to a tall parchment screen, painted with an exquisite Chinese winter landscape.

The smooth purring voice of Chang Ch'ien came from behind the screen.

"It will hurt, Miss Fraser. You may scream loudly. No one will hear—but our friend here in the chair. See—the iron is hot. It will burn deep. Be calm—you cannot break those straps...."

Val was behind the screen as the last words were uttered. A smooth wall panel was standing ajar. On the other side was another tall parchment screen.

The sounds were coming from beyond the second screen. The woman, choking, "Some day it will catch up with you!" Nancy Fraser's voice.

And Chang Ch'ien, smoothly, "Between the shoulders here...."

Val smashed the revolver through the parchment screen, tearing a great gap.

He glimpsed Nancy Fraser lying face down on a wide table, her arms outstretched, held firmly by leather straps around her wrists. Her dress had been torn down, exposing her back. Leaning over her, one hand on her left shoulder blade, was Chang Ch'ien on the point of pressing a smoking branding iron on the smooth white skin.

Startled by the ripping parchment Chang Ch'ien looked over his shoulder, saw the revolver coming through. Like a great cat he whirled, hurling the red hot iron at the screen before Val shot.

The bullet hit Chang Ch'ien's shoulder instead of the head where it was aimed. And Val bent double as the smoking iron caught him in the middle, knocking the wind out of him before it clattered to the floor.

Gasping, he kicked the screen down; and as it fell the light overhead went out, leaving only a faint glow through the open panel.

Chang Ch'ien was not in sight.

A calm voice said: "Across the room through a wall panel. I think you hit him. The light switch is on the other side of the wall."

As his eye pupils opened, Val made out the speaker sitting stiffly upright in a chair which stood against the wall. Li Hung was tied there, a helpless spectator.

"Just a minute, Nancy!"

Val went to the opposite wall, looked for the panel, failed to find it and turned back to the table.

Li Hung urged calmly: "Cut these cords. He will have men here in a few moments. I will be more help than the young lady."

"Val—he's right! Do it!" That from Nancy, helpless as she was.

"Haven't a knife," Val muttered.

Then he saw at the end of the table a charcoal brazier in which two more irons were heating. He jerked one out, found the end red, turned to the chair, put the red hot metal against the cords.

They smoldered, flamed, parted—and Li Hung clawed the smoldering strands aside and came to his feet.

"Give me that iron!" he begged sharply. "I hear them coming!"

Coming they were, feet tramping, voices calling. A gun crashed out in the house somewhere. A second report followed.

Val swore with relief. "That's a headquarters squad mopping up the house. I had myself followed here, with orders to bring a detail of armed men as soon as it was certain where I went. I thought I'd have more time than I did. But he's finally brought 'em."

Val was helping Nancy off the table when Hopkins burst in, followed by three plainclothesmen with flashlights.

"Thank God!" Hopkins panted. "I was afraid we were too late! Where are they? We caught a white couple in the garage below and turned up a couple of small fry on our way up through the house. Found Crumpmeyer's daughter safe, too. But that's all. Men are posted out in front."

Li Hung brushed his coat sleeve negligently. "I'm afraid the fox has left the den," he stated calmly. "He boasted to me that if the street in front were filled with people he could still come and go. But his claws are clipped. I can deal with him myself now."

"You'll find a panel in that wall," Val said to the plainclothesmen. "Get it open and you'll find how he got away. Nancy, I'll take you back to the hotel, while Hopkins stays with Mr. Li. It looks as if you're not going to be tattooed this evening."

Nancy laughed. She could still do that, even if she was a bit shaky. "At least," Nancy said, "my back would have been a sensation at a formal dinner."

THE DRAGONS OF CHANG CH'IEN

OUT OF THE NIGHT THEY SWARMED—THE SONS OF THE DRAGON—THOSE SAFFRON-SKINNED EMISSARIES OF THE BLACK DOCTOR AND HIS CO-PARTNER IN CRIME, THE DREAD CHANG CH'IEN. AND ONLY ONE MAN—VAL EASTON, ACE ESPIONAGE OPERATIVE—KNEW THE EVIL THAT WOULD FOLLOW IN THEIR WAKE. KNEW THAT THE VERY PEACE OF THE WORLD RESTED ON HIS SHOULDERS—AND HIS ALONE.

CHAPTER ONE
TWO DEAD CHINESE

ON **SATURDAY** morning, at eleven o'clock, the Secretary of State received the Chinese Ambassador and a companion. It was an informal call; most informal. His Excellency, the Ambassador, made that plain when, departing with the companion, they were waylaid in the long, high-ceilinged corridor of the State, War and Navy Building by several members of the press.

Beaming through the thick lenses of his spectacles, the Chinese Ambassador spoke in the perfect English which had made him a valuable member of his debating team when he had attended a large American university, a number of years before.

"Nothing official about this, gentlemen," the Ambassador declared amiably. "Merely an informal visit to introduce an old friend. And a very pleasant visit too. The Secretary is a corking chap, you know; always delightful."

Perhaps the Ambassador's smile was a bit more bland than usual over that fulsome praise. Most certainly he was aware that the Washington correspondents had consigned the Secretary to posterity under the nickname of Sourface Sam.

"Who is your friend, Mr. Ambassador?" was the next question.

The figure went down and Val dived for the knife.

Tall, scholarly, solemn behind shell-rimmed nose-glasses, the Ambassador's companion waited with no sign of interest on his thin, aristocratic face. His manner was in marked contrast to the amiable reply of the Ambassador.

"This is my old friend, Li Hung, whom you may know as a famous authority on old jade, enameled ware and lacquer work. Li Hung, I regret to say, does not speak English."

One of the newspaper men commented with a trace of sarcasm: "I suppose you gentlemen have been discussing Chinese art with the Secretary?"

"You hit the nail on the head, old man," the Ambassador replied, beaming. "The Secretary is interested in Chinese art himself, as you know. Sorry there's nothing worth printing today. Drop around to the embassy after the week-end and I'll see what I can scare up. Good day."

The smiling Ambassador and his grave companion went their way, leaving a somewhat stunned gathering behind.

Wesley Kinnard, of the *Continental News Service,* put his reaction into words.

"Who in hell would have thought Sourface Sam had imagination enough to dabble in Chinese art?"

SOME THIRTY minutes after the Chinese Ambassador and his friend rolled away from the State, War and Navy Building in the embassy limousine, another group of newspapermen, women, and cameramen, gathered in a fourth-floor suite of the fashionable St. Stephanie Hotel, just off Central Park, in New York.

They were asking questions also, fast and to the point. Noon was upon them. Sunday editions were being made up. This information was important in its own way.

"When does your marriage to the Countess Waleska take place, Mr. Brinton?"

"What are your plans after marriage?"

"Is there any objection to stating how old the bride is?"

"Will the Countess tell us something of her earlier life?"

Samuel Townsend Brinton lifted a hand for silence among his interrogators. His heavy, florid face was smiling, but his manner was firm, with that quality obtainable only by the habit of power and command.

"Not so fast, not so fast," he begged. "I summoned you here merely to announce my engagement to the Countess, not to give our autobiographies."

If Samuel Brinton had been as candid as usual he would have told them bluntly it was none of their business—and reminded them that this interview was more than he had ever given to the newspapers before. Love and romance had softened the great man strangely.

The Countess Waleska, standing beside him, laughed delightedly.

"Of course they want to know these things, Samuel," she said with a piquant touch of accent. "I myself would want to know them. Oh, yes. It ees not every day such a famous man as Samuel Brinton announce his engagement, no? My friends, I tell you one little secret; I am thirty-one. Now, you see? And we will be married soon. Very soon. Now what you say?"

One of the newspaperwomen gushed: "You don't look a day over thirty, Countess. Honestly."

The tribute carried a ring of truth. The Countess Waleska had captivated them all. Her dark, vivacious beauty seemed to bring energy and merriment into the hotel room. Her open, cordial manner had no restraint and much friendliness. She was eager to be liked; she let them all see it—and they liked her.

Samuel Brinton glowed with pride. "I consider myself a very fortunate man," he said, with an artlessness which would have amazed the directors of some of the powerful boards he headed.

The atmosphere was so free and unrestrained that one of the newspaper men ventured with a grin: "How will it feel to be a father again, Mr. Brinton?"

"Great!" Samuel Brinton replied enthusiastically. He turned to smile at the Countess Waleska's seven-year-old daughter, who stood gravely at one side in the company of her middle-aged nurse. Samuel Brinton added: "Having had one daughter, it will be a pleasure to welcome another."

"By the way, Mr. Brinton, where is your daughter?"

The faint shadow which passed over Brinton's face vanished instantly. "Shirley is at Broad Acres," he replied. "The Countess and her daughter are motoring to the estate with me for the week-end. Shirley has already heard the good news. And now, gentlemen, if you care for any pictures, we can give you five more minutes."

THAT SAME Saturday noon, a coupé driven by one John Mills was rolling through North Trenton, New Jersey, at one twenty, on its way to Newark.

John Mills was a traveling salesman. He had been on the road all week, covering his territory in his car; he was headed now toward Newark—home, and a restful week-end. John Mills was traveling a bit faster than he should have been. He denied it later and there was no one to dispute his word. At any rate, he was on his own side of the street when the shabby old delivery truck coming toward him struck a hole in the pavement, blew out a front tire and wobbled over across his path.

John Mills shouted, blew his horn, stamped hard on the brakes, twisted his front wheels. But to no avail. The crash of the collision was audible the length of the block. The two machines stopped with their radiators locked together.

Spectators began to converge toward the spot, and John Mills leaped out of his car, red-faced, angry. From the dilapidated little delivery truck two slender Orientals scurried and surveyed the damage.

"What the hell's the idea of running in front of me?" John Mills demanded passionately of them. His bumper and fender were smashed, a tire was blown out and the front wheels were knocked awry.

The right front wheel of the small delivery truck was smashed beyond repair.

The two Orientals looked at the damage and turned bland, smiling faces to John Mills. One of them spoke rapidly to him in Chinese, waved his arms, shook his head, shrugged, pointed over his shoulder. They hurried away.

"Hey, wait a minute! Where you going?" Mills yelled after them.

The man waved toward the middle of the block where there was a garage. That was peculiar, John Mills recalled later, in view of the Chinaman's inability to understand English. He had evidently understood the question and answered it with the gesture. But at the moment it seemed logical that they go for help. And just then the first spectator, a young man, came running up.

"I saw it, mister!" he panted. "They ran in front of you. It was their fault!"

A motorcycle policeman arrived on the scene and took charge. He heard John Mills' version, corroborated by others who had witnessed the collision.

"Where are these two Chinks?" the officer asked.

"They went to that garage to get some help," Mills said. "Funny they aren't back by now." A sudden thought struck him. "Say, I wonder if they ran away?"

"You should 'a kept 'em here," the officer grumbled. "No telling what Chinks'll do when they get scared. But I guess they won't get far from their car at that. Let's see what they've got inside."

The officer stepped to the back and opened the doors. One look, and the officer uttered a startled oath. A young woman standing just behind him looked past his arm and suddenly shrieked with fright.

"It's full of dead men! Oh, my God, look at the blood! Take me away from here!"

Two bodies lay on the truck bed, one sprawled partway across the other, as if they both had been tumbled in hastily and the door slammed on them.

The officer gulped, swallowed, and then did his duty like a man. Climbing into the truck he made a hasty examination.

"Two Chinamen," he said when he lurched out, pale and shaking. He shut the door firmly and regained a measure of composure. "Now where'd them two go who were running this truck?" he demanded, unfastening the leather holster flap over his revolver. "Down to that garage, hey? Don't nobody open those doors until I get back."

CHAPTER TWO

THE GREGG SYSTEM

AT **FIVE** minutes past five on that same Saturday afternoon, the hand of duty reached out and touched Valentine Easton.

At the moment Val Easton was waiting to follow a redcap through one of the train gates in the Washington, D.C. Union Station. The touch of duty was unobtrusive. It was safe to say that not one of the fifty-odd passengers and luggage porters in the group before the gate noticed or suspected anything. The small, meek man edging up beside Val Easton had touched Val's arm only once. When Val turned his head, the man was not even looking at him; but from the corner of the stranger's mouth three words issued.

"Gregg wants you."

Val's face remained expressionless; but a moment later he tapped his porter on the shoulder. "Bring my bag," he directed.

Puzzled, the redcap pushed back past the meek little man and followed Val out to the taxi line, received his tip and watched Val depart in a taxi.

"Now what you think of that?" the colored man said to a fellow redcap standing near. "Dat white man standin' right at de gate ready to go to Chicago, an' he change his mind an' walk away. Sho' look funny to me."

But to Val Easton the circumstance was not peculiar. Incidents like this had happened before and would happen again. You never knew what would happen when you were a part of the far-flung web of espionage which centered in that one man whose code name was "Gregg."

In a bare, high-ceilinged office in the State, War and Navy Building here in Washington, threads of contact centered from the wide world. Orders, which only two or three people would ever know, often set in motion unsuspected forces affecting the destinies of people and countries.

When Gregg ordered, questions were never asked. Strict obedience was the first thing grilled into every person who had contact with that office.

Val was mildly curious. That he could be. In his pocket was a railroad ticket and a lower-berth reservation to Chicago. His instructions had been explicit; his plans called for an absence of more than a week. Now, not two hours since he had last talked with Gregg, those plans were abruptly countermanded. Something had gone wrong.

Val dismissed the taxi at Seventeenth and Pennsylvania Avenue, waited until it was out of sight, and then carried his bag across to the State, War and Navy Building and left it in charge of one of the uniformed guards at the front door.

The hundreds of clerks and officials who made the place a bee-hive of industry during the day were now gone. Val's steps echoed in the deserted halls. The aged Negro man, who kept watch all day outside of Gregg's office, was also gone. Val opened the door and walked in.

THERE WAS no anteroom. Directly inside the door a large, high-ceilinged room contained several chairs and a single desk; and at opposite ends of the room portraits of Lincoln and Washington looked down on all business transacted there.

From behind the desk Gregg said: "Good thing the train hadn't left. You'd have had to leave it up the road and come back in a hurry."

Heavy-set, saturnine, Gregg had a gruff, curt manner. But that, like his name, was a mask for the world to see. Those closest to Gregg knew the rare understanding, the great gift for friendship, loyalty and high patriotism which motivated this man.

Too often, Gregg's orders sent men and women into danger and death. Perhaps that knowledge, ever at his elbow, caused him to affect the saturnine cloak.

"Miss Fraser should be here in a few minutes," Gregg said. He knocked ashes from a cork-tipped cigarette into a copper ashtray and added: "She's bringing a car. Do you have dinner clothes packed?"

"Nothing in Chicago called for them."

"You can pack them before you leave," Gregg said briefly. He pushed a small newspaper clipping across the desk. "This was in the *Evening Star.*"

The item read—

DEAD CHINAMEN IN TRUCK

A small delivery truck entering Trenton today crashed into an automobile driven by John Mills, a traveling salesman. In the excitement the two Chinese driving the truck walked off and disappeared. In the truck were found the bodies of two Orientals. Examination of the bodies indicated murder, Coroner Hillsbury declared. The skulls of the dead men had been split with a sharp weapon, probably an ax. Efforts to find the two Chinese who were driving the truck have proven fruitless so far.

Val put the clipping back on the desk. "Two dead Chinese," he said thoughtfully.

"Exactly, Easton; two dead Chinese; and a most peculiar coincidence coming from that territory at this time."

Val waited curiously. Gregg would come to the point in his own time and way.

Leaning back, Gregg drew on his cigarette and looked moodily from under shaggy eyebrows.

"This morning, Easton, the Chinese Ambassador called on the Secretary of State."

"I hadn't heard it."

"With him, the Ambassador took a friend, Li Hung."

"Ah—Li Hung. You interest me."

"I thought so," Gregg said. "We succeeded in getting Li Hung safely from San Francisco to the Chinese Embassy. I thought that would be the end of the matter. Apparently not. Tonight's paper also carried a short squib stating that the Chinese Ambassador took a world-famous authority on jade to see the Secretary, whose hobby is old jade."

"I thought," said Val with a straight face, "that poker was the Secretary's hobby."

Gregg allowed himself the luxury of a faint smile.

"As far as I know, it is. Poker and Kentucky rye. Certainly not Chinese jade. I had the report before the Secretary went out to lunch. It interested me enough to look into the matter. All I can find out it that the visit was merely a friendly call. There seems to be a bit of secrecy about it."

"This is the third secretive Secretary we've had," Val murmured.

GREGG ALLOWED himself the further luxury of a burst of candor. "And that's three too many! How the devil does the government expect to get any results out of this office when we have to spy on the Secretary of State, himself, to find out what's going on? They come in with their pet policies, likes and dislikes, and try to work magic by their own sweet selves. Hell! Forget I said this, Easton."

Val nodded.

"At noon today, in New York," Gregg went on, "Samuel Townsend Brinton announced his engagement, to the Countess Waleska. You may have heard of her."

"Isn't she the widow of that Polish count who died in Shanghai about three years ago? The chap who got out of Poland in a hurry because it was rumored part of his income was traced back to French government funds?"

"The same woman."

"As I recall it, she was rather a beauty, and had a little daughter," Val said, searching back into his memory. "I never met her, but I heard about her more than once in those months I was working out of Shanghai. *Hmmm;* so she's in this country now, and going to marry Brinton? Did rather well for herself, I'd say."

"Tremendously well," Gregg said curtly. "If gossip can be credited, most of the eligible women of Brinton's acquaintance had set their hearts on marrying him. It isn't every day you get an eligible widower, worth a hundred million dollars or more, to work on."

Val thought, in passing, that Gregg had at his fingertips more bits of knowledge than any other person in the country. The man could talk accurately of intimate matters concerning world powers, and by the same token could sit here and reel off authentic society gossip like the best of tea-table chatterers. Yet Gregg's life was spent mostly in this bare, high-ceilinged room. The constant stream of reports flowing over his desk was the answer.

But there was more to this than mere gossip. Gossip did not interest Gregg. In searching for some key to the puzzle, one fact stood out above all others. Val put it into words.

"Peculiar that the Countess Waleska should be marrying our greatest munitions manufacturer."

Gregg answered softly, without changing his position.

"I was wondering how long it would take you to get around to that. Very peculiar, isn't it? This afternoon, Samuel Brinton and the Countess Waleska left by motor for the Brinton estate, Broad Acres, in northern New Jersey. With them they took the Countess' daughter and the daughter's nurse. Over the weekend Samuel Brinton's daughter, Shirley, will act as hostess to her father's future wife."

Val speculated: "It would be interesting to know how the daughter feels toward the new addition to the family."

"I can tell you," Gregg said drily. "She would stop it if she could. She's barely civil to the Countess."

"Indeed," said Val. "It appears to me, sir, we're paying rather close attention to the love affairs of Samuel Brinton."

Gregg countered bluntly.

"Anything which concerns the largest manufacturer of munitions in the country concerns us. The man is a valuable and a vital part of the national defense. Much army and navy ordinance supply comes from his factories. The foreign contacts and sales of the Brinton Arms Company are at times tied up with our foreign policy."

That was so evident it did not call for agreement. But Gregg's next statement was a surprise.

"In Shanghai, the Countess Waleska's French maid was indiscreet with a young man whose reputation was rather clouded. The Countess was forced to discharge her. By a lucky fluke the Countess was able to engage the services of an American widow stranded in Shanghai. The widow is still on the job. She is S-13."

Val whistled softly. "I've been wondering what happened to Norah Beamish the last few months. So she's been in Shanghai?"

Gregg nodded. "The Countess was a bit too brazen in her choice of friends even for Shanghai. It seemed a good idea to keep a check on her; and, as it happened, it was a good idea."

VAL SAID nothing more about that. He knew the procedure only too well. One need not inquire too closely into the young man whom the French maid had met. The fact that Norah Beamish, one of Gregg's most trusted workers, was on hand to take the vacated position, was proof of a well laid and neatly consummated plot.

And if the Countess Waleska was worth all that trouble in distant Shanghai, here in the United States, as the bride-to-be of Samuel Brinton, she was worth far more attention. Evidently she was getting it.

Gregg unfolded a large-scale map of New Jersey and spread it flat on his desk.

"Here," he said, indicating with a pencil, "is Trenton. This is the state highway leading north to Newark. Go north on it to here—and you find this road leading off east, which will bring you to Broad Acres, Brinton's estate. The place is staffed very largely, I understand, by Chinese. Brinton is partial to them, having spent some time in the Orient as a young man."

"Have they traced the ownership of that delivery truck?" Val questioned.

"I have had the local police make inquiries by long-distance. The tags were found to belong to an old Dodge sedan, registered by a man named Harrison, in Orange, New Jersey. The New Jersey police have checked the address and found that no such man ever lived there."

"Interesting, isn't it?" Val said. "A truck coming from Brinton's estate, and heading south, would be exactly where this truck was. Have you queried the estate to see if any of the Chinese staff is missing?"

Gregg leaned back in his chair again. "You're going to do that, Easton. You're driving up this evening. Stop in Trenton and have a look at those two dead Chinamen. Inspect their backs."

"It appears to me," said Val softly, "that we are moving to something."

Silence fell between them for a moment as they looked at each other.

"Chang Ch'ien?" Val said.

Gregg shrugged.

But Gregg's very lack of comment carried its weight of emphasis. Between them fell the shadow of grim experience out of the recent past.

Chang Ch'ien again; Chang Ch'ien, the golden-skinned killer who had formed a mad and magnificent partnership with the master spy, Carl Zaken, known as the Black Doctor. Control of the membership of that great Chinese secret organization called the Sons of the Dragon was their objective.

Val Easton and Gregg were the only living white men who fully understood what that would mean.

Grounds existed for believing the Sons of the Dragon were the guiding force behind the present government of China. Immense sums of money were remitted by the membership for use as the unknown leaders saw fit. Those who controlled the Sons of the Dragon had power at their disposal which was not pleasant to contemplate. Terrible power indeed if it fell into the hands of Chang Ch'ien and Carl Zaken.

Each member of the Sons of the Dragon was branded on the back with the Mandarin character of the Dragon. Only death could remove him from that secret brotherhood. And now, Val wondered, had death freed two Chinese in New Jersey from their oaths to the Sons of the Dragon?

One look at their backs would answer that.

Just then the door opened, and Nancy Fraser strolled into the room.

CHAPTER THREE

BROAD ACRES

NANCY FRAZER always gave Val the same lifting of spirit, quickening of the pulse and feeling of abject homage.

Few women were the equal of Nancy Fraser. Gregg had no other woman in his corps to match her in daring and resourcefulness. Nancy was in the way of becoming a classic in that service to which they all gave blind devotion.

But to look at Nancy you would never guess it, so softly feminine was she. Her face was tanned by the sun and her fine platinum-blond hair was cut short and waved close to her head. A little beauty, with a wide humorous mouth, Nancy's eyes were deeper and bluer than any Val had ever seen. She entered now, smiling and unconcerned, as if she might be on her way home from an afternoon tea, with an evening of pleasure ahead.

Nancy's eyebrows lifted inquiringly at sight of Val; but she spoke to Gregg.

"I came as quickly as I could. Unfortunately your orders to be extra nice to that *Chargé d'Affaires* worked too well. He wouldn't hear of my leaving."

"This is good enough," Gregg said briefly. "You're leaving in a few minutes for New Jersey with Easton. Accompanying you will be Miss Marjorie Stoneham, one of the local society girls."

"I've met her," said Nancy promptly. "She's rather a nice girl."

"She is going with you because she went to school with a Miss Shirley Brinton," Gregg said. "Miss Stoneham has been in communication with Miss Brinton this afternoon. She has secured an invitation for the week-end for herself and a young married couple who are visiting her."

Nancy Fraser's eyebrows went higher this time, as she looked at Val. "Married?" Nancy questioned.

"Regrettable, but necessary," Gregg told her. "As a married couple you will both have more freedom. I want certain information from Brinton's estate; but chiefly I want someone on the spot as quickly as possible in case anything happens. I've just been giving Easton a general idea of the situation."

Gregg hesitated, and added: "I'm more interested in what may happen than in what has already happened. I think that is all. Oh, yes, if Miss Stoneham's automobile has been returned from the garage by this time I suggest you use it. How soon can you leave?"

"I'll need fifteen minutes to pack," Nancy stated promptly.

"Ten's enough for me," Val said, smiling at her. "I've only dinner clothes to pack."

Gregg handed him a slip of paper. "This is Miss Stoneham's street address."

TWENTY-FIVE MINUTES later, Nancy Fraser waited at the wheel of her car while Val went to the door of the S Street house.

Miss Stoneham answered his ring herself. She was dressed to leave, and very presentable in a long-legged, youthful way, Val thought. Excitement had put a touch of natural color in her cheeks; she spoke to him eagerly.

"My car is waiting at the curb. Shall I telephone the garage to pick up your car and hold it?"

"Please do that," Val said.

On the spot, he decided that Gregg, as usual, had selected someone competent and capable. It was a source of never-ending wonder how Gregg could always produce the exact people needed for any particular job. Perhaps Gregg's driving patriotism and sublime belief in the value of his work was capable of arousing similar feelings in those of his countrymen whom he needed.

Marjorie Stoneham drove her big sedan north out of town with the three of them in the front seat; and as the miles dropped behind she talked freely. Marjorie Stoneham was twenty. Reared against the background of social Washington, intrigue was not new to her.

"Why don't you call yourselves Mr. and Mrs. Van Dyke?" she suggested. "I have friends in Los Angeles by that name. Shirley Brinton has heard me speak of them. Do you know Los Angeles, so you can pass it off?"

Val smiled. "Miss Fraser has just come from there. Suppose you tell us all you can recall about the Van Dykes."

Marjorie sketched the background, the habits, the life of her friends while driving the big car wide-open with the unconcerned skill of one familiar with automobiles since early childhood.

They were in Trenton before it seemed possible. A patrolman directed them to police headquarters. There Val introduced himself, and a detective took him to the morgue. The gruesome examination was quickly over.

The dead men appeared to be Cantonese. No articles or marks of identification had been found on their clothes. Neither carried the brand of the Dragon. Each man's head had been split open from the back. It was doubtful if they moved or uttered a sound after being struck.

These men at least did not belong to the brotherhood of the Dragon. To himself Val admitted relief at the knowledge Perhaps Gregg had been mistaken. Perhaps this gory bit of business had nothing to do with Chang Ch'ien and the Black Doctor; no proof existed that the double murder had any connection with the estate of Samuel Brinton.

It was beginning to look as if Gregg had taken a shot in the dark at phantoms; and in that case the visit to the Brinton estate would be nothing more than a pleasant experience. The munitions manufacturer was reputed to live with the lavish splendor of a feudal baron.

As they walked out of the morgue, the detective delivered himself of a disgusted observation.

"It's a hell of a note, isn't it? Two Chinks riding around with a couple of dead ones in the back of their car. They must have gotten an awful shock when they had that accident and knew the bodies would probably be discovered. I'll bet they haven't stopped running yet."

"Probably never will be found," Val agreed. "The Chinese take care of their own. One of the tongs, or friends of the dead men, may take it up. Has that delivery truck been traced yet?"

"Not yet. It's impounded, of course; but there are no numbers on file to correspond with the motor and body serial numbers. The fact that the tags were taken out under a phony name shows that someone was covering tracks pretty far back. Anything more we can do for you?"

"Nothing, I believe. Thanks for this."

IT WAS five minutes till ten when a uniformed gate-keeper, with a revolver strapped under his coat, unlocked high iron gates and allowed them to pass onto Samuel Brinton's Jersey estate. Orders had evidently been left with the gateman for their admittance.

Marjorie Stoneham laughed as she followed a wide, winding drive. "You'd think the place was a fort, and the Brinton's couldn't be contaminated by the common herd. But Shirley isn't that way at all. You'll like her."

"And Brinton?" Val suggested.

"I've met him only once. Perhaps he finds it necessary to be so stern."

Samuel Brinton's family had lived on this land for four generations, adding constantly to it. Broad Acres was a small empire in itself. One read that whole sections of land were given over to the prize herd of dairy cows; other sections were devoted to intensive truck gardening super-vised by agricultural experts.

The headlights thrusting through a moon-drenched night found none of that. This driveway to the house ran through a great park, studded with tall shade-trees.

The gatekeeper's lodge was almost a mile back of them when the smooth drive curved around the base of a small, wooded hill and revealed the vast flower gardens which the present Samuel Brinton had developed. Every variety of flower which the climate would support in the open was grown here, and tropical and rare varieties were cultivated under glass.

A long step, Val reflected, from munitions to the careful rearing of delicate flowers. The mind of Samuel Brinton had bridged it.

The main house lay there before them against the night, not so imposing as the entry would lead one to expect. It was built of dressed stone, two stories high, and its wings stretched away to right and left. Terraces and courts were banked with flowers and shrubbery. The stonework loomed white under the moon, and innumerable windows glowed with light.

An estate like this called for ceremony and solemnity. Instead, a girl waiting on the steps with a big police dog ran out to the car, crying: "Marjorie! You dear! Why don't you do this more often?" The dog moved around the car, barking.

They got out, and Nancy and Val were introduced as the Van Dykes. Shirley Brinton welcomed them, laughing.

"Isn't this fun? Father has the house full of his guests. I've been hostess with half of me, and wishing with the other half that some of them were twenty years younger. Come in. Your bags and car will be taken care of."

She hardly had to say that. Three figures had materialized noiselessly. In the moonlight Val saw they were Orientals, wearing, felt-soled slippers and black jackets and trousers.

Another impassive Oriental admitted them to the house.

Shirley Brinton said: "Come and meet father before you go up to your rooms."

She led them along a short corridor and into a huge drawing room.

Twenty-odd people were in the room, Val judged, scattered about in little groups. Against a hum of talk and laughter a radio was softly playing, precisely as other radios were playing all over the country.

But the music was a symphony concert; the radio was large, expensive; and the great drawing room was a marvel of perfect proportion, exquisitely chosen furniture and decoration. Formality was lacking. Some of the men wore dinner jackets and some business suits, the latter as if they had come straight from busy offices.

Shirley Brinton walked half the length of the room to a big, broad-shouldered man in a blue suit who was talking with two men and a woman.

"Father, may I present my guests? You know Marjorie Stoneham, I believe? This is Mr. and Mrs. Van Dyke."

Samuel Brinton's heavy, florid face was smiling as he acknowledged the introduction.

"It's a pleasure to have you," he declared with blunt sincerity. "Shirley was delighted when she heard you were coming."

Even before Shirley Brinton made the next introduction, Val knew who the woman was.

"The Countess Waleska," Shirley said colorlessly.

Val bowed slightly, regarding with interest this woman who was to marry Samuel Brinton. She was everything Val had expected from hearing about her in Shanghai—and more. An inch or so taller than Shirley, and years older of course, the Countess had attained that goal of all women— seemingly permanent youthfulness. But it was a youthfulness tempered with poise, assurance, and a suggestion of mental depth which might be interesting to explore.

She was a brunette with a straight nose and a finely chiseled face, inclined to thinness. Her smile, her manner, her faintly accented words suggested she might have been waiting all evening just to greet them.

And then, before Shirley Brinton could do so, with the easy, deft assurance of one who might have been the hostess instead of Shirley, the Countess introduced the men with whom she had been talking.

"His Excellency, the Chinese Ambassador—and Mr. Li Hung."

CHAPTER FOUR
SURPRISE MEETING

VAL BARELY noticed Shirley Brinton's faint color and the quick catching of her lower lip between her teeth at being so deftly shunted into the background. He was too surprised to find these two men here.

Had Gregg known or suspected it? Hardly, or he would have mentioned them. In the same breath Val wondered what had brought them here.

The Chinese Ambassador was beaming. He seemed to go through life with unvarying good will toward everyone. But Li Hung, the Ambassador's tall, scholarly companion had no expression at all as his hand met Val's hand with that lax grip of the Oriental to whom handshaking is an unnatural rite.

Li Hung's manner was reserved, distant. No watching eye would have suspected Li Hung of knowing them, of being aware their names were not Van Dyke. A faint smile came on the man's face as he bowed to Nancy.

"This is indeed a delight and a pleasure," Li Hung said in excellent English, touched with an Oxford accent. "But I am not sure that I caught the name right."

"Van Dyke," said Nancy imperturbably.

"Ah—Van Dyke? Will you pardon my curiosity? Have you and your husband ever been in China, Mrs. Van Dyke? I have the feeling that we have met before."

On the surface it was sincere.

Val knew it to be velvet-sheathed claws toying as only an Oriental could toy with a victim. Hadn't he himself, not two weeks before, met Li Hung on the ship before it docked in San Francisco? Hadn't Nancy herself almost lost her life in helping to save the man from those whom, in all the world, he had most cause to fear—Chang Ch'ien and the Black Doctor?

All that had happened; and now what did it matter that they carried the secret knowledge that Li Hung headed the brotherhood of the Dragon? They could not mention it—and yet with a sentence Li Hung could expose them to Brinton as imposters. He seemed to be considering that move.

Nancy knew it, yet she walked the tight wire of uncertainty quite calmly.

"It must have been some other Van Dykes," Nancy smiled. "Unless you met us in Los Angeles. Have you ever been there?"

"To my regret, no," Li Hung replied. He looked at Val with a faint ironical smile. "But if in Los Angeles I will find friends as charming as your wife, Mr. Van Dyke, I shall certainly go there as soon as possible. You must be very proud of Mrs. Van Dyke."

Val damned the man inwardly as he replied to Li Hung: "If you get to Los Angeles, look us up by all means."

Countess Waleska slipped her arm intimately through Samuel Brinton's and laughed delightedly. "Does that include us also, Mr. Van Dyke?"

"That goes without saying."

"You don't live in Hollywood? I have promis' myself a visit there some day."

"We live out beyond Beverly Hills, off the Santa Monica highway," Val told her, giving the right location of the real Van Dyke's home.

"Would you rather meet some of the others now, or go to your rooms and freshen up?" Shirley Brinton asked Nancy. "I warn you, this is Saturday night and we stay up quite late."

"If I could get into my bag for a few minutes, I'd feel more comfortable," Nancy said.

Li Hung bowed. The touch of ironical humor was still about his mouth as he watched them go. But the last impression Val carried away was the smile of Countess Waleska. It was a thoughtful smile—just a shade too thoughtful.

THE BEDROOM in which Shirley Brinton left Val and Nancy was large and comfortable. Their bags had already been brought up. The covers of the twin beds had been turned down for the night.

Nancy looked about the room and made a face. "Gregg certainly had a brainstorm when he thought of this arrangement."

Val chuckled at the look of disgust on Nancy's face. "I find I'm able to take it very easily."

Nancy laughed ruefully. "You would, darn you. The tender sensibilities seem to have been scrapped when most of you men were made. I suppose we'll make out some way. Meanwhile—what do you think of the company?"

"Rather a coincidence, isn't it? I'd give something to know why Li Hung is here with the Chinese Ambassador."

"After all, he came to this country to visit the Ambassador."

"Quite right; and yet from the Secretary of State to the Brinton Arms Company is some jump. I'd say the Secretary has given his benign approval to some undercover munitions contracts with the Chinese government."

"Doubtless," Nancy agreed as she opened her black traveling case on one of the twin beds. "A Secretary has to approve of something now and then. What concerns me most at this moment is the expression on the Countess' face while Li Hung was fencing in his delicate Celestial way."

"I noticed that. She had something on her mind when we left."

"What could it be?" said Nancy, carefully unfolding an evening dress.

"She's a very clever woman," Val said, taking off his coat and vest. "And she doubtless knows her Chinese. She may have sensed something behind Li Hung's words—and, as the wife-to-be of Samuel Brinton, was mildly interested. On the other hand, if she is half the woman Gregg supposed her to be, she may have been more than mildly interested. And if so, why?" Val asked, starting to remove his shirt.

"Wait a minute," Nancy said hastily. "You're taking Gregg's suggestion a bit too literally. Pause, please, while I transfer my half of the Van Dykes to the bathroom."

Nancy took her things to the bathroom, and with the door opened a crack continued the conversation.

"As one woman explaining another, I can tell you quite definitely the Countess is interested first in marrying Samuel Brinton. She will never let sentiment or emotion interfere with her chance at one hundred million dollars and a rather likeable gentleman who looks as if he might have high blood pressure. Write that down in your little red book and file it away."

"Being only a suspicious male, may I suggest the hundred million being practically in the bag, so to speak, still leaves room for an agile mind to be concerned with other matters?"

Nancy chuckled. "As a suspicious male, you are probably right. We women are usually open to suspicion in one way or another,"

"And as a long-suffering male who grew up with three sisters, will you please not take too long with your dressing?" Val begged. "I want to get downstairs and look around as much as possible before the evening is over."

NANCY WAS stunning in her simple blue evening gown. She had not been downstairs many minutes before several men were grouped around her. The fact that most of them were old enough to be her father did not seem to abate their enthusiasm.

So casually that it might have been accidental, Li Hung appeared at Val's elbow. By mutual agreement they moved off together. Li Hung was not smiling now; his glance was penetrating as he spoke bluntly.

"Why are you here, Mr. Easton?"

"That is a question I'd like you to answer also," Val countered.

"My friend, the Ambassador, has long known Mr. Brinton."

"Doubtless," Val answered with faint irony of his own. "Brinton is a fine fellow, isn't he? His guns and ammunition are well thought of too, I understand."

Li Hung's thin face, more hawk-like than was usual among his countrymen, was stamped with aloofness and authority; his sharp eyes through shell-rimmed nose-glasses had nothing aloof in them.

"Quite right, Mr. Easton. Your government thinks well of Brinton arms; well enough to encourage large sales to other countries." Li Hung paused. The latent cruelty about his thin mouth grew more evident for a moment. "I fail to understand why, when that encouragement has been given, the government finds it necessary to watch the buyer, especially by sending spies known already to the person they are watching."

The cat was out of the bag now. Li Hung was here to buy arms from Brinton. Nothing wrong about that.

"Sorry to have disquieted you," Val said. "We're not here to watch you. Had no idea you'd be here as a matter of fact. I don't suppose it would be any use in telling you we're here on a friendly visit also, despite the fact that we're not using our right names?"

Li Hung's searching look grew satisfied. "My apologies," he murmured. "I presume it would be bad taste to ask what really brings you here?"

"Merely a friendly visit," Val repeated cheerfully. "By the way, you haven't heard anything about our mutual friend, Chang Ch'ien, have you?"

All of Li Hung's facial control could not conceal the start of agitation that question gave him.

"Nothing! Not a word. The man has vanished. Can you tell me anything about him, Mr. Easton? Do you know anything?"

"I know nothing," said Val. "But I'm wondering when I will." He looked around the room. "Nice staff of servants, Brinton has. They seem capable. In fact," said Val cheerfully, "your countrymen always seem capable. They can be depended on to carry out an order—even in such matters as murder. Let's hope Chang Ch'ien has not been giving any orders lately."

Smiling, Val walked away, leaving that thought with a profoundly disturbed man.

Shirley Brinton was moving among her father's guests with the ease of a perfect hostess. Val watched her for a few moments, finding her not very much like her father. From Brinton's big head and body Shirley had inherited only wide cheekbones and a firm jaw line. The red evening gown she wore gave her a bit of vivid dash which was probably not there ordinarily. But she was cheerful and agreeable and rather pretty. At the first opportune moment Val joined her.

"I've been watching your servants, Miss Brinton," he said. "It's really an extraordinary staff. Have they been with you very long?"

Smiling, she said: "Some of them have. Old Wong, the number-one boy, has been with father many years. There's a certain amount of change among the others. We keep between twenty and thirty, you know, outside and in. They're very efficient."

"So I've heard—if one can keep them. Have any left recently?"

"Not that I know of." Shirley Brinton gave him a direct smiling look. "Have you any particular reason for wanting to know?"

"Idle curiosity. I might consider hiring one or two for our own house. I was wondering about their reliability."

Shirley Brinton nodded, smiling. Val felt she hadn't entirely swallowed his rather lame explanation.

"There is Wong now, in the doorway," she said. "I'll ask him."

TURNING, VAL saw her slight gesture bringing to them a tall, elderly Oriental, whose shoulders were stooped and whose hands as he walked were in the sleeves of a long black silk coat. His thin face was expressionless and his voice was low as he bowed slightly and said: "Yes, missy?"

"Is everything all right, Wong?"

"Yes, missy."

"You will have the buffet ready before midnight?"

"Yes, missy."

Shirley gave Val a mischievous smile. "Wong, have any of your men left us lately?"

Wong's left sleeve bulged out as the hand inside moved suddenly. He stood still, watching her from sunken eyes. Imperceptibly the gaze flicked to Val Easton.

Popular superstition among whites was wrong, Val knew. Orientals had feelings and they showed them, if one knew what to look for.

The question had startled Wong, put him on guard. Wong was suspicious of something. And it seemed to Val that Wong's long, thin face looked worn and harried as Wong bowed slightly and said in the same low voice: "I tell missy if boys needed. Ve'y busy now. You want moah?"

"That is all, Wong."

Shirley smiled as Wong's tall, stooped figure moved silently out of the drawing room.

"I did the best I could for you, Mr. Van Dyke."

"I'm grateful," Val said, smiling. "And now all that remains is to hope that I shall be allowed to see all of the house before I leave. And, of course, your flowers."

Shirley had glanced away as he said that. Unconsciously her face hardened. Her smile as she looked back at him seemed forced.

"Please consider yourself free to go anywhere at any time, Mr. Van Dyke."

"I might look about tonight," Val threatened, smiling.

"Do, if you feel like it. A buffet supper will be served around midnight. Some people think father's art gallery is worth seeing. I'd offer to show it to you now but I—I don't think I'd better leave."

Shirley looked rather forlorn as she said that and left him.

Val had seen the reason for it. When Shirley's face had hardened she had been looking at the Countess Waleska, who, still with Samuel Brinton, had been moving from one group of guests to another with that faint air of being the actual hostess.

An unpleasant situation was brewing here. It was a bit rocky, at best, for a girl to see another woman stepping into her mother's place; and the Countess Waleska was not trying to make it any easier on Shirley.

Val put that out of his mind as he strolled out of the drawing room and began to inspect one large room after another, until it seemed to him there was no end to the house after all.

Large sums of money and a discriminating taste had brought together objects of art and rare furnishings. The long art gallery, in which he presently found himself, was lined with paintings which ranged from the best of European masters to selected American moderns.

Midway down the gallery, Val became conscious of a vague feeling that he was not alone.

Turning abruptly, Val saw the tall, stooped Wong standing near with his hands in black sleeves. He had approached like a phantom. In his black coat, staring silently from sunken eyes, he had a somber, sinister look.

CHAPTER FIVE
THE DRAGON SIGN

EVERYWHERE HE had gone in the house these silent servants had been in evidence, moving about like expressionless automatons. They were beginning to get on Val's nerves. "Don't slip up behind me that way!" he said sharply.

Wong bowed. "Ve'y solly," he whispered. "Can do foah you anything?"

"No. I'm inspecting the house, with Miss Brinton's permission. I'd rather be alone."

Wong bowed again and glided out of the gallery.

Frowning, Val watched him go. Some motive must have been behind this sudden appearance. But what? Had Wong been following him? If so, Wong need not have shown himself. The house was big enough to keep out of sight, and still note every move Val had made. Wong wouldn't even have had to do that. The men under him could have gotten any information he might have required.

It must tie back to Wong's agitation at Shirley Brinton's question, and Wong's knowledge that Val had inspired the question. But how? Why? What was going on in Brinton's house to justify any agitation at all on Wong's part?

There in the gallery, Val smoked a cigarette over it, found himself no nearer an answer, and decided to walk out in the moonlight and clear his mind.

Just beyond the entrance to the gallery one of the house-boys was loitering; placed there, Val thought with a jump of interest, to keep an eye on him. Wong must indeed have something on his mind.

"How do I get out to the flower gardens?" Val inquired.

The man was young, intelligent-looking, but he seemed to fumble longer than necessary for the reply.

"Flowe' ga'den?" he said vacantly.

"Flower gardens," Val repeated. "If you don't know what to do about it, we'll look up Miss Brinton and see if she can give you the information."

"You come." The boy conducted Val a short distance through two corridors and opened a door. "Flowe' ga'den," he said.

Val stepped out into the moon-drenched night. The door closed behind him—and he found himself on a side drive near the front of the house. The flower gardens lay to the back reached by walks from the nearer parts of the house.

That slender, fumbling China boy had either deliberately let him out a wrong door—or had not known where the right one was.

Val walked back toward the flowers, keeping on the clipped grass beside the drive. It was not intentional, but it did muffle his steps, so his advance was practically noise-less. The moon, hanging high overhead, was white and bright, and the night was very still—almost brooding.

Then the flowers were about him, rows and banks of them beside the first winding path into which he turned. He crossed another path, and then another. A maze of paths stretched through these acres of loveliness. One could easily get lost—or remain hidden, as Val abruptly remained hidden behind tall banks of flowers when he suddenly heard voices nearby. Two men were speaking guardedly in Chinese.

They did not know he was there as they made their way slowly toward the house by another path. Val trailed them slowly, keeping back out of sight. He saw their shoulders and heads—and recognized them with something of a shock.

Old Wong was one. The other was Li Hung.

Li Hung's voice carried better than Wong's. Out of the gibberish of Chinese syllables Val suddenly heard his own name pronounced.

What they were talking about he could only guess. Li Hung's voice carried a curt ring of authority. Intrigue of some sort was going on here.

Li Hung stopped speaking. Wong murmured something, made his way alone to the back of the house. Li Hung lighted a cigarette, stood smoking it until a door closed audibly behind Wong; then Li Hung walked toward the front of the house.

VAL WAITED a little and moved toward the drive. He was emerging from the flowers by a different path than the one he had entered, and it was only by accident he happened to look down and see a dark shape lying half in the path and half in the first row of tall flowers.

It was a dog, apparently sleeping. Val spoke, stirred the animal with a foot, put down a hand—and jerked it back. The dog was dead; his hand had fresh blood on it.

Cupping a match, Val found a trail of blood where the dog had come along the path, to fall here and die.

The wound was in the side of the big police dog which had frolicked around Shirley Brinton when she first welcomed them. Shirley Brinton's dog. Dead. Stabbed with a sharp blade.

Why?

Vague forebodings took shape in Val's mind as he lit match after match and followed that trail of blood back to its source—out of the flowers, diagonally across the drive, across the grass toward the door through which he had left the house.

There, near the door, the dog had been stabbed.

Placing a cigarette between his lips, Val struck a match. If his senses had not been sharply tuned, he probably would have missed that swift swish of movement across the grass behind him. He turned with the flare of light in his eyes— to see a dark figure almost on him with a knife raised to strike.

With no time to dodge, to run, Val did the only thing possible. He dropped, threw himself at the legs; and as he caught them, a knife-blade ripped across his back.

Twisting hard, Val threw the plunging figure heavily on the ground beside him. Rolling, he came up to his feet a moment before the other staggered up. There were two of them. The other was running in at them. Setting himself, Val smashed hard at the face in profile as it turned toward him. The slender figure went down on the grass again, limply this time, and Val dived for the knife, scrambling aside from the second man's rush as he got the weapon.

But the second man whirled and leaped at him, striking with a knife also. Val threw up an arm, felt the blade cut in the flesh; and only then, when he knew one of them had to die, did he strike with the knife in his hand; driving it in low, and up, in the deadly disemboweling stroke of the good knife-fighter, and jumped back.

A second feeble stroke missed Val as he went back. Then the other caught his middle with both hands and tottered, gasping. Then—

"Vely good!" old Wong said in a thin, strained voice. "No can do moah!"

Wong collapsed slowly on the grass and lay there holding his slashed middle and breathing hard.

The other one was the slender house-boy who had let Val out into the night. No more of them were in sight. Val picked up Wong's knife and ran into the house. Quick work by a doctor might save Wong.

As he turned into the hall leading from the art gallery, Val almost ran into Samuel Brinton, the Countess Waleska and Nancy Fraser. Before he had a chance to speak, Val knew something else was wrong. Nancy was pale. Samuel Brinton was red-faced, angry.

"Ah, there you are!" Brinton exploded. "I've been looking for you sir! What do you two mean by coming into my house posing as the Van Dykes? Who the devil are you?"

Breathing hard, Val looked at Brinton and wondered hastily how Brinton had discovered it. Li Hung probably. Val gave himself a minute to find out.

"How did you know we're not the Van Dykes?" he questioned.

And the Countess Waleska, who had been smiling coolly, answered before Brinton could.

"So simple. I telephone Los Angeles and ask for the Van Dykes who live where you say you do. And they answer. They are home. I am suspicious of you, so I tell Samuel. I cannot see you pull the wool over his face. He is such a big, good-hearted foolish. Now what you say?"

Nancy was mad. "It seems," she said to Val, "we get our walking papers. Out in five minutes, he says."

THE COUNTESS gave a little scream and clung to Brinton's arm. "Samuel, look! His hand is bloody! And the knife! Run before he kills you!"

She tried to drag Brinton back.

"You're safe!" Val snapped at them. "Your number-one boy and another of your Chinese boys just ganged me outside and tried to kill me, Brinton! You can see what they did to me! I had to knife Wong to save myself! Is there a doctor among your guests?"

"No," Brinton stammered, staring with fascination at the blood slowly dripping from Val's slashed arm.

"Telephone for one then! Wong is dying. There may be a chance to save him! Hurry man! We can settle all this later!"

Whatever Brinton's weaknesses, he could act quickly in an emergency.

"This way," he said, and led them hurriedly along the hall, unlocked a door and let them into a small office and den.

Catching up a telephone from the corner of a desk, Brinton jiggled the hook. Nothing happened. He slammed the telephone down a few moments later. "The line is dead!"

Quickly Val asked: "Does it happen often?"

"This is the first time in years! I can't understand it. What are we going to do with Wong? Take him to a doctor?"

"I don't think he'd stand the trip," Val said. "You can try it. By the way, where is your daughter, Mr. Brinton?"

"I don't know, sir. I've been looking for her also."

"Can you telephone the gate and ask the guard who has passed in or out in the last hour?" Val demanded hurriedly.

"The estate system is connected with the gate."

"Call him then! I think something has happened to your daughter!"

A second telephone stood at the back of the desk. Brinton picked it up—only to put it down presently with a baffled and suddenly harried look. "This line is not dead, but the gatekeeper does not answer!" he said thickly. "What do you think has happened to my daughter?"

"I don't know. Get an automobile to take us to the gate. I'm going out and see if this Wong will talk. Nancy, scare up something to tie around my arm to stop this bleeding."

Wong was still holding his middle with both hands when Val bent over him.

"What happened to Miss Brinton?" Val asked the old man.

In the moonlight Wong's sunken eyes stared dully. Feebly he shook his head. He was lying half on his side. Val stepped behind him and with one of the knives slashed Wong's clothes up the back. He worked swiftly and callously, for on what he would find depended many things.

Striking a match Val held it close to the yellow skin of Wong's back—and there, branded plainly on the skin was the mandarin sign of the Dragon. Wong belonged to the brotherhood of the Dragon—and from the ties formed the day he was branded, there was no escape except death.

And Li Hung, who had been talking to Wong, was, if reports were correct, not only a high official in the Chinese government, but the head of those secretive and powerful Sons of the Dragon.

THE MAN whom Val had knocked out so cleanly was still out. Val laid his back bare also, certain he would find a second Dragon sign. He was disappointed.

Nancy came running out with strips of towel in her hand. "Take your coat off Val, and let me tie that arm."

Nancy was working on the arm when Li Hung hurried out to them. "What's this I hear from Brinton?" Li Hung asked crisply. "Ah, is that Wong? Did you stab him?"

"I did," said Val curtly. "And I've looked at his back; and I'm aware that Miss Brinton is gone; and by God, what are you going to do about it? Diplomatic protection or not, I'm going to get the truth out of you if I have to use both hands and a knife!"

"Wait, Easton! Are you certain Miss Brinton is gone?" Li Hung said quickly.

"I found her dog over in the flowers, dead. He left a trail of blood back to this spot. I followed it here and your men jumped me with knives. I heard you give the order to Wong out there in the flowers. Heard my name spoken. Nancy, let the arm go for a minute. I'll make this fellow talk!"

Li Hung stepped back, raising a hand.

"One minute, Mr. Easton. Your suspicions are logical. But I had nothing to do with any attack on you, and I have no idea what has happened to Miss Brinton. I am here on business. Do you think I would countenance any harm to Brinton's daughter?"

"Damn you! I looked at Wong's back!"

"Ah—yes, the sign. You heard me telling Wong to watch you. Nothing more. Wong would not act without an order."

"That," said Val grimly, "is the point exactly. You gave him the order!"

"No!" said Li Hung emphatically. "Someone else must have given it; someone Wong would obey. Can the man talk?"

Li Hung knelt by Wong, spoke in Chinese. He seemed to be pleading, commanding, accusing.

Wong moved slightly, answered so weakly Li Hung had to bend his head close. Presently Li Hung got to his feet.

"This wretched man has destroyed himself, Easton. Three weeks ago his two sons vanished in New York. Wong was informed that he could save their lives by obeying certain orders; but one word to his brothers of the Dragon would mean the death of his sons. Their lives were precious to him; and because the secret of the mark on his back was known, Wong was afraid. He agreed. Tonight when I talked to him he had already helped abduct Miss Brinton."

Behind the house an automobile engine raced.

Li Hung continued rapidly. "Last night Wong received orders over the telephone to discharge two men and replace them with two other men who would arrive this morning. They came in a truck and the men Wong had discharged rode away in the truck. Tonight the same man telephoned that Miss Brinton would be found upstairs in a certain clothes closet, tied and gagged. One of the new men was to get an automobile—any automobile—and take her away. It was done. The dog tried to interfere and was killed.

"Wong's further orders were to kill you, Easton. When he left me and went into the house, he was told by the second new man that you had gone outside. When they found you inspecting the spot where the dog had been stabbed, Wong knew he would have to kill you quickly. He failed, and is dying himself."

THE AUTOMOBILE rushed from behind the house and slid to a stop beside them. Samuel Brinton called hoarsely: "Get in, Easton!" The Countess Waleska was in the front seat beside Brinton.

Val lifted the man he had knocked out and pushed him in the back of the car. "Come along," Val said to Li Hung. "When this man can talk I want you to question him."

Brinton started the car with a jerk, calling over his shoulder: "My chauffeur will take Wong to the nearest doctor in another car!"

Li Hung answered calmly. "Wong will be dead before they can start."

As the big machine raced down the winding drive, Val reminded Li Hung sharply, "You didn't finish. Who gave Wong the orders? Who got Miss Brinton? Where did they take her?"

"Wong did not know," Li Hung replied soberly. "The telephone calls all came over long-distance. Wong merely discharged the two men, hired two more in their places, and carried out the other instructions which came over the telephone."

"Who tied and gagged Miss Brinton?" Val persisted. "It doesn't make sense. She hadn't done anything."

"Wong did not know."

The man at their feet stirred slightly.

The Countess Waleska had been listening. She burst out in her piquant accent: "Has something really happened to Shirley? I think Samuel is merely excited when he said she was gone."

"He was right," Val said.

"Oh, the poor girl! I am so frightened now! Why do we not get the police? Where are the police? Is it true the telephone wires are cut as Samuel says?"

Before Val could answer, the car came to another skidding stop at the stone gate lodge. The high iron gates stood open. The watchman's lodge was lighted. The door stood open. But the watchman himself did not appear.

The man on the floor tried to sit up. Val shoved him down.

"Watch this man, Li Hung!"

Brinton went with Val to the open door of the lodge. The watchman was not inside.

"Was the man trustworthy?" Val asked.

"Absolutely! His father worked for my father," Brinton said.

"He'll be near then."

A few minutes later as they both searched, Brinton called from outside the gates: "Here he is!"

CHAPTER SIX

LI HUNG READS
THE TEA LEAVES

THE WATCHMAN lay in coarse grass on the right of the road. He was face down. Val had to turn the body over to find what had caused death.

"Shot in the head," Val said as the match cupped in his hands died out over the pallid face. "Took his gun, too."

Li Hung's sharp voice speaking Chinese drew them back to the car. The dome light had been turned on. Li Hung had dragged the prisoner's head and shoulders across one knee. With both hands he was throttling the feebly struggling figure.

"Don't kill him!" Val warned.

"I know how to handle such swine," Li Hung panted in that faultless and utterly incongruous Oxford English. "In China I would have him bastinadoed or hung by the thumbs until he talked. Here unfortunately, I must be more gentle."

Shifting into spitting, sing-song Chinese again, Li Hung continued to throttle his victim.

The Countess hid her face. "I cannot look at it!" she wailed.

Nancy sat in her corner of the seat and watched silently as the victim's eyes bulged, his face contorted and darkened with congested blood, and his tongue finally protruded.

"I am telling him that no matter where he goes, torture and death will follow him if he does not talk now," Li Hung panted cheerfully.

The prisoner's right hand lifted weakly in lieu of speech. Li Hung eased up. Fully half a minute elapsed before the man spoke in Chinese, thickly, hoarsely, and almost unrecognizably.

Li Hung listened attentively. His face grew grave.

"Miss Brinton was taken away, right enough. This man does not know why. He was sent here to await orders. The orders came through Wong and he helped carry them out. Miss Brinton was taken away by the orders of Chang Ch'ien."

Brinton there beside Val was a man torn with grief. He was aging, breaking under it before their eyes.

"Where is Shirley?" he burst out pathetically.

His fiancée slipped out of the car and caught his hand comfortingly. "Who is this Chang Ch'ien you speak of?" she demanded passionately.

Li Hung gave her a shrug for a reply and spoke to Brinton.

"I cannot say where your daughter is. This man does not know. The car which carried her away was to be driven to a rendezvous several miles north of the point where this road joins the New York highway. It is an old white farmhouse with three trees before it. An automobile was parked there ready for an emergency."

Val said: "I don't see that we can do anything back at the house. Mr. Brinton, will you drive to the point where your telephone exchange is?"

BRINTON DROVE like a man devoid of reason. In an incredibly short time they drew up before a small two-story frame building in one of the small towns north of Trenton.

The lower floor was dark. A bell-button got them attention from an open window above. Brinton's name quickly brought a woman operator down to unlock the door. A few words of explanation to her put the exchange at their disposal.

"Get the nearest substation of the state police," Val requested.

With Brinton he waited at a booth in the office downstairs. Brinton said hoarsely: "Tell them I'll offer any reward! God, this is horrible. I—anything might be happening to Shirley!"

The state police came on the wire. Val reported the matter, gave them Shirley's description, told where the dead man could be found, asked that a doctor be sent to the house as soon as possible, named the exchange where he was talking, and where he would be waiting, and hung up.

"The reward!" Brinton reminded him feverishly. "You didn't mention it!"

Val looked at him soberly as he waited a moment, lifted the receiver again and gave the number of Gregg's private telephone in Washington.

"You're not going to understand," Val told Brinton as he waited for the call to go through. "But if you try, it will help your daughter."

And Val had to stand there in the cramped little telephone booth and tell the grieving man that money would not help his daughter. Kidnaping a girl for ransom was so far from the half-mad genius of Chang Ch'ien that it was not even worth thinking about.

Brinton stared at him with gathering anger. "I don't understand! Are you crazy yourself, man? Who is this Chang Ch'ien?"

Val sighed. "I hoped I wouldn't have to go into all that."

As briefly as possible Val gave Brinton the background of Chang Ch'ien, who, with a mixture of Chinese, English and Burmese blood in his veins, had come out of the far interior of China as a young man and made his name a terror in the European underworlds.

Listening intently, Brinton heard how Chang Ch'ien had joined forces with Carl Zaken, the dread Black Doctor, and the two transferred their partnership to America. At the end Brinton snorted: "Where did you hear rot like that? Who *are* you anyway?"

Val identified Nancy and himself. Brinton's attitude changed instantly. He had dealt with the government too much not to understand their background.

"But I can't see why Shirley should have been brought into this!" Brinton cried fiercely. "What has she done? What good can she possibly do anyone? If money isn't wanted, what is?"

Val had to confess: "I don't know. Everything possible will be done. I'm calling Washington now. You understand all this must not be made public. I'm a guest. Chang Ch'ien is an unknown Oriental. Li Hung will not talk."

Gregg came on the wire. Val talked in French in case the operator was listening. When he finished, Gregg gave an exclamation of anger.

"I thought Chang Ch'ien was up to something! But the devil of it is I haven't the slightest idea where we can find him. He vanished absolutely after his last fiasco in San Francisco. You'll have to work blind. And work fast!" Gregg said forcibly. "It looks bad for the girl."

Before leaving the booth Val asked the local operator to make quickly a list of all telephone calls in and out of the Brinton estate the past two days.

"This helpless waiting is ghastly?" Brinton groaned as they walked out.

"The state police will be here shortly," Val cheered him.

First to come were two uniformed troopers on motorcycles. Hard after them, from north and south, followed men from the county sheriff's office, newspaper reporters and cameramen out of Trenton, and more troopers. The telephone operator had done her work only too well.

Two troopers raced off to the estate. Brinton refused to follow them, saying: "I'm no good there now, where there isn't even a telephone. I'll stay here."

RESIDENTS, AROUSED by the activity, swelled the group before the exchange. The Chinese prisoner was taken over by the sheriff. A cameraman's flashlight glared as he photographed the arrest.

In the telephone office, with a sheriff's deputy and three state troopers, Brinton and Val answered questions. Brinton kept his head enough to suppress mention of Chang Ch'ien.

A trooper telephoned his substation and was informed all approaches into New York were covered. A general alarm had been flashed over the state and into neighboring states.

Val described the white farmhouse. One of the troopers said: "I know that place. It's been empty for months. It's about six miles north of here."

The operator brought Val a list of the estate telephone calls. One call had been made from the estate at twenty minutes to eleven that evening, to a midtown hotel in Manhattan. Miss Brinton had called a Mr. Garza. Six minutes later the same Mr. Garza had telephoned back to the estate stating he would speak to anyone who answered. The operator who had handled the call remembered that one of the Chinese servants had answered; after that moment she had been cut off the circuit.

"Queer, Miss Brinton telephoning," Val said. "That was just about the time she was tied up."

Brinton shook his head desperately. "I can't conceive why she should have called anyone by that name. I've never heard her mention the man, or the hotel."

A trooper asked: "Any chance of a love affair you didn't know anything about?"

"Certainly not!" Brinton denied emphatically. But it was obvious the idea worried him.

The law decided to go to the white farmhouse first. The newspapermen followed. Motorcycles and automobiles strung out along the highway, breaking all speed laws.

The weed-grown bit of property they came to held a small, dilapidated two-story frame house. The lower windows were shuttered. No automobile was visible.

The troopers approached the house warily with drawn guns. Val ran back to a wooden shed. The doors, unlocked, creaked loudly as he opened them. The moonlight struck against the gleaming back of a new car carrying New York State tags. Its radiator was warm.

Val called Brinton, who excitedly identified the car as belonging to one of his guests.

The state troopers were inside the house with flashlights. Val went in, told them about the car, and looked around as best he could. Bare, deserted, dirty, no part but the kitchen showed signs of occupancy. There newspapers, cigarette ends and scraps of food showed that one or more men had spent time there.

Two boxes did for chairs beside an old table. Food had been cooked on a dilapidated oil stove. A dirty frying pan and dishes were in an old tin sink; part of a loaf of bread, a coffee pot and a small, almost empty sack of tea were in a shallow wall cupboard.

Using his handkerchief so as not to leave fingerprints, Val lifted the coffee pot lid. Tea had been made in it. The small sack of tea interested him after he smelled it. A lighted match showed the white petals of jasmine flowers scattered through the dark tea leaves. Chinese characters badly printed on the sack had evidently been executed in China.

Val put the small sack in his pocket as one of the troopers spoke disgustedly from the back doorway. "Nothing around here to show where they went. Joe, keep an eye on things while I go back an' telephone in. No use going any further north. Everything is covered that way."

Li Hung was standing placidly beside Brinton's car smoking a cigarette. At Val's request he stepped to one side.

"I'm a bit weak on my Chinese," Val said. "What do the characters on this sack mean? Here, I'll strike a match."

Li Hung scanned the printing, sniffed the contents.

"Jasmine tea, eh? Someone has been indulging a culti- vated taste. This sack of tea was packed in Hong Kong by Lu Foo for Sui Gee."

"Who is Sui Gee?"

"I should judge a retail dealer somewhere in this area," said Li Hung. "I can get the information from New York by telephone. Sui Gee's place of business is probably in New York."

"If we can trace this package of tea to its buyer, we'll be getting somewhere. I'll see Brinton about borrowing his car. He can go back in the other one."

The request brought a hopeful question from Brinton. "Have you anything in mind, Van Dyke—er—I mean, Easton?"

"Something which may not lead anywhere. I'm going to follow it out alone."

"I'll go with you," Brinton decided.

SOME EIGHTEEN miles put them in another small town which had a hotel. Val accompanied Li Hung into the lobby and stood by while Li Hung consulted a small, thin leather-bound notebook, and telephoned a Manhat- tan number. Li Hung talked in Chinese, and was smiling with satisfaction when he stepped out of the booth.

"Sui Gee is the owner of a chop-suey restaurant and retail store next to it which sells imported Chinese groceries. His place is in Newark. It is customary for small Chinese dealers to have their names printed on goods they buy packaged in China."

As Li Hung paid the desk clerk for the call, Val said thoughtfully: "Newark, eh? That could mean a lot, or nothing. Perhaps the tea was bought by someone driving out of New York to the south, merely passing through Newark. Or the purchaser may live in that territory and be known."

"At least," said Li Hung, "he will be remembered. The drinkers of jasmine tea are not numerous."

Brinton looked at Val haggardly when he received orders to drive to Newark. "Did you find out anything? Are you making any progress?" he begged.

"We're making some progress," Val told him.

The Countess Waleska put a slender comforting hand against Brinton's shoulder. "Samuel, I am so glad! See, you must not worry. Everything will be all right. Tell us, Mr. Van Dyke, what are you doing?"

And Brinton insisted: "Please do. You're being very secretive about this."

Since there was no reason for being secretive among themselves, Val told Brinton about the tea sack and the chance of getting some trace of Chang Ch'ien through it.

"It sounds like a mighty slim chance," Brinton groaned.

Then Newark.

With little difficulty they located the side-street chop-suey parlor of Sui Gee. Called the Pekin, even at this late hour it was serving a number of patrons. A small shop next door, closed and dark now, had the name of Sui Gee on the window.

Despite his doubts, Brinton went inside with Val and Li Hung. The place was hot and smelled of food. A radio was playing loudly.

Behind the cigar counter a short, wizened man was working the beads of an abacus.

"Sui Gee?" Li Hung asked.

The wizened little man nodded.

Li Hung handed him the paper tea sack and spoke in Chinese. Sui Gee shook his head, shrugged. Li Hung spoke again, more sharply; and drew another negative.

A pencil stub was lying on the glass. Li Hung picked it up, drew a pad of paper close and began to make meaningless marks as he talked. Casually he pushed the pad over in front of the other.

Sui Gee looked at the pad. The sack dropped from his fingers. Fright was visible on his face. He began to talk. Val suddenly realized the aimless marks Li Hung had made formed the mandarin sign for the dragon; that deathless brand borne by members of the great secret organization which Li Hung headed.

Li Hung listened impassively, and then turned to them.

"He was able to remember, finally. This sack is from a new importation of tea. He has sold only three packages of the jasmine variety; two of them to the same man, who has appeared frequently the last two months, and who calls himself Sum Yung. He is very fond of jasmine tea. In talking, Sum Yung has stated that he drives an automobile for the owner of a small business called the Jersey Experimental Company, located just out of town on the edge of the Jersey meadows. That is all this man knows, and I think he speaks the truth."

"Let me have that telephone directory behind you," Val said to Sui Gee. Leafing through the directory, Val found what he sought. "The company is listed here," he said, closing the book. "Sum Yung must have other interests besides his job."

Samuel Brinton had started out to the car. As Val finished speaking the door burst open; Brinton stood there bursting with excitement.

"The car and both the women are gone!" he gasped.

CHAPTER SEVEN
THE DRAGONS OF
CHANG CH'IEN

THE CAR had been parked across the street. It was gone now. Brinton was almost incoherent. "Isn't there any end to this? What could have happened to them? They wouldn't have driven off voluntarily without notifying us!"

"Go back and call the police," Val said to them. "I'll get a taxi and run down this chauffeur some way. This is hooked up with Chang Ch'ien somehow, of course!"

Val left them there and ran to the next corner, where, he recalled, two taxis had been parked. One taxi was still there.

"Jersey Experimental Products Company! Know where it is?"

"Huh? Oh yeah, over in the Meadows, ain't it? O.K. The road ain't so hot but I can get you there."

This was new territory to Val. The last city lights quickly dropped behind; the last cobblestoned stretch of street gave way to a narrow, rutty road. Looking out, Val saw he was rolling through the reedy fringes of the great Jersey meadows, that stretch of ill-reclaimed salt marsh lying desolate and open between Newark and Jersey City.

Factories fringed the open wasteland, rough dirt roads and water channels traversed it, and here and there buildings stood alone where the ground was firm.

The taxi turned through a gate in a high, wire fence and stopped before a small, two-story brick factory building.

"Here y'are," said the driver.

A light burned over the gate. From behind glowing, opaque windows the sound of working machinery pulsed on the night.

"Wait for me," Val said, getting out.

Across the front of the building a sign read—JERSEY EXPERIMENTAL PRODUCTS COMPANY. To the right of a loading platform a door was marked, *Office.* Two automobiles were parked over at one side.

In the moonlight a dark figure met him. A gruff voice asked: "What d'you want?"

"I want to see the man in charge here."

"He's busy."

"This is important! I've got to see him!" Val snapped, and strode toward the office. The other, evidently a guard, followed him.

Lights were burning in the office. The louder sound of machinery met Val as he stepped inside. Through an open door at the left he could see into a large room filled with a maze of lathes, overhead pulleys and vibrating belts.

Everything was running busily, but not a man visible. The next instant all that left Val's mind as a door at the back of the office opened and a tall, stooped figure entered.

Greenish eyes in a pale cadaverous face riveted on Val in astonishment. They were both surprised. Recognition was simultaneous. This was Carl Zaken, the master spy, the dread Black Doctor, who had earned that name by his inhuman use of a surgeon's scalpel on victims who refused to reveal secrets the Black Doctor sought!

Fury twisted the pallid face. "You fool, stop him!" Zaken shouted at the watchman.

Unarmed, Val had jumped toward Carl Zaken. A terrific blow behind the ear sent him sprawling to the floor.

THE MACHINERY was still throbbing, but a closer, roaring sound filled Val's ears when he opened his eyes. He was standing up, held by ropes to a pillar at his back. His coat had been removed, his collar was open at the neck. The glow of leaping flames directly ahead made him blink. He thought at first he was dreaming, and then sick horror engulfed him and blotted out the pain in his head.

Nancy Fraser, pale and trembling, was tied to a pillar at his left. Directly in front of him was a large, solid platform of bricks, topped with fire-brick and lined to its rim with sand inside.

Beyond that table, roaring gas flames were visible in a small open-hearth furnace. Before the furnace stood four Orientals, stripped to their waists and dripping sweat.

At Val's elbow stood the tall, stooped figure of Carl Zaken. The man was smiling, but his face looked malevolent in fire reflected light from the great furnace as he spoke.

"I trust your head is not paining you, Easton?"

Ignoring him, Val stared at the big platform which had inspired the sick feeling that gripped him. Beside the platform stood a huge, golden-skinned man wearing a red silk robe and a round hat. Chang Ch'ien, master of murder; Chang Ch'ien, bending over and talking to Shirley Brinton, who lay flat on her back on the harsh yellow sand, with her arms chained out to her sides and her red, sleeveless dress sheathing a slender body which twisted and turned helplessly.

Shirley was crying as she shook her head in answer to Chang Ch'ien.

Val could not hear what she said, but Chang Ch'ien turned abruptly from her, saw that Val was conscious and came to him, smiling. "Ah, Easton, well met. This is more than I dared expect. I'm happy to have you with us."

Tall, powerful, the man overtopped Val by inches. The small goatee he had last worn was gone, but his wide, full-lipped mouth was still shaded by a long, drooping black mustache. Behind his smile, ruthlessness lay stark and unhidden.

Power and ruthlessness; and yet somehow the stooped, malevolent Carl Zaken seemed to dominate Chang Ch'ien and everything in the room. Which was not strange when you knew how incredibly clever and cold-blooded the man was.

"What the devil is this?" Val grated. "This factory—you dressed like that in here—and Miss Brinton and—and all that?" Val nodded at the big platform and the roaring furnace beyond.

A glistening film of perspiration covered Chang Ch'ien's face. He had to raise his voice to be heard.

"The robes, Easton, are ceremonial robes. I feel the occasion requires a certain amount of dignity."

"Why dignity?"

The sick feeling was still with Val as he asked that. When Chang Ch'ien was at his politest, he was most dangerous. From that mad, power-drunk brain, any fantastic scheme of horror was apt to emerge. Something ghastly was in store for Shirley Brinton.

She would not be tied like that, the fires would not be roaring, the setting so carefully arranged as this, if Chang Ch'ien had not decided on some course of action.

Chang Ch'ien spoke. "I am the Jersey Experimental Corporation, Easton. Neat, eh? My own idea. This location is ideal for a headquarters near New York. You would be interested in some of the experiments I have made lately. Fortunately, you are just in time to witness one—and then I can promise you the pleasure of participating yourself. Zaken wished the satisfaction of dealing with you; but I convinced him that since everything was ready you might as well be included in this little—er—experiment. You and the charming Miss Fraser, who has so often help to annoy us."

VAL LOOKED at the smiling golden-tinted face and shivered inside. He couldn't help it. Too often before, he had seen what the man was capable of. And he wondered now, as he had wondered before it Chang Ch'ien's half sister, the lovely Tai Shan, was present, giving her consent to any horror which might take place. He looked for her, and did not see her.

Val wet his lips and asked: "How did you get Miss Fraser here?"

Anything to keep the man talking, to delay what was on his mind so there might be a chance to think. The ropes which held him were tight; he could hardly move.

Chang Ch'ien waved the question away. "I have just been asking Miss Brinton to whom she confided her suspicions before being taken from her home. She denies confiding anything. Perhaps so. At any rate, it becomes necessary for me to make her a part of my molding experiments."

"Molding?"

"Metal molding," said Chang Ch'ien, smiling. "In a moment you will see more clearly. Perhaps then you will be willing to tell me quickly how you got to this place, and answer a few questions about which I am curious. If you do, it may be you will earn the very easy end with a knife, which your taxicab driver used."

Chang Ch'ien walked to the four waiting men and spoke to them; and Carl Zaken followed him and stood to one side.

What followed was like a swiftly moving section of a nightmare.

Two metal tracks on the floor ran on either side of the table. From each one of them, a metal framework on wheels rose higher than a tall man's head. Stretching out from each frame was a thick bar of metal, ending in a fantastic dragon head which supported, with its lower jaw, one side of a metal bowl lined with firebrick.

A long-handled ladle swinging from a chain-hoist moved into the roaring flames inside the furnace. When a heave brought it out, the bare room was transferred into a fiery inferno. The ladle, filled to the brim and dripping over with molten metal, swung through the air and emptied into the great bowl.

Then Val saw the reason for the tracks and the framework on wheels. Two of the men pushed hard. Rolling along the tracks, the tall frames carried the huge bowl directly over the table; directly over Shirley Brinton.

Val understood then. He hadn't believed it possible one human being could bring such horror to another. He understood the sand-lined table now. It was a small molding platform—and Shirley Brinton lay helpless there where the molten metal would fall and spread and cover and devour flesh and bone instantly. All that would remain would be cold, solid metal whose dull surface would carry no hint of the ghastly destruction it had brought.

Only a man, mad with the lust of power, and cruel beyond all comprehension, could do such a thing. Only a man like Chang Ch'ien, whose face, as he came to Val, was smiling again in the red glare which filled the big, bare room.

"I trust, Easton, you appreciate the symbolism of those metal dragons which hold destruction like I shall soon demand from all those branded with the Dragon sign."

Val was struggling; but the ropes which bound him to the pillar were too tight. He had to stand there helplessly as Chang Ch'ien turned back to the table and grasped an upright bar which would tilt the great pot and start a molten stream of death flowing down over the helpless face below.

Nancy Fraser closed her eyes. Val fought the ropes helplessly. He could not tear his eyes away from the ghastly sight, from what was coming. But, suddenly, he did. The ropes which bound him fast were loosening, one by one. From his feet up they were loosening, falling away as they were cut from behind.

It was too good to be true. There must be some catch in it—and there was. For, as he came free and turned to see who had delivered him, a gun pressed hard into his side. And when he saw the owner of the gun he caught his breath.

TAI SHAN stood there. Tai Shan, half sister to Chang Ch'ien. Tai Shan, face framed in jet-black hair, vivid red lips and expressionless face, was like a woman from some lovely old Chinese painting.

Tai Shan's face was as haunting and expressionless as ever, her pale cheeks carried a trace of color, and it seemed to Val that her eyes were disturbed and frightened. But she held the gun against his side with a steady hand as she spoke to him in that clear, musical voice he never forgot when away from her.

"Val Easton, you should not have come here. You should have known. Quick, come with me, but do not try to stop what is happening. It is written, and it must be. You are— foolish."

But the red lips which spoke to him were tender and the clear, musical voice was gentle and a trifle sorrowful as it spoke to him. Never, Val knew, would he know why Tai Shan felt as she did toward him; why, hard and ruthless as she must be, she always exhibited this strange softness toward him.

He turned his head toward the big platform. Chang Ch'ien looked like some evil monster as he bent over the table and put pressure on the bar. The big pot was tilting; and in the dazzling glare of molten metal, Carl Zaken was only partially visible as he stood watching with rapt attention, forgetful for the moment of anything else which might be happening in the room.

Tai Shan moved back a step, holding the gun on him. Her clear voice lashed at him, ordering: "Come quickly! It will be too late! They will see us! We cannot wait!"

Val saw one of the half-naked Orientals, standing off on one side, turn a head, stare at them with surprise, and then start toward them.

Shirley Brinton screamed once in an agony of fear that was maddening.

And Val forgot everything as he snatched for the gun in Tai Shan's hand. Better to die here quickly, trying to do something, than to live afterwards knowing he had walked out leaving Shirley Brinton—and Nancy Fraser—to that hell of torture.

Tai Shan tried to kill him. Or perhaps she did not. As Val's hand caught her wrist the automatic exploded with a loud crash. He felt the push of the explosion against his side; and a moment later he had wrested the gun away from Tai Shan and swept her back with an arm. He turned just in time to meet a rush from the half-naked Oriental and a companion, both of whom had witnessed the brief struggle.

The first man had drawn a knife from somewhere and was striking down at him as Val shot point-blank at his middle and leaped aside.

The man plunged on past, collided with the pillar, reeled off and went down on the floor. The man who followed him came plunging in also, his soiled, sweating face strained with passion and determination. A long knife gleamed in his hand.

Jumping back, Val shot the second one full in the middle also. He saw the little, dark hole where the bullet went in, saw the muscular yellow abdomen, contract spasmodically under the shock, and saw the man still coming at him.

Val put in a second bullet, higher than the first. The desperate rush broke. The man reeled aside. And suddenly, above the din of machinery and roaring gas, Val heard other shots, distant shots, in some far part of the building.

The great pot had leveled off. Its molten contents were yet inside. Chang Ch'ien had vanished from the side of the platform. Peering through the red glow, Val caught the flutter of red silk at the right side of the room.

Moving like a great fleeing cat, Chang Ch'ien was bolting through an open door, tearing off his red silk robe as he ran.

The robe dropped to the floor as Val lifted the automatic and sent one shot after the fleeing figure. He didn't know whether he'd hit flesh or not; the last thing he saw was Chang Ch'ien vanishing through the door wearing a plain business suit. And then the door slammed—and Chang Ch'ien was gone.

CARL ZAKEN was gone also. Tai Shan had vanished. The other two half-naked Orientals had fled somewhere. Only the two wounded ones were writhing on the floor— and Shirley Brinton was struggling weakly on her bed of rough sand while the great glowing pot of metal rested just above her.

Catching up one of the knives, Val freed Nancy Fraser with a few quick slashes. Nancy was pale, but master of her actions.

"Help me get that pot away from her!" Val ordered through tight lips.

Nancy had seen the pot moved, knew what to do. While Val shoved hard on one side, Nancy strained on the other. Slowly, gradually, the wheels rolled back on the tracks and the molten death moved with it, away from Shirley Brinton. The heat radiating from the big pot was fearful to feel and contemplate.

Two uniformed police officers burst into the room with drawn revolvers.

It took but a moment for them to grasp what was being done, and to lend their strength to it. Li Hung and Samuel Brinton followed them, and helped also. Samuel Brinton's face was terrible to see. His hands were shaking as he helped them release his daughter.

"Have you got the place surrounded?" Val demanded of the nearest officer.

The man shook his head. "We're the only ones. We didn't know what we'd find. Came here because that man"— he pointed to Li Hung—"said we'd better. Fellow in the front office took a shot at my buddy an' we had to kill him. Where's the men who were running this?"

Val shook his head ruefully. "You won't find them," he said.

Nor did they, when they searched. Chang Ch'ien and his men had faded into the night. Two of the automobiles out in front were gone.

Val walked back into the office with Li Hung. Samuel Brinton was holding his daughter close. His face was haggard.

"Gentlemen," Brinton said, "I don't know what to say. Shirley has just told me that my—my fiancée was responsible for this. The—that woman was talking over one of the upstairs telephones in Chinese, and Shirley heard her and stepped into the room. Before Shirley knew what was happening, she was facing a gun. She was tied up and left in a closet; and presently two of the servants carried her out and she was taken away in the car. She heard the gateman shot, and she was transferred to another machine and brought here and questioned. She was under suspicion of knowing far more than she did. I—neither of us know what it is all about. Am I going mad? Did the woman I was in love with, and was going to marry, do this to my daughter? She couldn't be sane."

Nancy Fraser's look at the man was pitying.

"She was sane enough, Mr. Brinton," Nancy said. "When you men left us, she pulled a gun on me and forced me to drive here. She would have killed me if I hadn't. But while I was driving, she couldn't resist being catty. She had to let me know what a wonderful and clever woman she was. She was going to warn Chang Ch'ien and his partner, Zaken, that you were getting warm on their trail; and later say we both had been kidnaped and she, only, had escaped. And shortly after she was married to you, she would be a widow and in full control of your fortune and your business. First your daughter, and then you were to die, and she would have it all."

"But—but married to me, she would have had all she wanted," Brinton stammered.

Val said: "But not all Chang Ch'ien and Zaken wanted. The woman was working for them. You undoubtedly were selected for a victim before you ever saw her. Your money wasn't all they wanted. They were seeking control of the Brinton Arms Company." Val shook his head wonderingly. "What a force for evil they could have made their control of Brinton munitions! I think, Brinton, you'd better forget about ever being in love and thank your lucky stars you weren't married to her. At least you have a chance of living now. You wouldn't have had after the knot was tied."

Brinton shivered. "I believe you. I—I'm through with love. All I want now is to get my girl home and forget about this."

A little later Val said to Nancy, as a car carried them out of the desolate waste of meadow land: "Going home and forgetting it is probably the wisest idea Brinton has had for a long time."

Despite the ordeal she had been through, Nancy was still able to chuckle.

"Very good if he can do so. But for a long time to come I shall laugh when I think about the Countess. She, I am afraid, being a woman, will never forget that hundred million she almost had, and didn't get, and now never will have. The clothes, the power, the position she would have had. I'm glad," said Nancy, "I'm not the Countess."

Made in the USA
Coppell, TX
01 September 2021

61631150R00260